The Antipodeans

Greg McGee

Published by
Lightning Books Ltd
Imprint of EyeStorm Media
312 Uxbridge Road
Rickmansworth
Hertfordshire
WD3 8YL

www.lightning-books.com

First edition 2018
First published in 2015 in New Zealand by Upstart Press Ltd
Copyright © Greg McGee 2015
Cover design by Ifan Bates

British Library Cataloguing in Publication Data
A catalogue record for this book is available from the British Library.

The Author was the 2013 Katherine Mansfield Menton Fellow and gratefully acknowledges the support of the Katherine Mansfield Menton Fellowship and the Trustees of the Wynne-Manson Menton Trust.

Printed by CPI Group (UK) Ltd, Croydon CR0 4YY

ISBN 978-1-78563-058-3

*For Family
and
I miei amici Caimani*

About the Author

Greg McGee writes for theatre, film and television, in which he has won numerous awards. More recently he has concentrated on prose. Under the pseudonym of Alix Bosco he won the 2010 Ngaio Marsh Award for best crime fiction novel for *Cut & Run*, and was a finalist the following year with *Slaughter Falls*. He has since written his first novel under his own name, *Love & Money*, and the biography of Richie McCaw, *The Open Side*. He was the 2013 Katherine Mansfield Menton Fellow. He lives in Auckland.

The past is in us . . . not behind us
Tim Winton, *Aquifer*

Venice, 2014

1

He'd insisted they take a boat, an Alilaguna, so that her first view of Venice would be from the water. She'd asked whether that was wise — there was a low drizzle floating out of the early dusk at Marco Polo airport, and he was already shivering as they walked to the jetty.

'Drizzle's good,' he'd said, hauling on his suitcase. She'd offered to pull it for him, told him she could easily do both, but he wouldn't have it. Now he was labouring, as they arrived at a short gangway leading down off the jetty. 'You'll feel the ghosts of the place.'

That seemed so unlike him. 'Ghosts, Dad?'

He didn't answer. Perhaps he hadn't heard her. He'd always been selectively deaf, even when he was well. It had been one of the things that had driven her mother mad.

As the boat-bus droned along the channel, leaving a white wake trailing in the brown water and falling darkness, they passed a couple of islets with scruffy trees hiding all but the roof-lines of industrial garages. There were boats on cradles having their bums wiped. It could have been one of the less attractive indentations of the Auckland isthmus, lacking only mudflats and mangroves.

He refused to sit. That didn't surprise her: the osteoarthritis in his knees had given him pain throughout the long flight. He stayed on his feet, hands gripping the rail, staring out across the barely ruffled water. 'Shallow,' he said. 'Treacherous.' He pointed towards some lights out to the left, barely visible through the gloom. 'Franco and I used to fish off Murano.'

She saw his hands were shaking. Big hands, more so recently as the flesh withered on his frame. Hands that looked as if they'd crutched lambs or milked cows or pruned vines. They mostly lied, those hands: he'd been brought up on a farm but had spent his working life as a solicitor, a self-styled 'paper-pushing all-rounder' who did conveyancing, corporate, trusts, estates — and matrimonial property, in which he was not pleased to be currently acting for his only child. She wished it wasn't such an unholy mess. It was hard to say whether it had taken a toll on him — he wasn't a man who allowed emotion to leak — but she'd resolved before coming with him not to let her pain show.

He was pointing to a cluster of lights on the other side, told her it was Mestre, the mainland city, then looked puzzled. 'There used to be huge gas flares and light towers over there.' He addressed a question to the pilot, dour and overweight, who hadn't said a word to them or the other three passengers as he'd taken their tickets and loaded their suitcases. He seemed to have trouble understanding the question, and her father the answer, but he eventually reported that many of the installations at the mainland port, Marghera, had been closed down 'because the pollutants were rotting her'.

Her? She'd read a lot of guff about Venice — there was an awful lot of guff about Venice — and a fair bit of it had been so purple it could have been written by a desperate real estate agent. She should know. But her father's use of the female pronoun for a collection of old stones made her wonder. He was looking away, into the darkness ahead. 'There she is,' he said.

Clare looked and could see nothing, still blinded by the lights of Mestre. Then she saw a wide, muted light, sitting low on the water, which became buildings, none more than four or five storeys. The boat motored straight at them, slowing slightly, but not enough, she thought, instinctively looking for the wharf where they would surely disembark. Suddenly they were among those old stones, between them, moving up what she should have known was a canal, which soon brought them to what her father told her was the Grand Canal.

He had also told her Venice wasn't a picture postcard, and he was right: it was an illustration from a fairy tale, the unimaginably ancient and detailed facades of the palazzi, lit to show their Byzantine bones, seeming to float just above their reflection on the water. Between some of the grand houses, other smaller lanes of water led off into a gentle rose light thrown by lanterns, danced through by the drizzle. And everywhere, boats, barges, big and small, carrying all manner of people and produce.

She shouldn't have been surprised, and yet she was. She'd imagined Venice as a kind of theme park with canals and stripe-vested straw-hatted gondoliers singing 'O sole mio', not a working city where the main street was water, plied by truck barges and boat-buses carrying Coca-Cola and building materials and people.

She heard her father say something in Italian, quietly, almost muttering to himself. An impeccably dressed man in a hat and coat at the rail nearby overheard and turned in surprise, clapped his hands once and said, 'Bravo!'

'What'd you say?' she asked.

'The words of a Venetian song,' he said. 'O beautiful Venice, I can never leave you, you've made me fall in love with you.'

She was stunned into silence. She'd heard him speak Italian before, but never heard him sing a song or even quote poetry. Like most of the lawyers she'd known through him, he fancied himself as a writer. She'd seen the florid letters and e-mails they wrote to each other. But, with her father at least, the orotund wordsmithery on the page had seldom come from his mouth. In that too, he was true to his southern origins.

'It's pretty gorgeous, Dad,' she said, but found herself thinking that almost anything can look good at night, particularly if you've got a bit of water to reflect the lights.

As the Alilaguna approached another bridge across the canal, and slowed, she could see his hands were shaking. 'I came to hate this place,' he said. 'I felt trapped.'

Okay, she thought. That's real.

2

What happened next was real, too, and disconcerting. The Alilaguna stopped at Sant'Angelo, which wasn't what her father was expecting. After an exchange with the pilot in which neither seemed to understand much of what the other was trying to say, her father told her that he'd thought the boat stopped at Accademia, another couple of hundred metres further, but that was apparently a vaporetto stop, not an Alilaguna stop. Why such a short distance should be of any consequence became clear once they'd lifted their suitcases off the pontoon and hauled them to the end of a long narrow alley. He seemed lost.

Worse, when he asked a local where Campo Santo Stefano was, the local corrected his pronunciation. Then he didn't appear to understand the man's reply.

'Don't worry,' he said to her. 'You're never lost in Venice, it's too small. You just temporarily don't know where you are.'

They seemed to remain that way for quite some time, going round in a circle of endless labyrinthine alleys punctuated by nasty little humped bridges over small canals, which forced them to lift their suitcases. He weakened quickly and looked bewildered.

After more instructions and gesticulations, they arrived at a large, rectangular piazza that turned out to be the one he was looking for, Campo Santo Stefano. They plunged into various blind alleys along one side before they found the right one, which led to a smaller piazza, San Maurizio. More blundering, more infernal humped bridges, before the third door he tried turned out to be their B & B, though there were still three flights of stairs to carry the suitcases up. He was struggling but wouldn't hear of her suggestion that he should leave his suitcase and she'd come back for it.

A serene young man sitting at the small reception desk at the top of the stairs must have been deaf not to hear them coming, she thought, until she saw the little white pods in his ears.

'*So* sorry to disturb, you,' she said, as her father stood gasping with his hands on his knees.

There was another reality check when the young man showed them their room. She knew space was tight in Venice, and he'd warned her they were sharing a room, but the sight of a double bed, one old wardrobe and a single that looked as if it had been requisitioned from a jail cell was depressing. The claustrophobia wasn't helped by dark purple curtains over a window that scarcely justified them. They'd surely heard of venetians? She could easily redress this room to make it feel much more spacious, but even then, you'd only ever advertise it as a single.

Her father had caught his breath sufficiently to complain to the young man that he'd booked a room for four, a double bed and two singles, so they'd have a spare bed to lay their suitcases out on.

'Oh no, Signor,' he said, 'no mistake.' He pulled a trundler bed out from under the prison cell single.

Her father just nodded, his fight gone. When he'd proudly explained on the flight over his cunning ruse in booking a room for four, he'd seemed on top of it, ahead of the game. Now he seemed pitiful. They couldn't put their suitcases on the trundler because she'd have to climb over them to get into bed. There was room for one suitcase on a narrow bench beside the wardrobe, so hers went on the floor, impeding any access to the window.

Before she unclipped her suitcase, she stepped over it, pulled the dusty curtain back and looked out onto a dreary internal square. It was about three metres across and looked like an open lift shaft someone had forgotten to fill in. There were shuttered windows on three sides and the lower floor looked abandoned, the flagstones covered with seeping mould. One of the books she'd read lamented that Venice was crumbling, eroding, liquefying, being reclaimed by the sea. The sooner the better, she thought.

She'd fallen asleep easily enough, but something woke her. She lay awake and thought she'd quietly cry herself to sleep. Her woe-is-me litany was easily summoned: How did I end up like this, thirty-one years old in a crappy hotel room with my father? This is it, me and him, I've got no one else in the world. How tragic is that? It was something of a relief to have some variation on the same old grief-stricken riff about her husband fucking her best friend, etc., etc. She was so bored with it, so sick of it, yet still so enmeshed in it.

Moments would come back to her and she'd pore over them like entrails. Sarah, now she thought of it, had once said she didn't like hairy men. When had Nicholas started having those crack sack and back waxes he said were for her? She'd always thought he'd had them because no pubes made his penis look bigger. That penis he was so proud of — 'Say hello to Pedro!' *Pedro*? Nicholas was a Greek from Melbourne! Nick the Greek — it's why he hated that diminution of his name. Olive skinned, hirsute, except on his balding pate, and overweight — she could say it now: fat. Fat hairy arse. Hairy back. She'd thought she liked that, it had seemed so exotic once, though when her counsellor pointed it out, she could see that it might be just a reflexive thing, a reaction against the tallish, blondish, emotionally austere males in her family. So. Her upbringing, her conditioning, had given her a weakness for fat, a weakness for short, for hairy, for swarthy. Not to mention volatility. Great. Say hello to Pedro? She was *so* fucked.

She tried to heed her counsellor's advice and not lose herself in what had gone wrong, but couldn't help it. Maybe Nicholas's waxes had been for Sarah all along. She felt so humiliated. It was such a public betrayal and rejection — all their friends, the social media. And being business partners just made it so much worse.

Where would they be now, the two of them? It would be early afternoon in Auckland. Late winter sun would be falling across the matrimonial bed in their *Sunny, Mount Eden Treasure, Grammar Zone.* They'd be fucking on those virgin white pure cotton sheets that had cost a small fortune. After he'd admitted they'd done it on their bed, she couldn't bring herself to take them back, or even that Belgian linen throw, which would probably be lying crumpled on the shag carpet — how appropriate — along with their clothes . . .

She'd unfriended both of them on Facebook and that would have automatically worked the other way as well. She wasn't so masochistic as to go to either of their sites any more, but there was always Twitter. @clarebelle was still being followed by @ sarahbelle — she wished there was a way of remotely renaming it @slutbag — and she just *had* to get a message out there. Nicholas was still there through the agency. She knew they'd be checking. Tweeting was the only means left to her of maintaining a public presence with a bit of dignity. In her tweets, she'd been terribly excited about the upcoming trip, accompanying her father to the romantic little village just inland from Venice where he'd once lived for a reunion in his honour . . . A last hurrah, though she didn't tweet that.

Now she was actually here, she needed to tell the world, or at least Slick and Slut, that she was feeling no pain, that she was having a ball. She opened her iPhone and got into Twitter. *Loving Venice and Venetians*, she thumbed. *Wild. Say hello to Paolo! LOL.* On second thoughts, she deleted *LOL*; it seemed both a bit young and a bit old, not to mention desperate. Adding a hashtag like *#betrayed* or *#lovelorn* would have been more honest, real, but she didn't want the company of her own kind.

She pressed *Send* and felt better for it. She was sure she could get back to sleep now. But then she realised what had woken her earlier. It sounded like a rhinoceros about to charge.

He'd warned her that, 'according to your mother', he snored and she'd told him not to worry, she was a heavy sleeper, she could sleep through anything. But she was thinking of Nicholas's deep, sonorous snoring, not these epiglottal, arrhythmic snorts.

When she'd mentioned, not complainingly, that Nicholas snored, he, typically, defensively, had said she snored too. That was the way he responded to anything he perceived as criticism. Ping-pong. No further discussion, no attempt to address the situation. So she'd asked him if her snoring was a problem for him. Was it keeping him awake?

'Next time, I'll let you know,' he'd said. It had sounded like a threat. Nothing happened until he star-fished one night, and kicked her shin so hard she yelped and woke him up. 'Can you keep it down, for Christ's sake!' he'd told her.

There was no point explaining. She'd slept on the sofa in the still warm living room, then next day made up a bed in the spare room, the one they'd designated the nursery. Once that single bed was there, it was enticing. Nicholas seemed permanently exhausted — now she knew why! — and would fall asleep on the sofa in front of the television after the best part of a bottle of wine over dinner. He'd already be half cut most evenings by the time he got home, after meeting some 'client/banker/valuer/ solicitor/mate' in a nameless bar along the strip. He'd get angry over almost anything she said. It was easier to sleep undisturbed in the spare room than have him crawl into bed in the early hours already hung-over, and often horny. Sometimes in the morning she'd lie there and try to remember what she might have said to upset him. And she'd tried to work it out since, whether there was any sort of pattern to their arguments, a consistent complaint that she might have picked up on if she'd been more attuned, whether there might have been a clue she'd missed . . .

Her counsellor had told her not to do this, to stop trying to unpick *what* had gone wrong, stop remembering him as he was *before* it had all gone wrong, the man with huge energy and charm and big brown eyes, who had made her laugh and dance drunk to Springsteen . . . *Stop that.* 'Surrender to what is,' she'd said.

During the day, he'd be strung out or speedy. There never seemed to be time to discuss anything: the real estate partnership seemed to devour them both. Her father had warned her when she and Nicholas had set up the agency that a cautious, diligent businessperson could protect himself or herself against most calamities: the one big, uncertain, almost uncontrollable vulnerability was to your partner. That was her father's way: he hadn't tried to overtly dissuade her, but he'd seen something in Nicholas she wished she'd seen herself.

The trouble was, her father's *noises* were so unpredictable. She'd almost be off, convinced he'd stopped, then he'd rear up again. She knew he wasn't well, that he must need his sleep, particularly after their hike to get here. She'd seen his chalky, thin old man's calves under his robe after he'd had his turn in the tiny bathroom, which had only a shower. That was a shock. He'd always had powerful legs; she had the thighs to prove it, worse luck. He'd been your typical Kiwi male prototype, legs like strainer posts and surprisingly spare up top. In little more than eighteen months, he'd gone from indeterminate late middle age to old: from healthy to sick, she reminded herself. She had to grin and bear it and get to sleep between blasts. She had to. She was almost off again, when the rhino was overtaken by a bull elephant, calling to its mate across the vast plains of the Serengeti.

'Dad! Please!'

'Please what?' he mumbled.

'Please stop! *Please*!'

'Stop what?' he asked, then realised. This had clearly happened before. 'Oh, sorry, darling,' he said.

She felt sorry for her mother. How on earth had she put up with this for so long? Oh hell, she thought, Why did I come? What am I doing here? He was still awake, so she tried not to let her tears become sobs. She should cry for him too. Though, as her counsellor had pointed out, he was very much part of her problem. Why she'd believed in love. What a fool.

3

He, at least, was quite chipper next morning. After he'd worked his way through his blister-pack of pills, he decided he didn't want the breakfast they'd already paid for. She had no quarrel with that, after seeing the dining room. Small tables had been pressed along one side of the entrance hallway, so that a motley collection of tourists could down stale croissants and beaker coffee in whispering polyglot huddles.

He led her back through Campo San Maurizio to Campo Santo Stefano, carrying his tatty old leather briefcase. When he'd turned up at the airport with that briefcase as carry on, she'd tried to persuade him to upgrade to a lightweight shoulder bag at duty free, but he'd baulked. He was a rational man — no one had ever described him as emotional, unless coupled with the word 'stunted' — but he seemed afraid that if he changed his briefcase he would somehow lose all its contents.

Once they were seated in a small cafe where the piazza pinched into the alley they'd entered from the night before, he opened the briefcase, pulled out a bulging manila file and began thumbing through the foolscap pages. No explanation. She tried to see the name on the outside but there didn't seem to be one, just some numbers beginning with *1* — the rest of the sequence was obscured by his hand.

'That's not mine, is it?'

'Hell no,' he said. Her relief was tempered when he continued. 'Though I did bring yours with me, just in case.'

In case of what? Nicholas wasn't about to change his stance in the next two weeks while they 'did' Venice, Florence and Rome.

She said nothing, and watched as he went back and forth through what looked like old typewritten pages. She could see the indentations on the backs of the pages where the keys had punched through the ribbon. He was looking for something he never seemed to find, and not just in the file. Every so often he'd look up at the passers-by, and either stare at them or quickly dismiss them and get back to his pages. She noticed there was a pattern to this. Those his gaze lingered on were all older women, elegantly dressed Venetians. His eyes would devour them, almost desperately, as if he didn't want to miss one detail, as if there must be a clue there somewhere if he looked hard enough. It was so obvious it was embarrassing, and she was about to say something when their macchiatos and pastries arrived. He closed the file, looked around the piazza again and said, 'It's all changed.'

Yes, Dad, she felt like saying, they're nearly forty years older and so are you. 'What's all changed?' she asked. 'This place doesn't look like it's changed in a thousand years.'

'Not the surroundings, the people. There are fewer people. You won't notice it once the day-trippers arrive, but there are only fifty thousand Venetians left here. There used to be at least a hundred thousand. They're abandoning it to the tourists.'

That figures, she thought. You wouldn't want to be trying to get over those dreadful little humpy bridges if you were old or disabled or a mother with a pram. How many families did that disqualify? *Close to bus and shops* would be meaningless in Venice.

When they'd finished their coffees, he said he'd show her the Rialto. At the other end of the piazza was a wooden footbridge that spanned the Grand Canal. He seemed to have regained his energy and sense of direction, as he explained to her that this was Accademia, where he thought they'd be disembarking last night. He stopped at the top of the bridge, breathing heavily, and pointed back down the canal towards one of the grand palazzi. 'Byron stayed there,' he said. 'He swam the canal. He had a club foot and probably felt he had to prove something. Venetians were very superstitious and thought those sorts of defects were contagious.'

I'm in the right place, she thought. Her counsellor would be appalled by the thought, but their work had convinced her that all sorts of contagions, which medical science hadn't yet considered, could be transmuted through blood and ether.

Then he swung round the other way and pointed to a huge domed church, Santa Maria della Salute, which he said stood sentinel over the entrance to Venice from the Adriatic. The low autumn sun was doing its best to break through the cloud cover and was lancing off the water into the old stone, giving the blue and grey a wash of pale yellow, like looking through gauze. She loved Turner and tried to remember if he'd ever painted Venice.

Water and light, she thought. Hard not to like. She'd been brought up in Herne Bay, had wanted to buy somewhere there, nearer the water, even if it had meant an in-fill do-up, but Nicholas wouldn't have it. In retrospect, she saw it may have been because she'd been brought up there, and because her father still lived there. He'd wanted to isolate her from all that.

They boarded a vaporetto on the other side of the bridge and found seats easily enough. The canal became a churning mess of water as they worked their way through boat traffic from stop to stop towards the Rialto Bridge. All the boat-buses coming the other way were full, standing room only, with people hanging onto straps and hand-rails.

'Day-trippers,' said her father. 'It's cheaper to stay outside

Venice and come in and out by train each day.'

How sensible, she thought. She wished it was Carnevale. He'd told her about that. Disneyland for adults. You got to dress up and behave badly before Lent, when presumably you confessed your sins and did penance before Easter. How Catholic. Although, saying that, Nicholas was theoretically Catholic and had shown no sign of penance. He seemed to regard his adultery as an understandable response to her shortcomings, though he'd never been specific about what these were. The way he explained it, his adultery was her fault, a kind of *constructive* adultery. And for that she was grateful: she didn't need to know why Sarah was better in bed than she was, what Sarah might do to entertain Pedro that she wouldn't.

Her father wasn't interested in the jewellery and trinkets in the Rialto stalls. He seemed preoccupied and then relieved once they'd traversed the bridge. 'Follow me,' he said, 'I'll show you where the locals buy their stuff.'

That sounded promising, until he told her it was food on sale, not handbags or shoes. She tried not to let her disappointment show as he led her among stalls of fresh vegetables and fish, which seemed a bit of a waste of time since they weren't able to cook at the B & B.

'Tomorrow morning,' he told her, 'we'll get up at the crack of dawn and you'll see the real Venice. Everything has to be brought in by boat and handcart, and all the rubbish taken out. It's like the tide, an army of workers, in and out, every day, and the tourists never see them.'

Once more, he seemed to be gazing at people, as if there was a clue somewhere there if he stared hard enough. At one stage, there was a yell from behind them, and she saw him turn, his face full of happy expectancy, until he realised that the big swarthy guy in the apron wasn't calling to him. That's it, she thought. He's expecting to meet someone he knows. He's *looking* for someone.

That made sense. In 1976 he'd lived for a year in a town on the mainland, somewhere close by, and had spent a lot of his time in Venice. It stood to reason that he would have known people here. But why doesn't he know where they live? Give them a ring, send them an e-mail, get on Facebook: Hey, I'm in town, what are you guys up to? She guessed she'd find out more tonight at the reunion.

He tired quickly. After drawing a blank at the market, they crossed back over the bridge and followed the signs for Piazza San Marco. After about ten minutes walking down narrow alleys they reached an intersection with signs for San Marco and Accademia. He told her he needed to sit down and might head back to the B & B so as to conserve his strength for tonight. Would that be okay with her? Would she be able to find her way to San Marco and then back to the B & B?

She was relieved, if she was honest. They'd passed several bag and shoe bottegas where she would have liked to have browsed. There'd doubtless be more between here and San Marco. And there was something else she'd made a decision about, that she didn't quite know how to broach with him.

Sometime before dawn, she'd realised that she couldn't brave another night on the Serengeti. She was going to get her own room in a decent hotel, whatever the cost. It would be much easier if she presented it to him as a fait accompli. He might not like the idea of her spending that money, but this morning's decision to skip breakfast notwithstanding, the Southerner in him would regard it as a greater sin to pay for a room and not stay in it.

Bari, 1942

4

Joe stood propped on one leg against the stable door listening for the dogs, while in the darkness Harry moved among the beasts with an easy, calming confidence. Harry was murmuring to them while he mucked out with his hands between their back legs, scraping shit and urine-infused cornstalks and hay across the earthen floor towards the wooden door.

Joe had wanted to hide in the hayloft, but Harry told him it was the first place Jerry would look: he'd be skewered by a bayonet. He got Joe to lie down in a shallow culvert that drained under the door, smeared him with shit, basted him with urine, then covered him with more of the muck he'd scraped from the floor. 'Jerry doesn't like shit on his boots,' said Harry. 'Or on his bayonet.'

So Joe lay in the dark culvert as Harry ministered to him and made it look as if the farmer had been halfway through mucking out his byre, and had left a smallish pile of old straw and shit blocking the drain, with the piss gradually pooling behind. 'Just as well it's cold,' said Harry. 'Your body temperature won't cake the shit.'

Harry spread some of the muck on his own boots and was

gone into the night. Joe didn't hear the wooden bar lift and latch as the door was opened, then closed.

He was as cold as death, which he thought might come before the Germans. For what seemed like a long time he shivered and had they come then, he would have been a goner. Then something surprising happened: a warmth suffused him, working out from his core. He was as comfortable as he could remember being since lying on the warm rocks beside the river at Clifton Falls, where the Kakanui's glides and riffles squeezed down a limestone gorge. He and Dan would dive into the deep blue green of the water and come out truly clean, white as they dried in the sun, all the coal dust and flour husks washed away. He'd clasped that image close, used it time and again to try and forestall the other images, the one from El Mreir where he'd dropped his rifle and tried to scrabble through the rock into the safety of the earth as a cloud of molten metallic fire broke over him. The shrapnel that sliced his head from crown to cheek had saved him from seeing much more.

But he'd seen everything on the *Nino Bixio*, somewhere out on the Mediterranean between Benghazi and Bari, though he'd been desperate to look away. His stretcher had been lashed to a mezzanine above the compartments in the forward hold where the able-bodied Kiwi prisoners of war were crammed. When the British torpedoes hit, bodies exploded upwards through the hatches. Some of the debris was recognisable. Legless torsos, arms, hands, feet, an eye among brain tissue splattering his blanket. As the ship listed, many of those who could had leapt into the sea. Joe saw a lifeboat out there with Italian crew and some prisoners on board, others clinging to rafts and flotsam, but he distrusted the sea and knew he had no chance in the water. He'd resigned himself to death and closed his eyes, but the horror of what he'd seen was imprinted on the back of his lids.

It had been at least a year now, but both El Mreir and the *Nino Bixio* were red-hot embers of a bush fire in his head, waiting for the nor-wester. While he could keep his head full of other thoughts, the flame spluttered and smouldered but never really died. In unguarded moments it would flare and all he could see was burnt and shredded flesh as the sky closed over him with concussive waves of fire. Feeding that blaze was the shame of his cowardice: that he'd dropped his rifle when the Panzers came and, in his terror, had scraped at the rock with bare, bloody hands, and that when he'd woken up in the Benghazi hospital and heard the nurses whispering in Italian, he'd been relieved that he was a prisoner, that his war was over.

He thought he'd lost the sight in one eye, but it was covered in bandages supporting his fractured cheekbone. When the dressings were lifted, his left eye had been slightly displaced by the force of the fragmented shell but he could see enough to notice that the patients with rosaries hanging above their beds got an extra piece of bread and other kindnesses and care from the nurses, nuns called suore. He'd been cowardly enough to ask for a rosary. Suor Teresa brought it to him. She spoke a little English, but not nearly enough to understand Joe's whispered confession of cowardice.

* * *

Some weeks later, after the *Nino Bixio* had been towed to Greece and they'd been transferred to a smaller vessel to run the Adriatic gauntlet, he'd done the same for Harry in the hospital at Bari.

Joe hadn't recognised anything about the motionless body on the stretcher when they'd carried it into the ward but heard the sisters trying to pronounce his name when they were writing up his chart. It took some imagination to get Henry Spence from what they were saying but he remembered a Harry Spence back in Ngapara just before the war.

Joe had been sixteen, lined up in the players' tunnel waiting for the referee to whistle them onto the field for his first senior club game. Nervous steel sprigs on concrete, an overpowering stink of liniment and players sneaking measuring glances at their opposites. Joe felt his bowels go and only just made it back to the dunnies. While he was in there, he heard the ref's whistle and pulled up his jock-strap and shorts and ran back to the tunnel, anxious not to be left behind. Most of the players had already taken the field. One opposition player was still in the tunnel, a tallish loose forward in white shorts and a black, red and amber hooped jersey, who was taking a last deep drag. He'd stubbed out the cigarette on an exposed joist, given Joe a teasing smile and jogged out onto the field, still exhaling smoke, all knees, elbows, angles and gristle. As the opposing half-back, Joe had done his best to let the ball go before that loosie got anywhere near him. From the side of the scrum and the back of the lineout he could feel those predatory eyes on him.

After the game, in the clubrooms beside the dressing shed, Harry Spence had been a striking figure in the local cockies' uniform of tweed jacket over checked shirt, off-white moleskins and brown riding boots, his dirty blond hair plastered down, a raw scrape of red on the bridge of his nose between powder blue eyes.

When the sisters were done, Joe went to have a look. The man didn't look much like the Harry Spence he remembered.

His eyes were closed. The only sign of life was the wound on his upper thigh already suppurating through the army blanket. The man's face was drawn back in a rictus grimace and Joe thought he might already be dead, until the fever wracked him, made his teeth clatter like a machine gun and threatened to throw him and the thin kapok mattress right off the wire springs. Spooked, Joe quickly retreated. By the time he got back to his own bed, the spasms had passed and the man was as quiet as a cadaver again.

At the Benghazi hospital, Suor Teresa had told him in halting English that she always knew which of the wounded soldiers would survive. 'Short neck,' she said, holding her hands a couple of inches apart as if she was about to pray. Joe thought Suor Teresa was trying to encourage him when he'd been so sick and weak. But Harry, if that's who he was, had a long neck and he looked as good as dead when later that night Joe took the rosary from above his bed and hung it above Harry's.

It might have been too late but at least the suore seemed to notice. Next day they cleaned and redressed the stinking wound and did what they could for him. But that night they called the local priest and Henry William Spence was given the last rites. Joe woke to the whispered Latin, the priest and two suore bent over Harry's waxen face. Joe thought about trying to stop it but watched and said nothing as Harry was commended unto God, the act of contrition or extreme unction, something like that. He ought to remember but couldn't. Instead he lay there wondering if he, not Harry Spence, would end up in hell because the fraudulent rosary wasn't Harry's sin, but Joe's.

There'd been no wife after the match at Ngapara, but a posy of local girls eager for Harry's attention. Joe was sad for whoever loved and was about to lose Harry Spence. It became more difficult to remember as the war went on and so many thousands were lost that back home there'd be a rippling circle of grief every time another one died. But not for him any more. Only Dan would mourn Joe now.

He was undecided these days about God and an after-life and thought it might be better for him if there wasn't: there'd be no room in heaven for a man who was thrice a coward when so many thousands of brave men were arriving every day at the pearly gates.

But Harry Spence didn't die that night.

Later, when Joe knew Harry better, he began to think that maybe indirectly the rosary had indeed saved Harry. That the last rites had ignited some small anti-Catholic spark that had flared into anger and brought him back from the brink. The following day Joe could see by the hour the infection releasing its grip as Harry Spence flowed back into the wasted husk. The fever had done its worst and was beaten.

One of the first things Harry noticed was the string of black beads hanging on the iron bedstead above his head. 'Who put those there?'

'The sisters,' Joe lied. 'You get better treatment if they think you're a Catholic.'

Harry reached up a bony hand and lifted them off. 'Bugger that,' he said. He went to throw them away, but was too weak and the beads fell on the bed and lay in his lap.

'I'll get rid of them,' Joe said.

Harry's faded blue eyes bored into Joe, but he said nothing and Joe couldn't tell whether there was any recognition in them before they closed again.

Over the weeks that followed, Joe watched Harry's resurrection as the infection retreated to his thigh and the ulcerated wound gradually healed. Early on, Joe told him they'd played against each other at Ngapara on the footy field cut from a paddock at the edge of town.

'Who'd you play for?'

'Athies,' said Joe. 'Half-back.'

'You're a Mick.'

'I was brought up that way,' said Joe.

'Which school?'

Joe shook his head. He'd desperately wanted to go to high school. When he was twelve, his last year at Ardgowan Primary, his teacher had argued that point with the old man but she had no chance. 'I started in the mine at thirteen,' he told Harry.

Although the coal mine at Ngapara was tough at first, he was used to hard work. He and Dan had always risen before dawn to get the cows in for milking by their sisters, then feed the horses, muck out the stable, put the team in harness. The old man made sure there was no time off: there were always jobs either side of school, from grubbing thistles to stooking hay to chopping wood. Nothing changed when he began at the mine except that he started earlier and finished later. The owner of the mine, Captain Nimmo, was a softie by comparison with the old man.

5

Despite Harry's contempt for Catholics, the home link seemed to count for something. He would wave Joe over to his bed to talk, or ask him to cadge a smoke from the suore, who were different from the severe sisters he'd seen at Sunday school and at the basilica in Reed Street. These ones chatted among themselves and laughed. Harry, who had a nose for these things, had spotted a couple of the younger ones having a furtive durry out on the terrace and thereafter he was at them all the time for a smoke. He'd make them laugh then hit them up. When Harry first wanted to get out of bed, the suore said no, but he did anyway, with Joe's shoulder supporting him as he hobbled painfully down the ward to a terrace with some chairs. There, Harry looked out at the drop of stone streets and houses to the wharves and the sea beyond. 'Where's this?'

Joe told him that he was in a converted barracks in Bari on the eastern seaboard of Italy, that there were a lot of Kiwi and other prisoners of war in a camp just out of town.

Harry didn't seem very interested in the view, but Joe sat on the terrace a lot, looking out at the town. The buildings were the same colour as the earth they sprang from — no paint, no wood. Oamaru had some grand old whitestone buildings, banks, courts, an opera house, yet none of those looked as old as any one of the ordinary houses and apartments here. He could see a breakwater like Oamaru's but much bigger, and a lighthouse and a castle with a moat. There were palm trees and a still fierce sun.

Joe wasn't sure what day or even month it was. He knew the

exact date they'd lined up for the advance on El Mreir: 21 July 1942. Time became hazy after that. Weeks had passed, but Joe had lost count of how many. He suspected that, despite the heat, it might be well into autumn. Bari reminded him of a smaller, tidier Cairo, and Benghazi, what little he'd seen of it when he was so sick. You could look out from Bari and feel North Africa just across the water. That gave him no comfort.

Other times, Harry seemed happy to have Joe sit by his bed. As they talked, Joe realised that the easy egalitarianism of the footy field had its limits, because the Harry Spence who came back from the dead was the sort of man that Joe had never really known before. It wasn't just that Harry was five or so years older, mid-twenties to Joe's just-turned nineteen, though that was significant. Nor was it just that Harry had some stripes — Joe wasn't sure how many currently, because in Harry's stories from Crete he'd been a sergeant, but by the time of El Alamein he was a corporal. Harry never overtly pulled rank yet everything he said had an unstated authority that might have come from his rank or experience or age, or might have come from home.

In Ngapara, hunched at the end of the Waiareka Valley before the hills rose up to Tokarahi and Danseys Pass, there'd been a geographical and social distance between the town and the upland farmers and Joe had heard the villagers, who mostly worked in the flour mill or the mine, say that the hill country people thought they were a cut above. Joe didn't know whether that was true, but the country beyond Ngapara was certainly different — huge limestone ridges that ran along the skyline like hand-hewn battlements — so it stood to reason that the people might be too.

Harry didn't give the impression of thinking he was a cut

above, but maybe he never needed to. It was embedded in everything that he was, all the props and struts and joists of background that went into the construction of the man Joe was gradually piecing together.

Harry had been a boarder at Waitaki Boys' High School down on the foreshore at Oamaru, whose famous rector, Frank 'The Man' Milner, seemed to know a war was coming. The stories were legion of boys having to sleep in huts named after the battlegrounds at Gallipoli, like Chunuk Bair and Lone Pine and Anzac Cove. These huts had no glass in the windows, just canvas blinds that would be lowered only in the worst weather. The boys would be woken to a trumpeted reveille, then had to muster in the quad in footy jersey and shorts and run to the end of the avenue where it met the main road and back, before stripping off, summer or winter, to swim a width of the school baths naked, encouraged by prefects with sticks. The school's Hall of Memories was draped with military flags and the rector made impassioned speeches about serving King and Country. The old man told Joe and Dan that if they thought they had it bad at home, he'd send them to Waitaki Boys' with the rest of the heathens for a bit of hell on earth. They never took his threats seriously because old Malachy Lamont didn't have the money, but from what Joe knew of Waitaki, it seemed like a school for soldiers and it was no surprise that a man like Harry would take to war like a duck to water.

Joe could see that the expectations arising from a background like Harry's were very different from his own, even though they came from farms that were less than thirty miles apart. Malachy Lamont's land at Devil's Bridge was a small-holding won in a ballot during the enforced break-up of the big estates late last century. Its name came from the way the water in the local creek disappeared into a limestone cliff on one side of the hill and reappeared on the other. The children had been forbidden to go into the cavern where the water came out, but Dan and Joe had once walked a little way in, until a gurgle of water from the darkness ahead had sounded like the devil clearing his throat and they'd run. Joe had gone straight from dux at Ardgowan School to the mine at Ngapara, because the Lamont farm couldn't support any more mouths in the aftermath of the Depression.

Joe had missed school. Since he was five, he and Dan and the three youngest of their six sisters, Betty and Agnes and Ida, had ridden to school together on an old horse, retired from the team. They'd followed a track established by their older sisters up a long valley and under the wooden aqueduct that brought water in an open race thirty miles from the Waitaki River to the Oamaru reservoir, just across the valley from the school. Ardgowan School never had more than forty pupils. It was just a big room with a steeply pitched corrugated iron roof set on a ridge that looked back west, past Devil's Bridge and the Waiareka Valley to the Kakanui Mountains on the horizon, the hill country where Harry farmed. Beyond the mountains was the basin of the Maniototo. Plain of Blood, someone said it meant.

Joe had always loved that view of blue hills and white tops. Sometimes in Benghazi hospital he'd tried to use that memory to help keep the molten sky of El Mreir at bay. But El Mreir had leached its way in one night when Joe was particularly desperate to leave it behind. The grand peaks of the Kakanuis had begun to melt and Joe felt something awful stirring behind them on the Plain of Blood. He tried not to think of it again.

Maybe Harry knew more about the Lamonts than he let on.

Maybe it was just that Joe was a coal miner, or a private, but the difference between them was clear mostly in the way Harry talked about the war.

Joe had seen only terror and confusion in his one action, the night attack at El Mreir. Three infantry companies from the 24th Battalion, about three hundred and fifty men, had fought their way towards a set of co-ordinates on someone's map, cutting a line through minefields, then making close-quarter assaults on nests of machine guns and isolated defensive strongpoints. As they waited for the off, fuelled by adrenaline and fear, seconds had seemed to stretch to hours, then compress again when they walked into a steel mesh of bullets. Joe had cursed the darkness to begin with, until the night lit up with flares and tracers and mortars. In those brief explosive brightnesses he could see the splaying and ripping of flesh and bone but was mostly spared what followed as his eyes tried to readjust to the blackness. For most of the advance they couldn't see the enemy until they were upon them and then thankfully it was all in monochrome: the faces Joe shot at, some as young as his. That had surprised him. In his imaginings the Germans had all been hardened veterans. Reason suggested that because he was still alive some of those Germans he had shot at must be dead. One of them might have been putting his hands up, or not. Maybe he was reaching for something. His mouth was open and he looked surprised when he fell.

By the time they reached their objective it was about 2 a.m. and fewer than a hundred of the three hundred and fifty were left, shocked by the hand-to-hand savagery of their first engagement and by the loss of so many of their mates. They lay battered and exhausted in what seemed like a sandy hollow as the trucks and mortars caught up. They were ordered to dig in while it was still dark and wait for the British tanks to arrive at dawn.

The sand proved superficial — six inches down was unyielding rock. They didn't have to wait long for the tanks. The British never arrived but just after 5 a.m., in the pre-dawn darkness, a Panzer division appeared on the lip of the low cliff just in front of them. The Panzers were shooting blind but the Kiwis were so close it didn't matter. What no one had told Joe about battle was the noise. He'd thought the sounds of close combat were horrific enough, the cries and screams, the expulsions of air and blood when the body was punctured by bullet or bayonet. He was used to explosions in the mine, the dull whump of dynamite drilled deep into the face and packed. But when those Panzers had opened up with their big barrels so close, his ears popped with the shock-waves of air from the shells as they hit the rock and fragmented and went right through flesh and blood and metal. The ammo truck took a direct hit and if the Germans had been struggling to see in front of them, that fireball solved the problem. Their machine gun tracer scorched the last pockets of air and Joe stopped looking, dropped his rifle and tried to burrow his way back home through the rock. Until mercifully he'd been hit by a piece of shell, it must have been.

El Mreir was all Joe knew about the real war, but Harry had come over in the Second Echelon — said he'd pulled a favour with an old Waitaki mate in Wellington to get into the 22nd Battalion so he could get to the war sooner. He'd fought in every battle the New Zealand Division had been involved in, from Greece to Crete to North Africa. According to Harry, every one of those, until El Alamein, had been either a SABU, a self-adjusting balls-up, or a GAFU, a general army fuck-up. It seemed the stronger Harry got, the angrier he got, but not with the Germans, whom he always referred to as 'Jerry'.

'What happened to you at El Mreir had already happened to 4th Brigade at Ruweisat Ridge the week before. We reach our objective by night, then come dawn we're sitting ducks for the Panzers because the Pommie tanks we've been promised are nowhere to be seen.'

In Harry's view, most of the Div's defeats — and they were all defeats from Greece through to El Alamein — were GAFUs and could be laid at the feet of Churchill or the English commander of the 8th Army, 'that twit Auchindick', who'd split the New Zealand brigades up into digestible portions for Rommel's benefit and had left the Kiwi infantry to fight battles against entrenched enemy positions that should have been attacked by British tanks. Sidi Rezegh made Harry particularly bilious, the way the Kiwis were abandoned and nearly five thousand men killed, wounded or captured in two days. Joe had heard about that. The 20th Battalion, which included most of the South Island intake Joe had trained with at Burnham, had been pretty much wiped out.

Joe had no idea what communications had taken place at El Mreir while they were waiting in that wadi for dawn and the arrival of British tanks, but Harry's suggestion that the British tank commander might have spotted a grammatical mistake in the Kiwi request for support, a misplaced comma, perhaps, into which ambiguity could be read, seemed to make a bitter, futile sense.

Most days, towards evening, Harry would manage to cadge a smoke from one of the younger suore, and with a cigarette between his lips, seemed more reflective. Joe saw an opening to talk about something he was struggling with.

At Maadi he'd been separated from the southern Burnham intake and put into the 24th, an Auckland battalion, as filler. He hadn't made any real friends by the time of El Mreir, but even so, almost all the faces he recognised were no longer there next morning. He'd seen some of them go down — one, Darby O'Neill, another filler from Dunedin, right alongside, calling to him, but he'd been ordered to keep going, told the medics would come for Darby. Joe heard later that Darby was among the hundreds who didn't make it that night. Death became commonplace so quickly, so easily. Joe couldn't mourn anyone, because there were so many. Where did you start? And the guilt. Because what he was thinking as his comrades died screaming or silently all around him was mainly 'It's not me. Yet.' Joe worried that he wasn't responding correctly to the death all around him, that there must be something wrong with him. How had Harry coped with so many more lost mates?

But for Harry, the dead had simply 'copped it' in an unquestionable cause. Hitler was evil scum and had to be stopped. He wasn't interested in talking about the mates he'd lost, but only about his opinion of what had gone right or wrong, who had won, who had lost. He was particularly incensed that he'd been wounded and captured at El Alamein when they finally 'had Jerry by the throat' and had learnt how to beat him, with night attacks supported by tanks that could be relied on to turn up when they said they would.

Joe admired Harry's strategic perspective on the terror and confusion of war, but was left wondering if he should be feeling something more than fear and guilt.

6

Joe's wound was healing. The scar tissue down his temple and cheek had pulled the edge of his left eye up and open so it always looked a bit startled. From what he'd seen in the wards at Benghazi and Bari he thought it was a small price to pay.

One morning Joe said goodbye to Harry: he'd been cleared by the doctor to join the rest of the POWs at the camp on the edge of town.

'Me too,' said Harry. 'I've had enough of this lark.'

Joe said nothing, certain the doctor and the suore would stop him, but when the carabinieri came to escort him to the camp, Harry was there too, propped up with one crutch in what was left of his fighting kit, his lemon squeezer hat, a shirt with the black *New Zealand* shoulder tab and boots. His shorts had been cut off him in the field hospital, but the sisters had found some trousers that hung baggy from the waist. With Joe's regulation shorts and a borrowed singlet, they had the makings of one uniform between them.

The contrast with the carabinieri couldn't have been greater. The older one, who might have been an officer, was an elaboration of dark blue serge and gold braid, with a three-cornered hat surmounting jowls and dewlaps that hadn't been anywhere near serious work, let alone fighting. The callow youth beside him, who stared wild-eyed at Harry and Joe with his rifle raised, was more modestly uniformed.

'You're an absolute picture, mate,' said Harry, as the senior carabiniere waved his rifle to usher them in front of him.

The man gave no indication as to whether he'd understood

but when it became apparent that Harry wasn't going to get far using a crutch and Joe's shoulder, he said, 'Stop.'

After a rapid exchange, the younger man hared off down the street and the older man said, haltingly but clearly, 'We are waiting here.'

They were on a narrow footpath near a corner that looked out across a small square. There was washing strung out to dry above them, and a small shrine of Mary and baby Jesus set into the wall nearby. Joe was happy to stand there, watching the small intimate transactions of everyday life.

Harry relaxed onto his crutch and asked the carabiniere if he had a smoke. The man shook his head. Satisfied that the policeman would understand, Harry told Joe a story in slow and careful English, about finding an Italian tank in the desert, abandoned, not a scratch on it. The hatch was open and inside it was immaculate, the gun turret pristine, the magazine and gas tank full. Clearly this machine had never fired a shot in anger. 'But you know the really amazing thing about that Italian tank?' asked Harry. 'When we started it up, we found it had one forward gear and four reverse gears.'

The carabiniere pursed his lips but it was unclear whether he'd understood until he hoicked a fat glob of spittle, which landed dead centre on the front of Harry's shirt. It was the first time Joe had seen Harry smile so broadly. 'Bull's-eye,' he said.

They were blocking the footpath and people had to step around them. The carabiniere's action seemed to unlock some animosity in the passing townsfolk, women particularly, and mostly towards Harry. He was spat at more than once, although others clearly tried to remonstrate. By the time the small truck arrived with the young carabiniere riding shotgun both men were grateful to ease themselves onto the tray and get out of

41

there.

The truck worked its noisy way parallel to the bay through narrow streets towards hillsides of olive groves. When they crossed the main road up from the wharves, Joe saw a huge poster that might have explained the reaction of the Italian women. There were smaller words that neither Joe nor Harry could understand but across the middle was one word, *Difendila!*, which was easily translatable in concert with the cartoonish drawing underneath: a wild-eyed, dark-skinned man attempting to ravish a beautiful Italian girl who was trying desperately to push him away. As he thrust himself on the crying woman, the devil's hat was falling off the back of his head.

'The hat's definitely a lemon squeezer,' said Harry, adjusting his own.

After inductions at the camp were completed, they were given a groundsheet and some bundles of straw and shunted out into an orchard riven by a dry canal bed. It seemed there was a choice of lying under the trees or in the canal. Thousands of men were spread across the land, trying to find some shade. They were dirty, malnourished and thirsty. While Joe and Harry were taking it all in, a noticeably pudgy individual appeared before them, waving a bag full of bread rolls.

'You fellas will need a couple of these,' he said, in a broad Kiwi accent.

'Will we?' asked Harry.

'You'll find out soon enough. When you do, come to me at the cookhouse, I'll do you a deal.'

'What kind of a deal?' asked Harry.

'I like the look of that wristwatch,' said the man.

'Do you?' asked Harry, slipping it from his wrist and holding it out to him. When the man reached for it, Harry swung his crutch into the back of his knees. By the time he hit the ground, Harry had handed Joe the crutch and his hands were at the man's throat. He struggled for a short time, then convulsed and was still. Harry calmly asked Joe to hand him the bag of rolls. Harry took out one and broke it open. The inside was green with mould. The man on the ground was gasping and coughing, trying to get air back into his lungs as Harry stuck the bread roll in his mouth, mould first.

'You're a fucking disgrace,' Harry said. 'If I see you again, you're dead.'

The cookhouse wallah scurried away as Harry manoeuvred himself back onto his feet, cheered by twenty or thirty skeletal soldiers who'd been attracted by his efforts. Some of them were from Harry's 22nd Battalion, had thought he was dead.

Joe left him to it and wandered out into the orchard, hoping to see someone he knew from his battalion or from Maadi, but didn't recognise any of the gaunt faces that occasionally looked his way. Back at the gate, another large truck arrived with more prisoners so Joe found the first spot he could and laid out his straw and groundsheet near an emaciated fair-haired man with skin the colour of old leather.

'Where you from, cobber?' the man asked.

'Down south,' said Joe.

'Lot of Kiwis here,' said the man. 'And Aussies, worse luck.' He introduced himself as Howie from Adelaide and told Joe there was fuck all food, water or shelter going around, but an abundance of amoebic dysentery and lice.

And queues, Joe discovered, when late in the afternoon long lines formed in front of the cookhouse for a foul-smelling broth with lumps of something floating in it. Joe tried to ignore the smell. He looked in vain for the bread roll man among those serving up. His eyes were drawn to the battle tunic of the man in front of him. The seams round the shoulders and down the back were crawling with lice. They looked like there was no more room inside and were trying to escape.

Later he lay on the straw, using the groundsheet as a blanket against the cold. When he looked up at the stars in a black sky he remembered the teacher at the one-room school at Ardgowan, who had told him that the sky wasn't a blue canopy decorated with lights that came out at night, but infinity. Nothingness. That had seemed unimaginable. He'd thought there had to be an end out there somewhere. Now he knew that her story of a black void lit by fiery burning suns was true. He'd become afraid of the sky. He yearned for the mine at Ngapara, the carefully excavated and buttressed shafts, the secure earth above.

In the six years between leaving school and presenting himself as a volunteer at the drill hall in Itchen Street, right above the lovers' lane he'd heard about but never walked through, he'd spent six days a week of eight-hour shifts underground. There'd been lots of explosions down there, dynamite drilled and packed into the coal face, a carefully controlled combustion that sent clouds of black dust back up the shaft, then silence, always silence. Joe stared at the black sky and listened for the sound of an engine, the low drone of an aircraft, the clanking of armoured tracks on rock, waited for the fire and flesh and intestine to fall and spit on hot hard metal. Nothing but the sound of cicadas, mosquitoes, and the curses and wet splatters of the men wracked by dysentery squatting below him in the canal.

* * *

He must have slept. When he awoke, there were no stars above him. He was lying in the drain in some contadino's stable. Jesus Christ, he was cold. The embers inside him seemed to have died. Even the flaming sky of El Mreir couldn't warm him now. Dying smeared in cow shit would be a suitable end, he thought. He'd been raised a farmer's boy. There were worse ways to go.

Sometime later he heard voices. The sounds came from the back of the throat like a tui's glottal stops, so different from the thrush song of Italian. They seemed to come from far way, though they must have been right above him because he could also hear their boots. 'Jerry doesn't like shit,' Harry had said. 'He won't imagine that anyone would hide themselves in it.'

But when Joe heard the boots hard and clear on the packed earth right beside his head, he braced himself for the bayonet and found himself hoping for God rather than black infinity and fiery suns.

San Pietro di Livenza, 2014

7

It was already dark when Clare and her father crossed the bridge at Accademia again and took the vaporetto back up the Grand Canal. She was grateful it was full of day-trippers heading back to the train station, because there was no space to talk. He'd accepted her move to a hotel — 'so that they could both be more comfortable and get a decent night's sleep' — in that phlegmatic way of his, but she could tell he was a bit hurt. They passed under the Rialto and continued on past the train station stop to Piazzale Roma, a huge roundabout ringed by parking garages.

Her father had received a message from his contact at San Pietro to look out for a black Audi Q5 opposite one of the garages, and it was already waiting when they walked up the steps from the pontoon. As soon as he saw them, the driver got out of the car and came around to shake their hands. Beautifully dressed in a subdued earth-toned jacket over a V-necked pullover and buttoned-down collar, he radiated warmth and welcome. Lorenzo — Renzo, he insisted — looked to be in his early thirties, with the kind of stocky, athletic frame that to her father spoke mid-field back.

'Inside centre, yes,' said Renzo, 'recently retired, but never very good.' His accent was American, with only a hint of Italian in the r's and vowels. Clare was disappointed: there were enough Americans speaking like that, it just sounded wrong in a European. But he was very solicitous, opening the front passenger door for her father, making sure he was able to step up. Then Renzo opened the rear door for her. 'Age before beauty, Signorina Clare,' he said to her. 'I'm sure you understand.'

As they drove back across what her father called Mussolini's causeway, spanning the lagoon to the mainland, Renzo explained to her father that he'd been too young to see him play, but had seen many photos of him and heard many stories. 'You and Franco are still the inspiration for running backs at our club.'

Her father seemed to have trouble knowing quite how to respond to such praise. He nodded and stared out the window at the lights of the Mestre tower blocks. He might have been more comfortable in the back seat by himself.

'Did you play professionally?' she asked Renzo, leaning forward.

'Oh no,' he said. 'These days our club moves between Serie B and C, not like the glory days of your father's era. I also played in Boston, when I was doing my doctorate at MIT. Now I'm retired from rugby, I contribute as a member of the dirigenti, the committee that administers the club. My day job is at Padova University, where I teach physics. Education was very important to my family.'

'You've come all the way from Padova for tonight?'

'I live in Treviso, half an hour away,' he shrugged, 'and I have family in Venice. Your father's return is a big moment for us.'

Renzo's lionising of her father set the tenor for the evening.

He'd spoken from time to time about his sojourn in Italy and she'd seen a couple of photos of him and his team-mates at San Pietro di Livenza, but the more detailed her questions about his time there, the vaguer his answers seemed to become.

They left the lights of Mestre behind and continued north on the autostrada for about twenty minutes, then took an exit onto a flat two-lane black-top across what Renzo said were the plains of the Veneto. They could see the lights of houses on both sides of the road. To her they were spaced far enough apart to seem much less urban than where they'd come from, but not to her father.

'Lights everywhere,' he said finally. 'This used to be countryside.'

'Ah,' said Renzo, 'since you were last here we joined the EU, and suddenly having a few campi became profitable, so . . .'

'Agricultural subsidies,' agreed her father. 'We canned ours about the time the EU ramped yours up.'

There was a hint of bitterness in his tone. He had sold the family farm in the mid-eighties, just after agricultural subsidies were suddenly withdrawn and farm prices tanked. 'If I'd only gone earlier or hung on' was a fairly frequent refrain.

Renzo made a call ahead and shortly afterwards they crossed a bridge spanning a substantial-looking river and entered a little town that seemed to have nestled in close to the water with high levees either side.

'How much do you remember?' asked Renzo.

'Everything,' said her father, though it was apparent that some of the blander square-fronted buildings in the main street could not have been more than a decade or two old.

They turned left around the fountain of the central piazza and drove slowly down a wide cobblestoned street past the grand municipio building towards a small gathering of people, late middle-aged men, some older, some a little younger, filing out of the big double doors under *Bar* and *Peroni* neons.

Renzo stopped in front of them and turned, smiling expectantly at her father. 'Your old friends,' he said, 'here to welcome you.'

Now that they were here, having travelled twenty thousand kilometres for the occasion, her father seemed frozen, staring as if he'd seen the ghosts he'd mentioned on the Alilaguna. She got out and opened his door. 'Dad?'

As soon as they saw him, the men began smiling and clapping and calling out something that sounded like 'Broochay! Broochay!'

'It's Italian for Bruce,' said her father, snapping out of it with a wry grin. 'An old joke.' As his legs hit terra firma, the men were upon him, around him, grabbing his hands in both of theirs, some embracing him. Gradually they opened an aisle to the doors of the bar, where a much older man, maybe eighty, thick head of tousled hair, almost as wide as he was tall, was standing with the aid of a walking stick. He was weeping.

'Aldo,' said her father. As he climbed the steps towards his old friend, Aldo dropped his stick and hugged him like a long-lost brother.

Renzo meanwhile had one gentle hand on her upper arm and was introducing her to a succession of grey-haired men with names that ended in 'o' — Marios and Giorgios and Claudios. Some greeted Renzo by name, but many of them acknowledged him as 'Professore' or 'Dottore'. When she asked him which he was, he told her he was both. When she said she was terribly impressed, he looked bashful. The men she was introduced to gripped her in strong hands and pulled her to them for sometimes whiskery kisses on both cheeks with exclamations of 'Che bea!' When she asked Renzo what 'bea' meant and was told it was dialect for 'bella, beautiful', it was her turn to look bashful.

They were ushered inside, through a bar area to a restaurant where many tables had been pushed together to make one long table. Renzo seated himself beside her directly to the left of the head of the table, occupied by her father and Aldo.

Once everyone was seated, Aldo's wife Beatrice and her two middle-aged sons appeared from the kitchen, laden with bottles of prosecco and baskets of bread. More tears, this time from Beatrice. She had a beautiful face, stretched tight by grey hair pulled back in a French roll. She hugged her father, then held his face between both palms and kissed him, before introducing him to her sons, who both made what sounded like practised speeches.

'They remember him fondly,' translated Renzo quietly, 'though they were both very young.' When they'd finished, her father looked briefly uncertain about what to do next, but then stepped forward and shook both their hands — rather like the Pope, she thought, handing out benedictions.

Once everyone was seated, Aldo produced a well-worn clipping from a newspaper and, according to Renzo, asked her father to translate it for her as he read it.

'"Addio e auguri" dice Bruce,' said Aldo, reading the title.

'Goodbye and best wishes, says Bruce,' translated her father. It was an interview he'd given to *Corriere Dello Sport* just before he'd left Italy to come home.

As Aldo began reading the body of the article, declaiming every word as if it were Shakespeare, it became apparent that her father didn't understand very much at all of what he'd been quoted as saying. Renzo translated for her, somehow including her father's bewildered nods and smiles as much as Aldo's words. It was a David and Goliath story: little San Pietro pitted against the great cities of Milano, Torino, Roma and Padova in Serie A. San Pietro may not have had the money and playing resources of the giants, but it had demonstrated an exceptional combination of rugby spirit and ethos.

'And grinta,' said Renzo, struggling to translate the word.

'Guts,' said her father, and the table burst into applause.

'Ghe sboro mi!' exclaimed her father, much encouraged.

The table roared. Renzo looked a little embarrassed. 'It gives me a small ejaculation,' he said. 'An old Venetian saying.'

Aldo beamed his approval and the rest of the speech was punctuated with much acclamation by the men around the table.

'He says that he came to San Pietro with no expectations, and although he has to return to New Zealand for personal reasons, he feels as if he is leaving a part of himself in San Pietro, and would always value his time here and the wonderful friends he made,' finished Renzo, as Aldo drew Bruce to his feet and hugged him, then sat down, leaving him staring into an expectant silence.

She felt sorry for her father, aware that he had to somehow honour the occasion and concerned that his failure to do so was inevitable. His response would be dry and terse and, surely, in English. She was grateful Renzo was there to translate and was wondering how to suggest that he add a bit of emotional colour, when her father began speaking. In Italian. Fluently, without notes and at a pace Renzo's whispers in her ear struggled to keep up with.

'I have lived in a far-off land and never came back for nearly forty years, for reasons which some of you will understand, but my time here has remained with me always, in my cuore' — he thumped his heart — 'and in indelible memories which have accompanied me every day of my life since I lived among you.'

Christ, she thought, as Renzo translated, Who is this man? Where's he been hiding?

'I'm so sorry that my Italian is no longer good enough to speak to you with the eloquence and profundity which such old friendships deserve, but rest assured that though my tongue is tied, my heart is full of love and respect for you all.'

She could feel her eyes watering. Absolute silence. Renzo's whispers were growing softer and softer as he tried not to break the spell. *That's* what he's been doing in his room, she thought. He's been writing this speech and learning it off by heart.

Then he spoke about absent friends, named about five men, beginning with Angelo someone and ending with Domenico. Then something peculiar happened. He choked on another name, had trouble getting it out. It sounded like 'Franco', but when she turned to Renzo for clarification, he had tears streaming down his face and couldn't talk. Aldo was dabbing his eyes, and when she looked back to the table, they were all similarly affected.

'I'm sorry,' said Renzo. 'Emotion is contagious.'

'Who was Franco?'

'Your father's playing partner in the centres. You remember, we talked about him in the car.'

'Yes, but what on earth happened to him?'

'He died.'

So had the others her father had named, but their collective pain about Franco seemed to be of a different order. For all the deep emotion in the room, and all the words that had been spoken, she sensed that something important had been left unsaid. So, instead, they cried. Her father too. Those blue eyes, which mostly looked as if they were focused on something far away, were streaming now. She'd never seen him *close* to crying, and would never have believed it possible that the first time she saw him weep would be in public, at a table full of retired Italian rugby players.

She had no idea whether they'd received news of her father's illness, but the ravages of chemo and the bone marrow transplants were writ large in the deep ravines of his face and his skinny angularity, and you could hear his attempts to drag energy into his voice, which made his words all the more poignant. They all knew there'd be no encore.

He'd stopped speaking, she realised, seemed exhausted. 'Bravo,' the men said, 'bravo, Bruce.'

Aldo lumbered to his feet and hugged her father and they stood there for some moments comforting each other, before Aldo began singing in a powerful baritone. Everyone stood, Renzo included, and sang with passion.

O che bea Venezia
Non posso andar'via
M'hai fatto 'nammorare.

At the end, they raised their glasses of prosecco and toasted 'Broochay', then Beatrice and Aldo's sons arrived with the first course, prosciutto and melone.

Clare felt as if she'd witnessed something special, but also bewildering, that underneath the tears and laughter of nostalgia there was something melancholic, perhaps even tragic, that she hadn't understood.

Gemona, 1943

8

When Joe regained consciousness, he could hear a voice through the lingering fog. He lay there listening. His body felt heavy but comfortable. Warm. He couldn't feel his ankle. If the sounds were German, he wouldn't open his eyes, he'd let himself drift off again without attracting attention. But there was no mistaking the Italian, even though it was too low to distinguish many words. It was a woman's voice and Joe thought he might somehow be back in hospital with the suore. When he ventured a glance, there was only a young woman in quarter profile looking down at something, her head bowed and angled towards the low light, her lips moving. Joe strained to see the baby Jesus in her lap. When he lifted his head, her serious hazel eyes left the book she'd been reading and he realised she wasn't a heavenly illusion. Beyond her was a very ordinary room: one curtained window, rough plastered walls and wooden furniture, a small table with a bowl on it, and two straight-backed wooden chairs facing his bed, the closer of which she was sitting on.

'Eccolo!' she called out to someone. *Here he is.* He understood that.

Presently, her face was replaced by a man's, older, perhaps

her father's, a big forehead pressing creases around the same widely spaced eyes. He could understand the man's carefully enunciated Italian. 'Come stai?' *How are you?*

Joe tried to say something, but initially no sound came.

The man said 'Permesso', put a calloused hand to the back of Joe's head and lifted it to a long-necked bottle. He drank as much water as he could.

Finally he croaked 'Bene', his voice giving the lie. He felt the weakness and lassitude that he'd known in the Benghazi hospital and then in the drain of urine and shit. He shivered. How had he got from there to here? How long had he been here? Maybe the room was a cell, but the three people now in the room — the man and young woman had been joined by another woman, older, perhaps the mother — seemed more like a family than jailers. He must have been looking alarmed. The man put a finger to his lips, said, 'Stai tranquillo.' Joe could see his relief when he indicated he'd understood.

'Dove sono?' he asked. *Where am I?*

'Lei parla italiano?' asked the younger woman.

'Un pochino,' he said, *a little*, though he hoped it was better than that. The man told him he was safe, for now. He should rest, he'd been very sick, he should sleep.

He must have. The next time he woke, there was just her. She was sitting in the chair, again reading, but ready this time for his return, her face front on, looking down. He had time to take her in, dark lashes above broad cheekbones, and below them, down almost to her jaw, the scars of what must have been smallpox. The curtain was drawn back a little, letting in daylight, giving the tresses that framed her face a copper sheen. When she sensed his eyes on her, she looked up and smiled at him and called softly — 'È ritornato.'

The older man and woman came back into the room. 'Sei inglese?' the man asked.

'Neozelandese,' Joe croaked.

They stood there looking at him, a grave little circle. This must be the family who lived through the wooden door that adjoined the stable he'd hidden in. Joe's ankle had deteriorated to the point where he could no longer put any weight on it and Harry had left him propped against the main entrance to the stable while he crept to the door at the far end. When he came back he said there were people in there, they had to be quiet.

The man was holding out his hand to Joe. 'Mi chiamo Bepi,' he said.

'Piacere,' said Joe, grateful that this big square hand had found him. So far the family had not betrayed him, were giving him food and shelter, but he knew the Germans would still be looking for him and wondered if he should tell them his name. They had found him covered in shit, freezing, cleaned him, warmed him. Whatever happened, they had saved him. 'Mi chiamo Joseph,' he said.

'Joseph?' said Bepi, then pointed to himself. 'Giuseppe! Joseph, Giuseppe!' The coincidence seemed to give him huge pleasure. He introduced his wife, Nina, and daughter, Donatella.

'Piacere, Signora, Signorina,' said Joe.

Bepi explained with much gesticulation that the Germans had completed their rastrellamento of their house and stable, tipping over beds, stabbing the hayloft with bayonets, without finding him. After they'd gone, Bepi had gone down to check they'd latched the stable door behind them and had noticed the build-up of urine in the drain. He couldn't make out what the obstruction was in the darkness so he put his foot on it. Bepi mimicked a low moan or groan and stepped back, startled. 'Che cosa è?' *What is it?*

Harry had been right. He'd left Joe where the Germans wouldn't find him, but someone else would. What happened now?

Bepi seemed to understand his anxiety. 'Stai tranquillo,' he repeated. 'Noi,' he said, indicating the three of them, 'Noi siamo amici. Capito?'

Joe understood. *We are friends.* He was safe, for the moment.

He must have fallen asleep again in front of them. When he next woke, it was dark and he was alone. He was busting and pulled back the covers and laboured into a sitting position. The privy would be outside, if he could find his way there. He could flex the ankle when it had no weight on it so he tried to stand up. The blood immediately filled the damaged tissue so that he almost swooned with the pain and sank back onto the bed and waited for the throbbing to subside. He'd seen a basin at the end of the bed: he'd use that.

Bepi had been reassuring, but he had no idea that there had been two of them out there being hunted by the Germans. Where was Harry? If he'd been caught, Joe's refuge here was on borrowed time. They were after them both: one would not be enough. They'd come back here to where Harry had left him, find him right next door to the cow byre. And then Joe himself would not be enough: this little family would also suffer.

He consoled himself with the thought that Harry was the bravest man he knew. The Germans were brutal and efficient but it would take them a long time to break Harry, even if they caught him. Harry had always been intent on escape, and finally he'd managed it, although it'd taken him the best part of a year to do it. He wouldn't have been retaken easily.

9

When the prisoners had been herded onto the train heading north out of Bari, Harry ended up in the same cattle truck as Joe. It was the first time Joe had seen him since they'd arrived at the camp two or three weeks before. He was much stronger than when Joe had last seen him, hardly limping and simmering with a belligerence that threatened to provoke any guards in his vicinity. For that reason, Joe tried to keep his distance but Harry, oblivious, passed on to Joe the consensus: they were going all the way to Germany. 'Not how I thought I'd get there,' said Harry.

They were in the cattle trucks for two nights, not always moving, and had no idea where they were when the doors were rolled back and they were ordered out. The wintry blast of air and grey-green landscape might have signalled a different country, it was so unlike Bari and North Africa. When they saw the name of the station, Cividale, on the pale yellow wall of a verandahed two-storey building that looked to Joe like a grand homestead, they realised they were still in Italy. Joe had been aching for green and relief from the heat but as they were marched from the station, the seeping cold and the trees standing bare bones against a grey sky made him suddenly homesick for colour and light.

Campo Prigionieri di Guerra 57 at Grupignano was a huge purpose-built prison about a mile from the railway station. There were rows of wooden barracks, administration and communal buildings, all surrounded by intimidating twenty-foot-high barbed wire, arc lights, machine gun posts and sentries. It was late November by the time they got there, and PG 57 was already home to four or five thousand, most of them Australians and New Zealanders, but also many South Africans and Canadians.

That first night Joe climbed into a top bunk and watched the man below him, Ernest he said his name was, put striped pyjamas over his underwear and kneel in whispered prayer beside his bunk. Joe could see the bald spot on his crown. He looked older than most, mid-thirties perhaps, though it was hard to tell because he was so gaunt. When he finished his prayers Ernest stood up, said, 'Ah well, that's that then.' He walked past the wood stove to the door of the barracks. Joe thought he must be going to the dunny, but shortly after they heard, directly outside, shouts of 'Halt! Halt!' from the guards, then the chatter of sub-machine guns. The other POWs rushed outside — Joe made sure he wasn't among the first. Ernest, in his blood-splattered pyjamas, was lying out in no man's land almost under the first wire.

Captain Calcaterra had addressed them en masse the next morning. They were shivering and hungry. They didn't have to know a word of Italian to understand that he was another vainglorious peacock of a carabiniere, stocky enough to stay upright under the weight of medals strewn across his chest. The translation made it clear that he was also a ruthless martinet: the men should stay at attention until he was finished speaking; any interruption would be dealt with severely; they would salute any Italian officer they encountered and stand at attention when the Italian flag was raised and lowered at the beginning and end of each day. Joe had been relieved at the restraint Harry showed, restricting himself to a muttered 'The man's a fucking joke'.

Calcaterra had a persuasive weapon in his arsenal. Hunger. The prisoners got enough to keep them upright and ambulatory, but nowhere near enough to encourage energetic pursuits like digging or running or even calisthenics. Food became of overpowering importance that winter. In the morning the prisoners received a cup of what they called coffee to wash down a small bread roll, and in the evening a ladle or two of skilly, a thin, watery soup with bits and pieces of pasta or green stalks in it, or, once a week on average, some small shreds of what might have been meat.

Joe supposed that it depended what you were used to, and would never have said so to the other men, but he came to think that PG 57 wasn't too bad. The huts provided adequate shelter, there were beds, ablution blocks, latrines, plenty of drinking water, enough food to stay alive, and time. Joe had never had much time to himself; the closest he'd come to it was at school. His regret at having to leave so young had never gone away, and he was keen to resume learning, something, anything. The prisoners were organising all sorts of activities and courses. Joe went to every dramatic performance, musical, lecture and quiz, but didn't have the confidence to participate in any of them.

He looked at courses in accountancy, agriculture and French, because he wanted something challenging, the kind of learning that would burn up the oxygen in his head that might otherwise feed the embers of El Mreir and the *Nino Bixio*. He decided that he knew as much as he wanted to know about agriculture, so chose accounting, where he was drawn to the logical symmetry of double-entry bookkeeping.

Arch Scott, a lanky, genial native of Papakura, and his best mate, Paul Day, were fluent in French and running classes, but Arch persuaded Joe that if he had to learn one language in his present predicament, with escape a possibility, Italian might be more useful.

But the winter still seemed interminable and so much colder than home. Devil's Bridge was relatively sheltered, though the easterly would rush from the sea up the valley to Ngapara, or a southerly blast would coat the foothills with snow and close Danseys Pass behind the town, but it never felt as cold as this. At PG 57, there was a stufa, a heater, at one end of each of the bunk huts, but neither the stufas nor the men huddled around them ever had enough fuel inside. As stomachs contracted and fell, bladders came under pressure and many men lay in their beds in agony, trying to hold on until dawn rather than going out to piss in the snow.

Joe didn't see much of Harry, for which he was grateful. Harry's contempt for the guards was unsettling. He would mutter that he'd been captured by 'Jerry, not these buffoons' and Joe sometimes felt that Harry would have been happier in a German camp, where the guards would be worthy of having him as a prisoner.

When their paths next crossed, Joe told him about the Italian lessons and suggested they might be handy if he was still planning to escape.

'What's Italian for "escaped"?' Harry had asked.

'Scappato,' said Joe.

'That's me,' he told Joe. 'Scappato. Gone.' It was a clear day and they could see the formidable Dolomites enclosing them to the north and right round to the west. 'We'll go for the mountains,' Harry said. 'Switzerland. One day.'

Venice, 2014

10

As the courses proceeded at Aldo's bar — a meat dish that was just that, a pork chop on a plate, unadorned, followed by a separate dish of salad — and the prosecco and verduzzo and merlot were drunk, different groups coalesced and dispersed as her father moved among them.

Renzo showed her a team photograph, framed and glassed, that was being passed from hand to hand like a precious relic. She could recognise some of the faces around the table, and Aldo, standing to one side, the proud manager. It wasn't a formal pose and it was after the game: the players were muddy and dishevelled, and the beaming smiles indicated they'd won. 'They'd just beaten Rome in Rome at the Foro Italico,' Renzo said, the wonder still in his voice.

The grinning men in the photo confirmed what she already knew, as a childless, relationless woman who wanted a family: age is a tyranny. Most of the faces were adorned with such ridiculously big hair and moustaches and sideburns that they looked as if someone had drawn them on, but underneath all that they were so young and so happy that their joy caught in her throat. She couldn't bring herself to look across the table at her father: the contrast was too awful. In the photo, he had his right arm over the shoulder of the most striking figure in the shot. He was stockier than her father and not quite as tall. He had shoulder-length black curls tied back with a red bandana and a full black beard from which perfect teeth flashed a wide white smile. 'Franco,' confirmed Renzo.

The photo had been signed by all the players. She recognised her father's signature, though it had a lot more of a flourish than the one he put on his letters. Under his and Franco's signatures, someone had written a phrase in Italian, 'I Due Coglioni di San Pietro'.

When she pointed to it, Renzo laughed. 'The two balls of San Pietro.' He told her that it referred to an expression in Italian, 'Non rompermi i coglioni — Don't break my balls. When the balls were broken, so was San Pietro.'

By the time they got to the tiramisu — 'pick me up', according to Renzo — her father was back beside Aldo. His Italian seemed much improved as the two men had what seemed like a very intense conversation, sotto voce. He looked as if he was asking for something and Aldo was shaking his head. This seemed a strange dynamic after what had gone before, when the keys to the town seemed to be Broochay's for the asking.

Whatever was going on seemed to become a stalemate. Her father began visibly fading, and she worried about how much he'd had to drink. Aldo, too, was looking at him with a worried expression, and at Renzo.

The timing may have been entirely coincidental, but when Renzo excused himself to go to the toilet, Aldo immediately called Beatrice over and whispered something to her. She disappeared into the kitchen and returned soon after with a folded piece of paper, which she slipped to Aldo, as if discreetly giving him the bill for the evening. Renzo came back and she thought no more of it until they filed back outside the bar and her father was farewelled by being passed from hug to hug, from kiss to kiss. Last in line, before the rear door being held open by her, Aldo gripped her father's right hand in both of his, pulled him close and kissed him. She saw him quickly look down at the piece of paper Aldo had palmed him, before his fist closed over it. She saw the look of gratitude on her father's gaunt face as he hugged Aldo again.

Once they were back in the car — her father had insisted on the back seat and quickly slumped into exhausted quiescence — Renzo talked to her mainly about New Zealand, its economic situation, its health system. He seemed extraordinarily well informed and she had the feeling, though he was too polite to say so, that none of what she told him was new information. He was curious and empathetic and gradually they segued to more personal subjects. She found him easy to talk to and told him far more than she'd intended about the break-up of her marriage and the end of her business partnership. Until now, it had all seemed too raw to talk about except with her counsellor, and she was surprised that she was able to navigate her shitty stuff without bursting into tears. Maybe the high emotion and tears of her father's speech had provided a kind of balm. Her father was slumped against the window and a subdued snore indicated he was asleep. She could only hope that the rhinos and bull elephants wouldn't start calling to one another before they got to Venice. Let him sleep, she thought, it's been such a big night for him — and for her.

She looked across at Renzo, who'd stayed at her side throughout and made it possible, subtly and unobtrusively, for her to understand what had gone on. His face, lit by the dash lights, looked more hawkishly Arab in profile than Italian.

Deep lines ran from his cheekbones to the corners of his mouth. Laugh lines, they'd usually be called, except he didn't seem to laugh much.

The silence between them now, as he drove back through the light-sprinkled countryside, felt companionable after so many words, though not many of them had been about him. In their continuing conversation since she'd first got into the vehicle and right through dinner, Renzo had asked all the questions. She knew next to nothing about him other than his job at Padova Uni. How do you work *physics* into a conversation?

'So should I call you Doctor or Professor?' she asked him.

'Neither, really,' he said. 'I'm a lapsed physicist, probably.'

'Probably?'

'Theoretical physicists are in trouble. Experimental physicists may be about to make us obsolete — our theories to date, at least. I've lost faith, I think, so I teach rather than do research these days. That probably makes me a hypocrite.'

'Do physicists need faith? I thought science was about empirical proof, all that.'

'Yes and no.'

She smiled. 'That's not a very scientific answer.'

'It's a paradox, which is more or less what physicists have to live with.'

Renzo gave her a quick glance but enough, it seemed, to prompt a decision. He waved his hand at the quarter-moon, barely visible over the approaching light-stacked towers of Mestre. 'There's an old story about Einstein and his philosopher colleague,' he said. 'Einstein asked his colleague if he really believed that the moon wasn't there when nobody was looking at it. His friend asked Einstein to prove the opposite — that the moon *was* still there when nobody was looking. That was of course impossible, even for Einstein, partly because it's a question of philosophy as much as physics.'

The moon illuminated a drainage ditch running alongside the verge of the road. She told him that they weren't looking at the moon but could see its light.

'Ah,' he said, 'but those photons know we're looking.'

She thought this silly and circuitous but also funny. 'Looking?'

'That's a paradox physicists have been trying to unravel for decades. Several paradoxes, in fact. That a single particle of light, a photon, can be in many places at the same time, which is against Newton's laws of physics. In that sense, you could say that photons misbehave, except that, from a physicist's point of view, photons do what photons do and if that doesn't match our theory then the theory is wrong. We've tried to formulate new theory to describe this quantum reality. Quantum mechanics looked promising, then quantum field theory — I won't bore you with the details, but we've had a great deal of trouble applying any theory because of another paradox: photons won't allow us to observe their errant behaviour. We can shoot them through a laser gun and know exactly what they're doing at source and on arrival at the target, but as soon as we try to observe what they're doing in between, when they "misbehave" according to the laws of physics as we know them, they stop doing it.'

'They must be shy,' she suggested.

He laughed. 'Timido? Maybe.'

It was a sound she wanted to hear again. 'Or are they duplicitous and don't want to be found out?'

That worked too. 'Are they naughty children or cunning adults?' he laughed. Then seriously: 'It's fun anthropomorphising them, but can photons form intentions? We have no idea.

Anyway, the secret life of a photon, that is or was my life's work.'

'Why is it important?'

'Because the behaviour of these particles — if that's what they are — questions the very nature of our reality. Quantum mechanics was exciting because it was extremely precise, mathematically brilliant and it described everything we could observe back then. The problem is that the behaviour of photons made it nonsensical.'

'Does that really matter to anyone in the real world?'

'That is exactly the question they pose: what *is* the real world? Quantum reality is turning out to be much stranger than we ever imagined. Everything has the power to be in several places at once, but we can't see it. Even though we can't see it, we can't ignore it, because it may be about to change our lives in a huge way.'

'Yes?' Clare briefly wondered whether Renzo was constructing a complex analogy for her, providing an alternative reality from the painful one she'd described to him earlier.

'Until we can understand how quantum reality works, we can't really understand how our universe works. What if what we see is not what is, *because* we can see it?'

The autostrada was delivering them to the causeway across the lagoon. She looked ahead to the lights of Venice, a city that had been sitting there since 400AD-ish. Or not. What did she know? She wished the causeway were longer, that the misbehaving photons could make Venice disappear for a while so that Renzo could keep talking to her with that light American lilt.

'My problem with physics is a fundamental one,' he continued. 'There are things we don't understand, but is that because we *can't* understand them? There's a difference. If I'm

67

a physicist and believe that maybe we're inherently incapable of understanding our universe, does that make me a heretic? What if the truth has an author who wants to preserve his anonymity?'

She was clinging to the edge of understanding. 'God?'

'Alas, I'm also a lapsed Catholic.'

'Can you believe in God and still be a physicist?'

'With a great deal of difficulty. You would have to accept that, despite our best endeavours to explain it, our universe remains such a mystery that there mightn't be any other explanation.'

'Aren't they looking for the God particle with that Hadron Collider thing?'

'They've found it. The Higgs boson. But that discovery just deepens the mystery. We'd hoped that it would point the way forward. And it does, but we don't know where to yet. It indicates a fork in the road ahead: to one side, super symmetry, where our theories would give us a coherent view of our universe; to the other, multiverse — universes on such an unimaginable scale that our theories of how this minute one of ours works are localised, irrelevant and useless, and life here on earth is nothing more than a happy accident in the midst of chaos.'

'Meaning what?'

'That what we thought was true may be mostly untrue, and yet . . . We managed to predict the existence of the Higgs boson. So we stand between symmetry and chaos, awaiting further developments.'

'That's me,' she said.

He laughed.

'I do have a tendency to take everything personally,' she said.

Renzo chuckled again. Maybe they were laugh lines after all.

He looked into the rear vision mirror. 'Your father seems to be asleep. Do you think that happened before or after I began talking?'

When they arrived at Piazzale Roma, she woke her father. As Renzo helped him down onto shaky feet, she wondered if he would make it back to the B & B unassisted. 'I can get a park here in the garage,' Renzo said, 'and accompany you. It isn't a problem.'

His grey-green eyes had a softness she'd noticed when they were sitting so close together in Aldo's bar. Olive skin, black hair, neither tall nor short. Her type. *There's no hope for me.* 'Thanks,' she said, more firmly than she'd intended, 'but we'll be fine.'

He gave her his card. 'Anything I can do for you or your father,' he said. 'I am entirely sincere.'

Of the many words and phrases he'd used across a long evening, that was the only one that a native English speaker would never say, unless in irony. But he was looking into her eyes as he said it and there was no irony: Renzo was entirely sincere.

* * *

On the vaporetto she told her father she was proud of him. She cuddled up to his bony shoulder against the cold and told him that sometimes you lose perspective on people you love and need to see them in a different context to appreciate them. Tonight she'd seen him as she'd never seen him before. The evening had been a triumph.

True to previous form he said nothing and she wondered whether her words were wasted. He seemed frozen with fatigue and his smile of acknowledgement looked more like a grimace.

Well, it was done: mission accomplished. Now he can relax and enjoy the rest of the trip, stay in bed all day if he wants to, before we move on to Florence.

After getting him off the vaporetto at Accademia and making slow progress through Campo Santo Stefano and San Maurizio to the door of his bedroom at the B & B, she stopped on the first little bridge on the way to her hotel and tried to find that quarter-moon.

I'm a speck of dust on the face of infinity and chaos. *I don't matter.* She had no idea why that should be of any comfort, but it was. She walked on along the wide alley back towards San Marco, then turned down the narrower calle to her hotel. For the first time, La Serenissima seemed something other than a bad joke. There were no hawkers, no day-trippers, no shoppers, no gondolas in the narrow canals jousting with motorboats full of Coke and cartons, no tourists pulling suitcases, just the occasional couple leaning in against each other as they made their way through the cold clear evening from dinner to bed.

The thought came to her that Nicholas and Sarah's betrayal might be part of an immutable law of nature that nobody understood, that what had happened wasn't her fault. This, too, was a strange comfort.

As she lay in her clean sheets, undisturbed, she put one palm over her heart, as her counsellor had taught her, and the other across her belly and tried to think kindly of herself, letting the warmth flow around that knot of pain in her chest. It seemed easier than it had been before, looser, and her mind wandered. Would Venice still be sinking, she wondered sleepily, if no one was watching? If I can't see Nicholas and Sarah, do they still exist? If a tree falls in the forest . . .

San Pietro di Livenza, 1943

11

When spring finally came, Harry was still in PG 57, and still there in early summer, when he told Joe that the fighting in North Africa was over: 'Jerry's on the skids, the boys will be coming ashore here next.' Some took the news as if the war was as good as won, but Harry had his doubts. Joe thought he might be worried that the war would be over before he could get back to it.

In June, Arch Scott told Joe about a working party that offered a chance of getting out of PG 57. He said that under the Geneva Convention the Italians were entitled to ask them to work on non-military tasks. This was apparently agricultural work which, said Arch, ever the pragmatist, meant 'working with food'.

When the fifty or so Kiwis comprising the working party were assembled for the march back to the Cividale train station, Joe was surprised to see Harry among them.

The train stopped at San Pietro di Livenza, another pale yellow double-storey station with elaborate plasterwork and wooden shutters. There were horses and wagons waiting to pick them up and take them back across the tracks, away from the town. The Livenza, they discovered, was a river that flowed across the plains north of Venice down to the lagoon. It was hemmed in by raised banks called argines, built thirty feet or more above the fields, on top of which, on either side, were roads.

As they made their way downstream on top of an argine, they had a great view of flat plains spreading to the mountains, more distant than they had been at Cividale. To Joe it looked like the view from the military camp at Burnham, looking west across the Canterbury Plains to the Southern Alps. Arch was reminded of the Hauraki Plains looking across to the Coromandel Ranges. Joe felt his spirits lifted by the verdant early summer green of the countryside and by the friendly people they passed, out walking in their Sunday best, most of whom acknowledged them with a nod or a smile. Some of the younger ones waved and called out 'Ciao, ciao' to the hollow-cheeked faces staring back at them.

Joe, sitting close to Arch, turned to him after one such greeting and said, 'This is different.'

Arch was sitting there looking out, smiling, but with tears running down his cheeks. 'It is,' he agreed. 'But it does make you realise what you're missing.'

It wasn't just Arch. Nostalgia was burgeoning among the men. They'd heard by then that the Allies had occupied the islands of Pantelleria and Lampedusa south-west of Sicily and for the first time they dared to hope that their travails would soon be over, and began imagining what a normal life might feel like.

* * *

The Veronese Estate, several miles down the river from San Pietro, was well set up for itinerant labourers: a huge three-storey dormitory the size of a small hospital sat hunched into a shoulder of the argine on a bend of the Livenza and looked out across infinite flat fields of crops. At one end was a long single-storey implement shed with brick arches, at the other a kitchen garden and a chicken run. The Italians had simply put barbed wire around that end of the building, keeping the prisoners and chickens from straying, bricked up the other exits and called it PG 107/7.

A couple of fellows cooked and the rest went out each day in two groups to different parts of the estate to do variations of what Joe had done at Devil's Bridge since he was old enough to walk. He'd never struck sugar beet before, or castor oil seeds, but thinning and hoeing and picking and cleaning and topping and loading were common enough to most crops, and Joe settled easily into the long hours out in the fields, particularly since the work came with benefits unheard of at PG 57. At San Pietro, the prisoners got double rations and real vegetables pulled from the gardens they worked in — potatoes and onions and peas and cabbages — and Red Cross parcels came more regularly. They were also given quinine tablets because the land was reclaimed swamp and malarial. All of them began putting on weight and condition, so that they looked fit, rather than, as Harry put it, 'fucked'.

Although Harry outranked Arch by one stripe, he spoke no Italian, and since none of the guards or the estate overseer spoke any English, except 'Stop!', Arch was the one who had to act as interpreter and relay orders to the men. That didn't seem to worry Harry unduly, but it did impress on him the wisdom of learning Italian, and thereafter he was part of a much-expanded Italian language class.

The prisoners agreed among themselves to work at an easy pace and Joe found it a breeze compared with home, where Malachy would bang his stick on the ground and demand more elbow grease. The old bugger was a little more sympathetic with the girls, but if he or Dan complained, Malachy would dismiss whatever it was, blisters or fatigue or thirst or skinned knees or an aching back, with a 'Be buggered you have!' and then threaten in his hard and flat-as-slate Northern Irish brogue to give it to them, 'around the earhole'.

After Malachy and Capitano Calcaterra, the guards at PG 107/7 were also relatively benign. A sergeant, two corporals and three or four privates guarded the fifty prisoners. The sergeant looked apprehensive when they said they were Kiwis, then after a couple of days of very close scrutiny the apprehension turned to puzzlement and he kept asking Arch if he was sure they were New Zealanders. Arch thought it might be a joke he wasn't getting, but Harry remembered the poster they'd seen at Bari of the black man in the lemon squeezer hat attacking the woman, and speculated that the sergeant might be having trouble reconciling the propaganda with the reality in front of him.

A sure sign that the sergeant had adjusted to reality was the appearance of civilians out in the fields beside them. Since the young men were away in the army, the local workforce was mainly women, who seemed friendly and open — shockingly so for some of the men, who were unused to seeing women, young and old, hitch up their dresses and squat whenever they needed to pee. It was less of a shock for Joe — Ida, Betty and Agnes had all done the same out in the paddocks at Devil's Bridge in front of Dan and Joe, but there'd been something covert about it then, much giggling and blushing, and they'd never have done it in front of Malachy or Molly.

Another frequent visitor was Don Antonio, the priest from the church just down the river, San Anastasio. Don Antonio, who rode a bicycle around his parish, was an energetic cheerful man obviously much respected by the locals and seemed to have real empathy for the prisoners, particularly Arch, who would greet him like a villager. 'Sia lodato Gesù Cristo, Don Antonio.' *Praised be Jesus Christ, Don Antonio.*

'Sempre sia lodato, Aci,' said Don Antonio. *Be He praised forever, Archie.*

* * *

Joe's Italian was coming along, though he wasn't as adept as Arch. If the locals spoke slowly enough directly to him, he could understand most of what they said, but when they spoke dialect between themselves, he was lost. Harry knew much less than Joe, yet had some means of communication beyond the verbal that verged on magic. He picked up words of dialect and the hand signals the locals used, and could somehow make them laugh.

One day they were working on rows of sugar beet, which resembled bigger, uglier turnips or swedes. They had a leafy top and a long, sweet tap root that had to be pulled from the ground, topped and tailed with a special knife and thrown onto a horse-drawn dray. Joe had driven the team at Devil's Bridge, so would take the full loads back to one of the estate's storage sheds, where Harry and some locals would transfer them into jute sacks that were later taken to the wharf for barging down the Livenza to the Venetian lagoon.

When the shed seemed deserted for the last load of the morning, Joe assumed they'd all broken early for lunch. He was unbuckling the horse from its harness when he heard a low shriek from behind the stall. As he left the horse and went across to the shadows to investigate, he heard a slap, and then a laugh, a woman's, and knew enough to back off and make some noise. By the time he led the horse over to the stall, one of the more attractive women was coming out, flushed and adjusting her blouse.

'Scusami,' she said, and hurried out of the shed.

Shortly afterwards Harry appeared. 'You spooked her,' he said. 'She was coming along nicely.'

Joe wondered how that connection had been made. The locals and the prisoners were increasingly animated, particularly Arch with Don Antonio and the estate overseer and the friendly corporal, who'd helped Arch to translate 'Lili Marlene' into Italian, but Joe had never noticed Harry exchanging one word with the woman in the shed. During lunch in the shade of the chestnuts at the bottom of the argine, he watched carefully, but the woman's eyes never met Harry's, and Joe was none the wiser.

12

Harry's dalliance was a sign that the prisoners were becoming strong enough to contemplate pursuits other than working and eating and sleeping. Some of these new activities made the guards anxious.

After Arch cleared it with the sergeant, they were allowed to go swimming in the Livenza at a spot where the argine flattened out to a kind of beach. But when the prisoners all rushed into the water, the corporal and two privates who'd taken them down there were extremely twitchy. The corporal told Arch they were sure some of the prisoners would drown, because not many Italians could swim.

That first time, as Joe floated on his back and looked out towards the mountains, he felt a bit as Arch had when they first arrived in the wagons on that beautiful Sunday. The Livenza reminded him of the Kakanui where it was confined by the limestone gorge, a deep purity of greens and blues, though much bigger and with whirls and eddies out in the middle that might have been dangerous. Joe's tears were lost in the water, and the evening swim became a salve for the long hot days of July and August.

By the middle of August, the prisoners were sufficiently restored to look at a freshly cropped cornfield out in front of the building and see a rugby ground. On a Sunday afternoon, after great anticipation, bundles of clothing were set in piles at either end to simulate goalposts, which the ref had to imagine extending upwards to a cross-bar at about the right height. Harry and Arch were the captains and tossed a coin provided by the bemused sergeant to see who got first pick of the assembled men. Harry won the toss and chose Joe.

Joe hadn't been sure he wanted to play. The wound on his head was long healed into an angry scar, but he feared he might be a bit ginger in contact. Being Harry's first pick decided the matter. Those blue eyes that had seemed so predatory in the game at Ngapara must have approved of what they'd seen. And if Harry was prepared to play on his leg, Joe would risk his wound too.

The sergeant, guards and quite a few of the locals and their children gathered along the touchline with the rest of the prisoners as a ball that had arrived in a Red Cross parcel was kicked off. Harry took it in, then released it to Joe. It was another of those deeply nostalgic moments. The feel of the leather ball in his hands as he quickly juggled it into alignment and flipped his right palm over the top so that it spun long and low out left to Morrie Simpson from the Manawatu. In that split second, he realised how much he'd been missing the semi-civilised chaos of rugby.

The Italians had no idea what would ensue. After the first few minutes of contact, there were two bloody noses — one from a Harry Spence elbow at the back of a lineout — and a player left lying on the ground. The sergeant ran onto the field, waving his pistol, and told the players to stop. He told Arch that this was no game, that the men were deliberately trying to injure each other so they couldn't work and ordered everyone back to camp.

*　*　*

By then the news had come to Arch via the corporal that the Allies had landed in Sicily back in early July and that a couple of weeks later Mussolini had been outvoted by his own Grand Council of Fascism, then arrested and jailed. As August progressed, the guards seemed to become more jumpy and argued with each other in front of the prisoners.

Harry, predictably, was the first to notice that surveillance standards were slipping and put it about that it might be time to scappato. Arch cautioned him to bide his time a little, because he'd understood what the guards were arguing about: whether they should stay or go home. 'The way things are going,' said Arch, 'we might be able to walk out of here, not run.'

13

On 9 September 1943, in the fourteenth month of Joe's captivity, they were told by the corporal that there'd been a capovolto the day before, a *capitulation*, by Italy, and that an armistizo was in place. The prisoners cheered. They understood that Italy had surrendered and was out of the war, but no one seemed sure exactly what it meant for them.

Neither were the guards. They read out a provision of the armistice agreement that ordered all prisoners to stay put until further orders, which presumably entailed the Italian guards staying on duty until they could hand the captives over to the Allies. But the heated arguments between the guards increased, until a couple of days later the corporal, who lived locally, told Arch that the sergeant was andato via, along with a couple of the privates. The corporal distributed the latest Red Cross parcels to the prisoners, including a letter for Joe from Dan, then said, Basta, *enough*: he and the remaining guards were now going home and they'd leave the gates open behind them when they left.

Harry, first through the gates, led the men down the road back towards the town, where they stopped at the first taverna and found the locals more than willing to swap Red Cross goodies for wine and grappa.

On the way, Joe read Dan's letter. He knew it wouldn't be a long read, and it wasn't, but it lifted him up like a warm current in the Kakanui:

Dear Joe,

*Hope you're okay little brother. Didn't know whether
you'd copped it at El Mreir, so relieved to see you on
the Red Cross list of POWs. Can't say too much but
I'm with 18th Battalion Shermans now, and it's no
secret that we're on our way to Italy. Sandy's good,
gone to Trentham to train as a voluntary nurse aide,
do her bit. See you soon, Joe, with a bit of luck.*

Your loving brother,
Dan

The locals called their red wine nero, *black*. It stuck Joe's tongue to the roof of his mouth and was so astringent he tasted nothing but tannins and acids and alcohol. Predictably, the prisoners got drunk quickly and happily, most of them, Joe included, not giving a lot of thought to what would happen next.

Arch was one exception, talking earnestly to the locals, who included the estate manager and Don Antonio. The Italians who'd worked alongside the prisoners had come to know and like them and seemed opposed to Mussolini and the fascists and relieved that Italy was out of a war they'd never wanted to be in. But they warned Arch that not all their fellow countrymen thought the same way, that there were many fascists still around, particularly in powerful administrative positions, and the prisoners had to be careful because these people would sympathise with the Germans.

They suggested to Arch that the prisoners should consider moving out of the estate and into hiding around the district with sympathetic families, so that if the Germans came, they wouldn't all be sitting ducks. That seemed to be the nub of it —

would the Germans abandon Italy or occupy it? No one seemed to know the answer except Harry, who was certain Jerry was going to punish the Italians for 'going soft' and that the Allies would have a real 'shit-fight' as they fought their way up Italy.

Celebrations were at a peak, the locals and the prisoners had launched into 'Santa Lucia', when a heavy hand landed on Joe's shoulder. When he turned, he saw two faces, both Harry's. 'Come with me.'

Outside the taverna, the woman he'd seen Harry with in the shed was waiting with two bicycles. When he looked doubtful, Harry told Joe they had to get out while they could. 'Those buggers'll still be singing "Lili Marlene" when Jerry arrives.'

There didn't seem to be much choice. Joe wobbled down the street on the bike, following Harry, who was doubling the woman. They veered off down an alley and stopped outside a door that opened onto a small courtyard. With much shushing and giggling, they ended up in the woman's parlour, where clothes had been laid out on the kitchen table.

'Whose are these?' asked Joe, when the clothes turned out to be one size, a bit small for Harry and way too big for Joe.

'Her husband's,' said Harry, smiling at the woman. 'Signora or signorina?' he asked her.

It seemed to be an old joke between them. 'Signorina stanotte,' she said, laughing as she wrapped bread and tomatoes and cheese for them.

'But signora next week,' said Harry, 'when hubby gets home from the front.'

Outside, they put the food down the front of their shirts, mounted the bicycles. Harry kissed the woman, pulled a cloth cap down over hair blonded from the sun and said, 'Andiamo via.'

'Where are we going?' asked Joe as they turned into the main street, away from the tavern.

'To the mountains,' said Harry. 'Switzerland.'

* * *

A three-quarter-moon lit up the Livenza as they left the town environs and rode upstream. There was no one around, but Harry thought the argines were too exposed, so they crossed the river at the first bridge west of San Pietro and descended to the greater and lesser roads that criss-crossed the plains to the north and west. Harry reckoned the mountains they'd seen on clear days couldn't be more than a hundred miles away 'as the crow flies' and they'd make it easily in three or four days.

The trouble was, despite the moon, a crow would have seen a great deal more than they could once they got down on the featureless plains. Harry, though, seemed to have a grid in his head, and no matter how many times they reached intersections that forced them to leave their original course and go right or left, he always seemed to know where the mountains were, and which road would bring them back on course.

After several hours, they reached an intersection with a major road, which Harry said looked like the main road from Venice to Udine and the mountains. He was in two minds as to whether to take it. It was probably the quickest way of getting to the mountains, but they'd be a lot more exposed when dawn broke. While Harry was considering the pros and cons, Joe went to sleep for a moment and fell down on the road. The minute or two it took for him to pick himself and his bicycle up may have saved them. They saw hooded lights coming from Udine and heard big engines at almost the same time.

They threw the bikes into a drain that ran alongside the road and flattened themselves, as the light and noise grew into a column of five huge articulated lorries bearing the black Maltese cross. Each one of these monsters carried another monster, a great armour-plated behemoth of a tank the size of a small house with gun barrels as big as turrets, pointing backwards at Harry and Joe as they were enveloped by the darkness.

'Holy hell,' said Harry.

Joe hadn't seen a tank of any description since the Panzers at El Mreir. Those had assumed enormous dimensions in his nightmares, yet were puny by comparison with what he'd just seen.

They pulled the bikes out of the drain and returned the way they'd come. Harry seemed deflated, and once they'd gone a mile or two back into the maze of smaller roads, he decided they'd put enough distance between themselves and San Pietro, and they carried the bikes down into one of the summer-dry drains beside the road and slumped beside them.

'That confirms one thing,' said Harry, as he lit the last of his foul-smelling Italian cigarettes. 'Jerry's gearing up for a scrap.'

Joe looked up at the sky and tried to imagine it as a quilt, studded with gold, protecting him and Dan. He'd seen Sherman tanks and prayed that Dan would never come up against those monsters he'd seen heading south. He had to trust that Harry knew what he was doing, but fourteen months of incarceration had convinced him he could survive prison. When he saw those tanks, he was equally sure he couldn't survive any more war.

Venice, 2014

14

Clare woke just before dawn after the most complete sleep she'd had in a long time. She listened for the familiar hum of a city awakening, but heard nothing, so thought she'd slip out into the empty streets and watch the sun come up from the top of Ponte dell' Accademia.

Outside the hotel, the narrow stone ravines skirting La Fenice were wreathed in fog and alive with people, mostly men in blue overalls manoeuvring tall, thin, rubber-tyred handcarts back and forth from long, high-prowed wooden boats with outboard motors. The carts were loaded with cartons of produce from the boats, then rolled through the alleys, returning minutes later with crushed cardboard and detritus.

Instead of making for the bridge, she found herself following one of the boats as it took off along an impossibly narrow canal, with a muscled helmsman controlling the outboard. As he approached a blind right angle, he let out what sounded like a high-pitched yelp, which must have served as a warning to any oncoming traffic, then seemed to swirl the boat around the corner like a matador with a cloak.

Remembering her father saying that you're never lost in

Venice, just temporarily unaware of where you are, she decided to follow whatever interested her — boats, carts, old women shuffling to churches with doors that seemed unprepossessing, but opened to huge naves with statuary and frescoes that were probably priceless. At first she wished she knew more about what she was seeing, but there were compensations in looking at it all with an almost childish innocence and openness. She eventually reached a wide canal that opened out into the misty lagoon, then tried to retrace her steps, but couldn't. It didn't matter: she saw a yellow arrow with *Rialto* stencilled on it and followed that.

When she got to the bridge, she could see the vegetable stalls across the far side of the Grand Canal where her father had taken her yesterday, when he'd seemed to be listening for ghosts.

From the Rialto, she followed the yellow arrows for Accademia and eventually arrived at Campo Santo Stefano, and walked on through Campo San Maurizio to her father's B & B. She thought it might be too early for him after last night's emotional demands, but when she climbed the stairs to the breakfast hallway, the woman warming the croissants recognised her and said, 'E' già andato via', then took pity on her and provided a translation: 'Is already gone out.'

She retraced her steps to Campo Santo Stefano, thinking she must have missed him sitting at the little bar near the entrance, having his coffee and croissant. When he wasn't there, she was at a loss. She walked right along Santo Stefano towards Ponte Accademia, looking in at all the cafes. Her father was nowhere to be seen, but she did see someone she recognised, coming towards her from the Accademia vaporetto stop.

Ishmael was one of the African hawkers who had tried to sell her a rip-off Chloe handbag yesterday near San Marco when she was searching for a hotel. She'd made the mistake of stopping to check out the leather and the stitching. Both were perfect, as was the washed-out green colour of the soft kid. All the while, Ishmael had been lowering the price, from fifty euros to forty-five, from forty-five to forty, his eyes dancing up and down the alley, looking to his African mates who were working in leathery clumps of bags and briefcases about fifty metres apart. The more she dithered, the more agitated he'd become and the lower the price fell — and the more suspicious she'd grown. In the end, he was imploring her to give him twenty euros for it. 'What do I have to do?' he'd asked, arms wide.

'I'm just not sure,' she'd said. His face had closed, then he'd got some signal from his mates at the San Marco end of the alley, suddenly thrown his strung-together sack of bags over his shoulder and walked off quickly. Shortly afterwards, two carabinieri appeared from the direction of San Marco, wandering down the alleyway like window shoppers in uniform.

She'd stood there watching Ishmael hustle off, feeling awful. Why hadn't she just *given* him the twenty euros? The money was obviously so important to him. She'd been to a bottega just off San Marco and inspected the real thing, with a price tag of twelve hundred euros, and couldn't tell the difference, so what was her problem? No one she knew would be aware it was a rip-off. Was it just that *she* knew it wasn't a real Chloe?

Now, when she saw Ishmael coming towards her with his long languid strides under the sack of bags that made his legs look even thinner, she thought of Renzo's shy or wilful little photons. She could see analogies everywhere: not just her behaviour about buying the bag, but Ishmael's too, when he thought the carabinieri were watching and when they weren't.

'Do you think you're quite suggestible?' her counsellor had asked her at one point. If I say yes, Clare thought, does that prove her point?

Ishmael saw her and she could tell, by the way his face hardened, that he remembered her. When she stopped him and offered him forty euros, he beamed the most perfect smile, and it was this, as much as the fake Chloe over her shoulder, that seemed to make the view from the top of Ponte Accademia more pleasing. She looked down the Grand Canal towards the Rialto, then turned towards Santa Maria della Salute. The fog had almost been burnt off by the sun, but there were shrouds of sea mist still lingering out on the lagoon and feathery strands still trailing along the sides of the canal, masking the transition between water and air, softening the facades of the palazzi. As her eyes followed the sinuous water and vapour back past the low white incongruousness of the Peggy Guggenheim museum and arrived at the far side of the bridge, she saw an angular, slow-moving figure she recognised.

There was no point in shouting to him, so she hurried down the other side of the bridge. Her father had shown her how the map of Venice resembled the shape of a fish and she remembered that the area on the other side of the bridge was the fish's spine, Dorsoduro. By the time she'd plunged into the maze of alleys, he'd disappeared, so she followed the signs for the museum, thinking that must be where he was making for. After all, he'd hung two Milan Mrkusich paintings on his office wall, plain oblongs of dark grey and blue, and seemed to enjoy the fact that most of his clients found them impenetrable.

Before she reached the museum, she crossed a wide canal running at right angles to the Grand Canal. From the top of the bridge, she saw her father making his way down the footpath beside the canal, away from the Guggenheim building. She was about to call out, when she saw him stop and look up at the name of a street sign, then compare it with something he was holding in the palm of his hand. It was a piece of paper, surely the one Aldo had given him last night.

She kept her distance as he worked his way along the canal, checking the names of the side alleys. The fourth time he checked she saw him hold himself taller, straighten his jacket lapels and nervously wipe his mouth, before disappearing into the alley. And she knew in that moment he was looking for a woman, perhaps the same one he'd been looking for at Campo Santo Stefano and at the market below Rialto.

She stopped at the top of the alley. The houses were tiny, three storeys high but barely a room wide on each level, with doors painted mostly in pastel colours, yellows and blues, turquoise. The door where her father waited was a deep red, almost maroon, and was barely taller than him. He must have knocked once already and got no answer. She saw him knock again, and once again perform that hopeful pantomime, standing taller, patting his hair, wiping his mouth. The door opened. Whoever stood there was not welcoming: she saw her father become agitated, arms wide in supplication, then the door closed on him. He looked bereft, shrunken, raised his hand as if to knock again, then slumped against the wall beside the door. She couldn't bear to watch any more.

Clare walked on some twenty metres and stood gazing out towards the wide water at the end of the canal. He'd played her for a fool. Telling her he was coming for a reunion when all the time he'd had another quest in mind. If he'd been honest about that, she could have got him onto a few internet sites and he could have trawled through those and saved them both the trouble of flying to the other side of the world to have a door slammed in his face.

Perhaps she was too raw from her own betrayal, but she felt like challenging him. *Poor Mum.* A big, ebullient woman who'd been gradually worn down by her father's indifference. The rational part of Clare accepted that a stroke was a combination of bad luck and genetics, but a loveless marriage may have played a part. Even on her deathbed, her mother kept insisting, 'He's a good man.'

Another of her mother's mantras had been 'We've got you'. As if her daughter's existence justified everything. That old joke about the only child that someone cruel recited to her: they tried it once and didn't like it. It could almost have been true. He'd been so polite and stiff with her mother. She'd thought that was normal until she was old enough to notice the sly nudges and knowing winks and surreptitious little taps on shoulder or bum between her friends' parents, the shared secrets of true intimacy. There'd been none of that for her mother, who'd come to remind her of one of those sheep dogs, running all day for a rare pat on the head or a word of praise. It was like living with a pair of polite monks.

When she turned to confront him, he was resting on the iron rail at the edge of the canal, lost in his own misery, staring at the water.

She knew she should go to him, offer him some comfort in his wretchedness.

She couldn't even look at him. She turned and walked away.

15

She found herself sitting on a wooden jetty, just a collection of piles really, projecting out from the old customs house at the end of Dorsoduro. The dome of La Salute was at her back, and she could look out across the wide water to an island her father had told her was Giudecca. To her right, a wide sea wall ran back towards the mainland. The tide was coming in and the water was just a couple of metres below her. She felt as if she was at the very edge of Venice, away from its claustrophobic centre.

She knew she'd overreacted. It was partly because she was so raw and broken by her own betrayal, but it was more than that. Her counsellor had suggested she go back through what she knew of her family, and as she did so a pall of gloom had fallen over her that was far harder to shift than mere tears. What a tale of woe it had been, her parents' marriage, the little her father had told her of his own upbringing. For at least a couple of generations back, her family seemed to be caught in a repeating cycle of loveless marriage, misery and early death.

She'd left that session feeling as low as she'd ever felt. There'd been something almost reassuring in knowing that what she was going through was nothing more or less than hundreds and thousands of people endured when their relationships ended. The jumble of loss and grief. Her counsellor had talked about that, and given her some sort of emotional map to navigate with. But the examination of her family told her a different story: she was uniquely and irrevocably cursed, and there was no way out.

Seen in that light, or shadow, Nicholas wasn't just an unfortunate accident who might have happened to anyone: he was fire to her dry tinder. It hadn't just been his looks, but his emotional extravagance, his willingness to engage, even his volatility had offered her a warmth and overt humanity that had been missing between her parents. Seen in that shadow, Nicholas had been her fate.

She resented seeing herself like that, as a victim of both nature and nurture. With her counsellor's help she'd been gradually moving herself out of that penumbra towards the light, until she'd seen her father abasing himself at that little red door. She'd wanted to shake him, tell him *Too late!* He should have had the courage to follow his feelings back when he could have all those years ago, should have declared himself back then to whatever exotic creature lived behind that door, rather than condemn her mother to twenty-five years of marital half-life.

Maybe this discovery of her father's real reason for coming to Italy was an improvement on what she'd previously known about him. Once, albeit a long time ago, he'd fallen in love. *Fallen*, as in lost control of his emotions. She'd yearned almost as much as her mother to see some sign of that, but they'd both, without ever discussing it, accepted that he was incapable of letting go. Love might have been deep inside him somewhere, driving his always impeccable behaviour towards his wife and his daughter, but he had never been able to see how crippling it was. He seldom talked about his own upbringing but when he did, it was strangely objective. He didn't describe himself in the third person, but he might as well have: an only child in a huge landscape, which swallowed his mother. His father was never mentioned.

The more she thought about it, knowing that he had loved and lost someone here in Venice wasn't that much consolation: it simply added another stitch to the pattern of despair. A passionate mistake followed by a loveless marriage was also a template she recognised.

And there was something else, something she now wished she'd discussed with her counsellor. She was pregnant. She'd told no one, because she hadn't decided whether to go through with it or have a termination. These two weeks which, she'd calculated, would take her to twelve, were her time to decide. She desperately wanted children, a child, as she'd desperately wanted a good marriage.

She sat straighter on the wooden slats and dangled her feet over the edge, just above the rising water. She put one hand on her heart and one hand on her belly and tried to think kindly thoughts about herself and her baby, keep the fear at bay. Fear that the bad acids of anguish over the break-up would be harming the tiny bud of cells inside her.

The rhythm of the waves beneath her was comforting, like the moon last night. Your pain changes nothing, she told herself. The tide still comes in and out. Keep breathing. In. And out. *It'll be okay.*

* * *

She knocked on his door, resolved to extend her kindness to him too. After all, she, too, had come here with a secret. She was going to ask him questions, instead of throwing accusatory barbs. Who is she? Did you love her? What happened?

She knocked again. 'Dad?'

He had to be there. He'd been on his last legs. 'Dad?' He would have come straight back here. She knocked harder. 'Dad!'

Even as she hurried back down the hallway to ask the woman at the desk to open the door, she knew.

Gemona, 1943

16

Joe woke late with a start, hearing voices. There were workers in the field beside the drain picking rows of beet. There was no chance of getting themselves and their bikes out of there without being seen, so Harry stood up, smiled and said, 'Buon giorno.'

The workers couldn't have looked less surprised. Clearly they already knew the Kiwis were there. Harry looked at his watch. 'Christ, gone nine.'

By the time they'd hauled their bikes back onto the road, some of the workers had returned to their labours, but some were looking at them still, anxiously.

'Tedeschi,' said a woman, making a T with her hands. 'Dappertutto.'

'Germans,' translated Joe, anxiously and perhaps unnecessarily, unsure how much Harry understood. 'Everywhere.'

'Andiamo via,' said Harry.

Calling thanks to the woman and her companions, they rode off. 'Do you reckon she was trying to tell us something?' asked Joe, alarmed at how easily the workers had recognised them as foreigners, despite their clothes and their best buon giornos.

'Like what?'

'That one of them had told the Germans or their overseer where we were?'

'There's nothing we can do except keep moving,' said Harry, and that made sense.

The day was overcast and they couldn't see the mountains, but Harry reckoned he could feel the position of the sun behind the cloud cover. That gave him north, and he could plot a course that avoided Udine and took them more directly towards the mountains.

They felt safe enough on the small country roads that dissected the plain. There was vegetation to give them cover, trees and hedgerows, shoulder-height fields of maize and grapevines, and the roads were all busy enough to make them unremarkable among the traffic: people on bicycles, tractors and farm machinery, horse-drawn wagons, the odd car and many trucks.

Harry set a good pace, telling Joe they had to get across the major rivers before Jerry put guards on the bridges. The biggest one they crossed was the Tagliamento, braided like the Waitaki, with pale blue snow-fed waters. As they crossed, they saw a convoy of German trucks coming the other way. They dismounted and pressed themselves and their bikes back against the rails.

Joe forced himself to look at the trucks as they passed. German infantry were sitting shoulder to shoulder in Wehrmacht grey under the canopied trays. The only German troops Joe had seen until that moment wore the light tan of the Afrika Korps. The grim vacant faces flitting past stared out at the river and countryside and showed no interest in a couple of cyclists heading in the other direction.

On the northern side of the Tagliamento, they turned left onto a long straight road that followed the river upstream. Harry said they'd follow the river back to the snow. Joe marvelled at the way Italians used everything around them — here the farmhouses were made of round stones from the river, split and mortared. They stopped and ate their bread and tomatoes beside a field of maize by a sign for a village called Dignano. The sun had burnt off the cloud cover and they saw the mountains for the first time since they'd left San Pietro. They looked like a dragon's back, close enough to touch, formidable enough to make Joe shiver.

They'd been pushing it, and became drowsy in the heat. Joe closed his eyes for what seemed like a moment and was woken by a yell from Harry, who was leaping on a man struggling up the bank with one of the bikes.

'Get the other thieving bastard!'

Joe scrambled up the bank and hit the second man in the small of the back with his shoulder. When they fell on top of the bike, the handlebars smacked the thief in the ear. 'Jeez, mate!' he protested.

Harry had the other thief in a choke-hold, but it was clear from his desperate gurgles to 'Lay off!' that he wasn't an Italian either.

'There are hundreds of us around here,' said the Aussie when they'd all calmed down. He and his companion, a Canadian, had escaped from another huge work camp called Prati Nuovi just before the Nazis had arrived and put everyone on a train for Germany. They were making for the mountains with about ten others and had taken shelter in the maize because the Jerries were everywhere. They had no food or water.

'Or transport,' said Harry.

'Sorry about that, mate,' said the Aussie. 'We thought you were Eyeties.'

'Bullshit,' said Harry.

The Canadian sought to explain, said they were welcome to join them. They'd made huts in the maize, were going to hit up the locals for food. He talked about safety in numbers.

'We'll take our chances,' said Harry, and when they were back on the road, he told Joe they were better off on their own. Joe was in no position to dispute this: they had transport, which the others clearly didn't, but as of now they had no food or water.

By late afternoon, the field worker's warning took on substance. As they pedalled north and west, leaving the plains and having to work harder as the contour changed to hill and dale, the German presence grew more pervasive. They even saw a German bicycle patrol ahead of them, luckily cycling in the same direction.

*   *   *

Towards evening the signs indicated they were close to a biggish town called Gemona, which seemed to sit up on the side of a hill to their right. Harry wanted to keep going, could see a gap in the mountains behind opening up into a huge V, almost certainly a pass, he reckoned. But they'd crossed on a railway bridge further down the road and found they couldn't get back across the river or the tracks.

They almost rode into a German control point on one bridge. Without papers, they would have had no chance. Again they were saved by a warning from an Italian peasant who seemed to have no trouble recognising that Harry and Joe were not of his ilk. He put his scythe down and made the T sign. 'Al ponte,' he said, pointing ahead. He said the Tedeschi were looking for 'prigionieri e partigiani sulle biciclette', *prisoners and partisans on bikes.* This seemed to him a great joke, and he revealed a wide grin completely bereft of teeth.

When Harry and Joe dumped their bikes and crept forward to see whether the old man was having them on, they got a shock. There were four Germans on the bridge all right, but not in uniforms Joe had ever seen before. Their collars were black and they had the jagged lightning flashes at the throat.

Harry didn't say much after that, but they rode much more carefully, south and then west. Again, they came to a bridge over the tracks, which, when they recce-ed it, was also manned by the SS.

When they retraced their steps they realised they were trapped between the railway tracks and the town, which covered the flank of the hill in front of them. They were hungry, tired and thirsty as the day faded and lights transformed the buildings above them from bleak to seductive.

There were no barriers to the town itself, apart from its topography. The streets were canyons between old houses that clung to the steep hillside. They pushed their bikes up the narrowest alleys they could find, but couldn't avoid crossing larger streets and piazzas, disconcertingly full of German uniforms: on foot, on motorbikes, in the occasional car.

Most of them appeared to be off duty, and none of them gave Harry and Joe a second glance, but when they stopped at a larger piazza near the top of the town, a dapper young man stood beside them for a moment. 'You're English,' he said quietly. 'You should know that there are Republican soldiers in town looking expressly for escaped prisoners of war.' He walked off without waiting for confirmation or denial.

'Who the hell are the Republicans?' asked Harry.

Joe didn't know either, but by simple deduction they had to be Italian fascists, working with the Germans. That was a problem, perfectly illustrated by the young man who spoke such immaculate English, and also by the old toothless man with the scythe: they might look like Italians to Germans, but to Italians they stood out like dog's balls. Any confidence they'd had about working their way through the town and out the other side drained away. Now they felt as if there was a sign around their necks drawing everyone's eyes to them.

'We need to find a place to lie low,' said Harry. They agreed their best bet was to find the poorest part of town and knock on doors until someone was kind enough to take them in for the night.

As they stood there, undecided, a priest pushed past them, making for a church that fronted the far side of the square. He was a tall, spare man, quite unlike Don Antonio, but a priest is a priest, thought Joe.

'Sia lodato Gesù Cristo,' he said.

'Sempre sia lodato,' the priest replied.

'Ci da santuario, Padre?' Joe asked. *Can you give us sanctuary, Father?*

The priest looked troubled, then looked right and left.

'Soltanto una notte,' said Joe. *One night only.*

'Take your bicycles round to the side door,' said the priest in excellent English. 'I'll let you in there.'

With that he hurried across to the main entrance of the church. Joe looked at Harry, worried that he might not approve.

'You're not just a pretty face,' said Harry.

The side door led to the presbytery at the back of the church.

They left the bicycles propped in the hallway and the priest ushered them through to a small dining room.

After introducing himself, lighting the first of many cigarettes and offering one to Harry, Don Claudio thought it safe to reveal himself as an Anglophile, boasting that he knew the streets of Mayfair better than those of Rome. He asked them about the damage to London from German bombs and barely managed to hide his disappointment when Joe and Harry revealed they were New Zealanders and had never been to England. Perhaps as some compensation for not being English, Harry introduced himself as a captain and Joe as a corporal.

Don Claudio hardly endeared himself to them by insisting that 'you New Zealanders' could have had no better 'imperial masters' than the English, but by that time he was plying them with red wine brought by his housekeeper, an old woman with bowed legs wrapped in bandages, who also produced a plate of cheese and a loaf of bread.

'Congratulations on your promotion, Captain,' Joe said, when Don Claudio excused himself to 'procure' another bottle of red.

'And to you, Corporal,' said Harry, grinning, leaning back in his chair with a glass of red in one hand and a real cigarette in the other. 'God knows, you're old enough and ugly enough.'

'What do you think of him?'

'He's got his head so far up his own arse it's no wonder he talks shit, but at least he's on the right side.'

Joe wasn't so sure, but kept his doubts to himself as, over the second bottle of red, Don Claudio seemed to take some pleasure in spelling out how wrong 'my friends the peasants' were in thinking that the armistice was the end of the war for Italy. He told them that everything had changed since 8 September. Italy had gone from being an ally of Germany to being an occupied alien. Ten German divisions had poured down into the country since the armistice. Italian soldiers in their tens of thousands had already been disarmed by their former comrades and put on trains for Germany, along with the Jews, to become slave labour in German farms and factories. The Germans were scouring the countryside not just for escaped prisoners of war — Don Claudio gave Joe and Harry a conspiratorial smile — and for Jews 'of course', but also for any able-bodied Italian males, 'apart from those who have joined the Republican army'.

'We heard about them,' said Harry. 'Who are they?'

Don Claudio smiled like a comedian who realises this audience hasn't heard his favourite joke, and delivered the punchline. 'But surely you know?' he teased them. 'Mussolini has been liberated from the Gran Sasso by an elite German SS unit. He has already set up a new fascist government on the shores of Lake Garda and launched the Republican Army to fight alongside the Germans.'

Don Claudio's delight in their dismay was unsettling.

'Italians,' he shrugged, reaching forward and refilling Harry's glass. 'Things here are never as nicely ordered as in England, or indeed Germany. You mustn't expect too much of us. Salute.'

Joe had sat on his first glass. The red wine was vastly more sophisticated than the nero from the taverna in San Pietro, but he could still taste his hangover in it.

Don Claudio insisted that he and Harry finish the second bottle, and quite a few more cigarettes, before leading them up a long flight of stairs to an attic, where there was a single bed and an upholstered chair. Don Claudio apologised for not having another bed, but Joe reassured him that the chair would be comfortable.

'The benefit of rank, Captain,' smiled Don Claudio to Harry, wishing them goodnight and closing the door behind himself.

'Toss you for it,' offered Harry, generously.

'This'll do me,' said Joe, slumping into the chair. 'What'd you make of him?' he asked again.

'He's an Eyetie,' said Harry. 'What d'you expect? He said so himself.'

Harry stretched his length on the bed and sighed. 'Landed on our feet, Corporal,' he said. 'Don Claudio's a strange fish, but, shit, we could have done a lot worse.'

Joe was trying to work out what it was about Don Claudio that was so unsettling, so that he could frame a sensible question to Harry, but a gentle snore removed any pressure on that front.

Although he was utterly buggered too, Joe sat there for some time, decanting the evening's events. Was Don Claudio's insistence on more wine to give himself Dutch courage — for what and why? — or a deliberate ploy to get them both drunk? And, failing that, get Harry drunk, since he was an officer? Again, why? Was he just a boastful bore, eager to speak English? Was he just a drunk? He had that slightly emaciated look about him and had shown no interest in the food.

From his chair, Joe could see through a small window, back down the alley below to a narrow sliver of piazza. Apart from the unbarred window, the room looked like a cell. Joe took some comfort from that. Nevertheless, when he closed his eyes, his inner ear began listening for sounds in the sky, the low drone of an aircraft, the clanking of armoured tracks on rock, the revving of engines . . .

17

When he opened his eyes, he thought he saw a canopied truck slide very slowly across the sliver of piazza and disappear. He was about to close his eyes again, when he saw a black car with a swastika cruise to a halt and a small man in black Gestapo uniform get out. He looked like propaganda photos of Himmler or Goebbels, the one with the rimless glasses — Joe couldn't remember which. Then Don Claudio walked into view and shook the Gestapo officer's hand.

Harry was instantly awake when Joe shook him.

'The fucking cunt,' said Harry, when he saw the priest turning away from the Gestapo officer. The staff car moved off, but Don Claudio was gesticulating, 'This way', to someone else. He disappeared from view, but six soldiers in black uniforms, one carrying a Luger, the rest with sub-machine guns, followed him. They'd be heading across the front of the church and down the side alley to the door of the presbytery, which meant it was already too late to get out the way they'd come in, or to grab their bikes.

Harry put his shoulder to the window and bust it open without breaking the glass. 'You first,' he said to Joe. 'I might not fit through.'

There was no time to argue, no time for Joe to explain that he'd prefer to wait for the German soldiers and prison than get shot in the back trying to escape. He levered himself feet first through the window and was looking to suspend himself from the sill to lessen the drop when Harry pushed him too hard and he fell sideways, trying to get his feet underneath him before he struck the cobbles. He didn't quite manage it and his right foot landed on an angle and slewed sideways. It felt like a skein of rubber bands being stretched and torn. His shoulder hit the cobblestones and he tried not to cry out.

Above him, Harry had squeezed through the window and was hanging from the sill. As Joe rolled and tried to stand, Harry landed like a cat. Joe took a step on his right foot and fell forward. Harry grabbed him, put one shoulder under Joe's right arm and they ran down the alley, away from the piazza, like a couple of contestants in the three-legged race at a church fete.

Joe was expecting to hear the chatter of those sub-machine guns, feel the rip of bullets in his back. Surely the Germans would have made the top of the stairs and burst into the room by now? Perhaps Don Claudio was offering them a red wine and telling them how much he loved German culture and knew the streets of Berlin better than Rome. Nothing happened. They made the first corner and swung around it, out of the line of fire.

'Leave me,' said Joe, as Harry tried to catch his breath and bearings.

There was only uphill and downhill.

'We'll head for the bush,' he said, as if Joe hadn't spoken.

The big moon was a curse, but it cast heavy shadows in the narrow stone canyons, and they made sure to stay on the dark side as they careered downhill. Within minutes, they were on a wider, less sloping street, with stone-fenced plots on either side. This fed them into a larger country road and they worked their way down that until they heard the sound of a straining engine behind them. Harry helped Joe over the stone wall into a field of shoulder-high maize. Harry led the way and Joe tried to hobble after him.

From within the maize, they couldn't see the headlights of the truck, but they could hear its engine. It kept going as they held their breath, faded a little, then stopped, maybe a couple of hundred yards further up the road.

'Fuck,' said Harry. 'From their point of view, there's not too many ways we could have gone.'

Harry knelt in front of Joe and, supporting his ankle in one hand like a farrier, began gently manoeuvring the foot this way and that with the other hand, as Joe groaned in greater or lesser pain. 'If you were a horse I might consider a lead pill,' Harry said when he'd finished, 'but I don't reckon there's anything actually broken.'

He stood up and listened. 'They'll sweep from where they've stopped back to town, maybe bring in reinforcements. We've got to try and get beyond their starting point, otherwise we're buggered.'

Once again, Harry seemed to have a grid in his head as they worked their way through the maize. Joe took strength from Harry's diagnosis of his ankle: if it was just sprained, he couldn't really do much damage by continuing to use it. But the pain and swelling got worse. It felt like a tube of scalding blood around the joint, and he was in agony every time he tried to put weight on it.

When they arrived at the edge of the maize field, it seemed to fit with Harry's internal map, and they crossed a drain and immediately dived into another field of maize on the other side. Periodically, Harry would stop and they would listen. Shortly after they entered the second field they heard more engines whining their way up the same road, the noise reverberating off the hills to their left. Harry waited until the trucks stopped.

'Roughly parallel to us,' he said. 'We're on the right track.'

That moment of optimism was quickly dashed by another sound that carried clearly on the night air. Barking dogs.

'Bugger,' said Harry. It might have been the first time Joe had seen him slump, but it was only for a moment. 'They'll have to track back to pick up our scent,' he said. 'We might have time.'

For what? thought Joe. Maybe it was his half-heartedness that had buggered his ankle when he dropped. He implored Harry to go on without him, said he'd work his way back towards the trucks and muddle the scent, delay them.

'Like hell,' said Harry, and put his shoulder back under Joe's armpit.

When they reached the edge of the second field of maize, there was a stretch of more open land, rows of grapes and, fifty yards beyond, a cluster of buildings. The barking dogs didn't seem any closer or further away, but certainly sounded more excited.

'We need animals,' said Harry. 'Horses, cattle.'

In his pain, Joe thought that Harry meant to ride the animals rather than walk, and it wasn't until they'd unlatched the big wooden door at one end of the nearest building that Joe understood: the dogs wouldn't be let in among the animals. Harry was leaving him here embalmed in shit, while he went out to take on the SS and their dogs.

Treviso, 2014

18

Treviso seemed so normal after Venice, even if nothing else about her life was. There were streets, cars, trucks, buses, pedestrian crossings. And the kind of shopping that took her breath away, along with any resolve to be moderate. Clare had bought two pairs of Church's brogues, one white and one light tan because she couldn't decide between them. Then she'd worried about spoiling the exposed stitching if she got caught in Auckland's rain so she got a pair of conventional black brogues just in case. That was the best part of a thousand euros right there. She'd already spent another grand in a little shop called Adriana, where the woman who served her told her all the shoes were handmade and that she had an interest in their manufacture and that's why they were so incredibly cheap and well produced. And they *were* so cheap — 100 euros on average and every one of them would have been 300 New Zealand dollars at least so she was saving big money the more she spent, which is why she'd bought so many: knee-length leather boots with dorsal zigzag laces that hugged the calf, and apple-green woven leather flat lace-ups, and red straight-back patent stilettos with platforms, faux jewel-encrusted gladiator sandals with ankle straps, cream sandals with wedges, and maroon nubuck ankle boots with stacked heels, not to mention gold lamé mules with fluffy pom-poms which could be slippers or evening wear, and blue court shoes that went with a fuck-off pin-striped business suit which she'd definitely need if she ever had to walk through the front door of the agency to sort Nicholas out. The Hush Puppies were from another shoe store just across the cobbled street from Adriana, because you couldn't go past Hush Puppies for kick-about comfort, so she'd got the red and white kid leather slip-ons and the tan and white ones too because the woman there agreed that they definitely lasted longer if you rotated them.

She refused to feel guilty about any of it, except that the shoe boxes had filled the closet of her room at the Continental, so she'd had to stack some of them under the window that opened onto the carpark at the back of the hotel. On the little writing table by the window was the letter she'd discovered in her father's tatty old briefcase after he'd been taken by water ambulance to Piazzale Roma, then by conventional ambulance to Treviso hospital, which had a specialist oncology and haematology department. It was inside a plain white envelope addressed to 'Clarebelle' in his copperplate handwriting. She'd read and reread bits of it from time to time, as much as she could stand in a sitting, so to speak.

> *Darling daughter,*
> *If you're reading this, the worst has happened.*

It hadn't. What *had* happened was worse, if anything.

> *I was always hopeful of making it back home, but*

Geoff made it very clear that things could change fast at any time and the end could come suddenly. I've been completely up front with the insurer and the premium has cost me a fortune but you'll see from the policy attached that everything is covered.

Geoff Paterson was an old rugby mate from Otago Uni, with a badly broken nose to prove it, who now happened to be *the* specialist on lymphoblastic leukaemia. She should ring Geoff but couldn't bring herself to do it: just one more instruction she'd ignored.

She hated seeing her father lying there in intensive care sprouting tubes. The room looked like a laboratory where plastic slippered, gowned and masked scientists carried out tests on people who already looked like cadavers.

Treviso hospital was quite the ugliest building in a beautiful town and the separate oncology and haematology building made the Auckland central police station look like an architectural masterpiece. The bile yellow foyer had wheelchairs stacked in a line ready for the patients arriving in the emergency bay just outside. Every time she passed them she swore she'd get her father into one of them and escape.

There was a room waiting for him if he ever got out of intensive care. It had a view of treetops hiding a carpark. His empty bed there was surrounded by flowers from all those people from San Pietro whom she'd so far managed to avoid by going into the trees opposite the emergency entrance for a fag and checking reception for faces she might recognise. Renzo had somehow fooled her and been in the room yesterday, quietly sitting there when she'd blown in, smelling of fags. She'd been so surprised to see him she'd probably been rude, asked him what he was doing there before she'd even said hello, but he seemed not to mind or even hear. He'd risen and kissed her elaborately on both cheeks, then simply asked her how she was. That surprised her too. When she said she was fine, he'd smiled gently and said, 'That's good.'

He'd asked where she was staying and she was hesitant about telling him. The Continental may not have been the best hotel in town but it was a perfect refuge for her, comforting old plasterwork with high studs and terrazzo floors and a discreet bar, the Americano, down under the arch by the street. It was close to the railway station where she could buy English newspapers, and a short walk the other way took her along the magic carpet — she'd never seen that before, a red carpet along the middle of the footpath — to Adriana and the Piazza dei Signori. She didn't want to have to cope with well-intentioned visitors from San Pietro. She couldn't speak Italian to them and didn't even know what to say in English to Renzo. She couldn't *not* tell him where she was staying, but how to tell him she wanted to be alone without coming across like Greta Garbo? In the end, she just said it. 'I don't want visitors.'

He responded as if that was the most rational thing he'd ever heard, said 'Of course' and enquired whether the hotel was okay or if she needed anything. She wanted to tell him that the Continental was her cave and she was filling it up with everything she needed, but that sounded slightly crazy, even to her.

19

This morning, she'd gone into Adriana again just for a look. There was a different woman there, who showed her the bags along the top shelf. She was stunned that she'd been in there three times yet there were still treasures she hadn't seen, particularly a beautiful bag in soft summery yellow leather.

The thing was, she kept telling herself, she'd never be back here and at home the warm weather would come and she'd need to be prepared. She hadn't realised how much she'd been depending on her father to sort out the mess. He'd passed her on to a colleague, Tania, who was an expert in matrimonial property, but he had still been patiently working through her options.

> You'll find a file in my suitcase with notes about your situation. I've tried to anticipate everything, but that's probably impossible. Tania will of course guide you through the matrimonial property options, but the other mess, the business, will be much more fluid and you'll have some difficult choices to make. I think you should cut your losses and move on. Don't pursue him for damages. Let the Real Estate Agents Authority sort him out.
>
> That's my real grief, Clarebelle, that I can't be there to help you through this awful time in your life. I'm sorry. While I can't anticipate everything that might happen, I can say with some certainty that fighting the likes of Nicholas never brings satisfaction.

> *You'll never get the revenge or the apology or inflict*
> *the shame or pain on him that you deserve. Don't*
> *waste more money and time trying: you're financially*
> *independent as of this moment. Until you let him go,*
> *you won't be able to get on with your life. That's my*
> *final bob's worth, darling.*

Easily said, even if it was written, probably laboriously. At times, she could contemplate letting it go, letting him go. But the *detail* of Nicholas's betrayal kept coming back. She should have seen the signs. The way he convinced her after their successful fledgling year that he would be better as the front man for the agency, the lone scout out there on the streets of the inner-city fringe while she ran the office, did the contracts, managed the deposits and commissions, banked the profits. He'd sold the idea — and she'd bought it, more fool her — that it was a better use of their *complementary* skills: hers sedentary, static, supervisory, composing and placing the advertising, keeping the website up to date, working the banks and the solicitors on the landline and by e-mail, doing the books; his verbal, mobile, working from the hands-free in his black BMW 5 series which she thought would alienate the clients but he *knew* would impress them and besides they needed the tax deductions.

That should have alerted her. Though he was always out doing appraisals, talking to valuers, particularly one, the month-on-month figures on agency exclusives didn't really improve in their second year, or third, despite the overall market volumes increasing by twenty or thirty per cent. The rising values and their commissions on the back of them disguised the reality that Nicholas wasn't bringing in any more contracts than he had the year before. The *volumes* for the agency were flat-lining, while the profits were going up on the back of the *values* of a hot market. She should have seen it, but dismissed it as an indicator of increased competition: a lot of agents who'd found something else to do after the meltdown in 2008 were back in the game.

She was sipping a prosecco under the vaulted arches of the huge loggia that projected out into the piazza from the Palazzo del Trecento, partly rebuilt after the war. There was a photo of it on the other side of the square, looking absolutely *wrecked* after the bombardamento in 1944, and if you stood there and compared the photo with the reality you could see — this was where the Italians were so cool — the deliberate zigzags of new bricks that perfectly delineated for future generations exactly where they'd had to start again. At home they'd have bulldozed it and put up something new, pretended that things didn't get broken, that people and buildings didn't have to find a way to endure in their imperfection.

To begin with, the fraud that Nicholas perpetrated on her was like a knot in the entrails of their business that she couldn't even find the ends of. But gradually, with her father's help, she'd got her head around the *mechanics* of what Nicholas did: classic contract flipping.

He would hear of a prospective sale, from the ether, from his myriad contacts, from his ceaseless quartering of their patch, but would tell no one at the agency. Instead, he would visit the prospective vendor to do an appraisal. Happened all the time, that was his job. But the real motive was to suss out whether the vendor was a potential mark, based on criteria like eagerness or desperation to sell, old age, isolation, naïveté, or, at the other end of the scale, openness to the idea of a back-hander.

As soon as he had the verbal nod, Nicholas would bring the vendor an unconditional agreement for sale and purchase, a standard Law Society template bought from Whitcoulls with no mention of any agency on it, signed either by a purchaser 'or nominee', and with a long settlement date. But that purchaser would not be the person Nicholas knew was interested in buying a property of this type. The first purchaser was a stooge, who was in on the deal.

Clare tried to scoot over the next stage, but it never worked: the stooge purchaser could be anyone, of course she knew that. But the fact that in almost every case it was her best friend Sarah didn't help. It was like Tourette's, leaping out at inopportune times — *Bitch!* — and she couldn't get past it. It was a mathematical equation that kept getting worse: trying to work out on how many levels she'd been fucked over by Sarah.

Somehow, the first glass of prosecco had gone, along with the cute little complimentary squares of egg sandwich. She felt she was on the edge of some important revelation and obliged to order a second glass. When she looked out across the piazza, the autumn sun had left it, and the ambling couples, old and young, were putting their hands in jacket pockets or taking their partner's hands in theirs. What a place this would be to share with someone.

Anyway, Nicholas would then flip the contract: take another agreement to the third party he knew was interested in a property like this and sign him up for an extra twenty or thirty or fifty k. The vendor on the new contract was, of course, the stooge purchaser on the original contract, and the dates for settlement of the two contracts were always contemporaneous.

On settlement, without putting up a penny, the stooge purchaser and Nicholas would walk away with whatever the difference was between their purchase price and the ultimate sale price — fifteen or twenty k mostly, but on three occasions it was thirty and once fifty, for a widowed pensioner who had no family and was selling a former state house she'd paid for over the course of a lifetime. That money was cash and a hundred per cent profit, apart from Sarah's cut and the back-hander to the valuer. There were no agency overheads and no commission to pay because the agency, being run by the faithful *gormless* wife, knew nothing about it.

It might have gone on for another couple of years, had it not been for New Zealand's two degrees of separation. One of the third party purchasers was represented by her father, who'd seen a contract come across his desk with Sarah Easton as the vendor. He'd mentioned it to Clare — he wasn't acting for Sarah and not breaching any confidence — who thought it more than passing strange that her best friend was buying and selling houses and had never mentioned it to her or asked her advice about the market. They'd made it through the terrible twenties together, cried over boyfriends together, got drunk together, shopped for clothes together, planned their lives together, yet Sarah had never said, even in passing, that she'd bought a fucking *house* and was selling it.

What Clare knew of Sarah's financial situation was pretty dire. Her flirtation with the law was short-lived (*boring!*) and she'd spent the fag-end of her twenties with Shanes and Dwaynes and Kanes, each younger and poorer than the last, doing an endless succession of courses from TM to Bikram yoga to dance therapy to drama to NLP to Zumba, some of which had qualified her to instruct. Sarah was in no position to pony up a deposit on a house, even in the days of ninety per cent mortgages. If she had been, Clare would have been on the case for her best friend, looking.

She'd met Sarah for a coffee to ask her the question. They'd sat in the wintry morning sun at Blake Street, just down from Jervois Road, Sarah in lycras under a puff jacket — she was currently a Zumba instructor at Les Mills. But something in Sarah's manner stopped Clare from opening her mouth. She wasn't sure how long it had been there, a kind of flitting, fleeting eye contact, a rush of words about nothing, skating and slipping across the surface of their intent, old coded signals that used to be shorthand for something meaningful and understood, but now seemed opaque. Something had changed. Clare had gone away, weighed down with worry.

20

Dusk had come to the piazza and given it a cosy shroud, an intimacy that seemed to encourage the couples to move closer together as they walked. Their happiness wrenched her heart and flooded her with regret and yearning.

She ordered a coffee from the tall, dark and not very handsome waiter who was at least looking less truculent than when she'd arrived. He even smiled when she said she didn't want any more sandwiches, grazie. She loved it here, she loved the anonymity, that there was almost zero chance that anyone would walk into the Piazza dei Signori and see her occasional tears and know her shame.

But amid the betrayal, the deceit, the emotional meltdown, she'd missed something. *Rewind.*

The original vendors. Most of them had been unknown to the agency but three of the dozen had been on the books. Another had rung her one lunchtime when Lana, the receptionist, was at the gym. Having used up her lunchtime, Lana would then eat her yoghurt and lettuce at the desk, which Clare had been meaning to talk to her about, but the girl was so emotionally fragile she didn't dare. Anyway, this woman had telephoned while Lana was out and it had come straight through to Clare. It was one of those exploratory calls — the market's going crazy, should I cash up? — the sort of query she'd refer to Nicholas to go and do an appraisal. She'd duly done this then heard no more about it and assumed the woman had been another tyre kicker. Until she saw her name on one of the flipped contracts a year later.

It came to Clare at the same time as the coffee. *Lana had to have been complicit.* Nicholas had to make sure all contacts to the office went to him first so he could vet them for potential marks. It suddenly made sense: she'd seen dates and times on Lana's telephone messages that were hours old, sometimes as much as a day. When Clare had taxed Lana with it she'd rolled her big blue eyes, then blushed so badly that Clare felt sorry for her. *She was fucking Nicholas.*

Clare swallowed the coffee, left some euros to cover it — the figures on the notes were blurred and she didn't want to wipe her eyes, was sure it'd be more than enough — and walked back down the magic carpet, oblivious this time to the warm glow of the shops.

At first she felt a kind of triumph. Over Sarah. She felt like texting her or even ringing her and telling her that Nicholas had made a fool of her too. But the feeling didn't last. Lana, hopeless, helpless Lana, whom she'd thought of as a charity case. She'd wanted to fire her but Nicholas always wanted to give her another chance. *Damn right he did!* Should she ring him? Let him know she had additional information on . . . What exactly? The magnitude of his betrayal? On what a deluded idiot she'd been?

It was always the detail that killed her. Those lunchtimes when Lana would get back pink-faced from 'the gym' and gobble her yogurt and god-awful health confection or whatever the fuck it was, spilling stuff on her keyboard and answering the phone with her mouth full of couscous and Nicholas's cum. *Say hello to Pedro!*

Clare walked past the sallow young man on reception and took the lift up to her room. She tripped over a shoe box in her tan and white Hush Puppies and booted it across the floor, sending the gladiator slave sandals cannoning into the boxes under the writing table. The room seemed suddenly stuffy and full. She picked up the empty box, gathered up the tissue paper and opened the shuttered windows to the night air. Below, the bland expanse of the mostly empty car park looked yellow under the lights. She saw two of those huge rubbish bins against the wall further along near the back entrance to the hotel kitchen. She dropped the box the three storeys to an empty park, screwed up the tissue and threw it after. Then she began emptying the boxes, throwing the shoes on the bed and the boxes and tissue out the window. It didn't take that long. When she leaned out the window again she saw that they'd made a messy sort of pile across one park.

She left the room, went downstairs and outside for a smoke, then remembered her mission and walked through the arch and round the back of the hotel to the car park. She lit the fag, then tried to gather an armful of boxes and tissue. Some of it fell out of her arms and she looked across to the rubbish bins through the curling smoke, so far away. It was hopeless, useless. She dropped the stuff she was carrying and went around the outside of her midden, booting the boxes and tissues into some sort of pile. The Hush Puppies were exactly right for the job. She had a last drag on the disgusting cigarette that disgusted her almost as much as she disgusted herself and threw it on the pile. She wondered how long it would take the cigarette to ignite the tissue paper or whether she'd have to use her lighter. She felt numb, becalmed, until the smoke grew into flames, quite spectacular for about twenty or thirty seconds. She thought about taking a photo and sharing it with someone — Sarah, probably, or Nicholas. Subject: My life. My dreams. You're such a drama queen, she admonished herself, even though she felt no emotion at all. She heard a siren, quite close.

Gemona, 1943

21

'Hai fame?' someone was asking him. *Are you hungry?*

Joe remembered a game at PG 57, where men would describe their favourite meals in great detail. When he had seen them salivating and swallowing, he had started to as well. That had made him feel worse, not better, so thereafter he'd stayed well clear. He heard the voice again, asking him if he was hungry.

When he opened his eyes, the mother, Nina, was there, offering him a bowl of soup, flanked by Donatella. Joe pushed himself upright and took the bowl in hand. He must have looked for a spoon.

'Così,' said Donatella, and mimed sipping it from the bowl.

The soup was thin, but tasted of chicken. Bepi came in with a torn chunk of crumbly bread, to soak up the last of the soup. They seemed to approve, as he slurped and swallowed. Nina was watching him intently and when he'd finished and handed her the bowl, she took it with one hand and with the other gently touched him on the temple, where the hair wouldn't grow, and traced the scar down to the lump on his cheekbone. 'Quanti anni hai?' she asked him.

'Diciannove,' he told her. *Nineteen years old.*

'Poveretto,' she said.

'Mamma!' said Donatella. There was a quick exchange between mother and daughter in dialect, which Joe didn't understand, but in which Nina seemed to be justifying expressing sympathy for Joe's disfigurement so young. Nina was either ash blonde or grey, Joe couldn't tell which, but was probably only in her mid-forties.

'Lei,' said Nina, turning to Joe and indicating Donatella, 'diciotto.'

'Eighteen, me,' translated Donatella.

'You speak English?'

'A little only. I study at convent school. To become a teacher.'

Nina had crossed the room to the dresser, and returned with a portrait photograph of a young man with fierce eyes glowering under the peak of what looked like the kind of stiff felt hat mountaineers wore, with a long feather pointing straight up from the left temple. 'Questo mio figlio,' she said. 'Luca.'

'My brother has twenty-four years,' said Donatella.

Nina explained that Luca was somewhere in Russia, she didn't know where, and she prayed that wherever he was, some mother knew that he was the son of another mother, like Joe, and would treat him like her own son. Joe nodded and said he hoped so too, though he'd never been treated like this by Molly.

'Where is your mother?' asked Donatella.

'Dead,' said Joe, and tried to explain that she died giving birth to him.

'Orfano?' asked Nina.

Orphan. He supposed he was. His sisters weren't his sisters, strictly speaking: they were his aunts. The youngest of the oldest three, by Mal's first wife, Patricia, had been his mother, Annie. When Annie had died giving birth to Joe, Mal Lamont,

Joe's grandfather, had grabbed both boys and taken them back to the farm at Devil's Bridge. By that time Mal had had nine daughters trying to get a son, the last six by his second wife, Molly, who'd been his housekeeper after Pat's death. Mal had formally adopted Dan and Joe and had raised them as his sons. By that time, Mal was in his seventies, and Molly, though twenty years his junior, would have been too old to have more children.

The youngest of the last six daughters, Ida, who had been more of a mother to him than Molly, had told Dan she remembered a man coming out from town on a horse, and Mal confronting him at the farm gate with his shotgun, telling him if he came again he'd shoot his horse.

But the man had come once more, according to Ida. He'd waited until Mal and Molly and the sisters had gone off to the basilica, as they did every Sunday morning, rain or shine. Ida had been left alone to look after Dan and Joe and when this man had ridden up to the house and demanded to see the little boys, what could she say? She was terrified, because Mal had told them the boys' father was a gambler and a drinker and a ne'er do well. 'Indeed,' said Ida, 'he might have been smelling a bit of whisky, but he seemed gentle enough.'

Ida told Dan that the man had done nothing, just ruffled three-year-old Dan's hair, then stared at Joe in his basket. Ida said he might have been crying, that at one stage he'd bent over and gripped the basket and she could see his knuckles were white. Then he rode away.

Ida had been worried that he'd come back the next Sunday, but he never did. She'd sworn Dan to silence and had never told her father about the man's visit. Malachy would have beaten her for allowing the man into his home and hearth, though Ida didn't know what she could have done to stop him.

When Joe was older, Dan told him about the man who'd come to see them. They both taxed Ida about the stranger: What did he look like? All Ida could remember was that he was darker than 'the rest of us' and polite and 'dressed like a townie, dapper'. She said he looked like Dan, though that might have been because she knew that's what Dan wanted to hear. What was his name? they chorused. But Ida didn't know, the man never said. Joe thought that, after the war, he and Dan would go to the Magistrates' Court or the Oamaru Borough Council or wherever the adoption records were kept and find out what their real father's name was.

Joe wanted to explain to Nina, so that she wouldn't think he'd had no one looking after him, that in some ways having so many of his aunts around had meant he'd had many mothers, but it was too complicated for his fledgling Italian. It was easier to say sì.

'Poveretto,' said Nina again, with a clucking sound, and made him lie back down. This time Donatella didn't disagree with her mother, but lifted Joe's head so that she could plump the cushion underneath.

For a moment Donatella's hair fell forward and enveloped his face. He breathed her in and felt as secure as he could ever remember feeling.

22

For three weeks, Joe scarcely left Bepi and Nina's house or the cobblestone courtyard that connected the Bonazzon house and stables to the similar sized Zanardi house and stables about twenty yards opposite. There was a long implement shed on the third side, through which an arch opened onto the gravel road. On its fourth side, the courtyard led to a dirt track between two fields, one planted in maize and the other in grapes, and more fields beyond, working up the hill towards a steep slope on which, further to the west, the town had taken root. Bepi explained that the two families farmed under the mezzadria system, which Joe understood to mean that they worked the land for an absent landowner or padrone, who took a share of all they produced.

The Bonazzons and Zanardis operated as one big family. Bepi and Gigi Zanardi had grown up together locally, and Gigi had eventually married Nina's much younger sister, Marisa. Nina and Marisa, from the Bolzano area, up in the mountains, were striking women with olive skin, but blue eyes and dark blonde hair. 'Austriaci,' Bepi joked. Gigi and Marisa's children, Paola and Leo, aged seven and five, were often cared for by Gigi's seventy-year-old mother, Nonna Isabella, who also lived with them. There surely would have been discussions while Joe was still bed-ridden, but he'd been accepted without question and with unfailing hospitality, even though there were constant reminders of the risks they were running. He didn't want to leave, but knew he had to.

They hadn't suffered any further rastrellamenti since the

night Harry had left him in the culvert, but the troop trucks had come up their road several times, stopping at farms further up. News would come back of German or Republican troops raking through houses and stables and storehouses with knives and bayonets. The word was that the Republicans were worse, because they had local knowledge. Each time they'd heard the trucks grinding up their road, Joe had limped into the casotta, a little bivvy Bepi had made out of stalks and hay in the middle of the maize, and stayed there until Donatella or one of the Zanardi children came to tell him it was safe.

Although the paranoia was difficult to live with, for Joe those weeks were idyllic. He tried to earn his keep, once the ankle could bear his weight. Bepi had held his ankle just like Harry and twisted the foot this way and that while he pressed his other hand palm down on the joint, 'listening' for signs of bone damage. Satisfied, he offered his shoulder to Joe and they hobbled outside, across the courtyard towards the fields. Joe knew it was the vendemmia, the grape harvest, but felt Bepi would be optimistic if he thought Joe could get through a day on the ankle out among the vines.

Instead, Bepi stopped at a tall vat with rungs up the side. Gigi was at the top, tipping a basket of red grapes into it, helped by Donatella, who was standing inside. When Gigi came down with the empty basket and crossed back to the vineyard, Bepi turned to Joe. 'Puoi andare dentro con lei?' he asked. *Can you get in there with her?*

'Venga,' said Donatella, leaning over the side of the vat and holding out her hands.

Joe removed his shoes and socks, then looked doubtfully at his dirty feet, but Bepi, untroubled, helped to push him up the ladder as Donatella pulled, with many exhortations of 'Dai!

Dai!' which, after some initial alarm, Joe realised was dialect for 'Come on!' or 'Go for it!'.

When he reached the top, he saw that Donatella had her skirt tucked into her pants and was up to her calves in a soggy purple mass. She helped Joe lower himself into the sludge and demonstrated the stamping motion that pressed the grapes through the filter at the bottom of the vat. The ankle was sore to begin with, but the repetitive and almost weightless tramping motion in the squelching morass soon freed it up. The other inspiration was being so close to Donatella. That proximity didn't last long, because once Joe had proved he could do the job, Bepi reassigned Donatella to the harvest, where her quick hands would be more useful. Joe tried not to watch as she climbed out of the vat, but couldn't help but admire strongly muscled white thighs that had seldom seen the sun.

Joe's mobility improved rapidly after a couple of days in the vat, and he was able to help scrape the residue from the top of the filter, stalks and leaves and skin, and load it into another smaller vat. There it would ferment and become the fiery spirit, grappa, which Bepi called 'graspa', and to which he ascribed magical properties.

Bepi had a limp that imposed itself late in the day and he would sigh and take a swig of what he called 'un po' di riscaldamento'. Joe translated that literally as *a little reheating*, so when Bepi offered him a swig of the clear liquid at the end of a long day cutting maize, he accepted. When the stuff hit the back of his throat, it burned like liquid fire and he almost spat it out. Gigi, particularly, and Bepi almost wet themselves as he staggered and sweated. Thereafter, the offer of un po' di riscaldamento, and Joe's refusal, were a source of great mirth.

Bepi was a big man with a high forehead and eyes that

drooped like a bloodhound's, but any appearance of dolefulness was alleviated by his happy, upturned mouth, even though it threw out curses like corn for the chickens. If God wasn't a dog, Dio cane, the Madonna was a pig, porca Madonna, or a prostitute, Madonna putana.

At the end of the day, when he began limping, Bepi could become testy with both Gigi and Joe. Gigi told Joe not to take it personally: Bepi had an old war wound that gave him trouble still. Joe had read articles in the *Oamaru Mail* commemorating Anzac Day, stories of Gallipoli and the Somme, but had never heard a whisper of the battles Gigi told him about, Caporetto and the Battle of the Solstice on the Piave River, and Vittorio Veneto. He said the Austrians and Germans and Hungarians had pushed the Italian population of Friuli south to the Piave and razed all the land between here and there. Bepi was a hero, because he was one of the indomitable warriors who had stopped the Austrians and Germans at the Piave in June 1918 with a last-ditch counter-attack from the Montello plateau.

There was a place on the Piave, Gigi said, a shingle bank called L'Isola dei Morti, *The Island of the Dead*, where the river was still giving up bones. That was where Bepi and his fellow heroes had used the stacked bodies of their comrades as cover to finally stop the Austrians. There were sayings and songs that commemorated that famous victory: 'E' meglio vivere un giorno da leone che cent'anni da pecora.' *It's better to live one single day as a lion than a hundred years as a sheep.* And the song of the Piave: 'Il Piave momorò, non passa lo straniero.' *The Piave murmurs, the foreigner shall not cross.* 'Yet here we are,' muttered Gigi, 'not thirty years later, reliving the same nightmare, and our heroes now old and crippled.'

Gigi said none of this near Bepi, who never talked about the

Island of the Dead, but simply said that Italy should be fighting on the side of the British against the Tedeschi, as they did in the Great War.

* * *

After the grape harvest, Joe made himself useful around the animals. So many of the rhythms and routines were similar to those he'd grown up with. Milking, feeding, mucking out. The cows never left the stalle, so he didn't have to bring them in from the fields in the morning, just milked them where they stood, then separated the milk from the cream by cranking the churner. The separator was similar to the one they'd used at home and just as hard to clean.

The Bonazzons and Zanardis were self-sufficient in milk, cream and butter, just like the Lamonts, and grew most of the rest of what they needed in a vegetable garden close to the houses. Out beyond the Zanardi house was a sty for the pigs, from which the salamis hanging in the cupboard behind the kitchen were made.

At Devil's Bridge, Joe and Dan had hunted rabbits with Dan's pet ferret, which would flush them out of their burrows. The rabbits were mostly fed to the dogs, but here they were hung, then cooked over a coal range in the kitchen that also supplied the hot water, just like at home.

Nina and Marisa's day went much like Molly's and the aunties', from daylight until dusk and beyond, milking cows, gardening, washing, ironing, knitting and sewing, in the light from candles and lamps. At their side for most of the time was Nonna Isabella, wizened, grey hair in a tight bun, dressed in widow's black, but in some ways quite unconventional: she told

Joe she didn't believe in God but went to church every Sunday just in case. In other ways, she was very conservative. When Joe attempted to wash the dishes after an evening meal, Nonna was affronted and chased him from the sink with a broom. When Paola and Leo recognised a similarity with a picture book they were reading and called 'Strega! Strega!' *Witch! Witch!*, Nonna put the broomstick between her knees and rode across to the children, who pretended to be scared witless.

Although so much was the same as at Devil's Bridge, it was also incalculably different. Orders were seldom given, voices seldom raised, except between Bepi and Gigi, whose constant banter and discussion and cursing was carried out at a volume that at home would have ended in punches being thrown. Gigi was taller than Bepi and wiry, not as outgoing, but the pair worked like a left and right hand with a mutual knowledge that looked instinctive but was born of thousands of man hours together. There was an easy rhythm to their tasks, whether out in the fields or repairs and maintenance in the implement shed when the first winter rains came. Work seemed to be an integral part of a joyful life, not an obligation to be tackled and beaten.

Books were precious and the whole family embraced the education of Donatella and Paola and Leo. The teacher at Ardgowan had let Joe take the odd school book home to read, but if old Mal had caught him reading, he'd find Joe some work to occupy his hands, 'Or I'll give ye this book around yer bluddy ears!'

Every evening, as the temperature dropped, both families would gather in one house or the other while dinner was being prepared. The houses were virtually identical, with the bottom storey divided into the stalle for the animals and a huge flagstoned room that served as kitchen, dining and sitting room. Behind the kitchen was a small room where meat was hung and food stored. In the aromatic warmth of the range the school books would come out and Donatella would go through the children's homework exercises, with everyone joining in. Joe quickly realised that neither Nonna nor Gigi could read or write and the others were semi-literate at best. So a circle of curious adults, including Joe, tried to pick up as much as they could, and often asked questions.

By all the standards that Joe knew, Paola and Leo were spoilt rotten, always the centre of the adults' attention and, as far as he could see, much the better for it. There was no evidence of sibling rivalry, no tantrums, no tears, and when they got home from school at lunchtime they did their jobs in the afternoon without being ordered to or even asked and then did their homework with Donatella when she got home from the convent school in the evening.

She would insist everyone joined in the action song that ended homework. They would all hold hands and sing about the pecorella, *little lamb*, Cibin, who kept getting lost and had to be looked for everywhere, in the river, the mountains, the sea and the forests. Really, Paola was already too old for the song and they all acted it out for little Leo, whose dark blond hair shone in the lamplight.

One evening Donatella asked Joe for a song. He was about to tell them there had been no singing in his house, not even hymns, when he remembered his first day at school, when the teacher had asked the new entrants to join hands in a circle and they sang, 'Ring a ring o' roses, a pocket full of posies.' Paola and Leo loved it, especially when Joe did the exaggerated sneezes, 'A tishoo! A tishoo!', then threw himself on the floor for 'We all fall down!'. The song became a favourite and Donatella and the kids clamoured for another.

The only other one Joe could remember was 'Twinkle, twinkle little star'. When he mimed looking up into the heavens, 'Up above the world so high, like a diamond in the sky', Paola and Leo both gazed skywards in wonder too, though they couldn't understand the words until Donatella translated them.

Although it wasn't as much fun as 'Ring a ring o' roses', 'Twinkle, twinkle' became a much requested lullaby, and several times Joe went up the stairs in the Zanardi house with Donatella and they sang the song to Paola and Leo in their beds. He couldn't remember all the verses but the ones he knew stayed with him as he lay under the photograph of the absent son Luca in his Alpino hat.

> *When the blazing sun is gone,*
> *When he nothing shines upon,*
> *Then you show your little light,*
> *Twinkle, twinkle, all the night.*
> *As your bright and tiny spark,*
> *Lights the traveller in the dark.*
> *Though I know not what you are,*
> *Twinkle, twinkle, little star.*

Joe would wish for the innocence that believed there was only one burning sun in the sky, and that it disappeared at night.

One evening when he was singing the lullaby to the kids Donatella took his hand in the darkness and held it between her own. He perhaps imagined that he saw her looking at him fondly sometimes but she seldom touched him in a family where touching was like breathing and she always called him the formal *lei*, in a family where they all called each other, and

Joe, *tu*. He called her *tu*, partly because everyone else did, and partly because he knew more of the verb endings for *tu*. That night, he cautioned himself that he shouldn't read too much into Donatella's touch. It was an instinctive thing, he knew, a response to a magical moment with the kids.

When the children went to bed, the families would retreat to their respective houses. Donatella would get out her own books and practise her English with Joe. To his embarrassment he wasn't able to answer some of her questions about grammar but he was at least able to help her conversational skills. She laughed easily and often, a throaty sound that belied the softness of her voice. Joe had never really known love, not even what Ida had called puppy love at school, but he instinctively recognised the feeling that rose in him at the sight and sound of her.

23

The constant threat of rastrellamenti by the Germans and Republicans was probably more difficult to live with than Bepi and the family let on. Paola and Leo had to be told not to mention the stranger to their friends or at school. Joe had to make sure he wasn't spotted by passers-by on the road and if visitors came through the arch he would high-step to his casotta in the maize field so as not to leave a track.

Bepi had told him that there were known sympathisers on the farms around them and known fascists, but most of their neighbours had learnt not to declare themselves politically after two decades of Mussolini. Bepi called them 'Chi lo sa', the *Who knows*.

Joe still might have tried to stay on had it not been for news Donatella brought home from the convent school about two and a half weeks after he had arrived. Once the children were in bed, she told them there'd been a scandal at the church further up the hill from the convent: Don Claudio, the priest, had been found dead in his presbytery. 'Strangolato.'

Joe had never heard the word before, but it was an easy enough translation, and he had to be careful how he responded. He'd said nothing as Donatella repeated the gossip: that there'd been rumours about Don Claudio's sexuality, and he may have been the victim of a sordid lovers' tiff. According to Bepi, it was also common knowledge that Don Claudio was a confidant of the district Gestapo commander, known universally as Il Pazzo, *The Madman*, because of the savagery of his reprisals.

Joe had told Bepi and the family very little of what had

happened in Gemona that night, or about Harry. He'd just said that his friend had run off after trying to save Joe by covering him in shit. Bepi had asked few questions: he understood that it was safer not to know.

Joe had heard nothing from Harry, but he remembered the corrupt cookhouse wallah at the Bari prison camp who almost died with Harry's hands clamped around his neck. Don Claudio's death and the manner of it was surely confirmation that Harry had escaped the SS and their dogs, and had gone back for vengeance on the priest.

There were no rumours about any connection between escaped POWs and Don Claudio's death, but a day or so after the body was found Bepi returned from the big market, where he had sold beets and greens and the last of the potatoes, with a copy of a poster he said was plastered all over town. It showed sketches of *Il Capitano Neozelandese*, who was supposed to be Harry, and *Il Caporale*, who was supposed to be Joe. Neither was very accurate, apart from the scar running down the side of il caporale's temple and cheek. The Gestapo could only have got those details of Harry and Joe's 'new' rank from Don Claudio. In Joe's mind, the timing of the posters confirmed that Il Pazzo and the Gestapo suspected that he and Harry had been involved in the priest's death. Joe remained silent, but knew that if he were captured, he would be recognised and interrogated by the Gestapo, and the reprisals suffered by Bepi and the others would be unimaginable.

Bepi, translated by Donatella, told Joe of other developments that upped the ante. Joe knew from Don Claudio that Mussolini had set up a fascist republican government on Lake Garda under German control, but he had no idea that the Venezia–Friuli–Giulia region had been informally annexed by Germany and was no longer part of the Italian state. The existence of the Adriatisches Küstenland, as it was known, incensed Bepi. It was administered by an Austrian Nazi who hated Italians, and particularly Venetians and Friulians, whom he considered alien even to the Italian race. 'Twenty-five years after we stopped the Austrians at the Piave, Mussolini has delivered us to them!' lamented Bepi. In response a clandestine Comitato Liberazione Nazionale had been set up in Milan, determined to expel the Germans and eliminate fascism. Part of the CLN's brief was to assist Allied prisoners of war and Bepi asked for Joe's permission to approach the local cell and get advice.

Two nights later, Bepi dressed warmly after dinner and disappeared into the darkness. At midnight, he returned with news of a plan. Joe would be supplied with a train ticket from Gemona to Monfalcone, a town to the east, not far from Trieste. There a group of Slovenian partisans in the hills above the town would lead him and others to an English command in the mountains, who in turn would get them across the border to Switzerland.

'Sloveni?' asked Joe.

'Comunisti,' said Bepi. 'Buoni.'

An Italian guide named Arturo would meet Joe and other prisoners of war when they arrived at the Monfalcone railway station, though Bepi wasn't sure who Arturo was or how Joe would be recognised. The plan seemed to lack a bit of detail but Joe was in no position to complain.

Two nights later Joe said goodbye to Paola and Leo and they sang two verses of 'Twinkle, twinkle little star' in almost word perfect English. Downstairs he hugged Marisa and Nonna, then shook hands with Gigi, who gave him one of his berets.

Next morning, Donatella stayed home from school and

helped Nina to prepare Joe for the trip. The scar was a problem. The women did their best to cover his cheekbone with pancake make-up but with limited success. It was autumnal enough for Joe to be wearing Gigi's beret with Bepi's scarf and coat, which Nina pinned so Joe didn't look quite as lost in it.

Joe remembered one Sunday morning when Agnes was excused the weekly expedition to the basilica because of illness, she and Ida had used Joe as a tailor's dummy for dressing up in Molly's clothes. When she got back and discovered her wardrobe in disarray she'd gone to Malachy, who'd demanded the truth, then berated the two girls for 'perverting the boy'. Joe was given a beating, but it was one of many and the memory of it had faded: what had stayed with him was standing in a trance of pleasure as the two girls fussed over him.

Nina and Donatella told Joe he might pass for an Italian as long as he didn't speak. If he was questioned, Donatella thought it safest if he pretended to have a terrible stammer. That way, people would probably finish his sentences for him and at least he would be understood. She encouraged him to practise his stammer, but when he did, she laughed so hard she had to hold her belly, while Nina tried to hide her smile with a tragic expression, and said, 'Poveretto.'

When it came time, Nina hugged Joe as if she'd never let go, with many poverettos. At the arch by the side of the road, Bepi looked as if his eyes were about to fill as Joe and his daughter set off on foot for the railway station.

* * *

Joe and Donatella had to skirt the lower reaches of the town before joining the street that crossed the valley floor to the station. As they entered the lower alleys of town and crossed the first piazza, Joe recalled Don Claudio's warning that ten divisions of Germans were about to pour down into Italy. The cobbled streets and narrow footpaths were disconcertingly full of men in uniform — German soldiers and officers, Republicans in grey and carabinieri in dark blue.

Joe feared that he stood out like a dog's balls until he realised that the eyes cast his way were focused on Donatella. Clearly accustomed to the attention, she kept her head up and her eyes ahead while she gripped his elbow and directed him through the maze of skinny streets and onto the strada leading down to the railway station, a grand two-storey building with many chimneys above shuttered windows and stuccoed arches. Back in Oamaru the townsfolk were very proud of the wooden station where Joe and the other volunteers had boarded the train for Burnham, but this looked like the house of a prince. There were many vehicles parked outside, military and commercial. Gemona was obviously an important stop on the line down through Austria, and the main platform was full of people, most of whom seemed to be in uniform.

Donatella had told him that they would time their arrival so that they didn't have to wait long for the train to Udine, and indeed there was a train pulling into the main platform as they arrived. To reassure herself, she checked the departure board. Right beside this, visible to almost everyone on the platform, was a glass-fronted notice-board that featured the poster of Joe and Harry.

Joe went weak at the knees and Donatella must have felt his dismay. She turned him away from the poster, took his face in her hands, hiding the scar on his cheek, kissed him on the lips and whispered, 'Coraggio, ragazzo. Ci vediamo.' During the embrace she tugged the beret further down over his temple and pulled Bepi's scarf higher up his cheek. She put his ticket in his hand, closed his palm over it and held his hand for a moment in both of hers. 'Ti voglio bene.' Joe watched her make for the exit, his fear overtaken by the shock that he would never see her again.

He kept his head down as he boarded the carriage and found a seat on the polished wooden slats against the window, opposite an overflowing woman who kept up an incessant monologue to a sullen child sitting beside her. His scar towards the window, he let his fingers brush his lips, which could still feel Donatella's kiss.

Joe knew it had been a gesture born of necessity, but the kisses he'd been given by his sisters who were his aunts had never felt like that. Then there were Donatella's last words, which he knew meant something like 'I think well of you' or 'I wish you well'. But the important thing was not so much what she said as how she had said it: for the very first time, she'd called him *tu*, not *lei*.

The train began moving, and Joe relaxed in the warm balm of his thoughts of Donatella. He looked at the ticket that she'd pressed into his hand. Bepi had told him that Monfalcone was just a stop or two before Trieste. When he looked up he could see a group of German soldiers at the front of the carriage talking loudly among themselves as if they owned the space. They seemed happy enough, maybe because they weren't going to the front, wherever that now was.

Joe hadn't heard any news of the Allied advance since he'd been with the Bonazzons. He hoped that their progress was rapid so that the war would be over before he could be thrown back into it. Maybe he'd be able to come back and thank Bepi and Nina and Donatella. She'd said, 'Ci vediamo', which was their way of saying, 'We'll be seeing you.'

While the mother opposite prattled on to her son, he said nothing and stared at Joe with a spoilt-brat confidence and a child's pure curiosity. Joe feared the boy was on the verge of saying something to him or about him. He could sense that Joe was somehow different.

Joe knew he couldn't survive any serious attention from Italians. Most of the German troops shared the English arrogance and didn't speak Italian so he had a chance with them. His Italian was much better and by necessity he'd learnt a bit of dialect, but it wasn't nearly good enough to pass himself off as Italian to Italians. He didn't want to have to test his stammer.

The train stopped at a couple of small towns. Joe was encouraged by the absence of uniforms on the platforms. He tried not to look at the boy, but every time he did, the unwavering stare met his. Joe managed to present his ticket to the guard without having to say a word. He was an emphysemic old fellow, whose coughing and spluttering made any response from the passengers redundant. Joe tried to ignore the boy and focus on what was happening outside the window.

The train slowed as it entered Udine. This time, as at Gemona, the platform was full of soldiers. To Joe's relief the boy's mother got to her feet, retrieved her bag from the shelf above and pulled the boy towards the exit, past the Wehrmacht soldiers. The child, twisting to look back at Joe, almost swung into a tall priest getting onto the train. 'Scusi, Padre,' said the mother. 'Sia lodato, Gesù Christo.' The priest nodded acknowledgement and stepped aside.

Joe stared resolutely out the window, breathing slightly easier. He could hear several muttered greetings from the passengers as the priest came down the carriage towards him. Then he was aware that someone was sitting right beside him. In his peripheral vision he could see a black cassock falling over bony knees. Then he felt the priest lean towards him, his mouth close to Joe's ear.

'Dog's balls,' he whispered.

Joe didn't trust himself to look at the powder blue eyes or teasing smile.

'Bit of a turn-up for the books,' murmured Harry.

Treviso, 2014

24

Renzo had come to get her from the small polizia locale office near the station. He'd been directed to the woman sitting weeping in the corner by a stout, truncheon-bearing signorina in short sleeves, who was as mystified over what to do with Clare as the older male officer who'd retreated outside for a smoke.

Renzo didn't say much as he walked her back to the hotel and she said nothing. When they arrived at reception to ask for her key, she winced with embarrassment but the sallow young man apologised to her for calling the police. 'I didn't realise it was you,' he said.

Her room was a mess, brogues, boots, ballerina flats and sandals scattered across the bed and the floor. Renzo made a good pretence of finding it unremarkable and suggested she have a shower, then they'd go for a walk. She took a change of clothes into the bathroom and tried to wash away the deranged, red-eyed woman in the mirror. By the time she'd showered and changed and covered as much as she could with mascara and shadow, Renzo had paired all the shoes and placed them in a row on the floor right around the bed, just under the edge, only their heels poking out. The room looked almost normal.

She told him she wasn't sure she wanted to go out.

'Fine,' he said. 'Let's just walk.'

'Walking is out,' she said.

'Not really,' he said. 'I know what you mean.'

She was past debating. They left the hotel, crossed the Ponte Martino past the most discreet McDonald's she'd ever seen, then turned left and right and two hundred metres later she was lost in a maze of old stone and coursing water. Renzo showed her wrought iron statues of horses dancing on the water, walls of roses falling into it, how it flowed under buildings and drove greater and lesser waterwheels, floated dinghies of flowers, made an island of the fish market, provided inspiration for Dante at a little bridge where the Sile and the Cagnan met. He told her the water came from a spring so its flow hardly varied, all the way to the Venetian lagoon. 'In the old days, my grandfather ran a barge and took fresh produce from just downriver to the markets in Venice. These days the only cargo on the river is tourists.'

She looked down from the bridge and the water seemed so clear and unhurried. Renzo leaned over the parapet and wafted air into his face. 'Although it's water,' he said, 'it brings oxygen to the town.'

Near the fish market, he asked her where she thought the centre of town was, the Piazza dei Signori. 'Left?' she guessed.

'Left is right,' he smiled, 'and so is right. And straight head is also right.'

He asked her the same question at Dante's bridge. She had no idea but said right.

'Right is good,' he answered, 'but so is left and straight ahead.'

When she asked him how that could possibly be, he shrugged

and said that Treviso might mean three faces and that might be how it got its name.

Renzo knew a lot of people who had to be hugged and kissed and introduced to 'my friend from New Zealand'. She didn't really want him to do that but was gratified at the way the faces lit up. Quite often there was mention of the All Blacks, which surprised her. Renzo said that Treviso was a rugby town with a team in the Heineken Cup.

At one stage, near the vegetable market, they passed under an arch upon which a pair of discreet modern apartments had been built. 'I live there,' he said, 'the one on the right.' It was quite late and she was tired but he didn't ask her in and they kept walking.

They passed skimpily dressed young girls walking alone in dark alleys with buds in their ears and eyes on their screens, not one sense alert for danger. It was their town and it was populated by their own and they felt safe. It struck Clare then that she had hardly seen a face in Treviso that wasn't white. A group of Africans gathered at a cafe near Ponte Martino morning and evening, but those were the only people she'd seen who didn't look as though they'd lived here for centuries.

He must have realised she was tired and he showed her to a bar beside a waterwheel. Once they were seated, the waiter put a spritz and some antipasti in front of them.

'I thought you should eat something,' he said.

She felt she owed it to him to explain what had happened, how she had ended up in the hands of the local constabulary, but she didn't want to provoke an inquisition.

'I'm in a black hole,' she said. That might be the kind of wisecrack a physicist who'd done his doctorate at MIT would appreciate, but then as she was trying to add, 'I can't get out', her tongue caught on the top of her mouth, her breath became constricted and she gave what sounded almost like a sob. She was trying not to cry but she was having trouble seeing him clearly.

'I too have known sorrow,' he said.

She sniffled but was too surprised to speak. His statement had an archaic formality. The same quality of strangeness as when he'd said in Venice, 'I am entirely sincere.' Maybe he reverted to that when he was on unfamiliar or emotional ground.

'My wife and parents were killed on the autostrada between here and Padova.'

'How awful! When?'

'Five years ago. They were returning from Christmas celebrations with my grandfather in Venice and got hit by a drunken driver. The irony was that Papà had only just stopped drinking himself and that Christmas was the reconciliation between my father and my grandfather after many years of estrangement, many years of trying to get them to come together. Sofia — my wife — would still be alive if I hadn't tried to mend fences.'

She reached across the small table and held both his hands in hers and their tears dripped onto their food.

'We won't need salt,' she said, taking her hands back.

'Enough of that,' he said, blinking back tears but still smiling. 'My grandfather's seen a lot of tragedy, but he is still alive. More than ninety years old. There is hope for us.'

Remembering what he'd told her as he'd driven her and her father back to Venice from San Pietro, and how that had made her feel, she asked him to tell her another story about misbehaving particles.

He looked at her with those careful, considering eyes. Maybe

144

he thought she might be making fun of him. Then he told her that those duplicitous particles that can be in several places at the same time can also be different things, a particle and a wave, and might be about to change everyone's lives.

'You know how computer bits work,' he said. It wasn't a question. She had no idea but nodded. 'A computer bit can be either one or zero at any given time and that ability governs all the complicated software that enables us to do everything, from flying unmanned spacecraft to making reservations on the internet. But what if you could harness electrons and develop a quantum bit that can be either one or zero at the same time?'

'Wouldn't that just be confusing?' she asked, already downcast.

'If these quantum bits could be linked, they could do vast numbers of calculations at an atomic level: they could process information in ways that normal computers cannot comprehend. So that a quantum computer, so small that you cannot see it even with a microscope, might be more powerful than a conventional computer the size of the globe.'

That was *so* disappointing. She'd been looking for another story that made her feel, however insignificant, part of a grand and majestic or even chaotic universe, something to make her concerns resemble a speck in the sky that might eventually be extinguished. She said nothing.

'Let's stay with black holes then,' he said.

Was he piqued? Was he insinuating that she'd rather wallow in sorrow? His tone hadn't changed and he was still talking with that mesmeric timbre. As much as she'd been disappointed with his American accent, she had to admit that it had a seductive cadence.

'For hundreds of years,' he was saying, 'Newtonian physics

has been able to explain the universe around us, then Einstein's theory of relativity. Gravity perfectly described the motions of stars and galaxies. Gravity holds and binds the galaxy and the solar system together. If gravity were to be shut off now, the sun would explode, the earth would fall apart and we'd be flung into outer space at a thousand kilometres per hour.'

'Yes please,' she said.

'Yet the discovery of black holes means we don't fully understand anything.'

She puzzled fruitlessly over possible analogies as he continued.

'We can't see black holes because nothing can escape them, not even light. But we know enough about them to be able to say they are the greatest destructive force known to man. The point of no return for getting sucked into a black hole is called the event horizon. Past it, space is travelling inward faster than the speed of light, which means that even one of our misbehaving particles of light that wants to get out, can't: it'll be sucked into oblivion. So once past that event horizon you're doomed, there's no way you can ever get out again.'

Right, she thought, I've got it. I'm completely stuffed. 'What a good news story!'

'It is!'

She could already see that she'd been wrong. He wasn't telling her this story out of pique, she was sure of that. She wasn't sure what other motive he might have but the light in his eyes was neither anger nor frustration.

'At the centre of the black hole, equations predict something so strange that Einstein's equations spiral wildly out of control. At the centre of a black hole gravity is infinite. Infinity is just a number without limit to a mathematician, but to a physicist

146

infinity is a monstrosity, because that is the point where physics breaks down. If gravity is infinite, it means that time stops, that space makes no sense, it means the collapse of everything we know about the physical universe.'

'Okay,' she said slowly, as if she understood. She might have been somewhere close but even if she hadn't grasped everything, she didn't want his voice to stop. Somehow it was lifting her again, above her own morass and into the heavens.

'If you apply Einstein's theory, at the bottom of the black hole all the mass is contained within an infinitely small point which takes up precisely no space at all. This is described as an impossible object of infinite density and infinite gravity and is called a singularity. Okay?'

'A singularity.'

'Now we get back to our misbehaving particles. There were *two* great encompassing theories that explained our universe. One was Einstein's theory about gravity, which black holes have demonstrated is flawed. The other related to our misbehaving particles: quantum mechanics. Newtonian mechanics and Einstein's theory beautifully described the very large and the very fast and then we had quantum mechanics or quantum field theory, which was supposed to describe the very small. Most of the time, these theories could ignore each other — gravity wasn't a problem in the quantum world because atoms were so light that the effect of gravity was irrelevant. But there is one place which is very small but where gravity is very large . . . I haven't put that very well. But the singularity at the heart of a black hole is both astronomically heavy and infinitesimally small.'

'A perfect place for the meeting of the two minds?' She surprised herself.

'Exactly, particularly given that we now believe that the beginning of the universe, the Big Bang, exploded from a singularity. The singularity, the impossible object found at the heart of every black hole, is the same impossible object found at the very beginning of time that caused the creation and expansion of the universe. If that's true, we all came from a singularity. So if we could solve the problem of the singularity we might also solve the problem of how the universe began and where we came from. Except that when we try to combine the theories, we find a familiar difficulty. When you make the equation, at the end you get an infinite sequence of infinities. In other words they won't talk to each other. *Neither* of them works completely, not gravity or quantum. The equations no longer make any sense and nobody knows exactly what we're supposed to do about that.' He threw his hands wide. 'It may be the collapse of physics as we know it.'

'What does that mean? You're out of a job?'

'No, no. It means we don't know what we don't know. It means nature is smarter than we are — nature has a particular way of operating and we humans don't seem to be able to find that way. But what we do know is that the secret to discovering a unifying theorem to explain the universe and how it operates is at the bottom of the black hole. So, far from being the end of the road, the black hole, that hugely destructive force, is the catalyst for creation and contains the secret for enlightenment.'

'So the moral of the story is that in the midst of misery, there is hope?'

'I'm telling you what saved me.'

She'd broken the spell and didn't know how to restore it. The vaulting mysteries of the heavens. That mesmerising voice. The dark infinity of his eyes. She wanted it back.

'That was stupid,' she said. 'I'm sorry. I disappoint myself.'

'I'm something less than I could have been,' he said. 'But I'm reconciled to what I've become. Is that a bad thing?' There wasn't a trace of self-pity.

'No,' she said, shamed.

'No,' he agreed. 'It's a difficult truth, but I prefer it.'

She was anxious for the conversation not to end on this note. 'Your students are very lucky,' she said, 'and so am I.'

He shrugged. 'None of this is original, I just teach it. And it may already be out of date due to what they're discovering with the Hadron Collider.'

'What does that mean for you?' she asked.

'Happiness,' he said, and his eyes lit up again to prove it. 'It's the greatest time to be a lapsed physicist. Almost everything we thought we knew we now know we don't know. The challenge in front of us is fantastic. Imagine finding that unifying theorem! Where it might lead us!'

'Could that be you?'

'As a theoretical physicist, I can calculate that likelihood as being extremely low. Infinitesimal.'

'That's not a no.' He looked embarrassed. 'You have a theory!'

'No, no,' he said, 'but I do have an idea about an idea. A concept about a concept, you might call it. This is just between us.'

'Believe me, Renzo, there is absolutely no one in the world I can share this with.'

'Okay,' he said, not laughing. 'So, what everyone is looking for is a theory that unifies what we already know, quantum theory and gravity. String theory or Hawking's theory of everything or supersymmetry might all be overarching possibilities for explaining how the universe works, but we already have a name for the resolution of this particular problem: the quantum gravity theory — even though we don't know what quantum gravity is! We found both quantum mechanics and gravity theories through observation, but quantum gravity is so much more difficult because we can't even *see* a black hole. So we're stuck with pencil and paper, with theory, with calculations, equations. But what if the answer lies somewhere beyond both quantum and gravity?'

The waiter arrived with the bill, which Clare went to pick up but was intercepted by Renzo, even though he was in full flow and would not be diverted.

'I may have an advantage in that I come from the particle side of physics, the quantum mechanics side, the sub-atomic world, which is stranger than you can imagine. As you know from the misbehaving photons, in the quantum world the mere act of observing changes what you see. You can't say where something is, only where it's *likely* to be. And anything that is possible, no matter how unlikely, happens all the time. So all our notions about how things behave change. For example, objects have a known location: I'm sitting here, you're sitting there, but in a quantum reality, objects can be in many different places at the same time. Yet strange as quantum mechanics is, physicists believe that the world it describes is the true nature of reality. It's been more successful than any other idea in physics: it's allowed us to make the best predictions we've ever made. So like it or not, quantum mechanics describes our world and just about everything in it: there's no escaping it. Every object is a quantum mechanics object and is subject to the laws of quantum mechanics . . .'

'Except the singularity.'

'Except, of course, the singularity. But here's the thing.

Maybe the clue to the unifying theory *is* in nature, but we can't see it because we are limited by what nature gave *us*. *Nature* gave us imagination but also gave us limits to what we could imagine. The equations all lead to infinity, an infinite sequence of infinities. So infinity is clearly not beyond calculation, but it is beyond our human imagination. Even if infinity was truly *conceptually* possible for a physicist, which I doubt, the practical ramifications are horrendous. How can there be no end to the universe? And if there is no end, there can be no beginning. Chaos. What happens then to the Big Bang? Does everything we know as physicists fly out the window if there is such a thing as infinity in nature? If so, maybe that's the clue: to find a theorem that embraces the concept of infinity. It might not be physics any more, it might be closer to metaphysics, but it might be true.'

'And it might take a lapsed physicist to find it.'

He laughed. 'Or he might be talking through a black hole in his head.'

What could she say? She didn't know enough to impose any sort of critique on what he'd told her: it might be half-baked theory dumbed down for her benefit, but it sounded like the truth, his truth, despite his self-deprecation at the end. She told him she felt privileged. She might not understand half of what she was hearing, she wasn't sure she was intelligent enough to even know how much she wasn't getting, but what she did grasp was giving her that feeling again, lifting her so far above the petty fornications and sick commerce of human beings that, for just a few moments, none of that mattered, and the pain that crippled her loosened its grip.

25

At the entrance to the Continental, he kissed her. Just that courteous European on-both-cheeks thing. She was floating above the sordid little circle of her own concerns, up among the stars, and if he'd just kissed her on the lips . . . He smelled right. She thought they would fit.

There was a different man in reception when she collected her room key, and she felt like a different woman when she let herself into her room. She had that same feeling of elevation and excitement she'd had after Renzo had dropped her off in Venice. She was thinking about the light in his eyes and how people used to say she had that. She didn't used to be bitter and unhappy, but what had her happiness been? Perhaps she was happiest when she felt part of something larger than herself. Family would have given her that but now she had none. In the absence of family, being a tiny part of a majestic and mysterious and potentially chaotic universe seemed to be some sort of spiritual balm. Or was it just that she was attracted to Renzo and any attention from him made her happy?

He was a strange man, used to multiple realities, and a survivor of far worse tragedy than she'd had to cope with. Perhaps it was too soon for him, but if he *was* interested in her, and she thought he was, his chat-up lines must be the weirdest in the history of the world, or the universe, or what we know of it, which apparently isn't nearly as much as we thought we knew. Weird but almost irresistible. She hoped that brain sex wasn't all he wanted.

An unsettling thought came to her. How had he known she

was at the police station? Clearly the hotel rang him, but how did the staff know who to contact? Had Renzo left his number with reception once he knew she was here, telling them if they had any trouble with that crazy woman in Room 302, ring him?

She didn't want to think about that. She didn't look down at the burnt smudge on the concrete of the car park as she pulled the shutters to, but upwards to the stars, peering through a lattice-work of clouds. She slept like a doll, on her back, unmoving, one hand between her breasts, the other on her belly, profoundly unconscious for the first time since she'd found her father crumpled on the floor of his room in Venice two days ago.

It wasn't until she awoke next morning that she realised Renzo must know her secret.

Monfalcone, 1943

26

As the train trundled east, Joe sat tight-lipped beside Harry. A youth had taken the seat opposite so neither of them could speak.

When Bepi had reported the strangulation of Don Claudio, Joe had been shocked but had rationalised it as an act of vengeance that probably fell within the ragged boundaries of war ethics. For some reason it was more disturbing to think that Harry had killed the priest to acquire a disguise, or even that he'd been sufficiently opportunistic to take the dead priest's vestments after killing him in cold blood.

Joe gazed out at the wooded hills rising northwards to a grey sky. The trees were turning and Joe hoped that, wherever they were going, they'd get there before winter came down on them. He wanted to thank Harry for saving him and ask him how he'd escaped the dogs, but decided that, in the end, the details didn't matter, and Harry would probably dismiss it all with a few laconic words. But what were the odds against his path crossing Harry's? When the youth went to the toilet, Harry told him he, too, was heading for Monfalcone after being advised to do so by Carlo and the Udine cell of the CLN.

'Who's Carlo?'

Joe realised someone had stopped at Harry's shoulder, a compact, powerfully built balding Italian in his late twenties, and whispered something. Joe thought he might be asking for a blessing and waited anxiously for Harry's response. Instead, the man walked on to the end of the carriage, and Harry whispered, 'Dunny stop. Follow me.'

He rose and moved towards the end of the carriage. Joe had no idea what was going on but after a decent interval stood up too and made his way past the German soldiers and through the doors. Harry was standing as if waiting to use the toilet, which was *occupato*. Presently, the toilet door opened to reveal the Italian who had approached Harry.

'Joe Lamont, Charlie Farinelli from Chicago,' said Harry.

'Hi Joe,' said Charlie.

'Don't shake hands,' said Harry, as Joe held his hand out. 'What's the story, Carlo?'

'There's a couple of Republicans coming up through the carriages asking for papers.'

'How far away?'

'They'll be in my carriage now, one back from yours.'

Harry said nothing. Joe knew that disguises and speech impediments would count for nothing if they were asked for identification. 'Let's buy some time,' said Harry. 'Work our way forward, keep a bit of separation.'

Without another word Charlie took off into the next carriage. Harry pulled out some Italian cigarettes and lit up as if he had all the time in the world. He took a deep drag, then gave Joe the nod.

Joe worked his way through the next carriage, trying to move slowly, not daring to look right or left. He couldn't see Charlie until he entered the second carriage and found him happily chatting to some Italian women in uniform. Joe kept moving, straight past him, but heard enough to know that Charlie was as fluent as a native. When he reached the end of the third carriage he realised there were no more. The steel join plates outside led to the steam and the fury of the engine. Joe waited until Charlie joined him. 'The end of the line,' said Joe.

They waited a couple of minutes that seemed a lot longer, until Harry appeared.

'Sia lodato, Don Enrico,' said Charlie.

'Don't push it, Carlo,' said Harry.

'I'm saying we're gonna need divine inspiration.'

They were trapped. To break the silence, Joe asked Harry how he'd decided on his new name. Harry told him Charlie had christened him.

'Harry is Henry,' said Charlie. 'Henry is Enrico.'

They rocked forward as the train slowed for another small village, then stopped.

'Looks like you've delivered, Father,' said Charlie.

Don Enrico opened the door and peered out at a narrow platform thronged with people, civilians. 'Andiamo via.' Through copious blessings, he walked across the platform towards the exit, followed at a distance by Charlie and Joe. Then he stood and looked back at the stationary train. 'Where are they?' he whispered to Charlie.

Charlie walked back towards the train through the confusion of embarking and disembarking passengers and began working his way down the windows, looking inside as if searching for a relative. He didn't have to go far. One carriage down from where they'd disembarked, he turned back to catch Don Enrico's eye and nodded. The Republican soldiers had been right behind them when the train pulled into the station.

Harry was already onto their next move. 'Follow me but keep your distance,' he said and headed down the platform towards the other end of the train. Charlie was ahead of him, looking into the carriages. The second to last carriage seemed to pass muster and Charlie climbed the steps and disappeared inside, followed shortly afterwards by Don Enrico, then by Joe. They found wooden slatted seats facing each other and spread themselves across both sides.

'That's them,' said Charlie, pointing to three Republican soldiers who'd now left the train up by the engine and were trading cigarettes as they waited for the next train to take them back the way they'd come.

'We should be killing the bastards,' said Don Enrico, 'not dodging them.'

'Sia lodato,' said Charlie.

27

The Monfalcone railway station wasn't as imposing as Gemona's but still a beautiful double-storey square-fronted building at the north-eastern edge of the town.

Their Italian contact and guide, Arturo, turned out to be Arch Scott, looking singularly Italian among a group of eight other prisoners whom he'd collected from around the Livenza and Piave. Joe recognised some of them from PG 107/7 and there were hushed greetings, as if keeping their voices down would save them from standing out like the proverbial. Joe couldn't put his finger on exactly why they seemed foreign, even though, like him, they'd been dressed by their Italian families. Maybe it was just a different way of walking, or even of standing or holding themselves, that gave them away as aliens who were accustomed to keeping their balance on the other side of the globe.

Arch gave Joe a friendly nod, then caught sight of Don Enrico. 'Well, bugger me,' said Arch, shaking his head.

'The Lord moves in mysterious ways,' acknowledged Harry.

The only uniform in sight belonged to the stationmaster, who was regarding them with interest. Arch looked across the tracks to where the gravel gave way to a scrub-covered hill. 'The only way is up,' he said. As the bedraggled group followed Arch across the tracks and into the scrub, Joe turned to see the stationmaster making a beeline for his office.

Arch led them straight up the slope through light scrub until they reached a ridge running parallel to the tracks below them. Arch turned left, to the west, and they made their way along the ridge back the way they'd come. The going wasn't too difficult. There were long expanses of smooth, bare rock poking like bald patches through the shoulder-high scrub.

Harry and Charlie quizzed Arch about the arrangements, but he didn't know much more than they'd already been told. The San Donà di Piave cell of the CLN had told him that the Slovenians had shepherded eight Kiwi prisoners across the mountains to safety about six weeks before, and Arch hoped to establish a regular link with the partigiani to gradually repatriate the hundreds of Allied prisoners who'd escaped into the Veneto but were now trapped in their freedom and being hunted like hares. 'That's what the locals call us,' said Arch, 'Il Battaglione Lepre, the Hare Battalion.'

'Who're these Slovenians?' asked Charlie. 'Where do they come from?'

Arch explained that Slovenia was the nearest Yugoslavian province to Italy, and under Marshal Tito, Yugoslavia was claiming this area of Italy, as far west as the Isonzo River, back towards Udine. 'So once they finish fighting the Germans,' he said, 'they're likely to start on the Italians.'

'Great,' said Charlie, already spooked. 'Where are we supposed to be hooking up with them?'

'The CLN told me the Slovenians wouldn't give exact rendezvous co-ordinates,' said Arch, 'but if we walked west-north-west along the ridge behind the town, they would make contact.'

'Shouldn't be long,' said Harry, 'we're being watched now. Hope they're the right buggers doing the watching.'

Harry was looking out towards some craggy higher ground to their right. Joe looked too, but could see no sign of anyone among the rocks. Perhaps it was just something that Harry sensed. But he was right. A single shot cracked the silence.

Joe, like most of the men, dived for the ground. When he looked up, there was someone standing about ten yards in front of Arch and Harry, neither of whom had reacted to the shot. The man didn't introduce himself, and was looking at them with one eye along the barrel of his rifle. He was wearing a military cap with a five-pointed red star, and a battle tunic with the collar obscured by a checked red and white scarf that might have started life as a tablecloth.

'Buon giorno,' said Arch, then in English, so there could be no mistake as to their identity, 'Nice day for it.'

When the man lowered the rifle, Joe could see an empty socket of puckered skin where the other eye would have been. The man spoke fluent Italian, but had barely identified himself as the leader of the Slovenian partisans when more shots rang out and he ran back into the scrub.

'Wonder what happened to that eye,' said Harry.

'Jack the One-Eyed Terror,' said Arch. 'Do you remember that one? "Are you really called The Terror? asked the leader of our Push. You make no fuckin' error, said the Bastard from the bush."'

'Do you reckon he'll come back?' asked one of the men.

'Should we stick around to find out?' asked Charlie. 'This is shoot-first-ask-questions-after country, and we've got our balls hanging out in the wind here.'

Joe felt the panic rising. They were totally exposed on a ridge in the middle of nowhere with not a pocket-knife between them. In the silence, Joe saw Arch looking anxiously at Harry, who pulled a cigarette out of his cassock and lit it.

Arch, taking his cue, told them a story about another tough bastard called Jack who had only one ear and lived in an isolated block of bush. 'They reckon his ear was chewed off by pigs. My mates stayed with him in his shack one night and wondered where he'd got the milk for their tea. The milk was sort of bluish, they reckoned. There was no sign of any cow or goat out there but there was an old bitch with pups on a sack that did for a mat outside the back door. Next morning old Jack put the brew on, then disappeared out the back door with a mug. They heard the squeals as he shoved the pups aside.'

Some of the men laughed. Charlie stared at them uncomprehendingly. Before he could say anything, One-Eyed Jack was back, short of breath but now showing what was left of his yellowing teeth in a menacing grin. He told Arch someone had not followed orders, but it had been fixed. Then he asked them if they were ready to fight the Germans.

'We've been fighting the Germans,' said Arch. 'In Greece, in Crete, in North Africa and now in Sicily.'

'Those places are far away,' said the man. 'Non sono qua.' *They're not here.*

The conversation continued. Joe's understanding of Italian wasn't as good as Arch's or Charlie's, but what One-Eyed Jack wanted was fairly clear: he was looking for well-trained recruits. He didn't seem interested in establishing an escape route for Allied prisoners of war.

Arch kept trying. 'We're not here to fight as partisans,' he said. 'We want to be taken to the English command so that we can rejoin the New Zealand army and fight with our comrades.'

'No,' said One-Eyed Jack. 'Qua, la guerra.' *Here, the war.* He threw his arm wide to encompass the surrounding terrain of Italy to the west of where they were standing. 'Yugoslavia.'

'Oh fuck,' said Arch. 'This war won't be won by you or me,' he said, reverting to Italian, 'but by the Allies when they reach

161

Trieste.'

'That will be a different war.'

'Senta,' said Arch wearily. 'We only want the same as the last group of New Zealand soldiers. The eight prisoners of war you delivered to the English command six weeks ago.'

The Slovenian's response was a wider grin, then a high-pitched whistle. More heavily armed soldiers with the red star on their caps appeared from the scrub around them. Then five men, dirty, lousy, living skeletons, filed into sight under guard. Their faces were blank and hopeless, until one of them recognised Arch and burst into tears. 'Please get us out of here!'

A shocked Arch asked the questions that proved their identity. 'Where are the other three?'

'These bastards shot them where they stood when we said we wouldn't fight.'

'There's been a misunderstanding,' said Arch, trying to contain his anger and fear as One-Eyed Jack enjoyed the spectacle. 'These men are no use to you. We'll take them with us and go now.'

'Sei sicuro?' *Are you sure?*

It sounded like a threat to Joe. Arch seemed unsure how to respond. It was a stand-off, except that they were surrounded and had no weapons.

There was a long moment of uncertainty before Harry broke the impasse. 'Ce l'hai armi?' he asked One-Eyed Jack. *Have you got weapons?* 'Munizioni?' *Ammunition?*

'Who is this priest?' the Slovenian asked Arch.

'Captain Spence, 22nd Battalion,' said Harry.

'Congratulations on your commission,' said Arch, without looking at Harry. 'That happen before or after you took the vows?'

'You stay and fight?' asked One-Eyed Jack, somewhat taken aback.

'Jesus, Harry.' Arch appealed to him directly. 'It's not our fight.'

'A fight's a fight,' said Harry.

Then he nodded to One-Eyed Jack. 'Voglio stare qua,' he told him. *I want to stay here.* 'Voglio uccidere tedeschi.' *I want to kill Germans.*

28

After trying to dissuade Harry, they left him up there with the Slovenians and made their way down towards the lights of civilisation before darkness made it impossible to see their way. They were some miles west of where they'd started, which seemed to suit Arch. He agreed with Joe about the suspicious stationmaster at Monfalcone and thought there might be a reception committee waiting for them if they went back there.

Joe felt sorry for Arch. His dreams of setting up an escape route for prisoners was shattered. Not only would he have to find a way of getting the eight he'd brought from the Piave back whence they came — he was the only one with a return ticket — and rehoused there, but also find transport and refuge for the men they'd picked up. Then there were Charlie and Joe.

The five survivors were in such bad shape a couple of them had to be piggy-backed down the last slope and through the streets of a small town to the railway tracks. They drank from every tap and fountain they passed, but were tired and hungry by the time they crossed the tracks and saw a station, with a sign, Ronchi dei Legionari.

A light was still on in the stationmaster's house, a square two-storey place about fifty yards down the track. Arch asked Joe to come with him and look as tough as possible. 'Keep your forearm in your jacket, as if you might be carrying a pistol.' They left the others in the darkness and crossed to the stationmaster's home.

A sleepy moustachioed man in braces opened the door. When he saw Arch standing there before him any drowsiness instantly disappeared. Joe made sure his scar caught the light, as Arch told the stationmaster he was English, and his comrades knew where he was. 'If anything happens to me—'

Arch didn't need to finish the threat. 'I am only too pleased to help,' said the stationmaster, 'and that goes for anyone who works on the railways. Tell me what we can do.'

The last train for the night was long gone. The waiting room at the station was quickly transformed into temporary barracks as the stationmaster and his equally portly wife brought pillows and blankets so that the men could sleep on the benches and chairs. When they went to lie down the wife said, 'Aspetta, aspetta.' *Wait*. Soon, half a dozen men and women arrived with food — cold chicken, bread and cheese.

'These are townsfolk, not farmers,' Arch told the men. 'They're giving you their last reserves of food.' He made an emotional thank-you speech, as the railway workers and their wives regarded the men with shy curiosity, then left.

During the night, the survivor sleeping closest to Joe had some sort of fever and his groans and clattering false teeth kept him awake. Joe was reminded of when he'd first seen Harry at the hospital in Bari, and he lay there wondering what had possessed Harry to go with the Slovenians. And he thought about what he should do come morning. He would have liked to go back to Bepi and Nina and Donatella but nothing had changed. He would have to go with Arch and the others and try not to be a burden.

* * *

Arch roused the men before dawn and organised the clean-up so the waiting room was pristine for the arrival of the first train.

Then Arch asked Joe and Charlie how they were placed.

'I'll head back to Reant,' said Charlie. 'Harry and I were well set up there.'

When Joe said that he couldn't go back to Gemona, Arch shrugged and was about to get him a ticket with the rest of them back to the Piave when Charlie said, 'Come with me, why don't you? Take Harry's place.'

This took Joe by surprise. He asked Charlie if he was sure, hoping that he'd retract. Joe wanted to go south with Arch back to San Pietro, but if Charlie's offer was genuine he'd have to accept it. One man less for Arch to house in the Piave.

'Hell yes,' said Charlie. 'There's room at the Ritz.'

* * *

Joe and Charlie changed trains at Udine without incident and got off at Cividale, the end of the line. Joe remembered the station there, the pale yellow stucco with its verandah running along the streetfront, so pretty it could have been a mansion on some southern plantation in *Gone with the Wind*, the fat book that had kept him engrossed for six weeks from embarkation at Wellington until landing at Port Said. What a singular pleasure it had been, reading as much as he wanted whenever he wanted, without wincing in anticipation of a clout.

They'd seen plenty of Wehrmacht grey on the train but hadn't attracted any attention despite being pretty dirty and tattered. Charlie's fluent patter to any Italians had undoubtedly helped.

When they began walking west Joe kept his mouth shut and let Charlie talk to anyone they met. About a mile down the tarmac road, Charlie waited until it was clear then led Joe to an unruly hedgerow dividing fields of maize stumps, where they retrieved the bicycles Charlie and Harry had hidden the day before. Now that they weren't on foot, people were less likely to speak to them and they made good progress to a town called Togliano before turning north towards forbidding wooded hills.

Outside the Cividale station Joe had looked back towards PG 57 at Grupignano and marvelled that more than a year had passed since they'd been delivered there from Bari and had endured that awful winter. In the camp they'd at least had shelter, some heat and food. Charlie kept talking about the Ritz. It seemed like American code or shorthand for something, but Joe wasn't sure what.

The road became narrower and steeper. Occasional banks of houses that from a distance looked like dams opened up as the road carved through the middle of them. There was no one to be seen, near the houses or in the fields, but it was early afternoon so that wasn't surprising. The road became a pitted, rutted forestry track, so steep that they had to get off the bikes and walk. They reached a fork in the track and stowed the bikes in the bush. Charlie led them up the left fork. He was as short as Joe but muscly, and he walked on the balls of his feet, a bouncy confident stride. Always climbing, the track wound across the face of a steep drop until they came to a clearing with six or seven houses behind a sign saying *Reant*.

'Nearly home,' said Charlie, as he left the main track and led Joe onto a barely defined trail that crossed a heavily wooded drop to the plains of Lombardy, visible below them in the blue distance.

Charlie admitted that the Ritz was a cave the locals had told him about. 'They said this buca has been a sanctuary for hundreds of years for people on the run, folk heroes some of 'em, and not a one of 'em ever got caught.'

After slipping and sliding down and around a face of scree above a cliff, Joe could understand why. There were straggly trees that could support a careful hand but would have slipped a rope. When they finally made it to an opening that was all but invisible from any direction, Joe was initially disappointed. The cave mouth was low: wide lips with a tongue of scree that had to be crawled over. But then the tongue opened into a capacious throat that gave about ten yards of scuttling room before tapering away to nothing.

Charlie and Harry had collected hay and blankets and old coats and had made two beds on the dry rock floor. There was a tin of water, no food. They were hungry, but too exhausted to consider doing anything about it. Joe lay down on Harry's bed, used Bepi's coat as a blanket, and was asleep in moments as he felt the solid earth fold over him.

29

The surrounding country was a tangle of rocks and trees, sharp hills, deep gullies and rushing water, torrenti, but supported three tiny villages: Reant, Valle, another mile and a half down the same road, and Masarolis, a mile or two back up into the mountains from the fork. Charlie told Joe that he and Don Enrico were well known in all three, and proved it by introducing him to the villagers at Reant, right above them, next morning.

They were squat, strong-legged, tough-looking men and women who didn't say a lot but who seemed friendly enough and accepted Joe after he told them he was from the same country as Don Enrico. The dozen children of various ages adored Charlie, who did tricks with cards for them and made handkerchiefs and scarves disappear. The villagers had hardly any food but gave them dried meat and greens that looked to Joe like weeds.

Every house had firewood stacked high and smoke coming from the chimneys already, as winter closed in. Before they went back down to the cave with their food, Joe made sure Charlie had matches, then spent the rest of the day building a fireplace far enough inside the entrance to give some warmth. Charlie was worried about the smoke but Joe excavated a thin shallow ditch back up the cave to the entrance, then covered it with sticks and fern and tamped it all with earth to seal it. When they lit the fire, this chimney conveyed the smoke to the mouth of the cave. As they watched from outside that first time, the woodsmoke merged with the grey rock of the cliff-face and more or less disappeared by the time it reached the top.

'Attaboy!' said Charlie, slapping Joe on the back.

After all day in the cave, Joe was sure he could survive the cold, but not at all sure he could survive a whole winter of long hours with just Charlie for company. Charlie stopped talking only long enough to ask Joe, 'Right? Am I right?' He had opinions about everything and told long stories to justify whatever opinion he'd advanced, which always seemed to go back to some episode or other from the south side of Chicago, where he'd grown up. His stories often involved friends with funny names, like Four-Hands Hanrahan or Lefty Stinato or Big Belly Livassa. It seemed an exotic and incomprehensible world, where someone was 'on the make' or 'one down in the last'. And if he wasn't asking Joe 'Right? Am I right?' he was asking, 'You know?' Joe found it exhausting: he was used to men who spoke little and, for the most part, made silence companionable. When he realised that Charlie wasn't really looking for any reply, the pressure came off. How had Harry, who said bugger all, put up with the American? On the third day, when Charlie drew breath, Joe asked him how he'd met Harry.

Charlie said he'd been on his bicycle on the outskirts of Udine, trying to go south towards Allied lines, 'wherever the hell they were', when he'd been overtaken by this priest, pedalling hard, cassock billowing. When he'd called out, automatically, 'Sia lodato,' he was sure he'd heard the priest say, 'And up yours too.' He'd managed to catch the priest and ask him, 'What the fuck?', and the relationship was born.

'How'd you end up here?' asked Joe.

When they'd got to Udine it was as full of Nazis as Gemona, so Harry had looked around and said, 'Let's head for the hills.'

'And that was it,' said Charlie. 'We got up here, found Reant. The folks up here say they've always been their own men. They laughed fit to die when they found that the only Italian this priest knew seemed to be blasphemous curses.'

* * *

Mid to late afternoon, they would climb up to the road and head to one or other of the small villages 'to score some chow', as Charlie put it. He insisted that they follow the procedure set down by Harry: that Charlie walk about a hundred yards ahead of Joe and give a signal if he saw or heard someone ahead. Then Joe would immediately leave the track and hide. If it was an Italian civilian Charlie would have a conversation. If it was soldiers, Republican or German, Charlie would dive for cover too or try to brazen it out.

Simple but effective. Once, on the fork below Masarolis, Charlie signalled, then dived off the track himself. He'd heard an engine in low gear labouring down the hill, and the two of them watched from the bush as a Republican troop carrier eased past. The villagers at Masarolis confirmed that the Republicans had been combing the forestry tracks for partisans, Italian and Slovenian, but didn't seem to suspect the villagers themselves of harbouring or supporting, which was good news.

To lessen the burden on any one village Charlie and Harry had rotated themselves through Reant, Valle and Masarolis, so they would be reasonably welcome when they turned up at dinner time. Charlie sang well for his supper, doing magic for the children and telling stories to the adults round the fire, of a world of tall skyscrapers where everyone had a car and an education and plenty to eat. Joe listened too, trying to understand as much as he could, and said little.

On one occasion when Charlie was entertaining the children

down at Valle, Joe heard an old woman mutter something in the local dialect that sounded like a curse: 'Terrone.' She was clearly using it to describe Charlie.

Charlie was oblivious to any reservations the villagers had about him. He was also a very recent prisoner and perhaps hadn't had time to develop the doubts and defences that had been necessary for survival in the camps. He'd been a tanker in the US 5th, driving a Sherman that had thrown a track soon after landing in Salerno. 'A real bitch', according to Charlie, because he and his crew had been picked up by a truckload of German infantry without firing a shot in anger. His main disappointment seemed to be that he hadn't been part of the invasion of Sicily. His parents had emigrated from Palermo and he'd wanted to be able to tell them he'd been 'home'.

He'd been immediately sent to Germany by train. He'd attacked an air vent in the roof of the cattle truck with a pocket-knife, and he and some others had jumped into the darkness when the train slowed in the mountains above Gemona. He didn't know whether the others had survived the fall.

Joe told him about Dan, and Charlie said he'd be fine as long as he didn't run into any Tigers. That was the first time Joe had heard Charlie express any doubt about the US of A's capacity. For him, American technology, know-how and can-do was unbeatable. He hadn't seen one, but he'd been told a Tiger could easily destroy a Sherman, that it would take four or five Shermans to have a chance of taking out one Tiger. They'd been warned that they'd have to go in with up-gunned M10s to have a show, if the rumours were true. Joe recalled the steel monsters he'd seen on the back of the trucks rushing south when he and Harry had taken off from San Pietro. They must have been Tigers, and the fear in Charlie's voice was unsettling.

According to Charlie, the Allies would be close to Rome already and would be here before the end of the winter. Joe knew that Dan would be in the vanguard of the Div and if North Africa was any indication the Kiwis would be among the first into Trieste. He allowed himself to think about seeing Dan again, and about the life they might have when they got home. There'd just be Dan and Sandy and him, the nucleus of what used to be a huge family. Old Mal would never relent, and Dan would never forgive him. The farewell party at the Ardgowan Hall for the local boys who went away was an embarrassment when not one of the Lamont clan turned up to see their eldest son off. Mal told anyone who'd listen that he didn't want any son of his fighting for the English, but none of the clan had come to Dan's wedding either.

Dan and Sandy's courtship and marriage had been really quick. Sandra Goode worked for McKenzie's department store in Oamaru. Dan had first seen her on a Friday, late shopping night, when those who had cars would park in the trees in the middle of Thames Street and join the rest of the townsfolk walking up and down in front of the brightly lit shops pretending to be interested but really looking at each other, stopping for a catch-up with those they knew. One of the female mannequins in McKenzie's had fallen over and Sandy had to go into the window to restore it.

Dan was quiet like Joe, but much more likely to speak up if he had to. He waited until Sandy had gone back to her counter, then went straight in and told her he really liked the woman in the window. When she asked him which one, he smiled at her and said, 'This one.'

That's what Dan reckoned happened anyway and Sandy never gainsaid him. They became engaged within six weeks.

Sandy wasn't worried that Dan was from the Devil's Bridge Lamont clan or that he worked in the flour mill at Ngapara. Joe knew her father Fred. He was a coal merchant and ran his old Bedford out to Ngapara to fill the tray with big sacks direct from the mine, and sell them off the back of the truck around the streets of Oamaru.

Sandy said she wasn't 'religious' but had been brought up Church of England. To begin with she said she'd become a Catholic and was welcomed into the bosom of the Lamont family. But something changed in her, though she never said what prompted it. Maybe it was seeing the way Mal treated his daughters, maybe it was as simple as that. Or maybe the way he treated Dan. Whatever it was, Sandy decided she wouldn't convert. When he heard, Mal called her and Dan out to Devil's Bridge and read them the riot act. Sandy would never talk about what Mal said to her or what she said to him, but Dan told Joe that Sandy, blonde and small and pale, stood up to the old man and gave as good as she got.

Dan said that after that he loved her more, if anything. He showed it by becoming Anglican for her, and they were married in a small service at St Luke's at the bottom of the South Hill at the end of town. None of the Lamonts came, just Fred and Iris and quite a few Goode cousins, because Sandy was an only child.

Ida had tearfully entreated Joe not to attend Dan's wedding, because if he did Mal would cut him out of the family too. She was distraught, knowing she was about to lose her two brothers. Joe cried too, but there was no question that he would stand with Dan. That was the last he'd seen of Ida or any of his 'sisters'.

The wedding had been brought forward because New Zealand had declared war on Germany, the second country to do so after Britain, according to the newspapers. Dan used to laugh that Hitler must have been shitting himself. Dan was twenty-one and there was no question he would enlist, call-up or no. Sandy never once tried to stop him and in the two years between Dan's going and Joe following him, Joe had got to know her. She was very direct and matter-of-fact and Joe had never seen her feeling sorry for herself that her husband of a few weeks had been called away to war. She lived modestly, carried on at McKenzie's and saved Dan's army pay for the deposit on a house when he got back.

When Joe enlisted and was asked about next of kin and who he would entrust to oversee the bank account his army pay would go into, there was never any question. And now Sandy, according to Dan's last letter, had joined the war effort. Joe would have expected nothing less of her.

By the time he joined up there was some sort of provision for brothers to get younger brothers into the same units, and Dan said he tried to get Joe into tank or anti-tank, keep him away from the infantry. But whatever Dan had done hadn't worked, and Joe found himself among the infantry grunts at Burnham.

There were no more farewell parties this time. Only Sandy had turned up at the Oamaru railway station to say goodbye.

* * *

Thoughts of Fred Goode covered in coal dust as he manoeuvred those sacks off the tray of his truck and onto his back, the white worry lines in his black face, came to Joe when he woke next morning and looked at Charlie. Although the smoke from their fire was largely taken away by the chimney, some leaked out and curled round the cave to join the grit and dust that adhered to their sweat.

There was a big stone trough with sloping sides up at the village. When he saw the late autumn sun hit the far side of the valley, Joe took off his underwear and trousers, wrapped himself in Bepi's coat and carried his dirty clothes up to the trough. He started washing them, then wringing them out. A woman came down from one of the houses and gave him a bar of carbolic soap and showed him how to do it properly, beating the wet clothes on the splayed side of the trough. Others came down with their own washing and laughed at Joe's attempts. At least he thought that's what they were laughing at until the kids started lifting up the back of Bepi's coat. His bare legs had given away his nakedness underneath.

Joe managed to get his clean clothes and nakedness safely back to the cave, hung the wet clothes on some of the ropy saplings nearby, then crossed to a stream about a hundred yards away to wash himself. That all took some time and gave him respite from Charlie, who was inside the cave.

Early afternoon Joe was out to one side of the scree in front of the cave pulling his clothes from the saplings. They weren't quite dry but the winter sun was going behind the hill soon and Joe reckoned his body temperature would take the rest of the moisture out. It was the turn of Masarolis to host them — a stiff uphill walk and then, with a bit of luck, they'd be sitting in front of someone's fire for the evening.

Joe had dropped the coat and was struggling into his underwear when he heard a footfall on the far side of the scree. It was just an instant, but unmistakable. Joe froze and listened. One of the great virtues of the cave was that it was impossible to sneak up on. You couldn't get across the scree without sliding and making a noise. Joe heard the sound again, of someone trying to move very carefully across the slope.

The saplings still had most of their leaves and Joe was struggling to get a clear view of the cave entrance. As he shifted carefully he heard another footfall. His heart almost stopped when he saw the figure who was trying to ease himself around towards the cave. He had his back to Joe, but the checked scarf and the cap with the red star were unmistakable. It had to be One-Eyed Jack. The Slovenians must have tortured Harry for information; they would be all around them.

The intruder looked like a one-man munitions depot. He had belts of ammunition criss-crossing his back from shoulder to waist, German stick grenades hanging off his belt, and Joe counted four weapons, two rifles, a semi-automatic and a pistol. It was a wonder the bastard was able to stand upright under that load, let alone get across the scree. As Joe was wondering how or when he should warn Charlie, he caught sight of the man's bare calves below rough serge breeches cut off at the knee. They were long and white and he'd seen them before. And he was wearing black patent leather shoes that were almost cut to shreds, but which Joe had also seen before, first on Don Claudio, then on Don Enrico.

'Harry!'

'Don't just stand there,' Harry called, unable to turn from the cliff. 'Give us a hand, for Christ's sake!'

Treviso, 2014

30

Her father's instructions were very clear. They were on the page lying face up on the little writing table:

My old mate Geoff has done his absolute best for me but warned me at the beginning that the cure might almost be worse than the disease, 'except that you get to live'. Which, if you're reading this, won't happen.

Best laid plans and all that. I'm not complaining, but what I've endured since this bloody menace was diagnosed has been brutal beyond anything I could have imagined or that Geoff could have described, and is now beyond endurance. I mean that. The pros and cons may once have made sense but they don't any more. The only power I've got left is to say 'Enough'. I've discussed this fully with Geoff and he agrees. If I relapse, it might be sudden if it's my heart and all over quickly, and there'll be no decision to make. But if it's renal failure or something of that ilk — God knows, the possibilities seem endless — I might end up in a coma. Refer the local specialists to Geoff — his number is below. His advice was to make my position absolutely clear by way of declaration, which you'll find attached. If I survive the initial relapse and am incapable of speaking for myself, please show the declaration to whoever is treating me.

Renzo had to have read that when he was tidying her shoes away. How could he not? The declaration was attached by paper clip and it would have been easy enough for him to read that too, particularly when she recalled a conversation they'd had walking back from the bar. She'd told him that she had a meeting with the specialist tomorrow 'to discuss procedures and outcomes' for her father and that she was dreading it. He'd offered to come with her, if only to make sure that there were no 'linguistic misunderstandings'. She told him that was very kind of him, which probably meant that he'd turn up.

So far she'd ignored her father's instructions. Worse than that, she'd told the hospital they must do whatever they could to keep him alive. The only phone call she'd made had been to the insurance company. But if Renzo came to the meeting with the specialist there would be someone in the room who'd know she was going against her father's express wishes.

Should she ring Renzo and tell him not to come? Would that be worse? It might be better to tell him *why* her father couldn't die. Not here, not now. Not after she'd turned away from him in his moment of need in Venice. He'd already been lost in misery after whatever rejection he'd suffered at that little red door.

If she told Renzo why she was lying to the specialist, would he understand? She couldn't live the rest of her life knowing that was her last response to her father. They had to make him well enough to hear her say she was sorry, tell him how much she loved him, how much he had given her, how central he was to everything in her life, and how much she would miss him when he was gone. Surely then she'd be more able to let him go.

Last night's euphoria had been replaced by a nexus of anxiety in her diaphragm. She was fearful of the effect of all this stress on the baby, and that didn't help either. There were life and death decisions to make yet she didn't feel up to choosing whether to have a cup of tea or coffee.

She dressed as if she'd be giving evidence in court and needed help in appearing credible — that pin-striped suit and the black brogues. She'd been brought up to tell the truth and wasn't looking forward to being cross-examined on her lies.

* * *

In the event, she hardly got to say a word. The specialist, Signor Abruzzi, looked like a mad physicist, bald on top with a fringe of wild straggly hair and a goatee, while the mad physicist turned up in a stylish jacket, looking like Harley Street on holiday. Renzo didn't get to say much either, as Signor Abruzzi ran through the history of her father's 'bloody menace', acute lymphoblastic leukaemia, and its treatment.

The insurer had put him in touch with Mr Paterson in Auckland, who had confirmed her father's medical treatment. Signor Abruzzi consulted his clipboard as he read, and it sounded like a list of heinous tortures: the monthly lumbar punctures, induction chemotherapy, a battery of drugs, followed by radiation of the head and injections into the spine, then the bone-marrow transplant after his first relapse. Clare had fragmented memories of her father during some of those procedures, a bald skeleton struggling to draw breath.

Reciting the list served its purpose. The attempts to beat this thing were exhausted, as was her father. Signor Abruzzi hardly needed to offer a prognosis, but he did, saying, 'I'm sorry, Mrs Kostidis, but given his medical history and age, there are no more treatment options available to us.'

She said nothing, and Signor Abruzzi then told her that Mr Paterson was of the opinion that her father 'in any case did not want further attempts to prolong his life. Is that your understanding?'

There was no oxygen left for lying. 'What will happen to him?'

'The most likely outcome is gradual systemic failure. But it might be the heart first and quite sudden. In the meantime, we can make sure he feels no pain, that he is as comfortable as possible.'

'How long?'

'Almost certainly within twenty-four hours, perhaps a lot sooner.'

'Will he wake up before he dies?'

'We don't know. Probably not. Pain and discomfort would come with consciousness.'

She'd come dressed for a trial but it had turned out to be a funeral. She tried not to cry. 'I need to speak to him. Can he hear me?'

'There is plenty of evidence to suggest that patients in his situation can hear what others are saying.' Signor Abruzzi may have been trying to be kind, but it was enough.

* * *

Renzo drove her back to the hotel. He was sympathetic to her silence, didn't offer any platitudes, for which she was grateful. They were driving along a street which ran parallel to the old city wall, still with its moat, presumably the same water that threaded through the heart of the old town and gave it air.

'Your husband was Greek?'

'Australian.' She thought about saying more but couldn't. It'd been quite a jolt when Signor Abruzzi called her Mrs Kostidis.

She'd taken Nicholas's name without a second thought. She'd been looking forward to being adopted into some Australasian version of *My Big Fat Greek Wedding*. But Nicholas always had an excuse for not taking her back to Melbourne and she didn't get to meet his family until after the wedding in Auckland, to which only his brother Tony came. When they did finally get to Melbourne for a post-wedding party put on by Tony, it turned out to be a backyard barbecue in a scruffy suburban brick and tile that trapped the heat like an oven. They sat round on plastic chairs with cans of beer and Clare could feel the resentment in the oppressive air as Nicholas's mother said nothing to her while his father tried to hide behind shitty bonhomie. Maybe they thought she had lured their son away from Melbourne and had deprived them of a wedding.

After quite a few cans of beer Tony's wife Jaclyn — call me Jackie — blonde, with a low-cut dress that revealed a sun-damaged sternum, told her between burps and in 'total confidence' that it didn't matter how long the marriage lasted, and 'knowing what Nick got up to before he left town' she 'wouldn't put the house on it lasting', Clare would never be accepted into the family. She'd always be 'a skip'.

'Skip?'

'Skippy the Bush Kangaroo?'

Clare was none the wiser.

'White trash, that's what they think,' Jackie said.

Renzo offered to wait at the Continental while she got her things together. In her room, she took off the silly authoritarian suit and brogues, which she knew she'd never wear again, changed into jeans and a loose top that she'd brought from home, and a warm cardigan.

There was another instruction she'd ignored.

> *You should read it. There's no excuse for what happened, but there is an explanation, though lawyers always say that. And after so much time and so much pain, maybe something good can come out of you knowing what happened back then.*

He was referring to a third manila file in his old briefcase, the one she'd seen him reading when they were having their coffee that first morning in Campo Santo Stefano. It was much older than her matrimonial property file, and her father had written 1976 in crude black marker pen at the top right. It was heavy in her hands.

Maybe something good can come out of you knowing what happened back then. She was afraid of the unknown, she didn't need any more pain and anguish. She remembered the reunion at San Pietro, when they'd all sung 'O che bea Venezia' and her strong feeling that beneath the tears and laughter there was something melancholic, perhaps even tragic, that she hadn't understood.

Now her father was asking her to confront it on her own. Well, she wouldn't. She'd read it to him, every word. She had to do something as she sat there in the chair beside his bed, waiting for the possibility that he would wake. And even if he didn't wake, Signor Abruzzi said he might be able to hear her. If he recognised his own words, and her voice, he might want to respond.

She packed an overnight bag with toiletries and a bigger jersey that she could use as a pillow if she needed to. And a box of tissues, because whatever happened overnight there was only one possible end to this.

31

They'd shifted him out of intensive care into the room with the flowers and placed a comfortable chair beside the bed. No oxygen now, no monitoring machines: the one tube was connected to a little cylinder beside him on the bed, a syringe driver, Signor Abruzzi called it, which delivered a slow, steady supply of analgesic. To begin with, she thought it wasn't him lying there. He didn't fill out the sheets or look as tall as her father should have. She'd have liked him to look peaceful but the illness had eaten the flesh from his face too, and he looked as beaky as a bird and wracked, even though drugged and unconscious. The rampaging beasts of the Serengeti were silent. When she put her cheek close to his, his breathing was so soft and shallow it might have been imagined, like the sound of butterfly wings. She laid her palm on his forehead to check he was still warm. *Oh Dad.*

There were venetian blinds at the window, and through the slats she could look at the tops of the trees and imagine that under them wasn't a carpark. There'd been no kiss from Renzo this time and no flights of physicist fancy. He'd just asked if she had his card — she did — and to ring him when . . . well, whenever.

She got herself settled in the chair, took a deep breath and opened the file. It now seemed like a silly idea to read it aloud. The quietness in the room, apart from the hum of the hospital around her, was intimidating. But she had only one plan and if she didn't stick to it she was lost. She looked at the first sentence or two and was dismayed. It was so full of typos that it looked like a different language. Maybe she'd need to translate it before she could read it. She'd try.

* * *

<u>May 6, 1976.</u>
I wonder if this hqppened to He?ingzay. I got
carried awqy in Paris, drinking rough red
at the Polidor, ?aybe qt the sqme table as
Ja?es Joyce and on the way back to the flea-
pit in the Buci I bought a portable Olivetti
Valentine, with its ozn plqstic shell in tomato
red. It's great, apart from the fqct thqt it
zon't fit in my pqck so I have to carry it
by hand. Looking like a pretentious zqanker
may be the lesser of the proble?s: the bloody
thing's got an Itqlian or French keyboard, so
every ti?e I try to hit a, I get q, and for
z I get w and vice wersa and m isn't where
it should be, I keep getting a comma or a
question mark, and when I go for a colon or
a semi, I get m. I'm just a two finger hunter
and pecker, but when the thoughts are rqcing,
I'll be buggered if I'm going to be stopping
and correcting every second zord - maybe I'll
do some tzinking later. I'm just going to hqve
to roll with it until I get the hqang of this
keyboqrd. At leqst I knoz whqt I ?ean. Heminzay
was a journo, so he would have brought his own
Imperial. Smqrt ?an!
  I'? sitting in Sthe dunny of a very slow,

186

very full trqin between ?ilan and Padua, where
I chqnge for Treviso qnd then I've got to find
a train going north ot Gemona. There were no
seats left whenI got on, there wasn't even
standing room in the cqrriage proper, we were
saueezed in like bloody sardines in the area
outside the dunnies at the end. The stations
and the trains are full of soldiers, conscripts
I guess, going to and from their bqses. Some
of them seem about fifteen, too young to shawe,
but they sit amongst the people, no big deal,
just like the ?ilitary jets that cross-cross
the sky with vapour trails. You get a sense
here thqt the cold war zouldn't take a lot to
heat up.

There wasn't even room to put my pack down,
so I looked across at the dunny and thought
there's no chance of anyone fighting their way
in there. I didn't get the seat I paid for, but
I've got a seat. Times like this, I'm thinking
I've made a terrible mistake. My mates left
London this month on the cultural failure
trail - running the bulls inPamplona, down
through France, Italy, Greece, and hospitalised
in Munich after the October Beer fest. Sounds
attrqctive, particularly from the perspective
of the shitter in a slow train fro? Milan to
Padova. Maybe I'll meet up with them later,
but I've got something to do first and I only
get one shot at this. I've got nine ?onths
left before probate of my father's will comes

through and then I'll have to farm the farm or
sell it.

I'm trying not to sweat about that, but
keep thinking about what I owe my father. It
?ight be unfair on him, but I keep coming back
to two imqges. The first wqs when I was ten
years old. I'd been sent to boarding school
over Mum's protestations, or la?entation,
she never stood a chance with Dqd. He'd gone
to Waitaki, so I had to follow him. I was a
solitqry child, used to being on my own on the
best part of a thousand acres with a fqther
who said nothing and a ?other who filled every
second with words. I didn't have to say much
to either of them.

Anywqy, when I came home from boarding
school thqt first year, I couldn't wait to
do what I was used to doing. Tqking Sheba the
Jack Russell out across the hills for a wander
and a gander, see what we could find. Sheba -
named by Mum because Dad was always asking her
who the hell she thought she was, the Queen of
Sheba? - was a great rabbiter. She couldn't
get the fully mature ones but she could get the
younger ones before they reached their burrows.
They'd be dead in an instant. Even the first
time she chqsed a rabbit and caught it - she
must have been barely 12 months old - she knew
how to kill it. She got her teeth into the bqck
of its neck and shook it and it was dead. How
did she know that? We'd bought her as a pup

when Dad zas pissed qfter a good day at the
Waiareka stock sqles, so she hadn't learnt it
from her mother or father.

Sheba and I were working our way across the
hils and they seemed to meet the sky and there
was no bullies there to chivvy me or punch
me. The farm is full of limestone formations,
great craggy cliffs and caves where Sheba and
I spent a lot of time pretending we were the
Maoris who once lived there and left drawing
s of animals and stuff. I'd light fires in
winter and pretend I never had to go home. This
day, it was the winter term break so it was
bloody cold, the sou- wester coming up over
the Kakanuis. I had no idea where Dad was, he'd
left the house early as he used to do, and I'd
wait in bed until I heard hi? coughing qnd
spluttering on his first fag of the day as he
headed over to the implement shed. I guess Dad
was used to having the farm to himself since
I went off to boarding school, because he was
making a hell of a noise. I didn't reqlise it
was him at first. There's these two huge crags
of limestone poking out of the pasture on the
far side of the farm. I called them the Moon
Man, because it looked like a giant had dived
off the ?oon and plunged head-first into the
earth. All that was left of him were his feet,
soles up to the heavens where he came from and a
bit of his ankles holding them up. Sheba heard
the noise first and started that low growl

which meant she wasn't sure. I shooshed her and
we went round the side of the slope tozards the
sound. It was him, Dad, standing on top of
one of the giant's soles. He was facing north,
arms wide like one of Mum's opera singers, but
there was no beauty in the sound he was making,
only the most godqwful pain and misery.
Howling.

I told myself to turn away, but kept
watching. After a while he began coughing, like
the noise he'd made had hurt his throat, and he
bent forward and put his hands on his knees.
Then he fell onto his hands and knees and laid
his head against the rock. His face was turned
away from me, east towards the valley and the
sea, but I coul;d still hear the sounds he was
making.

I didn't ask myself then what had reduced
him to this. I'd been sort of afraid of him
all my life and part of me hated him. Maybe I
got that form Mum. I can;t describe all that
I felt, but some of it was disgust. He was
always the man. I'd seen other men at the footy
club and at the stockyards give him deference,
hold him in a kind of awe. I'd sensed form very
young that Harry Spence was a someone in the
district. To make such a spectacle of yourself.
What if someone had seen him in his weakness?
But now I wonder what ailed him. What could
possibly have happened to him to wring him out
like that?

I grabbed Sheba and held her to relax
her, petrified that Dad would see us and be
furious in his shame. This was a man who said
virtually nothing, who had no friends that I
knew of, who seemed locked into himself. The
way he was killed Mum, for sure. She was a
big woman, with desperately happy eyes, who
loved opera. Dad was in Italy in the war and
reckoned he spoke a bit of Italian, though
he never did in front of us. But every time
Mum put her opera on the gramophone in the
lounge, Dad would tell her if he was around
that it sounded okay until you understood the
words those people were yodelling. Mum stqpped
playing it when he was in the house.

The other thing I remember was when I was
at Otago doing law, must have been my second
year, or later. Anyway the Vietnam Wqr was
in the news all the time, and the footage on
the tv was awful. Down in Dunedin, there'd
been a protest march against the war and I
watched them go down George Street and thought
if there's another one, maybe I'll join them.
Then I went home for the holidays and we were
sitting there watching the news on Channel One
which we always did and there was more footage
from the war. I could tell Dad was interested,
because he stopped sipping his whisky to watch
it. I made some kind of anti-war remark. It
wasn't so much anti war as just expressing
some pretty cliched doubts about whether the

Yanks should be there or whatever. 'You want the Commies here, boy?' he said. 'You happy to see tanks with the red star coming down that driveway?'

He left the room and I knew I'd really pissed him off. I wqnted to ask him what he'd seen in his war that made him fear the Commies, but you wouldn't dare ask Dad anything really, except how to do something on the farm, when he'd tell you or show you once, then say every time 'You might make the odd mistake, boy, but never make the same one twice.' I never did. But I mqde a big mistake that time, in front of the tv. Mum went through to the kitchen to finish putting the dinner on the table and I was going to give her q hand, when Dad must have come back into the room from the door to the hallway. I didn't know he was there, until I felt my arm twisted behind my back and his other hand at my throat. It was grip like a vice and I was helpless even though I was playing senior club rugby for the As and he was full of emphysema. His body was vibrant behind me, I could feel his hard power, and his whisky breath in my ear. 'You're deqd,' he whispered. 'You're fucken dead.'

And fuck me, I would have been. I'd blacked out in a second and found myself lying on the floor and he'd gone. He didn't turn up to dinner and Mum and I made the most of his absence and I didn't tell her anything because

I was too freaked to know where to start. This
wasn't the rage I'd seen before, like the time
he broke a ewe's back when she baulked going up
the race. This was. I don't actuqlly know what
it was.

I don't remember him always being like that.
He was still playing rugby when I was little
and I could see the other men looked up to him.
He was liked, made them laugh, but something
was eating him and it got worse as he got
older, though it was always there. We found
a lamb once that had its eyes eaten out by a
hawk, so it could get into its brain. Dad
looked up at the crags and saw him watching
us, waiting to fly down and have another
go. Dad hqd his rifle, could have shot it,
but told me that the hawk was the perfect
predator. That you could raise it from a baby
with chickens and a mother hen and it would
kill them all as soon as it was old enough.
That you could train hawks to hunt for you
like falcons, but they wouldn't know you or
relate to you if you'd had them for ten years
or twenty. And that they never grew old, they
hunted with the same muscle and sinew till
the moment they fell dead out of the sky. The
emphysema was getting to him by then.

I didn't come home much after he tried
to strangle me. I came for Mum's funeral of
course a year later. Breast cancer. They say
they don't know the cause but that cancer was

Dad. He ate away at her spirit until there was
nothing left. It was qs if he was punishing her
for something, but god knows what she could
have done to deserve him. By then he was an
emphysemic wreck, and probably qn alcoholic,
and when he died a year later, there were bugger
all people at the Tokorahi church. The locals
came, though he didn't mix with them any more,
even his old Union rugby club mates, they came
but they had bugger all to say about Harry
Spence: that he was a good farmer and a good
provider and good husband and father. I refused
to speak to those lies, pretended I was too
upset.

I didn't notice the stranger at church,
but they had a few drinks in the Memorial
Hall after Dad had been put in the ground at
Livingstone Cemetery up on the hill, and I
saw him then because he came up and introduced
himself. He was my father's age, lanky, balding
at the front with grey hair coming through
what must have been blonde. He said his name
was Arch Scott. He qsked me how ?uch I knew
about what Dad did in the wqr. I said bugger
all, that he never spoke about it. (Never spoke
about it to ?e, anyway. I didn't tell Arch
that I'm pretty sure he never spoke about it to
Mum before she died, because they never seemed
to have much to say to one another anyway,
and he wouldn't have spoken to it to his ?ates
from the RSA because he didn't seem to have

194

any and never went). I also didn't tell Arch
that while Dad never talked about the war, the
war obviously still talked to him. Those two
things that had scared the shit out of me, him
howling on the Moon ?an that time, qnd nearly
killing me in the front room.

Arch may have known more than he was letting
on, but what he did say was that my father
had been a hero of the Italian resistance
movement. Thqt was the first time I'd heard
that there was an Italian resistance movement
- I'd seen some movies about the French and it
all looked kind of exciting cloak and dagger
stuff. Arch said he hadn't had a lot to do
with my father, they'd been based in different
parts of northern Italy qnd they couldn't move
around much, but that he'd heard stories of
my father's exploits and seen him in action
once. When I say Arch might have known more
than he was letting on, I mean that he may have
sensed or heard about what my father was like
after the war. I'm not sure where he would have
heard that, because I don't think Dad ever once
went to the RSA in Itchen Street or did the
Dawn Parade with the rest of the veterans down
Thames Street. But maybe Arch, if he'd lived a
similar life to dad during the war, just knew
how fucked up it left some of them. Because I'm
convinced that's what stuffed Dad up. Mind
you, Arch seemed such a different kettle of
fish. A very wqrm man and generous. He told

?e that he knew my father's code name had been
Rico Zanardi and if I went to the town close
to where my father was based, Gemona up in
Friuli, and looked for a family called the
Zanardis or the Bonazzons, I might learn a lot
more about what my father did,

Then Arch let on that he'd seen me before.
The Otago University team had played a
champions of champions club tournament up in
Pukekohe the year before. It was a quadrangular
tournament with Petone from Wellington and
Lincoln from Christchurch and Manurewa from
the Auckland area. Arch said he'd been one of
the principal movers behind the formation of
the new rugby province, Counties, which played
a great brand of rugby and if I ever came
north, to look him up, he'd find a team for
me. He gave me his address and phone number,
then asked if I thought I'd ever get to Italy.
I didn't have any real plans at that stage,
but I knew I had a yeqr before probate for my
father's will came through and qt that point I
could sell the farm, which meant that I'd have
to make a final decision between farming and
the law. Maybe I already knew qs I was talking
to Arch: that I needed to go and find something
redeeming about my father. Maybe Arch could see
it in my eyes. Anyway, he took a note of my
address at the flqt in Dunedin and said he'd
write to me. He shook ?y hand and said he'd
have to get back to town to catch the train

and left. Two weeks later, a letter arrived, well two letters. The first said that if I was passing a town called San Pietro di Livenza on the way to Gemona, I should drop in there, seek out Aldo's bar and hand Aldo the attached letter. The attached letter is pretty brief and it's in Italian, so I've got no idea what it says. And it's signed 'Arturo', which must be Arch in Italian.

After the funeral, I had to clear out Dad's study for the farm manager who was coming in. I'd seldom been in that room, it was Dad's retreat and woe betide Mum or me if we disturbed him. It had some books and a radio, a desk with the farming accounts and bugger all else. Everything stunk of stale cigarette smoke, until I opened an old wardrobe and found these bits and pieces of uniforms hanging there. One was German, I could see that, then there was another grey tunic and a brown battle-dress, and a red and white checked scarf that looked like an old tablecloth and what looked like a steel bracelet or necklace linked to a flat metal crescent with the word Feldgendarmerie above an eagle or hawk in mid-flight, with a swastika on its tail. On the shelf above were three hats, one an ordinary looking old fashioned black baseball hat, one with a red star and what looked like an SS officer's hat, jet black with a silver skull and the German eagle. I'd seen the Gestapo hat in war comics. I wish I'd had Arch there to tell me what the others were. They were freaky just hanging there in the gloom, and they stank of something, much stronger than mothballs or cigarette smoke. Cordite or something, like someone had been celebrating Guy Fawkes in the wardrobe and letting off skyrockets. The stink of war. Acrid. Foul. I was about to close the door and leave it all for another day, when I saw a shoe-box on the shelf underneath, pushed to the back. There were half a dozen envelopes, addressed to Henry Spence, but when I opened them, they all began Caro Rico. I couldn't understand a word of them, but they were signed Donatella. I must have had the thought even then that I'd go to Italy, because they're in the side pocket of my pack here beside the dunny.

They plqnted oaks for some of the men from the district killed in the two great wars. There's one on the road from Ngapara into Tokarahi to Private J Dasler, Gallipoli 1915 and two for the Lamont brothers along the Devil's Bridge roqd. They should have planted one for Henry Willia? Spence. Lost in action. But maybe I can find him.

Someone's hammering on the door, so I better get my qrse out of here.

32

It was weird having her father's words so alive in the room and written when he was younger than she had ever known him, younger than she was now, while he was lying there, close to death. He'd once been someone else before he'd become her father. The details about her grandfather Harry's brutality had shocked her. He'd never talked about it.

She remembered driving her father down the Waiareka Valley early in spring almost exactly a year ago. He'd finished his last bout of chemo and, even then, must have known the cancer still had some purchase in his blood and that his end was near: he'd wanted her to take him back to the farm.

She'd thought he was asleep, head lolling, but he was taking it all in. He told her there'd been a lot of change to the valley, that much of the land's mixed cropping charm was gone. He remembered patchwork rectangles of wheat and oats and linseed and sheep-grazed pasture, all delineated by hawthorn and gorse hedges, which had been ripped out so that massive irrigation centipedes could crawl unimpeded across the huge bare paddocks, pugged and polluted by cows.

'But it's wonderful!' she'd said, and to her urban eyes it was: the valley undulated gently in front of them and rose eventually to the purple Kakanuis, snow still on the tops.

They'd driven to the end of the valley and stopped beside the old Oamaru stone flour mill at Ngapara, shuttered and quiet, then walked about fifty metres up the hill behind to a hurricane gate that used to lead to the coal mine. The gorse and broom had covered the track into the side of the hill. They could see the top beam of what must have been the entrance to the main shaft, battened off with corrugated iron and four-by-two.

'The town died with the mill and the mine,' he'd said, as they walked back down to the car. The village looked so cute, the old pub and the rows of workers' cottages behind the trees on the opposite side of the main road.

Beyond Ngapara the road began climbing up and around huge limestone bluffs. 'The hill country hasn't changed,' said her father. 'It's too tough for cows.' Too tough for her, too. Above them the stone ramparts soared, the striations pockmarked with caves like footholds to the sky.

Her father directed her further into those hills, then asked Clare to stop the car beside a huge oak with a small white cross at its base, with a name and a date: 1915.

'Dad should have had one of those,' he said. 'Missing in action, even though he came back.'

He was weak, but had insisted on climbing up the hill towards two limestone crags, which she now realised must have been the ones in his diary, the soles of the Moon Man's boots pointing skywards after his plunge to earth. Where her father had seen his father howling at the empty sky.

She'd helped him climb the boulders on the uphill side and they'd stood on one of the Moon Man's soles, braced against the wind coming, he said, over Danseys Pass from the Maniototo. He should have told her about his father. Instead, he'd stood there for five minutes and said nothing, then asked her if she felt any connection.

'To this?' she'd asked, looking out at the burnt grass burst through with mushrooming limestone. It might as well have been the moon. The closest she'd got to a farm was the spring lambs at Cornwall Park. That was enough. This looked alien and almost malevolent. The only sign of life was a green sheen of buds along the branches of the oak down beside the road. 'Sort of,' she'd lied.

'It was hard to leave,' he said. 'Perhaps I should have stayed.'

She wondered if his mind was there now. His face seemed unchanged, but she couldn't give up hope that he might be hearing her.

May 7th 1976.

So?ething terrible's happened. I got to Treviso last night, found a flea pit near the railway station where I'm writing this. One thing about trqins and railways is you don't get a great impression of places. There's always a Terminus Hotel and it's always crap and the station's in the crap part of town. Maybe I'm s bit biased because I've only really seen London and here and the papers keep saying that the UK and Italy are the two sick men of Europe. I can believe that. But Italy's just got sicker. The reason I'm still here writing this is because Gemona got hit by an earthquake yesterday. I went in this morning to buy a ticket for the last leg up to Gemona and the guy in the ticket booth, who looked a bit shaken to be honest, kept saying 'No train, no train', then said 'No Gemona.' I didn't get what the hell he was trying to say until he grabbed a newspaper off his desk and showed me the headline - huge headline - TERREMOTO. I didn't need to be able to translate that to see whqt had happened by the pictures underneath. There was one, must have been shot from q plane, of what remained of a huge church on top of a hill. One wall was half intact but in between there and the re?ains of the spire was just sky and rubble.

The spire was two thin shards of stone sticking out from the pile of rubble, like q two-fingered salute to God. The guy in the ticket office was pissed off with this insensitive tourist until he caught the look on my face. I'd like to say it was sympathy for the people cqught in that earthquake, but it was also dismay. I didn't realise until I saw those pictures of Ge?ona how much I'd been banking on finding out something good about my father.

I'm not giving up, I'm going to stick around for a few dqys, then see if I cqn still get up to Gemona. Venice is close, but I want to save that for on the way back, I might enjoy it more. One of the stops on the failure trail the guys told me about wqs a place called Fusina, a camping ground somewhere close to Venice. Maybe I'll try and find that, see if I know anyone there.

May 8th, 1976.
I found Fusina, got a bus there. It dropped me off down the road and I walked the couple of hundred yqrds to the camping ground. It's in the middle of the industrial area of Mestre

and the wharves called Marghera: surrounded by
great pipes and fat petroleum tanks shimmering
in the sun, soaring smoke-stacks and gas burn-
off pipes on huge gantries crowned with blue
flame. Weird place for a holiday.

There was a sign up at the gate, saying -
You Are Now Leaving Dagoland and Entering the
Republic of Fusina. A proper sign, looked like
it had been there for years. Do they think
Italians can't speak English? Do they think
Italians are as ignorant as they are? Right
inside the gate are Fosters signs and a big
bar, and on the other side are goalposts.
It was mid-afternoon so I went into the bar
and there were pissed Kiwis and Aussies and
South Africans, girls and guys, in stubbies
and jandals and T shirts saying 'All Pommies
Are Bastards' and 'What's Fuck Off in Frog?'
and lots of silver ferns and green and gold.
I didn't know any of them but I had a beer
and I qsked this girl who said she was from
Wellington if she'd heard about the big
earthquake. She was shocked. But as soon as she
knew it was here not there, she didn't give it
another thought. I finished my beer and headed
back to the bus-stop. I might be fucked in my
own way but I didn't come twelve thousand miles
across the world to end up in the same plqce.

May 9th, 1976.
I found out I could get a train up to San

Pietro di Livenza, so I thought of doing that,
taking Arch's letter up to Aldo's bar, then
found that I could get a ticket to Trentino,
north of Gemona tomorrow. So I'm doing that.
Who knows, they might let me off at Gemona.

<u>May 10th, 1976.</u>
Holy hell. The train went through Gemona all
right. Very slowly, they'd obviously just
cleared the tracks. It looked like it used to
be a beautiful old station a couple of storeys
high and now the whole roof has caved in and
most of the walls are gone. When you look from
the station up to the hill where the old town
was and where that spire is still pointing
to the sky, it's just a sea of rubble, with
cranes and rescue workers and red cross still
amongst it trying to find people, but how
the hell do they know where to start? In some
places you can't even see where the streets used
to be, the stones are just spread evenly across
the landscape, like a huge river alluvial of
rubble. The train didn't stop and even if it
had and they'd let me off, I had no business
doing that. It would have been disrespectful to
even ask. There are more important things than
my questions.

   I'm in another flea-pit at Trentino writing
this. Another terminus hotel. I'm trying to work
out what I do next, since finding out anything
about Dad seems to be a dead duck. Bugger.

Gemona, 1943

33

For once Charlie was full of questions to which he genuinely wanted answers. Harry, though, was played out, said little. But Joe knew. Harry was a hunter of trophies, like the ones Joe had seen on the walls of houses back home — deer antlers and boars' ears and tusks. He'd taken the red kerchief and the hat, so One-Eyed Jack was dead. The Slovenian leader hadn't been wearing knickerbockers, so Harry had killed at least one other, whose boots didn't fit. Joe had thought back a hundred times to what had happened up on the ridge above Monfalcone, trying to work it out. Harry had asked the Slovenians if they had arms and ammo. He knew now that Harry had planned exactly this: to kill them for their weapons.

Harry stacked the guns and began unfurling himself from the belts of ammo.

Charlie didn't get it. 'Nice of 'em to share.'

'I made my move when we were close to the border,' said Harry, 'and slipped them.' He lay down on his bed and was instantly asleep.

Charlie looked at Joe, realising he was missing something. Joe thought he could see a touch of fear. For once, Charlie said nothing.

Joe climbed carefully back up to Reant. The village was quiet in the early afternoon, the villagers inside resting after lunch. Joe stopped by the little stone chapel with the two-bell campanile. Set into a wall nearby was a tiny shrine to the Madonna holding the baby Jesus. After checking that no one was watching, Joe plucked an onion flower and laid it at the Madonna's feet. He thought about what he should pray for but didn't know any more.

* * *

Late afternoon, Harry woke and asked about food. When Charlie told him that it was Masarolis tonight, and Harry shook his head and said he liked the look of Valle better, Joe knew he was worried about the Slovenians. Masarolis was up high, only about a mile from the Yugoslav border, while Valle was further down the road from Reant, back towards the plain.

Harry had it all worked out. Charlie would go lead scout as usual, unarmed. Harry would follow with the Mauser semi-auto and pistol, and Joe would be the packhorse at the rear carrying two rifles and most of the ammunition. That role suited Joe: he'd have preferred not to carry a weapon again but there was no choice, so he dutifully trudged after Charlie and Harry down the pitted road towards Valle.

Harry was full of admiration for the Slovenians. 'Tough hooers,' he said, 'and practical. They all carry German weapons because that's who they'll be killing. Makes it easier to get ammo and parts.'

'If they're killing Germans,' said Joe, 'doesn't that put them on our side?'

'Whoever kills us is our enemy,' said Harry. 'They shot three Kiwis cold. They've only lost two.'

Joe wasn't sure if that was the way the Slovenians would see it.

As they dropped down to Valle, the smallest of the villages, a cluster of three or four houses on a track that led up from the road, they heard raised voices. Charlie stopped and motioned them into the trees. They found one of the foresters' trails that took them round above the village, from where they had a good view down to the small square.

The Slovenians were there. They had the villagers, men, women and children, lined up, except one. Mario, a strong charcoal burner in his forties, father of two small boys being held back by his wife, had his hands pinned behind his back and his head pressed against the stone trough by the barrel of a Mauser.

Joe didn't know him but Harry and Charlie recognised the man who had hosted them many times, feeding them whatever the family had while Charlie did his tricks for the boys in front of the fire. The Slovenian with his rifle at Mario's temple was shouting. They couldn't hear his words but they didn't need to. The villagers were stoic people, they weren't crying or pleading, not even the children. They stood awaiting the imminent execution of one of their few able-bodied men and stayed silent: this is what happened when the outside world came into their world. It had always been thus. They would suffer and endure.

While Joe was grimacing, waiting for the shot, Harry handed him the semi-auto and took one of the rifles. When Charlie realised what Harry was planning, he whispered, 'No! You'll bring them down on us!'

'They're here already,' said Harry. 'What's to lose?'

As he sighted the rifle, Joe's gaze went back to the tableau in the village square: the women trying to hide their children's eyes, the men flinching in anticipation of the bullet fragmenting Mario's head, the Slovenian executioner shouting louder, enraged at the villagers' intransigence . . .

Then one side of his forehead blew away and he fell backwards into the trough. Joe hadn't even heard the bullet.

'Three all,' said Harry.

34

What followed was the march from hell. Though it wasn't so much a march as a desperate scuttle-run across angry country. Joe thought more than once of Arch and his Hare Battalion. They were hares being hunted along a maze of foresters' trails. The Slovenians had started below them in Valle so they had to climb higher before coming west. There was no going back to the buca, they'd just bring the Slovenians down on Reant. Perhaps they'd already visited Masarolis and extracted information that had led them to Valle. Joe tried not to think of the warm cave as darkness fell and he strained to see the trail ahead under a half-moon that was often obscured by clouds and trees.

It had been Harry's idea that Joe would lead under his direction with Charlie, now armed with one of the rifles, in the middle and Harry bringing up the rear, the first point of contact if the Slovenians caught up with them. For the first hour, while the light held, they were close to running and Charlie had no breath to talk. But as dusk closed in Charlie began a breathless patter, thinking out loud, trying to justify an attempt to find a village or even a house, get some chow and a good night's sleep. They could slurp water from the streams they clambered through, but Charlie and Joe hadn't eaten for the best part of eight hours. God knows when Harry last ate.

Charlie's visions must have got to Harry. 'Shut up,' he told him, 'or I'll shut you up.'

Every so often Harry would stop and listen, sniff the air like a pig dog and say, with what seemed like a kind of satisfaction, 'They're still coming.'

At times Joe thought that Harry might be disappointed if they outran the Slovenians. Giving Joe directions according to the grid in his head, he seemed to be enjoying the chase and didn't really see himself as the quarry. A couple of hours into darkness he told Joe they were far enough ahead and could start working their way down. They didn't want to be caught up near the border in daylight.

By the early morning hours, even Harry was done in. They stumbled across a charcoal burner's hut in a clearing and he said they could rest a while. Charlie and Joe huddled inside the hut while Harry took the first shift, sitting propped against the outside wall, the semi-auto between his knees, looking back the way they'd come.

When Joe woke it was just light. He was stiff and sore from the wooden shelf he'd slept on and went outside to stretch. But Harry was nowhere to be seen. Joe went inside to wake Charlie. Harry was suddenly there, fingers to his lips: 'Let's go! Scappato!'

Joe and Charlie grabbed their rifles and stumbled after Harry. He was leading them back up the hill, on a right angle to the track they'd come in on. Joe wanted to ask why, if the Slovenians had caught up with them, they weren't fleeing further west, but the answer soon presented itself. A platoon of Republicans appeared and started sniffing around the hut. Joe tried to reassure himself that they hadn't lit a fire or eaten anything, so there'd be no trace of their occupation: all they had to do was stay quiet in their well-camouflaged vantage point and the danger would pass.

And it would have if the Slovenians hadn't appeared, still doggedly following their trail and closer than they'd imagined. There was a moment of shocked recognition, from which the Slovenians recovered first. Two of the Republican soldiers went down before they got behind the hut. Even then the Republicans outnumbered the Slovenians by about ten and their firepower and the fact they had cover soon drove the Slovenians back, leaving one of their number lying beside the track. As the Slovenians retreated a couple of the Republicans dashed sideways from the hut, then another two. The Slovenians, afraid of being outflanked, quickly melted away, pursued down the track by the gung-ho Republicans. They could hear the crackle of small arms becoming more distant.

Harry was looking at one of the fallen Republicans, a tallish smudge of grey and bleeding red on the clearing floor. 'He might be about the right size. These are shot.' He was indicating Don Claudio's brogues. The stitching had separated from the upper along the instep of his left foot.

Joe pointed out that if the Republicans came back and found their dead comrade's boots missing, there might be consequences.

Charlie was anxious too. 'First village. I'll get you some boots. Sure thing.'

Harry let the corpse keep his boots and they continued down the trail the Republicans had appeared from, adopting a new formation: Harry led because he reckoned that was where the danger would come from now that the Republicans and Slovenians had neutralised each other. Charlie was man in the middle, ready to chat if they met any potentially friendly Italian civilians, and Joe brought up the rear.

Watching Charlie and Harry in front of him, Joe wondered whether Harry had realised there'd be no more mingling with Italians, no more pretending to the Germans that they were civilians. Harry, still wearing his scarf and cap, looked like a brigand with bare calves and strange shoes. Charlie looked most like an ordinary Italian, albeit a filthy one, in jacket, loose trousers and buttoned-up shirt, and Joe was still comfortably lost in Bepi's coat. But the rifles and the belts of ammo looping from both shoulders and crossing chests changed everything. They were now partigiani and if they were caught by the Germans they'd be shot, regardless of whether their true identities were discovered.

*   *   *

Early in the morning they left the wooded hills and began moving through cultivated fields, many just ploughed, which gave no cover, but were divided by hedgerows and clumps of trees that had turned but hadn't yet lost all their foliage. The three men were ravenous and thirsty but the first farmer they approached ran away before Charlie could strike up a conversation. After that they were more cautious about being seen as they moved constantly west. By midday, on their last legs, they broke into a stalle that was separate from the farmer's house. Joe milked three cows. They'd already been milked that morning but he managed to get the best part of a gallon into the bucket.

Late in the day they found an isolated hut which a farmer used to store field implements, hoes and rakes, so that he didn't have to carry them out every day. Inside was a small sack of spuds that had been half eaten by rats. They dumped their arms and ammo inside and when Charlie whined to light a fire Harry said yes. Thoughts turned to what could be cooked, besides the spuds.

At dusk Joe and Harry left Charlie to set the fire and made their way back about a mile to a compound they'd seen that had chickens and geese. Smoke was curling from the chimney of the farmhouse so there was little likelihood of anyone coming out into the yard unless they made too much noise.

Joe let himself into the chicken run and looked for the fattest, slowest hen. As Ida had taught him to do, he put a calming hand on the centre of the bird's back, where the softest feathers were. She relaxed and quietened as he picked her up in the crook of his elbow, holding her feet, and carried her out of the pen. Harry had been looking through the implement shed for an axe or a knife but had found neither. Joe was about to suggest they take the hen back to the hut where they could slit its throat with a bayonet, when Harry put his palm over her head, his fingers under her neck, and flicked his wrist so that she corkscrewed on the end of his arm. She squawked once and was dead, her head almost separated from the body.

Back at the hut, Joe plucked the hen and gutted it with a bayonet. They roasted it over the fire on a spit and wolfed it down with spuds cooked in their jackets in the embers, then tried to lick and wipe the chicken fat off their hands and faces.

There was room on the earthen floor for the three of them, Charlie in the middle, Joe and Harry on either side. Joe, nearest what was left of the sack of spuds, was woken by sounds that he couldn't place. When he opened his eyes he saw a rat the size of a small possum looking at him with a half-eaten spud in its claws and chicken fat bubbling in its nostrils.

35

They left the hut at dawn and kept moving west through low rolling hills with cultivated fields and plenty of cover, keeping the saw-toothed range to their right and the snow-capped giants in front. Harry hadn't mentioned Switzerland this time, or any plan at all.

During the morning it began to rain and the mountains disappeared. They trudged on for a while until a cold wind got up and icy water came at them horizontally. They took shelter in a dense copse for about an hour, but had to move again when big drops began to fall from the trees. They were soon wet through and very cold. Warm shelter overnight to dry themselves and their clothes was the only possibility left.

They hauled themselves along in such cold misery that Charlie stopped talking to himself. They passed the odd farmhouse and towards dusk knew that they had to choose one and take their chances. Joe thought of Bepi's Chi lo sa and worried that they might strike a family Harry considered likely to betray them to the fascists. The way Harry now was, Joe couldn't see him just shrugging and walking away, leaving them alive. Joe shivered at the prospect but knew they would have to do something soon. At that moment the rain thinned and he saw, in front of them, a town that appeared to be sitting on a low cloud over the foothills. It had to be Gemona.

They were so tired, hungry and wet that there was never any question, though Joe did try to rationalise putting the Bonazzons and Zanardis in such terrible jeopardy. That it would be for only one night. That they had no other choice, it was life or slow death. That even in his guilt and misery the thought of seeing Donatella lifted him.

By darkness they were close, and Joe took the lead down familiar farm tracks through the empty maize fields and skeletal vines towards the cobblestoned square bounded by the two houses. When they were fifty yards away, Joe handed his rifle to Harry and asked him and Charlie to stay right where they were until he called them in.

As Joe walked forward he saw lights on in both houses, but the sound of raised voices was coming from the Bonazzons'. He turned that way and crossed the end of the stalle, where he'd been hidden by Harry what seemed like an age ago. He heard a couple of muffled steps behind him before he was hit hard on the back and fell to the ground. Another figure came running from the entrance arch and he was grabbed by the arms before he could rise and dragged towards the front door. There must have been an exchange with the people inside because the door opened and he was thrown inside to sprawl on the flagstoned floor.

The first voice he recognised was Bepi's, identifying his coat before he identified Joe. Then Donatella was there, with Bepi, helping him to sit up. There were a dozen men, including Bepi and Gigi, in the big room, and two young women, one of them Donatella.

Bepi and Donatella were explaining who Joe was to a man in a loose red shirt who looked much older than his photograph in the bedroom above. The left side of his face, from his hairline down into his collar, resembled loose plastic. Whatever had burnt him had taken his ear too. The way he held himself, very straight and still, made it difficult to tell at first that his left sleeve was empty.

Luca gazed down at Joe, now sitting up with Donatella on one side and Bepi on the other. Even without the photo and with all the disfigurement, Joe could see that he must be Donatella's brother, the same wide face and dark eyes, though his were much fiercer. Donatella had said her brother was twenty-four, but they must have been punishing years. The big creased forehead that pressed down on Bepi's brow was making itself felt on Luca. He had stubble and a moustache and something else that Joe had seen in the eyes of the veterans in Maadi and sometimes in Harry's too — a glazed look, as if they were focused on something or somewhere a long way off.

Bepi said something to Joe in dialect, then realised his mistake and repeated it more slowly in Italian. 'This is my son, Luca.'

Turned on Joe, Luca's eyes were disconcertingly direct, no politeness, drilling for defects, full of contempt. Standing now, wet and dripping, Joe wasn't sure what to do. Luca made no effort to offer his hand, only nodding at Joe as he asked, 'Vuoi combattere i fascisti?' *Do you want to fight the fascists?*

His lies had carried him this far, thought Joe, through three different deaths to this last-chance refuge. He was in no position to tell the truth. 'Sì, certamente,' he said.

He thought the time might be right to call Harry and Charlie in, but he was too late. They must have seen Joe being set upon and had worked their way forward while the lookouts were otherwise occupied. Harry came shouldering through the door, covering the room coolly with the semi-automatic, while Charlie followed with the rifle, yelling at everyone to step back and stay calm.

Bepi and Donatella stood up and moved back a couple of paces with everyone else. Luca stayed where he was, now right in front of Harry's barrel, confused rather than fearful. In front of him was a man with German weapons and enough ammunition to hold off a platoon, wearing a cap with a red star and a tablecloth around his neck, but speaking English.

Harry pushed him in the belly with the Mauser. 'Who're you, sunshine?'

Luca's eyes blazed and Joe could see things escalating rapidly. He told Harry that this was the eldest son of the people who'd looked after him, who'd saved his life, and pointed at Bepi and Donatella.

Harry looked around at the men and at Luca and smelled something in the air that he liked. 'Ask him what this little shindig is in aid of.'

'This is the Gemona del Friuli division of the Garibaldi Nationalist Brigade,' said Luca when Joe translated the question. 'I am its commander.'

'Who the fuck are they?' asked Harry.

Joe translated for Bepi, even though he knew Luca had probably understood the question. It seemed like a good way of keeping Harry and Luca from each other's throats. There was a long silence as Bepi considered the question and looked towards his son.

'Un po' di riscaldamento,' said Bepi finally, moving towards the cupboard where he kept his grappa.

*   *   *

Joe later thought that if Harry had any plan when he killed the Slovenians for their weapons, this must have been it: to meet up with a like-minded group who wanted to kill Germans.

The first thing Luca wished to know, after their glasses were filled, was whether Harry, Joe and Charlie wanted to escape from Italy or stay and fight, because if they didn't want to fight, the Garibaldi Nationalist Brigade would commandeer their weapons, whether or not they agreed. Joe had noticed none of the men in the room were armed, and so had Harry. 'Get your own,' he said.

That appeared to be the answer Luca wanted to hear: to get three trained and armed soldiers into his group of well-intentioned and mostly middle-aged farmers and artisans.

The grappa seemed to burn from the inside and make them steam in their wet clothes. Even Joe had a second glass as Luca told them they were henceforth Italian. He'd arrange for a simpatico local priest to make forged identity papers under their Italian names. He raised his glass to Charlie. 'Come ti chiami?' *What is your name?*

That was easy. 'Carlo Farinelli,' said Charlie.

They all drank to Carlo Farinelli. Then Luca raised his glass to Harry.

'Enrico,' said Harry.

'Rico,' confirmed Luca. 'We'll think of your family name.'

They drank to Rico. When Luca raised his glass to Joe, out of deference he looked across to Bepi. Was Bepi prepared to countenance another Giuseppe in the group?

'Gianni,' said Donatella clearly, as if she'd been thinking about it for some time. The way she said it, it sounded like an American saying 'Johnny'. 'Gianni Lamonza.'

They drank to Gianni Lamonza and Joe, finishing his third shot of grappa and steaming like a locomotive, thought it was about as fine a name and as fine a christening as could be had. And to be given them by Donatella.

Luca had a question that was of great relevance to the

Garibaldis. 'How did you get your weapons?'

'Courtesy of the Slovenians,' said Harry, touching the red star on his cap.

'Buoni comunisti,' said Bepi approvingly.

Luca was incredulous. 'The Slovenians *gave* you weapons and ammunition?'

Harry conceded that they'd needed a bit of persuading. Joe was fairly sure that Harry's laconic irony flew right past Luca. He was less sure where the Garibaldis fitted into the political scheme of things but Bepi's politics and the red shirt worn by his son might be a pretty good indication they were communist. Joe wondered what would happen when the Slovenians found out the Kiwi capitano who had killed three of their own was now fighting alongside their communist allies, the Garibaldis. On the evidence so far Joe thought it unlikely the Slovenians would just shrug their shoulders and say, 'That's life.' If the Slovenians got shitty about the Garibaldis' new recruits, how would that sit with Luca? Not very well was Joe's guess.

All that was in the future. The here and now was rejoining the war. A different sort of fighting but the same war. The way he looked at it, beginning his fourth shot of grappa as Gianni Lamonza, it was an acceptable price, to stay close to Donatella. But when he looked across at her, she was still looking at Harry. Joe tried to read the expression in her eyes, but couldn't.

Treviso, 2014

36

By one o'clock in the morning, Clare had read almost a quarter of the yellowing pages, but seemed no closer to her ultimate quarry, the woman behind the red door in Dorsoduro. And something else came to her out of the instructions her father had left her, and the phraseology he had used: *There's no excuse for what happened, but there is an explanation, though lawyers always say that* . . . She remembered enough from her short career in the law to recognise a classic plea in mitigation, delivered after a guilty plea or verdict had been entered. The deed was done, the crime committed: there was an explanation, but no excuse, for what had happened . . . But *what* had happened? What was he talking about? What crime?

The instructions had obviously been prepared before he left New Zealand, so he couldn't be referring to the mystery woman, surely. He might be referring to his loveless marriage, but that seemed a bit metaphorical for the father she knew, who had never once discussed that with her. *After so much time and so much pain* . . . What else could it be? And if it did tie into the mystery woman, why hadn't she appeared in his diary? If there was no woman, Clare's actions in Venice were beyond forgiveness.

She couldn't help skimming ahead silently through the shoe-leather stuff that didn't much interest her: the details of her father's journey by train back through Gemona to San Pietro di Livenza, where he'd presented his letter from Arch Scott to Aldo, the proprietor of a bar in San Pietro, and had been welcomed like a long-lost son. Arch Scott had obviously warned them that a Bruce Spence was coming, that he'd seen this boy play, because San Pietro had offered him a playing contract as soon as he arrived. That much might have been anticipated.

San Pietro's plans for their first season in Serie A were in turmoil because the man who'd been appointed coach had lost his wife in the Gemona quake, and had resigned. So Bruce was also offered a co-coaching role.

That meant learning Italian, so he'd enrolled in a six-week course at the Università per Stranieri in Perugia, down in Umbria, to fill in the summer before the rugby season started. His diary became even more patchy and irregular down there but there was the occasional interesting bit.

<u>June 12 1976.</u>
There's a General Election coming. Went
for a run early this morning before it got
hot, up Corso Vannucci and saw buses full
of policemen armed with Uzis pouring into
the buildings either side. They reappeqred
this arvo, creating a buffer between the neo
fascisti rallying in the Piazza Italia and the
communists rallying in the Piazza Repubblica.
I saw armed cops in New South Wales on the

NZU tour, but they were carrying holstered
pistols, not waving sub-machine guns in
your face. I saw the hammer and sickle flag
waving in the communist rally and something
that looked like a swastika amongst the neo
fascisti. Politics is different here.

There was a lot of guff about his preparation for the coaching
role, writing down what he remembered about positions he'd
never played, sending letters to friends who had played those
positions. Far from rousing her father from his coma, his
words threatened to put *her* to sleep, lulled by the comforting
hum of the hospital. But once he got back to San Pietro and
began the serious business of coaching, it got more interesting
and funny, as her father described trying to get to grips with
his Italian team-mates.

September 2, 1976.
I need to tell the guys a joke in Italian, so
they know I've got a sense of humour. Rifi
dropped off two more giant bottles in rope
baskets last night, one of red, Merlot, one of
white, Pinot Grigio. Rifi's own, he tells me.
I'm finding my ability to speak and understand
Italian improves by the glass. Rifi is a prop
by position and by nature - it's amazing how
you can come to the other end of the world
and find that a prop is still a prop. Rifi
is the pure heart of the team, always a big
smile, not interested in politics - he might
be unique in that respect - has hands like

plates from pruning vines and is desperate to
make me laugh.. So last night after he dropped
off the wine, he acted out a carabinieri joke,
virtually no words, just slapstick. I got it!

The relief on Rifi's face when I laughed.
I wanted to tell him a joke in Italian in
return, make him laugh, show those big teeth.
I tried the simplest one I could remember from
Enfield primary:

Fatty in the teapot,
Skinny in the spout,
Fatty blew off
and blew Skinny out.

I thought I was doing quite well:
Un grosso in dentro della teiera,
Un magro in dentro del becco.

Rifi was looking pretty interested, but more
puzzled than laughing. 'Come mai un grosso
in dentro della teira?' How did a fat man get
into a teapot?

Patienza, Rifi, I told him, but I feared
the moment was gone. Worse, I didn't know
the Italian for fart and had to ask him,
acting it out with sound effects and holding
my nose. Rifi pissed himself. So that's a
start. Your basic poos and wees breaking down
international boundaries.

Though the actual season began with a spectacular

win and a loss, the real news kept coming from Gemona, the place which had drawn him to Italy in the first place, but which seemed as impossible to reach as ever.

September 13, 1976.
Gemona was rocked by another major after-shock early evening yesterday. We felt them in San Pietro - no wonder, they were 7.5 and 8 on what the Corriere Della Sera calls the Mercalli scale. If that's the same as the Richter scale, jesus. There's more pictures. Some of the buildings that were salvageable are now rubble. I'd been thinking of going back there, but it'll be months now before anyone from outside is allowed anywhere near the place. Poor bastards.

37

Another entry a week later, which looked to be about rugby, turned into something else. She recognised the name Franco, whose photo she had seen at the reunion, the handsome one who had died, and who, with her father, had formed the due coglioni, the two balls of San Pietro. And someone else, who Clare desperately hoped would be significant, finally made an appearance.

September 20, 1976
Lost again, by two points. Missed a drop
goal in injury time. Perfect set-up, scrum on
their 22. Claudio hooked it wide from dead in
front. Could have thrown it over, as they say,
or in Claudio's case talked it over. Oh the
lamentations. Last week the dropped goal went
right between the posts. Ours, not theirs. I'd
tried to charge it down and lay there with
my face in the mud not daring to look, but
listening for the crowd reaction. Whistling in
derision. Our fans. Not happy campers, we were
going at fifty per cent, but have lost the last
two, not by much - we're good at making a game
but not so good at winning it. We're inventing
new ways to lose, traversing the many and
various ways of snatching defeat from the jaws
of victory.

The game is usually on Sunday. Monday is

market day in San Pietro, just around the
corner from my apqrtment. I try to get out of
town without being seen. The Straniero who's
bringing shame to the town on their only
national stage. Shame is vergogna in Italian.
Another of those words that sounds better than
the English. Like magari. How do you translate
that - indeed? Right on! I wish! If only . . .
Depends entirely how you say it.

I hightail it in the little Opel Kadette
across the plain to Venice, my refuge,
particularly Beppino and his brother Franco.
They both speak good English, which is a relief
- after two hours of Italian in San Pietro
where no-one speaks English, I'm bushed, have
to hide away to recuperate.

Beppino is captain and co-coach with me,
gets advice from his father, so there's always
lots to discuss. He runs the family vegetable
stall in the market below Rialto. His father
was the coach, but is in grief over the death
of Beppino's mother. Beppino and Franco were
late starting training for that reason, but
seem okay. Beppino is an irrepressible little
bugger, stocky wee guy, perfect half-back
physique, loves talking rugby, is steeped in
it from his father I guess and knows damn near
as much about it as anyone I know. Franco is
different, still stocky but taller, cascade
of black curls and beard, Che Geuvara but
better looking, wants to talk politics not

rugby. He's the other serious communist in the
team, with big bad Domenico. God knows what
Stalinist or Mao splinter group Domenico is
part of, but Franco's party calls itself Lotta
Continua, the struggle continues, the struggle
never ends, which says it all really: while
the rest of the communists are celebrating
Berlinguer and the Communist party finally
getting a share of power in the June elections,
these guys are calling it a cop-out. Franco and
Domenico believe in revolution, not evolution.
They don't want to see the communists sharing
power with the Christian Democrats, whom
they believe are corrupt and unprincipled.
They believe that sharing government with
the DCs will taint the communist movement by
association. When I ask Franco what sort of
revolution he's talking about, is it blood
on the streets, he tells me that I shouldn't
believe everything I read in Time magazine.
Franco's not as unattractive as that makes
him sound: true he wears a red bandana when he
plays, but when he smiles, those white teeth
flash through the black beard.

Beppino's a smart little operator on the
field, a good distributor, whereas Franco
is very direct. He tackles and runs like a
kamikaze pilot, so he's a great guy to have on
my shoulder. But he seldom passes, not because
he can't but because he won't. On Sunday he ate
- that's what they say here - mangiato - a try

by not passing when he'd beaten his marker on
the outside and only had to draw the fullback
and pass, to me back on the inside, or to
Massimo on his outside. When he went to ground
with the ball and we lost the ruck, in the heat
of the moment I called him a selfish bastard.
He took me aside after the game and explained in
that soft reasonable voice of his that far from
his action being selfish, he'd held on to the
ball and run into the opposition rather than
pass as a political statement of communist
strength and integrity. Well, what the fuck do
you say to that? I've never seen that addressed
in any coaching manual.

Beppino says his father is broken by the loss
of their mother and so he's helped in the stall
by Franco, if he's there. Franco's studying
Chemistry at Bologna Uni, so he's away during
the week quite often, but not as often as you'd
think for a full-time course. There's always
shit in the paper around the universities,
faculties being occupied here in Venice and in
Padova, riots on the street, hits on banks and
barracks by the Red Brigade. I don't understand
all the ins and outs of it, but to listen to
Franco, he goes to Bologna for meetings of his
cell of Lotta Continua, I never hear him talk
about his chemistry degree.

Franco wasn't at the market this morning,
but their sister Cinzia (chin, I've got to
remember, not sin), was. First time I've met

her. She's unusual looking for round here, five or six years older than Franco and taller with dark red hair, probably hennaed or whatever they do. She speaks English with a bit of an American twang, probably because she thinks it's hip. I asked her if she'd ever been to the States and she said no, but she's been to a lot more places than Beppino. I've been bloody nowhere, says B, someone's got to run the bloody stall! He calls her Tess. When I asked her what I should call her, she said Cinzia. Beppino said I should call her Tess. She told me Tess is short for Testa Rossa, Red-head (so I guess the hair colour is natural). Beppino said bull-shit, Tess is short for Testa Calda, Hot-head. They had a stand-up row in dialect - all I could understand were bits of the swear-words I know, cazzo (cock), culo (arse), figa (cunt, which doesn't seem to have the same currency in Italian - women use it quite often, who would never blaspheme), stronzo (turd), etc punctuated with a lot of blasphemies, God's a dog, madonna's a prostitute. The customers were being ignored but didn't seem to worry, enjoyed the spectacle, and a couple of the other vendors joined in and as far as I could see, Cinzia was proving every second that she was Testa whatever. Not many people out-talk Beppino. He gave up after a while and they started serving customers again, but still muttering away to the customers about each other. Cinzia had

quite a queue of mainly men in front of her and
didn't give a shit, just chatted on to whoever
she was serving as if there was no-one waiting.
She doesn't look like she belongs in the market
- she was wearing la moda, but it's the men's
style, which is kinda uni-sex - black winkle
pickers, tight blue stovepipe jeans and grey V
neck with a stiff light blue collared shirt.
She had a man's tweed jacket she took off when
she put on a leather apron. I 'd never seen
her at the stall before, but she knew what she
was doing. Afterwards, when she was having a
smoke, I asked her how her Dad was. It was a
stupid question, just something to say, because
Beppino had told me that he was drinking too
much and wouldn't come out of the house. Cinzia
looked at me with green eyes, and asked me if I
knew her father. I said I'd never met him. Ah
well, she said. He's, how would you say it,
pretty fucked. She said it just like that, only
she said fuck-ed. He's pretty fuck-ed. She had
green eyes, did I say that. Or sort of browny
green. With a bit of gold or something maybe.
Though when I try to picture her, I'm not
sure. I can see a weird likeness between her and
Franco, the wide cheek-bones under the cascading
hair, but not much between her and Beppino,
except for the verbals.

Clare tried to temper her sense of triumph. It didn't vindicate
her actions, but there *was* a woman. For some reason she no

longer felt outraged on behalf of her mother. She leaned over his beaky mask and whispered, 'Cinzia. Chinzia. Is that how you say it? Tell me about her. Please, Dad. Speak to me.'

There was no change in him. She stood and stretched and crossed to the window. She closed the slats, then pulled up the blinds so she could see the moonlight shimmering off the glossy leaves.

It has to be her.

Gemona, 1945

38

The Nazis were leaving partisan corpses hanging on butchers' hooks on trees and under bridges and arches as a deterrent. That was how they found Charlie. They almost walked into him the night after it happened.

The hook under the chin was a slow way of dying and a man might scream out many names before the spirit left him. Charlie had known a lot of names, his own, Charlie and Carlo Farinelli, for a start. Then there were Joe Lamont/Gianni Lamonza, and Harry Spence/Rico Zanardi and Luca and Beppi Bonazzon and Gigi Zanardi and the other ten men in the 8th Brigade of the Garibaldi Nationalists and their staffetta, *courier*, Donatella Bonazzon. And all the people who had helped them, hidden them, fed them.

If the Gestapo major, Il Pazzo, The Madman, had heard those names from Charlie, he would have lined the Bonazzons and Zanardis up, even old Nonna Isabella and little Paola and Leo, and shot them against the walls of their own houses, then burned both houses to embers. Or maybe he'd make them watch their houses burn down before he shot them. But Joe knew that Charlie hadn't named any names. When Il Pazzo had put his hook into Charlie, he was already dead.

* * *

Blowing up the railway bridge over the Orvenco River had been an Allied priority for some time, judging by the number of times the British bombers had tried to hit it. Joe had heard the roar of the engines and the whump of the bombs, but every time, come morning, the bridge still stood. The surrounding mountain peaks made it a difficult target. The message had come down from British intelligence via Major Ferguson, a kilted Scot up in the mountains behind Gemona, that the Garibaldis should finish what the RAF could not. But the orders never took account of the moon, which had become the Garibaldis' enemy as they tried to take advantage of the night.

Darkness was their friend, the blacker the better. That night it was a full moon on white snow: it might as well have been daylight. As Harry and Joe worked their way down the riverbed towards the concrete arches of the railway bridge, they could see the glint of helmets and rifles up on the steel superstructure. Donatella had cycled past the bridge yesterday so they knew it was manned by stormtroopers, with sand-bagged machine gun emplacements at both ends.

The moon left strong shadows along the bank, which they tried to take advantage of. It was impossible to eliminate all sound: the large pebbles sometimes moved and clicked under their feet, but the winter torrent took the sound away. In summer the Orvenco pretty much dried up and any approach along the bed would have reverberated to those above.

Harry was leading as usual, wearing a combination of victims' clothes that he thought appropriate for the occasion:

a Wehrmacht tunic, the knee-length breeches he'd taken from the Slovenians, with lederhosen borrowed from Marisa's uncle up in the Brennero and a dead stormtrooper's boots. He no longer wore his Slovenian cap. After one of their ideological discussions in the hayloft, Luca had taken the cap off Harry's head and handed it to him. The message was clear: it was sacrilege for a man of Harry's political naïveté, if that's what it was, to wear the red star. Harry shrugged but got it, and Joe never saw him wear the cap again. Tonight he was wearing one of Gigi's berets, which he'd stick in his pocket when they got close to the enemy.

Harry had urged the Garibaldis to tog up in enemy uniforms when they went out. 'There might be a night where Jerry catches a first glimpse of you and thinks you're a friend and that split second might be enough.' He told them it made no odds if they were caught in civvies or a German or Republican uniform, they'd be tortured and shot anyway.

But, for Luca, the Garibaldis could not on principle wear Nazi or fascist uniforms, and he tried to insist that Harry change his vocabulary: the Italian militia they were fighting were *fascisti*, not *Republichini*. Luca had fought for the International Brigade of the Republicans in Spain, and the name had been stolen by the fascists, just as they'd stolen the black shirts worn by the heroes of Isola dei Morti, like his father. He also told Harry he'd fought alongside Germans and some of them were honourable soldiers.

'Noi combattiamo i Nazisti,' he said. *We're fighting Nazis.*

That fine distinction meant nothing to Harry as far as Joe could see. He was still fighting Jerry.

That night, for some reason Joe couldn't fathom, there were just the four of them: Luca, Harry, Joe and Charlie. Joe wasn't sure why the other Garibaldis weren't there, whether they'd deliberately not been told of this attack. Was there suspicion of a leak? He could think of no other reason why their complement should be so reduced for one of the biggest and riskiest operations they'd attempted.

Harry was reading contour, giving hand signals to Joe, carrying the explosives. It had gone like clockwork: they'd got to some willows a hundred yards downstream and waited for the diversion they'd planted in the rails on the other side of the bridge. Harry had counted it off on his watch until they heard the explosion. There was no time to assess the German reaction; they had to assume it had got their attention. It was so precise these days with the new pencil detonators supplied by Major Ferguson that they'd started their hunched run towards the arches almost before they heard the device go off.

They made the concrete arches undetected and could hear the consternation above them. Joe's fingertips searched for the small indentations at the back of the arches where the join in the mould had been, taped the explosive in there and set the timers. Four arches. They knew there was no chance of getting back the way they'd come and instead they found some moon shadow close to the bank, checked their weapons and waited.

When the small arms fire from Luca and Charlie began they scrambled up the bank as quickly as they could. At the crest Joe saw a German officer, back to them, gesticulating and shouting to two stormtroopers manning the machine gun emplacement at the eastern entrance to the bridge. In the time it took Joe to absorb what he was seeing and aim his rifle at the officer, Harry had raked the machine gunners with his short-barrel Mauser and ripped the officer in half as he turned with his pathetic pistol.

'Ndemo via!' shouted Harry and they did. Joe had time to see the machine gunners draped dead over their weapon like fawning lovers as he followed Harry, weaving along the road as the bullets from the other end of the bridge carved the air beside them.

They dived into the copse of trees they'd scouted earlier and climbed to a vantage point where they waited a matter of seconds before Luca and Charlie arrived. Luca had become adept with a tommy despite his one arm, but wasn't usually called upon to fire it much when all the Garibaldis were involved. Charlie still had one of the rifles Harry had taken from the Slovenians. Harry asked Charlie to lead, he'd take the rear. That was pretty standard but asking Charlie to exchange weapons wasn't. Charlie was happy enough to grab Harry's semi — maybe it was out of ammo — and they began climbing. They knew they had about ten minutes' start before the Germans got themselves organised with men and dogs and they knew by now how to make the most of it. There were still bullets spattering through the trees sending splinters and twigs flying, but you'd have to be unlucky to be hit.

Charlie was unlucky. He took a bullet in the nape of the neck and was dead before he hit the ground. A man who was never lost for a word died without a sigh. Joe pitched forward beside Charlie and tried to turn his head to see his eyes, pleading with him to say something.

'He's a goner,' said Harry, pulling Joe up by the collar. Joe tried to stay down with Charlie, but Harry hauled him up to his feet and pulled Joe's face around to his. 'Get a grip, or you're gone too.'

Harry, still holding Charlie's rifle, switched it over to his back and grabbed his Mauser semi out of Charlie's dead fingers.

Joe looked across to Luca, standing impassively. Luca just shook his head once. 'Andiamo,' he said, as Harry pushed Joe between the shoulder blades with the butt of the Mauser and Joe stumbled forward and nearly fell.

39

They worked through the low hills behind Artegna, turned at the first flash of fire as the bridge went up, then heard the roar. They stood there for some time in awe of their work.

'Fergie'll be pleased,' said Harry and they pushed on through scrub that dropped snow when they brushed against it, as they moved round the mountain behind Gemona and began climbing towards Monte Canin.

In the early hours they saw a couple of recently burnt-out houses ahead. They'd learnt that the safest place was often where the fascists had just been, so they circled the house that seemed to have the least damage. The roof was still smouldering but Luca thought the stone walls would hold and they'd be safe enough.

The bodies of the families who had lived there lay in the snow by the stalle wall. There were eight of them, two men, two women and four children, the oldest about ten. The men had had their voice boxes cut out as a sign that they had talked, or hadn't. Joe asked himself what they could possibly have known or done, but then, in this war, there was no logical cause and consequence. Whispers in the right ear were enough to decide who lived and who died. It had become a charter for pay-offs, for settling scores, even for coveting thy neighbour's goods.

The animals had been incinerated in the stalle and the smell of burnt flesh was pungent. They couldn't be entirely sure that it wasn't also human. The fascists had cleaned out the cupboards and meat safe but the heat from the embers was some comfort and they lay down under the huge table in the centre of the family room, making pillows of their ammo packs. Sleep came quickly for Joe but so did the nightmares of El Mreir and the *Nino Bixio*. The sky was aflame with metallic fire and roaring like a lion when he woke to the roof collapsing in on them. The burning rafters hit the floor above them first and that gave them enough time to dive out into the snow.

As dawn broke they climbed higher towards their rendezvous with Major Ferguson, and came across another destroyed house, drawn to it by their hunger. This one was still burning and they guessed that the fascists weren't far ahead of them.

About a hundred yards away Harry stopped, so Joe and Luca did too. They'd seen enough to trust Harry's instincts: he was often aware of danger before anyone else. Once it had been a squad of stormtroopers waiting for them in the bushes on a track they often used to get back to the Bonazzon farm. Like here, there'd been nothing to see or hear. If Harry saw and heard things that others didn't, Joe reasoned it was because he was more alive. As Joe and Charlie got worn down by living like hunted animals, Harry was in his element. He saw himself as the hunter, never the hunted, happy in a war with no boundaries, no hierarchy and very few rules.

Joe and Luca watched Harry circle the farmhouse like a dog, and step back sharply when the front door was pulled open from the inside. A tall, slim Republican lieutenant came out, carrying a kitbag. He'd probably seen something valuable when his squad was setting fire to the place, put it aside and come back to get it. He pulled the drawstring on the bag, threw it onto his back and then staggered a couple of steps under the weight. By the time he'd regained his balance Harry's hands were at his throat, and he went down on his knees like a lamb. The bag was full of dried meats and cheeses, treasure indeed here in the mountains where starvation was insidious. Maybe that was all the bodies lying in the snow had been killed for.

When the lieutenant regained consciousness Luca cross-examined him, sitting in the snow. Name, number, battalion, all this would be useful to the major waiting up the mountain. A big part of what Donatella did on her bike was recording division insignia, giving Ferguson a picture of who was moving through the pass, to and from Austria. The lieutenant, who must have been a bit older than Joe but younger than Luca and Harry, told them he'd like to join the partisans, that he'd often helped them when he could, that he'd been pressed into service with the Republicans. As the Allies got closer, this was a refrain they were hearing a lot.

Luca was a good listener. As the man told them he'd tried not to do any harm to anyone, Luca didn't interrogate him about the trail of dead and tortured contadini they'd followed across the side of the mountain. When the lieutenant asked what would happen to him, offering to help them in any way he could, Luca turned away, picked up the kitbag.

'Stai tranquillo,' Harry said. 'Potresti aiutarci, certamente.' *You'll certainly be able to help us.*

Some of what the lieutenant was telling them might be the truth and Joe felt sorry for him: as soon as he'd seen his impeccable uniform and height, he knew the man was dead. As the man relaxed, Harry carefully removed the black cap from his head and almost tenderly touched his temple.

'Hai visto questo?' he asked. *Have you seen this?* Harry produced a Feldgendarmerie gorget that he'd taken from the neck of a German military policeman he'd killed on a bridge roadblock months before. It was Harry's most precious trophy, a linked necklace in machined steel holding a breastplate or brooch of an eagle caught wheeling in flight, displaying swastika tail feathers. He'd told Joe it reminded him of the hawks from home. Joe suspected the gorget might have killed more fascists than Harry's Mauser in the time he'd had it. Now he dangled the gorget before the man like a snake charmer.

The lieutenant must have had some acquaintance with the Feldgendarmerie, for there was a moment of recognition and fear, before Harry put the swastika'd eagle against the man's Adam's apple and tightened the steel chain, forcing it back into his throat. As he slumped backwards into his killer's embrace, Harry was already unbuttoning the man's pristine tunic so that he could strip him before the corpse stiffened in the snow.

40

They found Major Ferguson in his eyrie on Monte Canin, a large cave that had been his first refuge when he'd been dropped by parachute at the beginning of winter with, from what Joe had seen, a kilt, a rifle and a radio. Since then he'd consolidated his position with further drops of men and munitions.

By the time Luca and Harry and Joe got there, Fergie'd already had radio reports from photo-reconnaissance aircraft that the bridge had been knocked out, blocking rail traffic north and south along the flats of the Tagliamento, the main corridor between Vienna and Venice.

Fergie was of the same ilk as Harry and Luca, a tough bugger even to have survived that first couple of weeks up here on his own, and a man of few words, particularly when it came to praise. 'You boys deserve a gong for this wee bugger,' he said. They'd split the contents of the fascist lieutenant's kitbag with him. Joe wasn't sure whether Fergie was referring to the bridge they'd knocked out or the salami the size of a bazooka barrel he was holding.

They knew the major and his unit didn't stay up here, that like them he moved between the safety and rigour of the mountains and the food, warmth and danger of the plains. He never volunteered information on where he was, only the co-ordinates for their next rendezvous, mostly up here on Monte Canin, where the cave had become a safe storehouse for arms and explosives. Fergie had never asked exactly where they lived either. The fewer details they knew about each other, the safer they all were. But from what he let drop they knew that when he wasn't up on Monte Canin, he went to the area around the town of Nimis, one of three villages, with Attimis and Faedis, which had been burnt to the ground by Cossack troops under the direction of Il Pazzo.

Fergie had made it clear to them shortly after his arrival that he was there to assist them with behind-the-lines sabotage and intelligence gathering: he wasn't there to get them out. Charlie had asked if he could let Allied Command know that they were still alive so that their families could be told, but Fergie had refused to broadcast their names on his radio because it was 'too risky'.

As usual, over a cup of tea made out of boiled snow, he gave them an update of how the Allies were progressing. He'd cheered them recently, particularly Charlie, with news of the US 1st and 3rd Armies winning the Battle of the Bulge. Luca had drawn satisfaction from the Soviets taking Warsaw, even though he'd fought against them as a sergeant in the elite Italian Alpine Division at Kharkov and been horribly burnt by rocket artillery from a Katyusha. For him the Soviets were the vanguard of the new communism, and he gloried in their success.

The progress of the Italian campaign always seemed more problematic. The German army hadn't ceded one yard of territory easily and Italy's terrain made for natural defensive lines that were difficult to breach. Fergie reckoned the Italian campaign would end up taking more infantry lives than any other action in the west. In deference to Luca, he was careful not to include the Russian front in the comparison.

It was through Fergie that they knew about the hard slog of the Div through Cassino and across the Sangro River. Florence had been taken last August, just before Fergie was dropped in. He'd told them about the running fight between Shermans and Tigers across Tuscany. The Kiwi Shermans had knocked out at least five Tigers during the advance, but casualties were huge.

Joe had managed to find his voice to say that his brother Dan would be in one of those Shermans. Did Fergie have access to the published casualty lists? Fergie said he didn't, and that was the end of it. Maybe he didn't want to take up valuable radio and battery life with such stuff, or maybe he didn't want to risk rocking their boat with bad news, but Joe had had to hold his tongue and accept that until the war ended his name wouldn't be on any Red Cross list of prisoners and that if Dan had somehow survived those Tigers, he would probably think Joe was dead.

Even before Fergie arrived the Garibaldis and other partisan groups could feel the Germans being compressed into northern Italy by the Allied advance, an angry scourge of black ants being pressed back into the plains and mountains of northern Italy and scouring the land for vengeance on partisan scraps.

This war of shadows was so different from the war he'd seen in North Africa, vicious and brutal and almost as arbitrary, but somehow preferable. Joe got no comfort from the men and women and children he'd seen killed but he could at least remember every person he'd shot and why. That seemed important. It seemed more honest and human than what had happened in North Africa when impersonal metallic fire burned legions to cinders. At least he'd thought so until he saw Charlie cut down from behind.

Joe noticed that Harry no longer talked about getting back to the 'real' war; he seemed perfectly content with the one he was in. This war had no hierarchy, few orders to follow, no rules of engagement, no hanging round waiting for British tanks to turn up. This, he told Joe, was exactly the sort of war Kiwis were made for. No more following orders from dickhead generals into suicide assaults like Sidi Rezegh and Ruweisat Ridge. Harry was comfortable taking orders from Luca because, despite all his communist rants, he was a warrior who'd been tempered by fire, and despite his horrific wounds he still showed the same fierce joy for the conflict as Harry. 'Fuck all that communist stuff,' Harry told Joe, 'true brotherhood is forged under fire.'

In this war, Harry knew exactly where the enemy were — dappertutto, *everywhere* — and that seemed to suit him. Joe was tired of being hunted but that had never been how Harry saw it. In his view, he was the hunter because he knew where the enemy was, but they weren't sure where he was. Though the Germans certainly had their suspicions.

Il Pazzo had heard something and put one and one together. The Gestapo had reissued the poster of the capitano neozelandese and his off-sider with the scar, and put a large figure beneath it, which kept changing. It had gone from 350,000 lire to 500,000 to 750,000, a lot of money for peasant families struggling to the end of a long winter. And they had Harry's new name. *Rico.*

Luca had done his best to make sure any local fascisti kept their heads down, but much of the talk wouldn't have been from them. 'Rico' was fast becoming a local legend through word of mouth. Though Luca was the boss and had learnt to operate a tommy gun one-handed, he did nothing without Harry's okay, because out in the field Harry was in charge. He could read contour better than any local and his sixth sense about the location of the enemy was infallible. And when the bullets began to fly Harry became calmer, if anything. Dan had been a boxer and had told Joe that anyone could be a clever mover in front of a punch bag. Dan had given boxing away because he couldn't think straight once the punches started hitting him.

Today, over the cuppa, Fergie told them that the British 8th, with the Div and the US 5th, Charlie's old outfit, which had spent the worst of the winter dug in along the Gothic Line just south of Bologna, were just weeks away from the last big push. 'I'm nae a betting man,' said Fergie, 'but I'd be prepared to make a wee wager that this will be your last winter here.'

He talked about their next target. The Gemona marshalling yards had one steam locomotive left and if that was taken out the German troop movements would be severely compromised. Fergie acknow-ledged that Il Pazzo was a mad dog and taking terrible reprisals, so his demise wasn't an order but more of a wish.

Joe waited for Luca or Harry to tell Fergie that Charlie had been killed, or for Fergie to ask why Charlie wasn't with them. The subject never came up. So when Luca and Harry went into the cave to load up with explosive and detonators Joe found a moment with Fergie and told him they'd lost Charlie Farinelli at the bridge.

'Poor bugger.' Fergie didn't seem surprised at the news.

'Can you get word to someone? Now that he's dead, his name doesn't matter, does it?'

'No can do,' said Fergie.

Joe grabbed his sleeve as he went to turn away. 'Get me out of here, sir. Please.'

Major Ferguson looked surprised at the request. 'You can't go yet, son,' he said. 'There's work still to be done. But you'll be out soon enough.'

* * *

With ammunition from Fergie, they retraced their steps down the mountain and spent the night in another house abandoned to the stench of burnt flesh. They'd got a bottle of red from the major and shared it over a feast of cheese and sausage warmed by a small fire on the kitchen flagstones. Joe ate and drank and said very little, which wasn't unusual, so Luca and Harry continued teasing each other with the debate they'd begun shortly after meeting nearly eighteen months ago. Luca was fighting for a better world; who or what was Harry fighting for?

This time Joe didn't even feign interest. He didn't care any more about their rationales for what they were doing. After the attack on the Orvenco bridge, Harry had swapped his submachine for Charlie's rifle. The bullet Charlie took in the back of his neck was from his own rifle. Luca had colluded. Harry may have fired the shot but Charlie's execution had been planned by both of them.

Fergie had said this would be their last winter here. It was those words and Charlie's death that had forced Joe's hand onto the major's sleeve. Before that moment he hadn't considered leaving.

He remembered last September seeing the first golden leaf flute in the air. He'd watched that leaf all the way to the still-warm earth and his heart had fallen with it. It wasn't just the prospect of a third northern winter. It wasn't just the way the Nazis and fascisti stepped up their rastrellamenti and seemed to want to burn houses and spill blood to keep themselves warm. That first leaf had fallen just as he'd learnt that his love for Donatella was hopeless.

After they'd eaten their fill of meat and cheese and drunk the wine they slept under the table again. In his sleep Joe inhaled burnt flesh and fumes of cordite from old dynamite and detonators. In his nightmare he saw the first leaf from last September fall right through the fiery sky of El Mreir and land gently on Charlie's face.

Next day they dropped down to the plains and waited until dark before following the path that took them to the back of the Bonazzon farm. They never went straight to the houses when they came down from the mountains, but unloaded the gear and explosives into the cave they'd burrowed into the side of the hill up in the vineyard and spent the night there.

It wasn't until next morning that they saw Charlie swinging on the meat hook in the entrance arch to the farm.

41

Bepi's face seemed to have been drained of blood. Il Pazzo himself had come to turn them over. It had been a rastrellamento unlike any other they'd suffered. After going through the hayloft and stalle with bayonets, the Gestapo had taken their frustrations out on anything in front of them — the mattresses on the beds were ripped apart, the bedsteads broken, dressers tipped over, drawers kicked to pieces, and in the kitchen they'd snapped every stick of furniture and smashed every piece of glass or crockery.

'They told us not to touch Carlo,' said Bepi. 'They said they'd be coming back for him.'

Donatella asked them if Charlie might have said something to the Gestapo before he died. Joe felt absurdly relieved at her question: it confirmed she hadn't been in on Charlie's execution. Joe realised that was also why the rest of the Garibaldis hadn't been there covering the bridge: Harry and Luca had decided to kill Charlie and they didn't want the rest of the brigade in on it. Luca at least was honest and said there was no chance that Charlie had told Il Pazzo anything.

They were clear about the message The Madman had left them. 'Lui sa,' said Bepi. *He knows.* He said Il Pazzo had asked detailed questions about where the one-armed son was. Bepi had told them he was with a girl. When they asked him what girl, Bepi said he didn't know, that a son Luca's age who has served his country in North Africa and on the Russian front does not tell his parents too many details of romantic entanglements. Harry thought it probable that the stormtroopers on the bridge had caught a glimpse of Luca's empty left sleeve as he and Charlie had opened up on them. A man shooting a tommy gun with one hand was a fairly obvious idiosyncrasy, which is one reason Luca had stayed in the background of any firefights until now.

The Zanardi house was marginally less affected so they helped Nina and Marisa and Donatella clean that up first. Nonna Isabella was sitting silently in the only unbroken chair, her hands on the shoulders of Paola and Leo, who sat stone faced at her feet. Joe and Harry set to with the others until Gigi told them he was more worried about the Gestapo coming back than he was about cleaning up. They took his point and reluctantly went back to their burrows above the vineyard.

* * *

Joe lay beside Charlie's empty slats in the main cave and tried to piece it all together, how everything had become so personal and vicious. Harry was further along in a separate burrow but all his clothes were hanging here like ghostly mementos of their past three years: Don Claudio's cassock, One-Eyed Jack's cap with the red star, the Wehrmacht tunic, his collection of boots, and now the black kepi and full uniform of the Republican lieutenant.

Building the cave and the burrows had been Joe's idea. When Luca and Harry had first put their heads together it was fairly obvious, even to warriors like them, that they didn't have the numbers or the firepower for direct confrontations, so the Garibaldis set out to harry and hamper the local Nazi war machine. Gemona was an important junction for men and materiel coming down through Austria: it made sense to blow up railway lines, points, trains and bridges. Their first attempt had been an ambitious attack on the same Orvenco bridge. Back then there was no one guarding it, but even so it had been a disaster.

Joe's assumption that everyone around him knew more than he did had cost them dearly. He'd said nothing as the homemade dynamite sticks were taped to the underside of the rails. When the fuse ignited the basting cap and the dynamite blew, there was much noise and fury and the rails themselves were twisted, but the bridge remained in place, as a squad of stormtroopers proved by running back across towards them. As the partisans tried to melt into the darkness along the river track, the man who'd set the charges was carrying an extra stick he'd thought was superfluous. As he was sliding down some shingle the stick exploded and he and the man behind him were blown to smithereens.

Back at the Bonazzon kitchen, the gloom had been pervasive. They'd lost their first men in action to their own blundering. Angelo and Toni had wives and children. Joe told Luca that if he'd seen Angelo put the stick in his jacket pocket he would have said something. In the mine at Ngapara, Captain Nimmo had insisted that the sticks were never taken out of their wooden boxes until they were at the blasting site, and great care was always taken in placing and packing the sticks in the holes they'd drilled, because dynamite was sensitive to movement and shock, and if it was old it wept and degraded and was even more dangerous. By this time, Luca was looking at him with great interest and Joe feared he'd been insensitive.

He tried to backtrack. 'Maybe,' he said, 'the formula you use here is different, but . . .'

'What formula did you use?' asked Luca.

'Three parts nitroglycerine, one part sawdust,' said Joe, 'and we mixed in a bit of sodium carbonate.'

'We can get nitroglycerine and sawdust,' said Luca. 'Where would we find sodium carbonate?'

'Senti,' said Joe when he saw where this was going. *Listen.*

Luca cut him off. 'Tell us what you want and we'll get it for you.'

Now that Joe had time to think about it, that's where Charlie's end had begun, in a local leather factory that used the chemical they wanted. They'd broken in easily enough and Charlie had pointed out, once they'd loaded the truck with the chemical, that there was all this empty space on the tray and all these cured skins inside the factory. They'd filled the truck with pelts and taken off. Charlie had found a buyer for the pelts in town, flogged them off and brought the money home.

What Charlie did with the pelts was a forerunner of what he did with nitroglycerine. The Garibaldis had found an old fellow who had connections to a tunnelling contractor and could get them nitro. He'd wanted payment, but the Garibaldis had no money. Charlie said that wasn't a problem. He talked to the old man and persuaded him to take tobacco as payment. It was like gold — he could make a lot of money.

'But we have no tobacco,' Luca pointed out.

Charlie said there were tobacconists all over town who would like to help the cause. Luca had his doubts but Charlie was right, in a sense. He and Luca simply walked into a tobacconist and handed over a scribbled IOU from 'Il Governo Democratico dello Stato Futuro d'Italia', and took what they wanted. In the retelling, Charlie made it sound easy, though he admitted they'd produced their guns as the tobacconist looked up in surprise after reading the note.

Spain and Russia had made Luca a hard bastard. Early on

he'd shot and killed a known fascist in his home in front of his wife. The message to the Chi lo sa's was obvious, Stai zitto. *Keep it zipped.* The Gestapo were no longer the only bully boys in town. And the tobacconists had heard the bush telegraph and said nothing.

Joe knew that dynamite had to be dry and not allowed to freeze, so the first thing he asked for was safe storage. His every instinct said cave, and Bepi, Gigi, Luca, Harry and Charlie spent several days at his direction extending a natural buca at the end of the property where it rose to the hills. The good soil excavated was barrowed to the maize fields, and the stones and clay to the vineyards. Rocks were kept to cover the floor, then they brought lengths of flat timber to lay on the rocks so there was air between the ground and the boards. Anything stored there was off the earth and dry. They built a wooden trapdoor for the entrance and covered it with one of several heaps of rotting vine prunings that were scattered across the hillside.

Joe carefully stored the nitro and blasting caps and fuses and chemicals, then constructed a low bench out of rocks and boards that he could kneel in front of. He used a couple of old bowls from Nina's kitchen for soaking the nitro and sodium carbonate into the sawdust, before he wrapped the dry mixture in white baking parchment from which the pitch and tar had been removed. He tried to keep the dimensions of the cylinders to roughly the same size as the ones they'd used in the mine at Ngapara — about eight inches long, an inch and a bit in diameter and weighing about half a pound. He reckoned if he used the same formula in sticks of roughly the same size, he might be able to work out how many he'd need for any given job.

They'd used the concrete electricity pylons as practice.

Joe remembered how they'd looked for the natural flaws and fissures in the coal seam to drill the holes, into which they'd pack the dynamite. They couldn't drill the concrete of a pylon, but Joe felt the small indentation running down the back, a join in the mould the makers had poured the concrete into. Trial and error was possible in the early days because the pylons weren't guarded, but Joe had got it about right from the start: the first pylon was blown out of the earth.

Joe had gradually refined the power he needed so he didn't waste precious explosive. They'd blown up so many pylons that the Nazis began to replace them with timber, and these the Garibaldis had attacked with saws. Once Joe got the timing right, they'd knocked out railway lines, points, signals and two locomotives on the railway.

Joe's cave set a precedent for the other partisans, who needed places of their own to store arms, ammunition and, occasionally, themselves. The Garibaldis all developed a cave or a sump, the location of which no one outside the immediate family knew.

As Gianni Lamonza, the name he'd been given by Donatella, Joe came to be held in higher regard than he'd ever been as Joe Lamont. There was huge satisfaction in being part of a team. For the first twelve months, until Major Ferguson parachuted in, they were masters of their own destiny. Much of what they did depended on Donatella's intelligence. She would cycle past the potential targets and give very precise descriptions to her brother of the German presence and avenues of approach and escape. Luca decided what targets when, Joe decided what they needed to do the job, and Charlie would go out and get whatever they needed. On the night, Harry's job was to get Joe and his box of dynamite to the target and back out again, and the partisans under Luca provided cover and diversions.

Harry had worked out hand signals he and Joe could use in close proximity as they crept or crawled forward. One black night, Joe had missed the flat hand that said, *Stop. Lie low.* Harry's hand, strong, dry, found Joe's in the darkness and pressed it flat against the earth. Joe had lowered the box of dynamite and lain silent on the ground for what seemed like minutes. He could hear nothing but his own careful breathing, until a German patrol crept right past their noses. Harry's hand bunched Joe's into a fist and they crawled forward again. In the blackest of nights Joe stopped even trying to look, just followed that strong, dry hand clasping and releasing his, like flashes of torchlight through the darkness ahead.

By night, they all hung together on a thread of absolute trust. By day, Joe watched everything gradually fall apart.

Treviso, 2014

42

She was woken at 4.06 a.m. by her iPhone burping. She took a moment to realise where she was, quickly checked on her father, then opened the text. *Im so srry babe. Cn u evr 4give me? S.*

Auckland was three hours behind, tomorrow, so 4.06 here would make it just after one o'clock in the afternoon there. Sarah would have finished her Zombie session and maybe she'd had a glass of wine and seen her own reflection in the bottom of the glass. *Srry?* This was a woman of thirty-one who, like Clare, had completed an LLB. *Cn u evr 4give me?* Clare felt like texting back: *4get abt fcking my hsbnd, btch. i hate U 4 ur txt-spk.* Or ringing her up and screaming down the phone: *Say something real to me, girlfriend! Tell me why you did it? Did you slip in the lotus position and accidentally impale yourself on Pedro? Was ripping me off in your fucking stars?*

Sarah believed in astrology. She had plotted her stars and moons down to the minute of her birth and maybe believed that the only reason she fucked her best friend's husband was because Scorpio was in its fourth moon. How could anyone with half a brain believe in that shit when the reality of stars and black holes and the universe was so much more interesting?

Though, she corrected herself, if Renzo, Mr Infinity, was to be believed there were many realities. And who was she to doubt a man with a doctorate in physics, even if he was probably dumbing the whole thing down for her benefit? Some of the things he'd talked about last night in that bar beside the spring-fed waters of the Sile kept coming back to her: the limits of human imagination; that the sub-atomic world was stranger than anyone could imagine; and that anything that is possible, no matter how unlikely, will happen all the time.

Where did that leave the improbability of astrology? Maybe there *was* something in it. And since it was entirely possible, not even unlikely, that people fucked their best friends' spouses, maybe Clare could one day find it in her heart to forgive Sarah. But first she'd have to grow up and apologise in a language that was recognisably adult.

What did Sarah think would follow from forgiveness — that their friendship would continue as before? To truly forgive did you have to also forget? Clare didn't think she could ever forget. Particles might by nature misbehave while no one was looking — maybe that was the human condition in microcosm — but when they misbehaved were the particles still recognisably themselves? She must ask Renzo. But forgiveness was beside the point: Clare would never again be able to look into Sarah's lovely brown eyes and see the person she used to know, the person she thought she knew. Clare could only just imagine a day when the cheating and the fraud might be forgotten, but not the betrayal of character that had allowed Sarah to do those things. That was fatal. That was what made it unutterably sad. She'd lost her best friend forever.

Nicholas had at least tried to apologise face to face. He'd surprised her as she watched him walk up the path to her father's house. He'd lost so much weight. She could recognise what she'd once seen in him, that exotic olive-skinned hirsuteness that also described Renzo: the opposite of her own colouring, the sensual contrast of her skin on theirs.

He'd tried to kiss her in the European way on the porch when she'd opened the door — at least she'd assumed that's what he was planning — but she'd stepped back and waved him through the door.

'Okay,' he said, 'I understand. Where's your father?'

'Out.' He'd advised her against seeing Nicholas and had made sure he wasn't there when he came.

'I always got him,' said Nicholas.

He meant *liked. My father never got you*, she felt like saying. *He warned me against you.*

Nicholas had been in conciliatory mode, and she'd been grateful for that. She'd offered him coffee; he'd asked for tea, herbal. So unlike him. She hadn't wanted him to get settled in the sitting room so she'd placed the cup on the breakfast bar in the kitchen and stood in front of him, implicitly challenging him to get on with it and say what he'd come to say.

'I wanted to say I'm sorry for what I did, so sorry. I wanted to tell you that to your face.'

'Is that it?' she'd asked him. She didn't mean to be rude, but she couldn't believe the man she knew had come here with that solitary card to play. He'd looked disappointed. The spaniel eyes had pleaded with her. They'd always done the trick in the past.

'I understand,' he'd said again. 'You're entitled to feel the way you do. I behaved like a total dick.'

'That doesn't begin to describe what you did—'

'I know, I know. I don't expect you to forgive me but I want you to understand something. It wasn't the real me that did that stuff, babe.'

'What?'

'Well, of course it was me, but it was the addicted me, the coke-head me. The money I stole from the business I didn't spend on stuff for myself, it went to feed my addiction.'

She'd felt like asking him for the name and address of this third party, Adam Addiction, so she could sue *him* for the money she'd lost.

'The business was us,' she'd said. '*You* stole from *me*.'

'I want to you to know that I've gotten help, that I'm clean.'

'I'm pleased for you.' She couldn't understand why he was telling her this. 'I thought maybe once you knew, you might find it in your heart to forgive me. It's not as if I profited personally from the fraud.'

'What?'

'In the sense that I was stashing it away,' he'd added quickly. 'It went straight up my nose.' He'd held his palms up like a supplicant. 'I've got nothing.'

She'd watched his seminar, recognised the tells: eyes engaged, palms open. *See, nothing to hide.* This was a sell. Nicholas was closing. She knew what he was doing, yet still felt the pull.

'You'll have half the house. That's more than you deserve, but I'm not fighting it.'

Nicholas had put nothing into the matrimonial home. Clare had ploughed in everything she had: her savings and the proceeds of her one-bedroom apartment — half a million. And they'd borrowed another half million. They'd planned to do the house up and either flick it or keep it, depending on babies, but nothing had happened — Nicholas had always been too busy to even discuss it, and the business was too fragile to risk borrowing any more. And she hadn't been able to get pregnant; she'd thought maybe it was all those years on the pill. So now, four years on, the house was valued at 1.5 million and they might get more, and Nicholas, having put in nothing, neither dollars nor effort, was going to walk away with half the equity, $500,000, while she would get exactly what she'd put in less inflation. In what kind of perverted legal perspective was that fair? And as the marriage fell about her — the very day before her father had tried to console her by saying, 'At least there's no child, Clarebelle' — she found out she was pregnant.

'Okay. But does it need to come to that is what I'm saying?'

That had been a shock. She'd believed he'd take the money and run. Maybe he'd thought it was good business to stay. Her father wouldn't last long, and she was the sole beneficiary. Maybe he'd thought if they stayed together for a while, he'd get a half share of that too. Had she imagined those eyes appraising the rooms as she'd ushered him in? Making a quick valuation of what he could gain by putting in another couple of years' hard yakka with her?

He'd held his hand out to her and said, 'Babe', with those pleading eyes. 'We were so good together. Come here. Come to me. Give me a hug.'

That's what forgiveness meant, she'd realised: a sympathy fuck for starters. *Say hello to Pedro.* He looked pathetic. Contemptible. The cocaine admission simply confirmed his weakness. She'd thought she'd have so much to say to him, she'd rehearsed so many lines. But when he was finally sitting there right in front of her, easy meat, none of it seemed worth saying. 'I'm not buying,' she'd said.

'Babe!' He'd managed to look mortified. 'As if!'

She'd known what she had to do. 'Go. Get out.'

Once he'd known his play hadn't worked, he'd become petulant, then angry. 'I thought you'd be grateful!' he'd shouted as she'd slammed the front door in his face.

43

In those few moments, standing white-faced inside the door, listening to his steps down the path, making sure he'd gone, she realised that the baby would mean Nicholas would be in her life forever. She'd have to see him regularly, consult with him over life choices for another vulnerable human being, give credence to his opinions as if she had respect for them, watch him attempt to inculcate his values as if she didn't have complete contempt for them.

Since then he'd gone on the offensive. The bastard had used the shiny-panted suburban sole practitioners for his contract flipping, *Oh yes*, but when it came to his own matrimonial property he'd gone straight for the jugular: Sheila McLintock QC, a big-haired blonde who'd made her name getting huge settlements for wives betrayed by rich husbands, and was now the go-to legal pundit on television. *We note we have not received a reply to our last e-mail. We look forward to your response by return.*

In the matrimonial property file her father had brought all the way to Venice there would be the note he'd written to her, the one that ended, *That's my final bob's worth, darling.* Except that it wasn't. Underneath in his own handwriting he'd scrawled: *This isn't advice I would give to any other client, Clarebelle, but here it is: on balance, and with apologies to John and Paul, Let it Go.*

Was that what they called dry humour in legal circles or just wet? He could at least have got the name of the song right. What had happened to the hard-arse from 4 October 1976?

Tomaso was crying after the game. The
opposition loosehead was boring in and he
did nothing. He's only 19, still got his
baby fat and plenty of it. I told the ref who
did nothing, then warned their loosehead,
who gave me the old Non me ne frega un cazzo
bullshit. So I told our second rower Domenico
if he did it again, whack him. Next scrum
the guy bores in again and Big Dom hooks him
through the second row with one that comes
all the way from Tokarahi. So obvious, even
that blind bastard of a ref saw it. Domenico
got sent off. We lost again. After the game,
Tomaso was in tears because he thought he'd
cost us the game and that was true, though
I'd never tell him that, he's just a kid. But
I got the guys around me and told them a bit
about rugby etiquette. If you pull my jersey
or obstruct me or step over the fine line,
you get whacked. That's the way it goes. It's
not personal. If you let someone obstruct
you and do nothing, you may as well wqlk off
the field because you've been intimidated and
you're no good to anyone. But you choose your
moment. I looked at Domenico, sitting naked
on the bench, his huge shaggy head and beard.
Not in front of the fucking ref, Domenico! E
allora quando? When then? he asked. Fuck what
was I going to say?

Rumour has it that Domenico is a comunista
di base, one of the extreme left. The Red

Brigade is whispered, but if he is, no-one
here would know, except maybe Franco. Everyone
seems to be a socialist of some persuasion, but
it's almost like this year's fashion for most
of them, the political version of the winkle
picker shoes, tight stove-pipe jeans and V
necked jerseys they all wear. Not Domenico. He
wears workman's jeans, steel capped boots and
sleeves rolled up over huge fucking forearms.
Some of the guys are scared of him, they tell
me he's been to gaol, they didn't say what for.
Domenico seems to know their fears, sometimes
shouts out Bomba! just for the hell of it,
then pisses himself as he watches them cringe.
Bomba!

I'm telling this guy how to take care of
himself on a rugby field? I'd started it, so
I had to finish, otherwise I've made a brutta
figura of myself and the respect is gone. The
scrum breaks up, I told him. The ball goes
left or right, that's where the ref is looking,
that's where everyone is looking. Ah, says
Domenico, with a big grin breaking through his
beard. Si, Dio can', he roars, Yes, God is a
dog! Capito!

Christ, what have I done.

This man was telling her not to fight?

If you let someone obstruct you and do
nothing, you may as well wqlk off the field

```
because you've been intimidated and you're no
good to anyone.
```

That's the kind of advice she wanted to hear. She wanted to somehow, some way, stick it right up Nicholas. How could she let it all go when he'd shamed her so badly she didn't want to walk down the street in her own town?

And yet. If she had the baby forgiveness would be essential. She'd done the matrimonial files for her father when she'd graduated and seen enough custody and access battles not to wish that on any child. If she didn't have the baby, Nicholas would know nothing and she'd be able to move on, as per her father's advice. Which had been given with no knowledge of the fact that she was pregnant, but made letting it all go even more important . . . *Didn't it?*

What if the baby was a boy and looked so like Nicholas that she couldn't bring herself to love him? Could such a thing happen? What if she loved the baby but he wanted custody? What if it was a girl?

She wished she and her father had both talked about their secrets in Venice. The fact that he didn't know about the baby, and now never would, made it less likely she'd have it. And if she wasn't going to have it, she could see a way of punishing Nicholas. Her response to Sheila McLintock QC could be very simple: *I'm pregnant.* Nicholas would probably get very excited about that. He was the sort of man who might fight tooth and nail to pay no maintenance for his child, but whose ego and vanity would delight in the prospect of a little Pedro. Two weeks later, she could send another e-mail: *I'm no longer pregnant.*

Could she be that cruel? Could she do that and still ask her father to forgive *her*, if she got the chance?

She had to calm herself and start again. There seemed to be no change in her father. If he came to, she was going to get him into one of those wheelchairs down in the hideous yellow reception and push him through emergency arrivals to that little knoll of grass and trees across the driveway. When she'd arrived yesterday afternoon there'd been a guy out there in slippers and dressing gown pushing his drip along on wheels, dragging on a fag. Not a good look but a human look. As soon as her father came out of the coma she would do it. And say what she needed to say, how much she loved him but not how terrified she was of a future without him. While she was saying what she needed to say he could have a last look at trees and grass.

She put her cheek close to his to feel those butterfly wings of breath. 'Please come back, Dad,' she whispered to him. 'If only for a moment or two. *Please.*'

44

<u>October 11, 1976.</u>
A draw at Brescia. Feels like a win. Maybe this
is the turning point.

One weird thing. I could never understand
the strange words my father would yell at his
dogs between whistles. Ndemo via! Dai figa!
Avanti fioi! Fermati stronzo! Va in mona de to
mare! Now I hear his words during the game, the
players exhorting or cursing one another. He'd
trained his dogs in Venetian dialect, no wonder
no-one else could work them.

<u>October 25, 1976.</u>
On a roll, beat Roma at home in the mud and
Padova away. Feels like a different team -
problem now is keeping them from thinking
they'll win without working for it.

<u>November 8, 1976.</u>
A narrow loss away at Torino. Our prep wasn't
great. On the way here, our bus was overtaken
on the autostrada between Padova and Verona by
a police Alfa with siren and ordered to pull
in to one of those autogrill places. There were
armed Carabinieri with Uzis waiting for us.
The officer walked up the aisle of the bus and
pulled out Big Dom and then Franco. Both went

quietly enough, though you could hear Dom's Dio
can's outside the bus. I was stunned that no-
one said anything. If this happened at home,
the team would be challenging the cops, giving
them heaps probably. I guess the difference is
the Uzis. So we sat there until Dom came back.
We clamoured to know what the Carabinieri asked
him? Where I was last night, said Dom. No-
one else said anything so dumbo here asked the
obvious. What happened last night? The Brigate
Rosse had another funding drive, said Dom. Hit
a bank in Padova killing two security guards.
Bomba!

We waited another five minutes for Franco but
the Carabinieri put him in one of the Alfas and
took him away. He turned up later that night
at the hotel. When I asked them what they had
wanted from him, he just smiled and said, News
from the real world, caro.

I'm the naive straniero so I asked him
whether there were any connections between
Lotta Continua and the Red Brigade. He took
his time replying, his eyes carefully checking
who was around out on the garden terrace. Well
I guess that's what he was doing. He said
Lotta Continua and the Brigate Rosse were both
elements of the radical left, so yes, it stands
to reason that there might be some connections.
I must have looked a bit shocked. Every second
day, I said, there are headlines about the Red
Brigade maniacs blowing something up, killing

innocent people. Franco didn't respond for a
bit, probably wondered whether it was worth
wasting words on me. Then told me that in
the last war the resistance had fought the
Nazis and Mussolini's fascists. They blew up
railway lines, electricity pylons, factories,
they tried to disrupt by whatever means they
could the organs of the corrupt fascist
state. He said his father had been one of these
partigiani, and they are now regarded as heroes
of La Patria.

You listen to Franco and it all seems so
logical. Lo Stato is so corrupt that the
populace has no faith that it can do anything
to improve their lot. So they don't pay taxes
and they look to other groups in society to
help them and protect them. This is why the
mafia flourish. And this cycle of cynicism
feeds on itself to the point where right-
thinking citizens must take up arms against the
corrupt organs of the state to stop the cycle.

Later, in the hotel room, I realise I've just
heard a manifesto of violent revolution. At the
time, sitting there listening to Franco, it
sounded more like a blessing from St Francis of
Assisi.

His sister Cinzia challenges him all
the time, tells him the real world is too
complicated for him, he has to reduce it to
silly self-serving slogans. The only bit of
that which seemed to bother Franco was the

last. In what way self-serving?

You're as vain as any fascisti, she chides
him. Try a different coloured bandana at least.
What colour would you have me wear? Cerise, she
says. And away they go. It sounds as if they're
about to come to blows, but they never do and
it all just blows away, like the rain storm
you think will never end.

Clare tried not to be impatient. She stood up and stretched. She
was tempted to race forward through the pages, skim the on-
field battles of San Pietro. She wanted to see whether her father's
heart had been burnt by La Testa Calda, but she owed it to him to
try to understand the full picture, even though his diary was so
fragmented that it was like joining the dots. There'd be nothing
for a week or ten days, then a big cluster of days together:

<u>November 30, 1976.</u>
I've learnt that everything here is political,
but it's not often as overt as this.
    After practice tonight, the boys had their
hqir dryers out - I've never seen so many
hair dryers in a changing room - for soft-
voiced girls waiting outside in the dark,
bums pressed against the warm stone where it
abuts the hot water cylinder. I'd finished the
practice by talking to them about the next
game, the Calabrians on Sunday, tried to keep
them grounded, to concentrate on the little
things each of them had to get right to make a
team performance. I've kept my speeches shorter

after my gaffes with dialect. I thought they
were calling each other fiori - flowers - which
seemed strange, but I thought when in Venice. So
in my team-talks and on the field I'd be saying
Come on flowers, climb into them! Finally, Aldo
took me aside last week in the bar and said he
didn't know about the custom in NZ, but here in
the Veneto, men didn't call each other flowers.
Turns out they were saying fioi, which is
dialect for guys. There've been other fuck-ups
which the language course in Perugia couldn't
have prepared me for. The dialect for lui, him,
sounds like you. So they're talking about you
you you, which I think is me me me and it turns
out to be about him him him.

Anyway, after the showers, I'm dressed
and ready to head for Aldo's, when Domenico
comes over, still towelling his balls and
says he needs to speak to me. Now. So we go
back into the steamy shower stall and stand
on the boards. Big Dom's a fearful sight at
the best of times but naked he looks like the
closest thing I've seen to Cro-Magnon man,
huge forehead and covered from head to foot
with brown fur. He tells me he wants to jump
at number 7 in the lineout on Sunday, not at
number two, where he usually jumps. Why? I
ask. Because we play the Calabrians, he says.
I tell him he jumps at 2 because he can explode
into the air quickly and has great timing.
That's sort of true but it's also because he

270

can't actually get off the ground. At 2, it's
more of an all-in wrestle and Big Dom excels.
At 7, we need someone who can actually jump.
Si, si, dio can', he says, when I give him my
censored explanation, but these are Calabrians.
When I ask him what difference that makes,
he says that Calabrians are strange people,
terroni, poor but fascist, the quintessence of
stupidity.

I still don't really understand where this
is going and I'm worried that if Dom gets
excited, the acoustics of the shower will
broadcast whatever he's going to tell me right
through the dressing shed. What difference does
jumping at 7 make? I ask. He tells me that
the Calabrian captain jumps at 7 and he must
oppose him. Why? Because otherwise I might not
get to see him face to face - he plays loose
forward, I am buried in the tight. Why should
that matter? Big Dom has infinite patience.
Because, he says, the captain of the Calabrians
is a known fascist and I want to break his
arms, his legs, his neck, his head, I want to
break his balls so that he has to carry them
back to Calabria in his pocket.

My other home is Aldo's bar. I eat there most
nights, courtesy of the club. Good country
food. You ask for a bistecca and that's
what you get, a piece of steak on a plate.
The insalata is always separate. They eat
everything, small birds and what we'd regard as

weeds. Aldo's a strong voice on the dirigenti, the committee that runs the club and if I need anything, I ask Aldo. He's like the kind uncle I never had. His wife Beatrice is lovely, and the two boys are always in the bar too, with other kids. That's so different to home. The guys from the team drift in and out, either for a birra fresca or an aperitivo or to sit and eat with me. Tonight I told Aldo I needed to talk to him alone.

In the backroom, I told him what Domenico told me. I wasn't sure what to make of it. If it was anyone else but Big Dom, you'd take it as a bit of bravado. But Aldo pursed his lips, shook his head in sorrow and said we had to drop Dom from Sunday's game. He said that if Domenico felt that way about the Calabrian captain, the man's life was in danger. Fuck a duck.

December 1, 1976.
Franco was away in Bologna today, so Cinzia was helping Beppino at the market. Cinzia invited me to come with her to some do tomorrow night - I didn't understand exactly what it was, because before that she said her fidanzato couldn't come, that's why she wanted me to accompany her. After the word fidanzato, I didn't hear anything else. She's engaged. She's got a diamond cluster on one finger. I never saw it because I don't look for those things.

I've got no right to be thrown - I don't even know her.

<u>December 3, 1976.</u>

Last night, as instructed, I waited for Cinzia in Campo Santo Stefano. The sky had started dripping and the passeggiata hour was at an end, canopies being rolled up, chairs being stacked and chained, the god-awful roar and bang of the shop shutters coming down. Then the kind of silence you don't get anywhere else. Creepy - you know they're in there somewhere, but the shutters are closed, you might see a sliver of light. I read somewhere this is the real Venice, a place of conspiracy and brutal intrigue, where in the old days you didn't want to be wandering the dark alleys at night.

She turns up with Max, her fidanzato. I think he'd come to check me out. He's a big guy, kinda pudgy but dressed immaculately, tweed and brogues and cashmere scarf, looked every inch of what Beppino had told me he was: the son of an aristocratic Venetian family who had provided more than one Doge. I was in my best jeans and Max must have been reassured by what he saw: scruffy no-account. He was amiable enough and soon sloped off.

Cinzia took me under the arm and steered me towards San Marco then off to the left. She's doing straight-legged toe-hops down the steps of the bridges because her jeans are so tight she can't bend them at the knees.

We pass through a little square with a statue of a horse and rider. Cinzia tells me who the sculptor was and says it's famous because it's the first sculpture where the horse is moving, and because it's being ridden by a general with 'tre coglioni', three balls. He looks comfortable enough, considering.

I could have read that stuff in a tourist brochure, if I'd bothered. Venice is more or less what they say it is, canals, palazzi, gondolas, etc. which I've kinda walked past going oh yeah, that one, tick. I've tended to go straight to the market below Rialto, then go to a local bacaro in Santa Croce with Beppino and Franco when the market's finished. Could be a bar anywhere in old Italy, then I head back to Piazzale Roma, hop into the Opel and charge back across the causeway and up the plains to San Pietro. Last night was a glimpse of a Venice I could never have seen without Cinzia, and it was pretty strange.

She took me to a hall with old columns in front but plate glass behind, which opened up to an air-conditioned foyer of marble and carpet where mainly older people were removing expensive shawls and overcoats helped by uniformed attendants. Cinzia introduced me to a bald bright-eyed guy called Saul, a Fulbright scholar from New York. The guest speaker, says Cinzia. Not much I could say about that,

because I had no idea what he was to speak
about. Didn't matter, Saul talked non-stop and
it wasn't to me. He was so intense with his New
York spiel, weaving a web of words around us,
there was no way in, nothing to say. When he
was called away by a little guy with a white
moustache, Cinzia introduced me to a tall thin
blonde, Lady Phenella and her husband, Hartley,
who Cinzia maids for, and who had invited her.
They were polite and understandably completely
uninterested in talking to me - I got the
impression they'd been expecting Max - and made
for their seats as soon as they could. As they
went, Cinzia told me she was a 'Bloomsbury
bambina' and he was 'old Boston'. She had a
pithy little description of almost everyone,
as we watched the different groups filing
through the double doors into the auditorium.
That was the British Ambassador, and the two
behind him were 'Texan grandees' whatever the
hell that means, and the big old lady in the
kaftan with a walking stick on one hip and
a toy boy on the other was Peggy Guggenheim,
followed by 'bits and pieces' of exiled royalty
from Greece and the Balkans, fragile old ladies
and arthritic men who were princesses or crown
princes according to Cinzia, living in Venice
she said because it was as old and irrelevant
as they were. That last bit surprised me.

We got a seat at the back - I had to push
down on her shoulders to make her knees bend.

Saul, the Fulbright scholar was introduced
in English by the old guy with the white
moustache, as an urban meteorologist who
was going to talk about the horrors being
perpetrated on the old stone of Venice by the
pollutants raining down on it from Mestre and
Marghera. Saul rose and began telling us what a
pleasure it was to be spending a year in Venice
in the midst of such class and culture. Cinzia
sort of guffawed, and as he read the rest of
his speech - reducing whatever it was that
was happening to Venice to a series of bland
chemical reactions - I wondered whether Cinzia
was deaf. She hummed and hahed and muttered as
if she was the only one in the room or in a
sound-proof cage. At one stage, Lady P turned
and shot us a look that would have felled an
African elephant but which Cinzia ignored,
snorting shortly after when Saul said one of
Venice's problems was that it lacked the usual
countering effects of automobile emissions. The
moment Saul sat down Cinzia said 'Ndemo via'
and we bolted for the fresh air of a drizzly
Venetian night.

The cold air had no effect on Cinzia's fury.
Cretins! she said. Stranieri who understand
nothing! This straniero certainly wasn't going
to poke his head up. I waited for her to get
to wherever she was going and it was a pretty
strange place. Venice is a parched tongue,
she said. The lagoon is reclaiming it after

centuries of being denied. She might have been
quoting someone, a poet maybe, but writing that
now in black and white makes it seem a lot
weirder than it was at the time. The drizzle
was drifting in sideways like a heavy shroud
being held back by the rose glow of the street
lamps. We walked on cobblestones that glistened
black with a fluid skin that seemed to ruffle
and arch like wind on water.

She became calmer as we walked and she
talked about Venetians, the great adventurers
and traders of the old world who no longer
travelled. Franco and Beppino have been nowhere,
she said. Nowhere! She said it like it was a
place. She talked about the places she'd been
and it felt a bit like the hippy trail, Paris,
London, New York, Tangiers, Marrakesh and in
the lee of the Ponte d'Accademia she pulled out
a half-smoked joint and lit up. I had a toke
and passed it back to her. At uni I'd flatted
with a couple of guys who had put themselves
through off the back of the dak they sold, and
I found it was guaranteed to make me paranoid
then send me to sleep, so I stopped doing it.
Sure enough, I found myself becoming jealous
of Cinzia's history, all the men who'd touched
her, the friends she'd made, the places she'd
been without me.

I said something stupid about free love,
as if I knew anything about it. Love is never
free, she said, putting one finger to her lips

as if I'd spoken sacrilege. Everything you do
in your life has to have meaning, no? Si or si?
she laughed. Si or si?

I didn't want her to stop talking. She had
a way of pronouncing every syllable of a word
with equal emphasis as she would in Italian,
like no-where-e and touch'ed and sing-ing-a,
and it sounded kinda Shakespearean or Biblical.
On the other side of Accademia she thanked
me for calming her - I'd done nothing, said
next to nothing - and kissed me on both cheeks
but not pecks, sort of breathing me in like a
hongi. My head was still reeling as I waited
for the vaporetto. Or buzzing. It might have
been that joint.

45

December 6, 1976.

The Calabria game yesterday was a disaster. I'm
not even sure what happened but it had fuck all
to do with rugby. While we played that game we
were doing all right, still ten points up into
the last quarter. Then the crowd got confident
and started chanting Ter-ro-ni! Ter-ro-ni! at
the Calabrians. Big Dom was up there in the
concrete stand but I'm not sure he had anything
to do with that - he would have been the one
chanting Fa-sci-sti! Fa-sci-sti! Anyway, it
was a red rag to a Calabrian bull. It seemed
to remind them who they were and bring out all
our guys' fears. I know we Southerners pretend
to hate Aucklanders but that's just mild
parochialism compared to what goes on here. I
think terrone just means farmer but it's come
to symbolise something evil and misunderstood
or even unknown. These were Italians we were
playing, at least as far as I was concerned.
They looked like Italians, spoke like Italians,
but for our guys they might as well have been
from Mars. Anyway, once the terroni chants
began, the Calabrians got furious, we got edgy
and they smelt our fear and really began hooking
into us. When the ref - probably fearful of
the home crowd - disallowed a perfectly legit

Calabrian try, it really sent them over the
top, and most of our guys just caved. Beppino
was still plucky, but got badly nailed trying
to run the blind, and Franco stepped in to save
his brother and came reeling out with a split
cheek. Could only have been a boot or fist.
The sight of blood didn't help our guys any,
and we gave away a soft try shortly after that
even the ref couldn't find an excuse not to
give. They booted it high from the re-start and
Franco, red blood and bandana flying, ran it
back at them, straight up into their pack, no
sidesteps or dummies. He got done, but just got
up and did it time after time in that last ten
minutes, often coming in on the angle to take
a short ball from his brother because no-one
else in our team wanted the attention that came
with possession of the pill. I tried to take
the pressure off him by doing the same and felt
the boots searching for my head as I hit the
ground. When I got up, Franco told me to back
off, this was their fight. He was bleeding from
his nose by then too.

I didn't - don't - really understand what
the fight was about, but I wished to hell we'd
had Big Dom there because we were never going to
win it without him. With 5 minutes to go, they
got a push-over from a 5 metre scrum, converted
and that was the game. When we kicked off,
no-one was looking for the ball anymore. It
bounced ignored into touch while the forwards

shoulder-checked and punched and kicked each other. There was an all-in brawl which the most of the backs joined. The ref blew the pea out of the whistle but couldn't stop it, saw there was no chance of getting the lineout formed so blew for full time. The Calabrians threw their hands in the air and we all marched to the centre of the field to give the traditional three cheers for each other. I was bloody seething at the way we'd capitulated but led the three cheers for the Calabrians, and the Calabrian captain, the one Dom wanted to kill, led three cheers for San Pietro and then bugger me dead they all started hooking into each other again!

The crowd was still chanting Terroni! and had come down to the wire fence, which I saw Dom climbing over in his steel boots and khaki shirt. At that stage I decided my contractual duties were over and I headed for the dressing room, smiling and holding out my hand to shake whichever Calabrian came anywhere near me and saying Grazie in as foreign an accent as I could muster. On the way I saw Big Dom step into a melee, pretending to be the peace-maker - Calmati, calmati, Dio can! - and get grazed with a punch meant for someone else, whereupon he launched into them and there was skin and hair and Dio cans and porca madonnas and fascisti flying everywhere.

Later in the dressing shed, we could hear the Calabrians smashing benches, chairs and doors,

and when their bus pulled up, it was surrounded
by San Pietro fans who were baying for Terroni
blood. Poor old Aldo and the other dirigenti,
terrified I suppose that the club would be
banned, were out there with hunks of four by
two keeping our own fans back so the Calabrians
could board their bus and get out of town.

I'm not sure what the fuck I've got myself
into here. Our next game is against the
Sicilians in Catania, our last game before a
one month Christmas break. God only knows how
we're going to get through that.

December 7, 1976.
Franco asked me to come fishing in the lagoon.
He had a dinghy with an outboard tied up to
one of the little canals in Dorsoduro. Cinzia
was there too, big surprise, asking me what I'd
done to her beautiful brother. Franco's face
is a mess. One eye nearly closed, stitches in
his cheek and across his forehead. I thought
that's what Cinzia had come for, to call me
out for letting Franco get disfigured, but she
climbed into the dinghy with us and we buzzed
out through the Fondamenta Zattere and straight
across to Giudecca, through another canal and
out the back and round towards the Lido. I
couldn't see any rods or lines in the boat, but
there were spear-guns and wet-suits and scuba
tanks. Franco had a snorkel for me and q wet-
suit, but I didn't fancy the opaque cold of the

lagoon. Franco called out over the engine that
some of the lagoon was too shallow or too busy
to dive, but he knew a spot. When we got out
to his spot, closer to the Lido than Giudecca,
Franco cut the engine and Cinzia threw the
anchor over.

Franco began stripping off down to his undies
and Cinzia did too. I went to the bow so they
had room to get their wet-suits on and studied
the sea like I knew anything about it. She and
Franco are joined at the hip but not at the
brain. As they got their gear off and struggled
into their suits, they somehow from a standing
start got into a row about Cinzia's fidanzato,
Max, his pedigree.

From what I could understand, Franco was
saying that Max's family were frauds, because
they were given their title by Napoleon,
they weren't one of the old titled Venetian
families that existed pre-Napoleon. Cinzia
told him he seemed to be making the kind of
fine distinctions a true communist wouldn't
be interested in. Mid-argument, Cinzia kept
appealing to me as if I was the adjudicator, so
I had to turn my head to look at her. Had to.

So I've seen all of her. Her nipples are the
same dark red as her hair. In summer she looked
as dark as Franco, whose olive beauty doesn't
change. Now her skin is really pale and a
sprinkle of freckles is showing on the bridge
of her nose. Never seen anything more lovely or

exciting. But it's like looking at a Monet or
something. Drink it in: it might be something
you can love but it's not something you can
ever have.

After Franco flopped backwards off the boat,
Cinzia asked me to help adjust her weight belt.
She told me that if she married Max and became
una contessa, that would make a brutta figura
of Franco with Lotta Continua. Then before she
put her gloves on, she took off her engagement
ring and gave it to me to hold. She talks a
lot, impetuously, but her eyes are very quiet.
They study you. When she gave me the ring, we
were very close and she looked at me carefully,
as if she was looking for a meaning. Maybe
that's just how she is, or maybe I imagined it.

Once she'd rolled into the water, I sat there
looking out across the lagoon towards Murano.
There was no horizon between the islands. The
grey of the sky merged seamlessly with the grey
of the sea. It looked like molten metal, not a
living sea.

When he got back in the boat and took off
his mask, Franco looked awful. The mask had
left a red oval welt on his face and the mouth-
piece had split his swollen lip and he was
bleeding from it. His face looked pulped. I
was surprised that he'd surfaced before Cinzia
and left her down there, but that was partly
the point: he wanted to tell me that he wasn't
coming to Sicily. Looking at his face, I

thought I could see why - the stitches would inevitably be opened and his head would be a bleeding mess within fifteen minutes. But he wanted to make it clear that it wasn't his wounds that were keeping him from playing. This weekend was going to be a big one at Bologna, which now had a communist mayor. They were going to test his mettle with a manifestazione, and Lotta Continua were going to lead the occupation of the university. I deliberately asked him about his chemistry degree, how was that going? He's not slow. That brilliant smile flashed through his beard. Caro amico, he says, my pursuit of a degree is selfish careerism, whereas my work with Lotta Continua is about a better life and education for all.

Then Cinzia surfaced with a fish on the end of her spear. Not a very big one, but the fish had never been the point of the excursion. I know what Franco wanted from me, and maybe Cinzia was just along for the ride, but I've come to realise that everything is political here: everything has meaning.

On the way back, Franco was on the outboard, I was in the middle and Cinzia up in the prow shaking her hair dry in the wind. I was able to really look at her while pretending to be looking at Venice. How can you know what you want until you see it? If someone had asked me to describe my perfect woman it wouldn't have been Cinzia because I'd never met anyone like her. She's

beyond my ability to imagine her. I'd given her
back her ring, but she stuck it in the pocket of
her jeans. Did that have meaning?

Franco took care of the boat and Cinzia and
I walked back to the market with her fish.
I wanted to debrief the Calabrian game with
Beppino. When we were working our way through
the throng at the market, I could see him ahead
behind the stall with an older man, unpacking
vegetables behind the banco. I could only see
the top of the man's old-fashioned hat as he
was about to straighten up and look our way.
Cinzia was asking me about something and when I
looked back he was gone - well, going. Beppino
called out to him and so did Cinzia. Papa!
Papa!

So that was the old man, a stocky figure
melting into the crowd. Beppino and Cinzia had
no idea what had spooked him, maybe coming to
the market was a step too soon. Cinzia clasped
her hands to her heart, said he was fuck-ed
because his love for their mother had been his
life. She said that most men have love and life
whereas for women love is life. She wanted to
be loved by a man like her father, whose love
for his wife my mother was his life. And will
therefore be fuck-ed, said Beppino. That was
enough to launch an argument between them which,
as far as I could understand it, seemed to have
only a vague relationship to what they'd been
talking about. Who was closest to their mother.

Beppino made the case that if he was most like
their father, then his love for their mother
was also like his father's. He might have had
reason on his side, but he lost when Cinzia
burst into tears of grief. Beppino was instantly
remorseful, but Cinzia turned to me for comfort.
I drove back across the plains to San Pietro
with a wet patch on my shirt right above my
heart.

Gemona, 1945

46

Charlie had had the tobacconists in his thrall. He would carry a big basket about town, a few cabbages on top notionally for sale or trade, making his collections. He'd developed a limp to suit his story of being a distant cousin of Gigi who'd been wounded and couldn't get back through enemy lines to his home in Catania.

He would come back to the cave and boast that when one leg got tired he'd limp with the other and no one noticed. Joe wasn't so sure. The locals may not have noticed his changing limp but they could hear well enough and they knew where Charlie was from. On the few occasions he'd risked going into town to help Charlie bring the tobacco back, Joe saw faces full of unspoken resentment. Charlie seemed to believe that what wasn't spoken didn't exist. Trailing behind Charlie as he bounced forward on his exuberant limp, Joe heard that word again, usually muttered or barely breathed, *terrone*, aimed at Charlie's back like a dart.

When Joe asked Donatella what it meant, she said that it was a bad word used to describe people from the south. Joe wanted more but Donatella seemed increasingly impatient with his questions. She called him *tu* all the time now, but Harry and Charlie and all the partisans were also *tu,* so it had become meaningless. Joe consoled himself with the thought that she was equally impatient with her brother.

The hayloft above the stalle was closer to the fields and the cave than either of the kitchens, and easier to escape from if the fascisti came, so they would spend most of their winter evenings there, basking in the smelly warmth of the animals below. Luca seemed to regard Harry, Charlie and Joe as a captive audience and would try to inculcate them with the essential precepts of communism and the coming people's state. These exchanges would often turn into an argument between Harry and Luca, who was infuriated by the Kiwi's lack of any apparent political framework for what he was doing.

Initially Luca had been bewildered as to why someone could be so naïve about the fascisti, yet come so far to oppose them. He teased Harry: 'You rush upstairs from your cellar at the bottom of the world to fight for your colonial masters.'

Joe could see Harry bite his tongue. He usually took any opportunity to bag the Brits, but he was intelligent enough to know that wouldn't serve his argument here. Instead he told Luca he'd always been fighting for himself and his cobbers, that he'd only enlisted because he'd wanted a bit of excitement, an adventure. Luca thought Harry was joking, then became incredulous when he saw that he was, at least in part, serious. When pressed, Harry said the war was about 'good and evil, black and white, simple as that'.

Luca wanted to know what was evil about fascism, and whether Harry understood what it was, and why it was evil. 'Otherwise,' said Luca, 'you have no reason to be here except to shoot Germans.'

'Reason enough,' agreed Harry.

'But not all Germans deserve to die,' said Luca. 'What is the difference between a German who deserves to die and one who doesn't?'

'No difference if they put a uniform on,' said Harry.

It was an endlessly circuitous debate. Luca would become incensed with what he saw as Harry's simplistic obfuscation. Harry would tease him with that smile and tell him that where he came from it was all about doing. That if a dog didn't work or a heifer got sick or a ewe got too old, they got a lead pill. That was the way of the world. 'Jerry's a mad dog,' said Harry. 'Mad dogs need putting down.'

'Sì, sì.' Luca would then ask what Rico meant. What made the Nazis mad dogs?

'Adolf,' said Harry.

'What makes Hitler a mad dog?'

'You might have a better idea of that,' said Harry with his smile. 'He calls himself a National Socialist, doesn't he?'

Luca would become apoplectic about Hitler misappropriating the word socialist.

'Just goes to show,' said Harry. 'It's not what you call yourself that matters, it's what you do.'

Joe listened with interest but said nothing. It was one of the few times Charlie also kept his mouth shut. Donatella was the only one who had the courage to get between her brother and her 'cousin', usually on Harry's side.

She would ask her brother about the communist position on the emancipation of women. Luca would turn the good side of his face away from the light, and Bepi would put his head in his hands as his daughter harangued his son about the difference between theory and action: that Harry helped with the dishes and made his bed every morning, while Luca would not lower himself to do any housework because in his peasant heart he believed, just like all the rest of the men around here, that it was women's work. Donatella told her brother that his narrow ideological view was unrealistic and inhuman. And indeed there was something otherworldly about Luca in the soft lamplight of the hayloft. The burnt-plastic side of his face had no wrinkles or expression. He would sit there severe and still under Donatella's criticisms.

Joe noticed that her attacks on her brother usually came when Luca had been deriding Harry, whether simply because she'd had enough of her brother's cold ideological analysis, or out of some elemental sympathy for Harry. He didn't wonder until later how Donatella knew that Harry made his bed up in the Zanardi loft.

Harry spent most of his time in the Zanardi house. Marisa smiled when he called her 'Blondie', and he could even make Gigi laugh. For the children, Paola and Leo, 'Twinkle, twinkle little star' and 'A tishoo, we all fall down' seemed long forgotten as Harry showed them how to do magic tricks he'd learnt from Charlie. Joe watched the little boy become entranced by the charismatic straniero. When not at his lessons, Leo followed Harry around the campi, or to the implement shed, where Harry spent time hack-sawing off the muzzles of the Mauser semi-autos they'd captured, to eliminate the muzzle trap system that jammed too easily and corroded on dirty damp nights. Leo would sit patiently watching Harry work on the weaponry, or listen as Harry and Joe talked. Though he understood next to nothing of their rapid New Zealand speech, he did notice that one person's name seemed to keep coming up. Once he asked them 'Qui é questo Farkinell?' *Who is this fucking hell?*

As far as Joe could tell, the Zanardi house was happier for

the presence of a fictional son, whereas the real son's return to the Bonazzon household had changed everything for the worse.

Joe could understand why there were no more sympathetic 'poverettos' for him once Nina's own son came home so damaged. No foreign mother had stepped in to save her beautiful son. The worst had almost happened and she devoted herself to him.

Nina was the one person who didn't warm to Harry. Perhaps, Joe thought, she couldn't help resenting what the war had done to her son, while Harry seemed to sail through everything untouched. She'd tried to ask him about his family, but Harry had been vague and uninterested. Joe knew from his sisters' discussions about their beaus that they loved trying to put together the full picture of a man. In their case not knowing or knowing a little and guessing the rest had been part of the attraction, but Nina's perspective was that of a matriarch whose family had invited a dangerous stranger into their nest, a man who could at any moment of any day bring fire and death down upon them. She felt she had a right to know who he was.

Bepi seemed diminished by Luca's grim presence. Everything was more tenuous under the constant threat of rastrellamenti, and there were no more invitations to un po' di riscaldamento in the Bonazzon kitchen, though Bepi quite often brought a bottle of grappa up to the hayloft.

Joe would still help Bepi and Gigi in the fields when they were working far enough away from the road. After long nights in the hayloft Bepi seemed too tired to bicker much with Gigi, though sometimes they regurgitated the debates from the previous evening. Joe found Bepi's humane socialism easy to respond to. His ideal world might not, in essence, have been that different from his son's — one of equality and mutual respect, where accident of birth didn't give one person an advantage over another — but Bepi's way of expressing it emphasised the results, not the ideology. In Bepi's world everyone had enough to live happily and with dignity, with un po' di riscaldamento to help keep them warm.

These times in the fields with Bepi and Gigi were the best of it for Joe. They'd tell him stories from years before as if he'd been there, or assume he knew who they were talking about. To them he'd become Gianni Lamonza and they almost seemed to have forgotten that he'd once had a different name and life. Sometimes he forgot himself. His dreams were in Italian, but the nightmares were still in English.

That winter, as 1944 coldly expired into 1945, Joe noticed that the families no longer joined each other after dinner. The men and Donatella were often in the hayloft debating ideology or discussing plans, while Marisa and Nonna Isabella tended to the children in their house, and Nina sat alone in hers with her knitting and her thoughts. Maybe Nina saw before anyone else what was happening between her daughter and Harry.

Joe could understand why Donatella would like Harry — he was a less damaged and less ideological version of her brother. And he could see why Luca and Harry maintained a mutual respect, no matter how much they argued: they were both warriors. Harry was happy to accept Luca's orders because his experience as a sergeant in the elite Alpini gave him authority. And Luca seemed to understand that, just as Harry Spence had castrated pigs, put distressed beasts out of their misery, slaughtered and butchered sheep for home kill, shot dogs that didn't deliver, Rico Zanardi now found it meant no more when there were Germans or fascisti in his sights. After watching Harry at close quarters firing and under fire, Luca understood that his superficial motives for wanting to fight didn't make him any less of a warrior, any less unwavering. Joe could understand why Luca trusted that.

Charlie hadn't been so lucky.

47

From the beginning, Charlie had frequented the local taverna with Luca, Bepi and Gigi. Donatella occasionally went with them and Harry too, as Rico Zanardi, Gigi's oldest son and Donatella's cousin. The locals knew Gigi didn't have such a son and, if he had, he would have spoken better Italian than Rico. But Rico had an easy smile and a way about him that they liked.

Harry had to be careful because most able-bodied Italian men were at the front or on a train to slave labour camps in Germany. The locals had heard the bush telegraph on Luca, though, and if Rico was under his protection, that was enough to make them think twice before they said anything. The Luca they had known as a child and a youth wasn't the same man who'd come back from Spain and Russia.

Despite Luca's protection, Joe didn't go to the taverna because he lacked even the ghost of a story to link him to either the Bonazzon or Zanardi families. Luca had been as good as his word and had supplied Harry, Charlie and Joe with carte d'identità, but they weren't up to detailed examination: they were only ever supposed to be a sufficient distraction to draw a pistol or a knife and kill whoever was looking at them. And there was the poster that made Joe's scar so recognisable.

Charlie had used the local taverna to get his confidence up and had then ranged further afield. In one of the tavernas in town he'd befriended a young German lieutenant called Klaus, who was in some sort of administrative post. Charlie was quite open about his pal Klaus, said he was 'a regular guy' who wanted to 'get to know the natives'. Charlie saw all sorts of potential benefits from having a friend among the enemy and managed to convince Luca to meet the man.

That meeting at the local taverna early the previous summer had been a success. Luca spoke fluent German and Klaus was delighted to meet a genuine war hero who had fought the enemy on the dreaded Russian front. He was determined to share with Luca his worries and anxieties over how or whether German plans would succeed in stopping the Allied advance in its tracks. Klaus was also introduced to Donatella and Rico. Klaus's Italian was worse than Harry's so he was none the wiser about this cousin who spoke only incomprehensible dialect. Two nights later it became apparent that Luca hadn't been the only one to impress Klaus.

Charlie brought an invitation home from Klaus, requesting Donatella's company at a local dance. She protested but Luca had already seen that Klaus was useful and told her she couldn't refuse to go. Harry was laughing at her dilemma and Joe wanted to believe that it was this that did it: Donatella told her brother that she would go to the dance with Klaus if she could be chaperoned by her 'cousin' Rico. Luca considered that too dangerous but was persuaded by Charlie — he'd be there too, and he and Donatella could ensure that Harry's Italian wasn't too exposed.

Joe didn't know exactly what had happened at the dance but when Charlie got back to the cave around midnight he told Joe that Donatella had danced with Klaus but had eyes only for Rico. And her infatuation hadn't gone unnoticed by the German, who'd told Charlie at the end of the evening that Rico was lucky indeed to have a cousin who held him in such high esteem.

Joe had been trying not to notice how much time Donatella was spending at the Zanardi house. Paola and Leo's homework gave her every excuse to be there but Joe couldn't always be sure whether Harry was with her. Harry had a smaller burrow further along the hillside which was big enough to crawl into, but he used the main cave as a dressing room. He had to make sure he didn't leave any clothes or other evidence of his presence in the Zanardi house.

The night Charlie came home from the dance, Joe waited until he'd talked himself out. Charlie said Klaus loved his stories about America, which Charlie told him he'd heard from his relatives who'd emigrated. In his cups Klaus had told Charlie he might go to America after the war, that Germany was finished and a vengeful world would extract a high price from the Fatherland. Klaus was a dentist and was sure he could make a lot of money working on American teeth.

'He kept wanting to look at mine!' exclaimed Charlie. 'But I couldn't let him because he'd see work that he'd know could never have been done in Europe.'

So Charlie had kept filling Klaus with beer and schnapps and had obviously had quite a few himself in the process, as he fell asleep soon enough.

Once Charlie was happily snoring, Joe went out into the moonlit night and checked Harry's burrow. If Harry was there the door would be open to the night. But the pile of vine prunings hadn't been disturbed. Joe walked back down the track between the fields to the houses. There were no lights on in either house.

As he watched, the Zanardis' front door opened. Donatella closed it quietly behind her and began crossing the courtyard. She was wearing a floral print dress that left her shoulders bare and was barefoot, carrying her shawl and best shoes. Joe stood transfixed. If she'd looked his way she would have seen him in the moonlight. When she reached the middle of the courtyard she held her shawl and shoes to her breast with one hand and swept the other in a wide arc, and her bare feet followed the sweep of her arm. Joe realised she was dancing to music she was hearing in her heart. He had never seen happiness so pure.

He stood where he was long after the lamp in her room had flickered off. He couldn't drag himself back into the cave with Charlie and instead sat out in the vineyard on Bepi's wooden barrow and convinced himself of the rightness of Donatella loving Harry. The smile in Harry's blue eyes when he was happy. The power in that strong, dry touch. Joe had once thought he'd loved Donatella, but if that was true he ought to be feeling angry and jealous. The only emotion left to him seemed to be fear, a low-level icy dread that was almost unworthy of being called an emotion. It felt more like a void, a hole where feeling used to be. The terror of his nightmares of El Mreir and the *Nino Bixio* were almost reassuring, reminding him that he was still alive. But even they were receding and changing.

* * *

After Major Ferguson's arrival on Monte Canin at the end of summer, it had become apparent that Charlie was pretty much redundant. They didn't need nitroglycerine for Joe's homemade dynamite; it arrived in tins courtesy of Fergie, along with the detonator pencils that made timing easy. They didn't need any more tobacco to pay for nitro, nor money to buy weapons and ammunition: Fergie gave them whatever they needed.

With Fergie's explosives they blew up a munitions factory in Buia on the other side of the Orvenco. Then they crossed the snow-choked hills to Maiano to immobilise a silk factory making German parachutes.

Charlie couldn't help himself, asked Luca if they could take a good swag of silk back across the hills to Gemona. At the time, Joe had wondered why Luca had agreed: they'd had to battle through snow with the mule train to get to Maiano and lugging even silk back across the hills wouldn't be easy. Indeed Luca had said no but then, unusually, had changed his mind when Charlie began wheedling like a spoilt child. Maybe Luca just wanted to shut Charlie up, but most of the time he could do that with one look. He seldom spoke to Charlie or even acknowledged him and it had crossed Joe's mind that for all Luca's talk about the brotherhood of man and an Italy free of class and prejudice, he shared the same elemental suspicion and dislike of Charlie that Joe had seen from the townsfolk. Or it may just have been that Charlie was an American and a capitalist, and so obviously enjoyed being both.

So Charlie got his silk, which he took to town to sell to his contacts. When he brought the proceeds back to Luca, the notes were Reichsmarks not lire. Luca stared at the German currency for some moments, trying to come to terms with what Charlie seemed to have done. 'You sold the silk to the Germans?'

'Klaus,' said Charlie.

'Do you imagine the Germans won't know where that silk came from?'

Charlie said Klaus knew he worked through middle men.

'Don't you see?' asked Luca, very calm. 'To the Germans, *you* are the middle man.'

Charlie just shrugged as if it wasn't a big problem. Luca said nothing more, and in Charlie's world that meant the problem was over.

Perhaps it would have been if next day Joe hadn't discovered

Charlie's hoard under the slats of his bed. Joe had been trying to get rid of the stink of cordite that hung over everything in the cave from the old dynamite mixing days and had lifted Charlie's bedclothes off the slats to get at the floor underneath. There he found an old dynamite box full to the brim with lire and Reichsmarks. The box said that Charlie hadn't been passing on all of the proceeds from his deals, he'd been skimming, and it also said that the silk wasn't the first deal he'd done with the Germans.

Joe showed Harry before Charlie got back from town. Harry got Joe to put the box back where it had been. He'd said nothing to Joe but obviously told Luca. Yet neither man had spoken to Charlie that day, nor even that night, when Harry shot Charlie through the back of the neck.

* * *

Joe knew the Gestapo had arrived when Harry crawled into the cave beside him. Someone outside pushed the wooden hatch into place, then piled the vineyard prunings on top. He heard Donatella's voice say, 'In bocca al lupo.' *In the mouth of the wolf.*

Harry pulled a tommy down off the rack and began loading it. When he'd finished that one, he started on the next weapon, working his way along the rack. Joe understood that there was to be no surrender. That if they were discovered here they would die here.

That was no longer a shocking concept. Directed by Il Pazzo, the Nazis and fascists had come down hard on the partisans with the snow and ice of that terrible winter. They heard Il Pazzo had set up a direct relationship with the San Sabba prison in Trieste, run by a butcher called Colonel Globocnik, who had built an oven. Anyone of consequence taken locally now ended up at San Sabba. Code names were always used these days and the partisans had taken to carrying hidden revolvers so that they could shoot themselves if capture looked imminent. Donatella, the messenger between the various cells, knew more than any other single partisan, particularly since the other staffetta had become terrified and withdrawn her services. One night in the hayloft Donatella had broken down. She said she feared that she wouldn't be able to resist giving the Nazis information if they caught her. Luca had procured a cyanide capsule for his sister and thereafter she carried it with her.

Soon they heard voices that didn't pass on but stayed at a consistent volume. Joe and Harry knew that if the Germans were paying attention to this one spot, they must be discovered.

Harry didn't stop, just moved more slowly, loading weapons off the rack, but not pushing the bolts home. He had a line of loaded weapons along the ground in front of them facing the door. With a gesture he offered Joe first choice. Joe saw he was smiling, eyebrows raised. *How about this, eh?*

Presently, there was another sound. The soft splatter of liquid. A rivulet of urine trickled into the dirt under the hatch.

'Must have a bladder the size of an elephant,' whispered Harry.

The voices faded and they sat there in silence for a long hour, until they heard someone outside, removing the branches, quickly, carelessly. The hatch was thrown aside and in one movement, Harry rose into Donatella's arms.

'They've taken them!' she said.

* * *

Donatella told them that when the Gestapo burst through the door of the Bonazzon house, Luca and Bepi were standing there in full uniform, showing all their service medals: Luca as sergeant of the elite Alpini, Bepi in his black shirt from the heroics of Montello.

Il Pazzo was a small man with pince-nez glasses and a squint. Donatella thought he looked like a desk clerk or a Jesuit priest. He was initially taken aback by the uniforms, particularly when Luca told him that he hadn't seen any Gestapo in the battles he'd fought in North Africa and on the Russian front.

'Ha sbagliato, Luca,' said Donatella. *He made a mistake.* He'd shamed Il Pazzo in front of his men and now the little major would have to prove to them how ruthless he was. One of his men had pushed Klaus the dentist into the kitchen and asked him if Luca was the man he'd spoken to, the man who said that Rico Zanardi was his cousin. Klaus said it was, as Gigi and Marisa and Nonna Isabella and the children were brought across from their house.

Il Pazzo asked Gigi where this son of his was, where his papers were.

'There are no papers,' said Gigi. 'There is no son.'

Il Pazzo put his hand on little Leo's head, said 'But this is your son, surely.'

'My only son,' said Gigi.

Il Pazzo asked Klaus to describe Rico Zanardi.

'When Klaus had finished describing you,' said Donatella, 'Il Pazzo said they had other descriptions of this man Rico, and produced the poster.' He'd pointed to the capitano neozelandese and said, 'This is Rico Zanardi.'

'Loro sanno!' cried Donatella. *They know!*

Harry had been rolling and lighting a smoke while Donatella

talked. He'd always had first dibs on whatever tobacco Charlie had purloined. He was showing no particular alarm. When she exclaimed, *They know!*, he exhaled a cloud of smoke and asked how it had ended.

'They took my father and brother away, along with Carlo on the meat hook,' said Donatella. 'Then Il Pazzo patted little Leo on the head and said to Gigi: "Better one son than no sons."'

48

For Joe, whatever game they'd been playing was over. For Harry, it was just another move by the opposition, which had to be countered. The distress and anxiety of the Bonazzons and Zanardis washed over him like a wave on a rock.

In her son and husband's absence Nina held sway. When Harry tried to speak she cut him off with a curt 'Basta'. *Enough.* For Joe the message was clear. Go. Leave us alone. Don't bring us any more grief.

Harry was persona non grata in both households. Marisa, unlike her sister, was charmed by Harry, but the choice between her own son, Leo, and the interloper, was no choice at all. So Harry brought the bedding from his little burrow to the cave and put it on top of Charlie's. That evening he sat on Charlie's bed looking at the poster Il Pazzo had slapped down on the Bonazzon table. Harry seemed to be pursing his lips at the 750,000 lire sum, whether in approval or irony Joe couldn't be sure.

Joe was repeating that they had to go. Information had come from the CLN that Arch Scott had finally got his underground railway operating, that he was getting prisoners off the beach at Caorle into submarines. 'We've done the best we can,' said Joe. 'If we can get to Arch at San Pietro he'll get us off.'

'Our orders from Fergie haven't changed,' said Harry. 'What about that last train?' It wasn't like him to worry about following orders.

'We've done our bit,' repeated Joe. 'The war's nearly over — Major Ferguson said so. If we disappear, it'll be apparent to Il

Pazzo sooner or later and he'll let Luca and Bepi go.'

'You sure about that?' asked Harry. 'They'll get nothing from Luca. Bepi, who knows?'

*　*　*

Bepi came home that evening, and almost immediately sought out Joe and Harry in the cave. He was red faced and looked like an overstuffed sofa in his ill-fitting uniform, puffs of flesh straining between the buttons of the tunic. He seemed unsettled, found difficulty in saying what he'd come to say. He told them he'd been separated from Luca, then brought before the Gestapo major who wanted Bepi to take a message to Rico.

'I told him I knew no Rico, but he said he had no interest in who I said I knew or didn't know. But the message is the message, he said, and if it doesn't get through or if there is no answer, your son will be sent to Trieste to see my friend Colonel Globocnik at San Sabba.'

'What's the message?' asked Harry.

Bepi looked away, trying to find a way of answering. When he looked back at Harry, there were tears welling and he shrugged and said he was sorry, but there was his family, his son, Gigi's son . . .

*　*　*

That night Harry had a last smoke outside and settled beside Joe as if he hadn't a worry in the world. Joe lay there listening to Harry's gentle snore, wondering if he should take his own advice and try to get back to Arch in San Pietro. He'd created enough trouble here for Bepi and Gigi and their families by bringing

Harry and Charlie to them.

He was still awake when Donatella came. He woke Harry, who went outside with her. Joe thought he could hear Donatella sobbing and Harry making reassuring noises. When he came back in, his face was grim but he said nothing.

Joe must have found sleep because sometime later he was shaken awake by Harry, who was wearing the Republican lieutenant's uniform with the black kepi. He asked Joe to come outside. There was no sign of Donatella. Harry lit another cigarette. 'I'm going to see Il Pazzo,' he said, 'but there's something I want to do first.'

Joe was incredulous. 'You're handing yourself over?'

Harry looked up at the clouds obscuring the moon. 'It's a great night for it,' he said.

*   *   *

Harry's plan seemed simple enough. Gemona's last locomotive had begun working round the clock, and very slowly. The rails and points around the marshalling yards had been blown up and repaired so many times that the engine had to go carefully. It now pushed an empty coal wagon ahead of it to take the force of the blast in the event of a mine, which made it even slower. When it wasn't working, it was kept in a heavily guarded yard. Harry told Joe they didn't need to mine the rails this time, they could take out the engine itself.

Joe protested, but Harry made the point that if they made a big statement while Luca was in custody, just the two of them, no other partisans involved, there would be less reason for the Gestapo to think that Luca was the mastermind. 'Besides,' said Harry, 'Il Pazzo will be slavering for us like a rabid dog.'

There was no denying the logic. Maybe Il Pazzo would be so incensed he'd shoot them before he could torture them. After what he'd seen, Joe realised there was no point in worrying about being dead, it was all about how you got there.

He and Harry made for a cutting where they could see the marshalling yards. The engine was shunting rows of wagons from a siding off the main lines down into the yards. They waited until the engine came back for another row, then Harry walked up to the train in his Republican uniform and shot the German guard standing on the riding plate as Joe broke from cover, dodged round the front of the engine and came in from the other side. By the time he'd mounted the step, Harry had cracked the driver across the back of the head with his rifle butt and thrown him out. Joe quickly set the explosives as close to the boiler as he dared, broke the detonator pencil and jumped out. Harry stayed with the train for another fifty yards, pulling open the throttle.

Joe had made it back to the cutting by the time Harry jumped. When Harry picked himself up he stood and watched the engine gathering speed away from him. None of the workers in the marshalling yards had heard the shot or had any inkling that the train had been sabotaged, until they saw it bearing down on them and still accelerating. They scattered as the train began bucking and jumping over the uneven lines. Joe had set the timer for ninety seconds but there was always a margin and the engine got to the built-up part of the track first, took off like a long jumper, twisted sideways as it hit a low wall, blasting through it and down an embankment, where it turned on its back. The boilers hissed, then seemed to sigh in momentary repose before Joe's dynamite blew them up. It was like a fountain of steam and fire. If the crash hadn't been heard all over Gemona, the explosion certainly was.

49

After a job the partisans would take to the mountains until things calmed down, but this time Harry led them back down the track to the stream they used to put the dogs off their trail to the farm. Then he continued past the cave and down through the furrows of the maize fields towards the town, retracing the steps they'd taken that first night when they'd run from Don Claudio's betrayal.

Joe considered trying to talk Harry out of surrendering to the Gestapo, but part of him believed they were doing the honourable thing for Luca and the families who had given them refuge for so long. Maybe the end of the war would come quickly enough to save them, or whatever was left of them after The Madman took his revenge.

When they reached the road coming down from the town, Harry stopped, lit a smoke and surveyed the stone walls ahead of them on either side of the road. 'This'll do the trick.'

'For what?' asked Joe.

'He'll come,' said Harry. 'You take any outriders with the tommy, stop the car.'

'What?'

'I'll make myself known to the man himself.'

'I thought we were giving ourselves up.'

'Did I say that?' Harry took another drag.

'What if he brings a truck full of stormtroopers with him?'

'They'll come from the barracks by the station. Il Pazzo will come this way from his apartment in town, if he comes at all. I'm betting he will, after the train.'

Joe was used to being a step or two behind Harry, but this time felt completely misled. 'You said doing the train would tell them Luca wasn't involved with the partisans. Now you're saying the train was just to goad Il Pazzo? The train was bait?'

'Il Pazzo wants to meet Rico,' said Harry. 'That was Bepi's message. I'm making sure he does.'

Joe could think of nothing to say. He wanted to be gone. Harry knew it.

'You've got a choice, dog's balls. Help me get him, or run away. If you're going, fuck off now.'

Joe remembered Harry's eyes when he'd dragged Joe off Charlie. *Get a grip, or you're gone too.* Harry might let him walk, but he wouldn't get far.

* * *

As the sky went grey up behind the dragon's spine running east towards Trieste, they saw lights coming down the hill from town. More than one set. Joe had time to pray that one of them was a troop truck or carrier so that he and Harry could abandon this folly and slink back to the mountains. He'd resolved to get to Arch in San Pietro even if he had to run the whole way. That prayer went unanswered. The first set of lights was a motorbike and sidecar, the second was the Gestapo major's staff car.

Harry had Charlie's rifle on the high wall to the left of the road. Joe had the tommy behind the lower wall to the right. A slight bend to the left gave Joe a straight field of fire up the road, so narrow between the stone walls that the vehicles couldn't deviate.

At fifty yards Joe began ripping the tommy right and left and right across the sidecar. Harry had told him to go low for the engine and tyres but he must have hit the rider, because the motorbike slewed sideways and lurched into the wall before the SS in the sidecar could return fire. There was now enough room for the car to get through. That wasn't the plan. Joe had to stop the car. He stepped out into the road and ripped back and forth through ten degrees into blinding lights and roaring engine. He could see the radiator rearing at him before it began going sideways. Joe jumped left as it broadsided past him into the wall. Harry was right above him. He hadn't even lifted the rifle to his eye, but was pulling a piece of paper out of the inside pocket of his Republican tunic.

Joe could see past the car to the motorbike. The rider had been hit or had broken his neck going into the wall, but the SS man in the sidecar had adjusted his helmet and was retrieving his rifle. Joe killed him with another burst, then turned back to the car.

Harry had opened the back door and dragged a small figure in black out onto the road. Joe checked the front seat and found the driver slumped over the steering wheel but still alive. He pulled him out so they could keep an eye on him.

Behind him, Harry was shouting at the small man. He wore black boots and jodhpurs but had lost his hat in the crash and his glasses had slipped down below his nose onto the pencil moustache along his top lip. His breath was fogging the lenses as he whispered something. He had a holstered Luger at his hip but made no attempt to use it as Harry grabbed him by the collar and hauled him into a sitting position.

'Vuoi Rico?' Harry was shouting at him. *You want Rico?* 'Eccomi!' *Here I am!*

When Harry drew breath Joe could hear the man's whispers. 'Per Dio, per Dio. Aiutami.' *Help me.* Il Pazzo was an Italian.

And Donatella was right. Without his hat and henchmen, the Gestapo major who had brought so much death and misery to this region looked like a clerk. A clerk in fancy dress.

Joe was worried about someone coming, perhaps a truck of stormtroopers who might be following. The driver had recovered consciousness and was watching bleary eyed. Joe was concerned about leaving him alive to tell the story, but more concerned about having to shoot him in cold blood. 'Rico . . .'

But Harry was still standing over Il Pazzo, waving the poster at him. 'Soltanto sette centocinquanta mila? Per Rico?' *Only seven hundred and fifty thousand? For Rico?*

'Shoot the bastard, Harry, please!'

Harry put his rifle to the little man's temple. 'They reckon the difference between animals and humans is that humans have knowledge of their own death. I want to give this bastard enough time to know it. I want to see it in his eyes.'

'Please don't kill me!' said the little man in perfect English.

Harry smiled. 'That'll about do it.'

'Please! I can give you whatever you want!'

Joe wanted to ask him to free Luca, to promise to keep his animals away from the Bonazzons and Zanardis, but of course that would simply have confirmed their guilt.

Harry forced the rifle barrel into the little man's mouth, breaking rodent teeth.

Joe turned away to the horror on the driver's face, as Harry pulled the trigger. When he turned back, Harry had dropped the corpse and was reaching into the back seat of the car.

'What do we do with the driver?' asked Joe.

Harry had retrieved the major's hat from the back seat, was admiring the silver eagle and skull above the black visor.

'Let him tell the tale,' said Harry.

50

Joe woke with daylight streaming into the cave and Donatella kneeling beside him. 'Dov'è Rico?' she was asking, looking at the empty wire where Harry's stuff had hung.

Joe remembered Harry changing out of his Republican uniform when they got back just after dawn. He'd been expecting to go to the mountains but Harry had hung the uniform and the Gestapo major's hat up with the rest, then told Joe fuck the mountains, he was tired and would go to his burrow to sleep first. Joe had been surprised at the change of plan, but also exhausted.

Now he realised there had been no change of plan — Harry had never intended running to the mountains, he was running somewhere else. He must have come back to the cave as soon as Joe was asleep. The Republican uniform was gone, and Il Pazzo's hat, and the Wehrmacht tunic and One-Eyed Jack's cap and tunic and all his boots and leggings.

Joe told Donatella the truth, as far as it went. 'Rico non mi ha detto niente che se ne andava via.' *Rico said nothing to me about going.*

Her eyes filled, her head fell forward and she held her stomach and cried. When Joe put his arms up she crumpled beside him and he held her while she sobbed. It was the best moment of his life, and the worst: the only time that he'd lain with the woman he loved in his arms, a woman who was lost in grief for another man. When Donatella stopped crying, she looked at Joe with red-rimmed eyes and said, 'Sono incinta.' *I'm pregnant.*

Joe remembered Donatella and Harry outside the cave the night before — her crying and his reassuring tone. 'Did you tell Harry?' he asked.

She confirmed that she'd told him last night. She'd cried because he didn't seem happy, but he'd said everything would be fine, the war would finish soon and they'd make a life together. She'd gone back to bed reassured, while Harry had put on his Republican uniform and planned a last, famous flourish for the legend of Rico Zanardi.

'Tornerà, vero?' asked Donatella. *He'll come back, yes?*

'Certo,' said Joe.

But when Donatella was gone, Joe walked across to Harry's burrow, open to the day. Cigarette butts lined both sides of the bed slats, but the Feldgendarmerie gorget and his favourite short barrel Mauser were gone: it seemed fairly clear that the hunter had taken his weapons and trophies and fled.

* * *

Later that day Joe helped Bepi and Gigi in the vineyard, threading the ends of the vines into the wire so the new spring growth would be supported. They knew they might not see it, but what else could they do. There was no longer any banter between them. They'd of course heard about last night. Bepi said Gemona was pulsing with the stories — the train and Il Pazzo in one night! Rico was a hero. Was there anything the man couldn't do? Already the reward on the poster had gone up to one million lire. The rest of the Garibaldis were ecstatic, even though both actions had been taken without consulting or warning them. Bepi and Gigi knew Joe had been with Rico last night and he wanted to tell them that he wasn't consulted or warned either, that he'd had no choice. But there was always a choice.

Joe didn't tell them that Rico had gone. They thought he was hiding up in the mountains while things cooled. They didn't ask why Joe hadn't gone too. Gigi said nothing and Bepi dried up also, and they worked on with a dull dread hanging over them. When they heard the roar of the engines coming up the road, it was more confirmation than surprise. Gigi immediately began walking back to the houses like a man going to the gallows, while Bepi wordlessly shut Joe in the cave.

Joe was sure that this time someone would tell the Gestapo where he was. Nina probably, to save her son in jail. Or Marisa to save her little son, Leo. Joe knew he was no Luca and doubted he'd be able to survive Gestapo torture without naming names. It would be best if he forced them to shoot him where he was, or saved them the trouble. He took one of the pistols off the rack, loaded it with one bullet and lay down with it on his chest. He crossed his arms and willed the earth to close over him.

He lay there for a long time before he heard anything much. Shouting and screaming and a commotion that he didn't want to put a name to. He smelled or thought he smelled smoke and heard the crackle of flames. Joe tried to summon God for the first time since El Mreir, not praying but pleading. Almost immediately he heard a single shot and a piercing wail and knew that it didn't matter any more how soon the war ended. The damage was done.

Sometime later — he could see through the slats that daylight had gone — someone came to the trapdoor and began lifting off the vine prunings. He sat up, clicked off the safety catch and put the barrel of the pistol against his temple.

When the hatch lifted off, it was Donatella. She was covered in ash, her hair and clothes grey, her cheeks streaked with tears but her hazel eyes clear. The Gestapo had come with a copy of the poster, with a reward of one million lire for Rico. When no one said a word, they burned both houses, and when still no one spoke, the captain put his Luger to Leo's head. The child had looked puzzled and asked his mother, 'Che cosa vuole, mamma?' *What does he want, Mummy?*

Joe cried and Donatella waited for him to finish, then said, 'Sei un bravo ragazzo, Gianni. Non è colpa tua.' *You're a good boy, Gianni. It's not your fault.* 'Torna dai tuoi.' *Go back to your own.* She told him they had put Leo's body and what was left of their possessions into a wagon and were driving the last of the oxen over to relations near Osoppo. She kissed him on both cheeks and left.

Much later Joe came out into the moonlit night and walked towards the houses. They were still smouldering and he was hit by the stench of the cows that had been burnt in the stalle where he'd been found covered in shit eighteen months ago. He looked up at the stars in a cold sky. He hadn't known it at the time, but he'd brought the fire with him.

Treviso, 2014

51

<u>December 8, 1976.</u>
The team, the club, the town, is in disarray.
The collective brutta figura when we hosted the
Calabrians last Sunday has had repercussions:
a column on page 16 of Corriere dello Sport
condemning us, and a rap on the knuckles from
the Italian Rugby Federation. Aldo told me
about that this morning and wants me to attend
a meeting of the dirigenti tonight.

Aldo also told me we'll be struggling to
field a team for the next game in Sicily. I
know that Franco's going to be busy with his
revolution in Bologna, and it wasn't really
news that Big Dom can't be risked because,
apparently, the Sicilian team are full of
fascisti too. So there goes the fiery guts of
the team but that's not all: some of the other
players have decided that Sicily is a game too
far.

At Aldo's direction, I drove out to see

brothers who are two thirds of our loose
forward trio. They're both squat tough buggers,
hugely strong in hand and fore-arm and seemed
utterly fearless, until today.

They speak only dialect and are the Italian
equivalent of sharecroppers, living in what
turns out to be a pretty bizarre out-building
on someone's estate. It has dirt floors and
two rooms, a bedroom and a kitchen/dining/
sitting room. Pride of place in that room is a
glass-topped display case from a fairground,
the sort you put a coin in and an arm sweeps
across to knock some worthless trinket into
a pocket. Except there's nothing to plug it
into. From where we were sitting I could see the
wallpaper of their bedroom, culled centrefolds
from Playboy and Penthouse, blonde brunette and
red-head, wall to wall beaver. Fair enough,
they're bachelors but as we sculled home-made
grappa which would have incinerated my tonsils
if I had any, they told me they wouldn't come
to Sicily.

This was the younger one talking. I'm not
sure I've ever heard the other one say a word
through his handle-bar moustache. He always
wears a hat, a kind of stetson I guess, which
he only takes off at the last moment before a
game - weird because he's got a fine head of
hair. Anyway, the younger brother tells me
they can't come to Sicily because they won't
fly. We've been able to bus to all our away

317

matches so far but it would take the best part
of three days to get to Catania by train and
ferry. The thought of the two of them doing
that did worry me. These are guys who had
never seen a hotel atrium before our overnight
stay in Milan on our first away game, and
stared in wonder at the chandelier, then
thought the mini-bar in their room had to be
gifts from their hosts which would be rude not
to drink. But we were so desperate I told them
that maybe one of the dirigenti could travel
on the train to Catania with them, but they'd
be losing nearly a week of work there and back
for which the club would have to compensate
them. Was this an option worth discussing?

They looked at each other - I swear the older
one didn't say a word - then the younger one
tells me they have another problem. What would
happen, he asked, if either of them got injured
in the game and had to spend the night in a
Sicilian hospital? I was telling them I hoped
they'd be looked after, etc, when the older
brother began shaking his head. I thought he
might actually say something, but no. It was
younger one who told me that Sicilian women
were streghe, witches. He was surprised that
I hadn't heard this incontrovertible truth,
and 'that while we are lying defenceless in
hospital, the Sicilian witches will put an
evil spell on us from which our lives will not
recover.'

Bugger all point looking in the coaching
manual for that one either - I'll have to run
it past Aldo tonight.

I drove into Venice to talk to Beppino
but I was too late for the market so I rang
Cinzia, supposedly to ask where I might find
Beppino. Lady P answered and said Cinzia wasn't
here, she'd gone to church, the one off Santo
Stefano. That surprised me, I don't know why.
I'd just assumed she'd be a socialist atheist
like Franco.

I thought I might have a coffee at Santo
Stefano and who knows, run into Cinzia. I
wanted to position myself outside the church
but couldn't see one. Most of them - and there
are a lot of them - are hard to miss, but I
had to ask for directions and was pointed
towards a big door in a wall at the end of
the piazza where you exit towards Rialto.
It was so discreet that I pushed it open to
check, and this huge cavernous space opened
up with frescoes and stained glass and naves
and altars, so I quickly closed the door
and ordered a coffee at the cafe opposite and
pretended to be reading a paper while keeping an
eye on the door of the church.

I missed her. I must have looked away and
she was there standing beside the table. Are you
waiting for me? she asked.

I wasn't sure what to say. She looked quite
stern but it was better not to lie - Lady P

would tell her I'd rung. So I said yes, I was waiting for her.

She smiled, said Good! and punched me lightly on the arm. Can I have a coffee?

After I'd ordered an espresso there was a long silence and she said that church was a quiet time and afterwards she found it hard to talk.

I said I was surprised that she went to church. It was a stupid thing to say. I'd forced my assumptions on to her when I hardly knew her.

She said that she'd been brought up by her mother and the Canossian Sisters, who all believed. She hadn't been sure whether she believed, but when she was a little girl waiting for her father to come back, her great-aunt Isabella would occasionally come down from Gemona and take her to church. Her great-aunt told her not to expect anything of God but to pray anyway 'just in case'.

In case what?

In case God exists, she said, in case the world turns out rotto.

I knew rotto meant broken, but the way she said the word it sounded like rotten.

I tried to make a joke and said she was having a bob each way. Who's Bob? she asked. You fear there might be a God, so you go to church, I said. She looked at me with a kind of pity, and I thought if she's really La Testa

Calda I'm going to get both barrels and I
bloody deserve it.

It's got nothing to do with fear, she said.
It's respect. Not everything is explicable. At
the heart of everything is a mystery. Where did
we come from? How did this universe happen? I
want to respect the mystery of life, I want my
life to have meaning, I want to do something
good, but I don't know what it is. If God
exists, I cannot ignore him. But either way, I
want to do something with my life.

She swallowed her espresso, said she had to
go and kissed me, a bit brusquely and I drove
back to San Pietro cursing myself for blowing
it. Was she wearing her ring? I'd forgotten to
look.

Clare read Cinzia's words again. *At the heart of everything is a mystery. Where did we come from? How did this universe happen? I want to respect the mystery of life, I want my life to have meaning, I want to do something good, but I don't know what it is.* She found herself wishing that when her father had knocked on that dark red door in Dorsoduro, she'd at least glimpsed the woman who had answered it: the woman who could say something so true that it reached out across forty years to touch her.

52

December 9, 1976.

I've been sacked. Aldo told me after the
meeting of the dirigenti. He was wiping tears
with a big hanky. I'd appeared in front
of them earlier, and had come out thinking
it went pretty well, considering - we were
playing good, constructive rugby, etc, and
our win/loss ratio was about fifty percent,
not too bad for our first season in Serie
A, particularly given we'd lost a few that
we could have, should have, won. As I was
talking, I tried to engage the men sitting in
front of me. I know most of them. Aldo, of
course, the de facto chairman, and Il Dottore,
the local doctor who stands sideline most games
so he can pull my dislocated finger back into
place when it goes. From the look on his face,
it hurts him more than it hurts me. Vincenzo
the local grain merchant who talked about his
customers as 'my dear friends the peasants' and
who Franco told me was a fascist, and Orlando,
a handsome semi-retired well intentioned
blowhard who knows fuck all about rugby but
loves talking up a storm. But there was one
guy there I'd never seen before, who I wasn't
introduced to, but was addressed by the others
as Signor Gianni. Signor Gianni was sitting

at Aldo's right and obviously had some power
because they all kinda deferred to him even
though he said not one word. As Orlando blew
on about what a catastrophe Sunday's game had
been for the national standing of the club and
the town and the sponsor, Signor Gianni's eyes
never left me. Unsettling because one of them
was a bit wonky and looked like it was coming
at me from a different angle.

I thought that the Calabrian episode had
had nothing to do with me, so I didn't really
respond directly to that, but Aldo told me it
was basically why I had been sacked. The lack of
discipline in that game showed that my control
of the team was weak. The dirigenti have decided
that now the original coach has recovered from
his grief, he would take over the team. I can
live with that, given that he was the man who
had got them to Serie A in the first place. That
wasn't why Aldo was in tears. Signor Gianni
is the original coach and doesn't want me as
a player in his team. I was free to go. Merry
Christmas.

I was in a bit of a daze. My first thought
was, So that's who Signor Gianni was! Then I
realised. If Signor Gianni was the original
coach, then he's also Beppino and Franco and
Cinzia's father? Is he the same man? I asked
Aldo.

He is.

<u>December 10, 1976.</u>

Jesus.

Didn't sleep much. Kept thinking about the
man who'd made a dash at the market when he
saw me - that must have been why he took off.
Then turned up at the meeting to turf me out.
Signor Gianni. There've been so many strange
goings-on here, things I don't understand
that have fuck all to do with rugby or life
as I know it. I feel innocent and naive but
I've tried to act in good faith. Part of me is
more than happy to clear out, side-step the
whole Sicilian thing and go back to London,
find some mates to spend the rest of the
winter with. Xmas with Kiwis whose context
I can understand. But I'd be deserting the
boys. And I'm carrying a sense of injustice
about what's happened - I can understand that
he was the coach and he's ready to step back
up, but why doesn't he want me as a player? He
never said a word, didn't ask me one question.
    Then there's Cinzia.
    Franco was already gone to Bologna, but I
had plenty of questions for Beppino when I saw
him at the market. His father was nowhere to
be seen. Beppino was horrified when I told him
what had happened. He couldn't leave the stall
but told me not to worry, he would speak to his
father, clear up this 'casin', this mess.

So I went back to Piazzale Roma, hopped in the car, but just sat there thinking that I didn't want to drive back to San Pietro. Vergogna. Shame. I would be an embarrassment to Aldo in his bar because all the boys would know what had happened and I would be a reminder of his powerlessness to stop it.

I only had one way of contacting Cinzia. The number of Lady P's palazzo in Cannaregio. I rang her from the public box. If Lady P or Hartley had answered, I was going to replace the receiver. A woman's voice said Pronto and it was so formal that I wasn't sure it was her but took a chance.

How to describe what happened next.

Cinzia let me in to this grand palazzo and led me up curving stone stairs to a huge room with high stud and antique furniture and then to a little alcove with a chaise longue and carpet, looking out on a canal. She still wasn't wearing her ring - I look for those things now. She was already furious with her father, sat me down and started patting my head and neck like you'd comfort a dog. I felt my fucking brain was bursting and I started blubbing like a baby. Next thing she was kissing my tears, kissing me.

We fell into each other. Made love on the carpet. It wasn't sex as I knew it, hot breath and clumsy . . .

Clare's voice trailed off as she lost the sense of the story and came back to herself. She felt uncomfortable, reading aloud this awkwardly described sex, while her father lay comatose beside her. She quickly checked that he *was* still out to it, before allowing her eyes to get back to his description. He'd never once talked like this: she could sense his discomfort in the writing of it.

. . . two separate bodies, thinking about what to do next, who was doing what to who, skin on skin. I forgot where we each began and ended.

When it did end she took my head in her hands and said it was me she'd been waiting for, part of her had always been waiting for me. Since she was a little girl she'd always dreamt about someone coming from far away. Until she was six she and her mother had believed that her father must be dead. He'd been a partisan who'd been caught in the last days of the war and imprisoned in Germany and was then interned by the Americans because the Germans had destroyed his identity papers. That's why he is always a bit fuck-ed, she said cheerfully. And now there is you. Mi fai, tu. Mi fai.

I wasn't sure what that actually means, but it sounded good, so I said, Me too. I told her if I never love again I'll remember this moment and be grateful. Don't know why I said that. Why shouldn't it last? There's a part of me that's frightened by the perfection of

what happened. Has anyone the right to expect
this sort of happiness? There's nothing in my
upbringing that tells me it's normal or even
possible.

We talked as if it was. About London, her
coming with me. She's ready to fly she told me,
she feels trapped in Venice, in her life here,
it's too close and cloying. I worried about
overselling London, said we'd have bugger all
money and she might miss her family. She said
all adventures have danger but we'd have each
other.

That's the guts of it. We didn't talk about
NZ. But the decisions I have to make about the
farm or law, where to live, how to live, all
that I'll have to look at through a different
lens. Love isn't free and I'm prepared to
pay any price. Whatever happens, my life has
changed forever.

Jesus.

There was a knock on the door. Clare didn't want the
interruption. There weren't many pages to go and now she
desperately wanted history to be reinvented, to protect her
mother from a loveless marriage and for her father to be with
the love of his life. *Has anyone the right to expect that sort of
happiness? There's nothing in my upbringing that tells me it's
normal or even possible.* Yet he had tried to believe in love.
There was something so uplifting in knowing that. How on
earth could it have gone wrong?

It was light outside, as Renzo let himself in, with two coffees and a chocolate pastry. 'I thought we could share,' he said.

He kissed her as she took the coffees. This time she didn't turn her cheek but found his lips. He might have been surprised but he didn't show it. They stood there lips and hands locked, balancing the coffees. 'I must taste awful,' she said and stepped back.

She excused herself and went to the toilet, looked at her shiny face in the mirror. Her make-up had succumbed. How could he like what he saw? And yet he kept coming back, appearing in her life with impeccable timing. It came to her again, as it had outside the hotel: *He fits.*

When she re-entered the room, there was a nun in a grey smock with white collar, plain white wimple holding back white hair, kneeling beside the bed praying, one hand clasping her father's. Clare called 'Stop!' but the nun finished her prayer while Renzo looked embarrassed and Clare pleaded with him to intervene. 'Please tell her that my father is an atheist — he was brought up Church of England.' After she'd said it, she realised it was a pretty strange non sequitur. 'Please tell her to stop.'

By that time, the nun was finished anyway and rose to her feet, turning her face away and left the room.

'I thought, what harm can she do?' said Renzo. 'I'm sorry.'

53

Catania. Palm trees. Warm. So good to get out
of the seeping cold.

Aldo asked me as one last favour to come. San
Pietro could hardly get a team on the plane -
the two loose forward brothers weren't the only
ones worried about the witches of Sicily - so
I'm here strictly as a player to make up the
numbers. When Aldo put it to me, I couldn't
refuse, he's done so much for me and I owe it to
the boys. They all know I'm going and there have
been tears - no idea how moving it is to have
two giant props, Rifi and Tomaso, in front of
you blubbing their eyes out. I can talk.

Signor Gianni had the good grace to mutter
Grazie to me as we were waiting to board at
Marco Polo, but that's the only word he's
addressed my way. He's so unlike his children,
a man of few words and they're all dialect.
That's okay, I don't want him asking any
questions about Cinzia. Franco says he's a
committed socialist and was against Cinzia
marrying Max, but I can't imagine he'd be
terribly thrilled if he knew what his actions
in sacking lo straniero had precipitated with
his daughter.

Very weird feeling in the team.

<u>December 13, 1976.</u>
Weird is right.

I'm writing this in longhand from the
hospital at Catania - I'll type it up when
I get back. I'm told it's the day after the
match. Feel a bit woozy still, bad headache,
but at least the nurses here are fine - I
haven't seen a witch amongst them, but there
were definitely a couple at our hotel the night
before the game.

We got into Catania about 9 the night before
last and it was 10 by the time we got to the
hotel. The boys nevertheless decided they wanted
to eat before they went to bed, so off we
traipse down the street to a pizzeria with out-
door tables.

Beppino, who's sole captain now, ordered red
wine to wash down the pizzas. That was okay -
I'd seen them drink red wine at lunch before a
game in the afternoon and I'd never seen any of
my boys drunk. But there was something in the
Sicilian air this night, a powerful foreboding,
a kind of eat drink be merry for tomorrow we die.
Beppino was obviously pissed off with the coach,
his father. He'd told me that he'd tried to
persuade his father to reverse his decision about
me, but his father had been utterly intransigent
and couldn't really offer a reason why. When the
coach and captain are at loggerheads, it's not
a good dynamic and even worse if they're father

330

and son. Beppino ordered another round of red wine for the table, then another. I began to feel sorry for Signor Gianni - he couldn't call out his son so he sat there watching with his wonky eye as his team got pissed the night before the big game. Finally he gets up and says it's time to get back to the hotel. Time for you, old man, says Beppino, and orders another carafe of red wine. Signor Gianni stood there for a moment or two but there was nothing he could do and walked off.

By the time the team got back to the hotel, they were, we were, collectively, legless. Salvatore, Big Dom's replacement, who thinks he's a bit of a lad even though he's only got one word for every occasion - Oy! - saw a couple of beautiful mini-skirted women in the house bar on the way through and, wonder of wonder, discovered they were prostitutes and available on room service. Oy!

I flaked out in the midst of a party, a panicky, bawdy amoebic thing that slithered from room to room, with much singing, slamming of doors and fornication. I had sour red wine dreams and got up for a piss at one stage and there was one of these extraordinarily beautiful women squatting over the bidet washing herself. Un momento, she said.

By ten yesterday morning, game day, when we gathered for a late brunch, it was pretty clear that the Sicilian witches had already

cast their spell and we were fuck-ed, as Cinzia
would say. Red streaming eyes, sore heads,
tender tummies and, back in NZ anyway, that
traditional coach's nightmare, depleted gonads.

As we bussed to the ground you could sense
the fear rising through the hangovers. I wasn't
sure what the hell was going to happen out on
the field, but was kinda glad that this was my
last game. Everything we'd built was slipping
away and I could see the boys looking at each
other and thinking Oh shit. Beppino was trying
to talk it up but we desperately needed the
Franco and Big Dom steel. In the dressing shed,
Signor Gianni tried to rev them up, but he's
not a great orator. What he can do is pass the
ball. He was rocketing flat spirals off both
wings right across the room in the warm-up
with Beppino. I can't see where Beppino gets his
mouth from but I can see where his hands come
from.

On the field, a stony dusty track fenced in
by wire to keep the fans off us, it all turned
to shit pretty quickly, what I can remember
of it. I'd determined to just play it out,
do my best but not bust a boiler in what I'd
already accepted was a lost cause. But shit,
someone pulls your jersey, it's just instinct.
I whacked him with a back-hander, nothing
major, thinking well, that'll be the end of
that, we'll get on and play rugby. But no, this
guy with a moustache the size of a dead possum

takes umbrage and hooks into me. I was feinting and dodging, thinking I'd have to clock him again soon to slow him down, when what felt like the rest of the Sicilians descended on me. Franco and Dom would have been in there with me, but minus their steel, our team just stepped back behind the ref and left me to it. I might have been fucking killed except there were so many of them on me they couldn't get a clear shot. Well, someone did, obviously, because that's the last I remember before waking up here in hospital asking Where am I? - every ten minutes apparently. Blinding headache and sore ribs, struggling to sit up. One of the Catanian management, Silvio, has been here this morning. Lovely guy, he told me I was concussed and was in here for observation. I told him my ribs hurt, so they're going to keep me here for an X ray later today. Silvio tells me we got 'eaten', done for a dinner, fifty points, a rout. We've never lost like that. I'm glad I'm going.

I've been told to rest my brain, no reading or writing, so I'll stop.

All I can think of is getting back to Venice, picking up Cinzia and flying into the rest of our lives. Fuck this. With Cinzia at my side, maybe I could reimagine the farm, obliterate my father's taint. Would she find the empty horizons a revelation after Venice, or desolate and frightening?

After we made love, she said Mi fai, tu. Mi

fai. I'm not at my brightest and I'm trying to figure out what she meant. Why would she say, You do me, when we'd already done it? It wasn't the imperative, that would have been Fammi.

I thought it was safe to ask Silvio what it meant, without giving him any context. It's not something we would say, he said. Maybe peculiar to up north.

Later.

I'm out of here this afternoon – the Xray revealed no ribs broken, just contusions. The headache's gone, along with that feeling of a cloud between me and what I'm trying to think about. I thought about using the hospital phone to ring Cinzia, but Beppino will have filled her in.

I wanted to ask her if I've got it right. Mi fai, tu. You make me. It must be that because it's what I feel too.

Clare put the pages down and bent over her father, feeling for the ghost of his breath on her cheek. 'Is that what you wanted me to know?' she asked him. Now she desperately wanted Bruce and Cinzia to be together and wondered what could possibly have happened to prevent it. She almost feared what the remainder of the pages would reveal and picked them up with a feeling of dread.

54

December 14, 1976

Franco is dead.

I went straight from Marco Polo to the stall below Rialto, but it was closed, and the guy next door told me. All the stall-holders are in shock. Franco e morto. E morto Franco.

Clare's voice failed her. Or her will. To continue reading aloud would be selfish, even cruel. She couldn't do it. She read the rest in shocked silence.

It's been in all the papers I haven't been reading. The students of the radical left had surrounded the university at Bologna where a meeting of right-wing Catholics, Commune e Liberazione, was being held. The Dean called the Carabinieri and that provoked a violent riot. A carabiniere had singled out Franco and shot him dead. He was the only one. Shot like some sheep worrying dog. There's going to be an enquiry, but that's not going to bring Franco back. I hardly knew him, I shouldn't feel this bad. I can't believe he's gone.

It's a much worse blow to my head than that Sicilian's boot. Sometimes I think I'm getting an understanding about this place, then I realise I know nothing. Could this ever happen at home? I can't imagine that it has or ever would. I don't want to stay here, the volatile mix of charming, seductive hospitality and sudden brutality throws me.

I rang Lady P's from Piazzale Roma. She didn't seem terribly pleased to hear the NZ accent - I wonder if Cinzia's given her notice already, told her about me, and Max. She said Cinzia wasn't there, that the family had gone north to Gemona for Franco's funeral and burial in the family plot.

December 15, 1976.
Aldo's bar is a sad place. The boys drift in and out looking for solace. Aldo's big face is dripping tears half the time, as he pulls beers and delivers food. There are photos of Franco plastered up all round the bar. Even Big Dom is in tears, periodically thumping the table and calling God a dog. I thought maybe some of the boys might be going north for the funeral, but Aldo says the family wanted it to be private, they've suffered so much and Gemona is still a war zone.

I don't need the photos - I can picture Franco so clearly, the ties of his red bandana flying, the way his smile flashed out of the black beard as he patiently dealt with my political ignorance. Out on the lagoon, his damaged face as he told me he had to save the world in Bologna. He seems so present still.

336

I have another picture too, of Signor Gianni
at Catania, looking lost and desolate as the
ref came to check our sprigs, knowing he'd
lost the dressing room to an insurrection led
by his youngest son. That must have been about
the time his older son was dying on the streets
of Bologna. I didn't warm to the man but what
tragedy he's had to carry, losing his wife in
the quake and now this.

And Cinzia, losing the brother to whom she
was joined at the hip.

Aldo took me aside and said the obvious:
tutto e cambiato. Everything has changed.
He said Signor Gianni won't be coaching or
playing any part at the club for the rest
of the season. Sicily was a catastrophe and
showed the value of what I had been doing with
the team. He wants me to come back and carry
on for the rest of the season. The Christmas
break will give everyone a chance to go away
and recover, then come back in the New Year and
start again.

I didn't give him an answer, said I'd think
about it.

He's right though. Everything has changed
and in ways Aldo doesn't know about. In my
mind, I'd already left, was already in London
with Cinzia getting on with the rest of our
lives together. But Cinzia won't be able to
leave her old man and Beppino now, or for
months to come. And there's the boys. I don't

think I can walk away now they've lost Franco.
I don't think I can do it.

December 16, 1976.
Franco's funeral was yesterday, so Cinzia
and Beppino could be back in Venice some time
today. I'll try to ring her tonight. But
I've decided to go north to Gemona tomorrow,
finally, just for the day. Aldo's given me
directions to a cemetery just to the south of
the town. I can be there and back in the day,
pay my respects to Franco, and maybe begin the
hunt for Dad's past, the families mentioned
by Arch Scott, the Zanardis and Bonazzons.
Maybe I can find some relatives, if things have
recovered enough from the quakes to make that
okay.

*   *   *

Clare stood up. It was mid-morning out there in the world of
the well beyond the glass. She was shattered by Franco's death,
felt as if she knew him, even though she'd got mere glimpses of
him from the diary. She remembered the underlying sense of
melancholy at her father's reunion and the prominence of the
beaming Che Guevara among the photos on the wall of Aldo's
bar. She felt she was beginning to understand why.

55

I've got no-one to talk to about this. I've got
to write it down to see if it makes sense. I'm
hoping to hell it doesn't.

Cold grey plains as I drove north and west
towards Gemona. Following Aldo's directions
I didn't have to go into Gemona itself but
turned off to the right just south, towards a
town called Nimis, then went north west again
until I passed another town called Artegna. I
crossed the bridge over the Orvenco river and
saw a very old church up on top of a hill,
separate from the hills that grew into the
mountains behind Gemona. I couldn't drive up,
so I parked the car and walked. I wondered if I
might meet Cinzia or some of the family still
there, because when I rang Lady P's last night,
she wasn't back. But the place was deserted.
Beautiful, but bleak. From up top you can look
back across the plains of the Veneto one way,
and up towards the Dolomites on the other.

Franco's grave was hard to find because so
many of the graves are recent. Il Terremoto
features on virtually all the new ones I could
see and there's quake damage in the part of the
cemetery where all the ashes are stored, with
little photos on the front of the columns of

drawers, all twisted and broken.

I found Franco over in the corner that looked
back towards the Veneto. That made it final
for me, that he was gone, lying under that
earth, never to return. That's when I began
crying. Before that moment, it'd been hard to
accept that he was gone. They didn't have a
photo of him on the head-stone, just Franco
Lamonza, 1952 - 1976, beloved son of Gianni
and Donatella Lamonza. That made him only 24.

After I'd dried up a bit I looked at the
graves next to his. He was right alongside
his mother, Donatella Lamonza, who had died
in May in the first quake. Then I saw it:
Donatella Lamonza, nee Bonazzon. I thought what
an amazing coincidence, that Franco's mother
could be connected to the Bonazzons, one of the
families that Arch Scott had told me to look
up. When I explored further, there were Bonazzon
graves alongside: Donatella's mother and
father, Giuseppe, 'Bepi', who had died in 1954,
and Nina, who had died in the quake with her
daughter. There was a son called Luca, who had
died in 1945, 'ucciso dai nazisti'. Killed by
the Nazis. I wondered whether my father might
have known him.

The next section of plots were Zanardis and
I knew then these must be the families Dad had
known. There was an Isabella who died in 1958,
but the oldest grave was Leo, only 8 years old,
who like Luca had been killed by the Nazis. His

mother Marisa had died in 1968, but the father
Luigi, Gigi, and eldest daughter Paola and her
husband Mario, had all died this year in the
quake.

The dimension of the tragedies that had
befallen these families was almost beyond
imagination. I thought selfishly, Bugger, I'm
too late, but I kept going through the head-
stones of the Bonazzons and Zanardis, thinking
that these had to be the families Arch had
told me about, must be, and wondering whether
I could get a name of a survivor to track
down and talk to, when it hit me: they'd been
all around me. Signor Gianni had married a
Bonazzon, which meant Franco and Beppino and
Cinzia were Bonazzons as much as they were
Lamonzas.

Then something else hit me, right in the
guts. Those letters I'd found in my father's
study, addressed to Caro Rico. I was pretty
sure the name I'd seen at the bottom was
Donatella. Maybe not.

I jumped in the car and tore back down the
plains to San Pietro. I'd never opened those
letters since I'd got here. Stupid, because what
was hieroglyphics to me back in NZ when I'd
first seen them, was now a language I could
understand.

The heavens opened as I came down the
autostrada and the Opel started aquaplaning
in the puddles, then the water overwhelmed its

windscreen wipers and I had to get off the
motorway and stop. I was on a road out in the
featureless flat country, no idea where I was,
windows steamed up like my brain.

The way Signor Gianni had looked at me at the
meeting of the dirigenti. Who had sacked me at
his insistence. The way he'd taken off when he
saw me for the first time at the markets. Like
he'd seen a ghost. Like he knew me.

Signor Gianni knew who I was. He'd known my
father.

December 18, 1976.
Awful awful night. I wanted to go to the phone
box out in the street and ring Cinzia. But
I'm not sure what to say. And even if I say
nothing, I won't be able to hide it from her.

When I finally got back here last night, I
went to the side pocket of my pack and hauled
out the letters I'd found in the shoe-box in
my father's study. I should have read them
carefully, out of respect, but I skimmed them:
I looked first at the dates, 1945 going into
1946. I was looking for any mention of one
word in the early ones, incinta, pregnant, and
another word in the later ones, bambina.

I found both.

December 19, 1976.
I've been to see Signor Gianni. Beppino's back
at the market, really lost his pep, which is

understandable. We moped in silence. He told me
Cinzia is really cut up and needs to see me. I
lied and said I was about to ring her, then I
told him I needed to see his father, I wanted
to pass on my condolences personally. Beppino
tried to dissuade me, told me his father was in
a bad way and didn't want to see anyone, but in
the end he gave me an address.

I took the long way round to Dorsoduro,
staying away from the track through Campo
Santo Stefano to Accademia, where I might bang
into Cinzia. I walked in a curve along the
spine of the fish, got a bit lost and ended up
on the long bland Zattere. The water looked grey
and melancholy and with no sun to light up
the facades, Venice's old soul looked tired and
dispirited but maybe that was just me.

I cut back into Dorsoduro and with some
difficulty found a little house with a door
the colour of the bandoliero rosso and with the
right number on it. When he opened the door and
saw me, he tried to close it again, but we're
well past all that. I just put my shoulder
into it. He was red-eyed and smelt of sour
spirits. The house is tiny, just one room wide
with stairs leading to a room above. How had he
and Donatella brought up three children here?

I told him I knew why he wanted me gone. He
made out he only spoke dialect and couldn't
understand my Italian. I didn't believe him and
told him really slow and clear that I wanted

him, I needed him to tell me I was wrong, that
his wife Donatella Bonazzon had not had a baby
by my father, Harry Spence, aka Rico Zanardi. I
lost it. Dimmi ho sbagliato! I yelled at him.
Tell me I'm mistaken! Tell me!

He closed his eyes for a long time, and I
knew I was lost. I knew what he was going to
say when he opened them. I knew what he was
going to say but no idea how he was going
to say it. In mangled English, with a sort
of Kiwi accent which he must have picked up
from Dad. The words were like boulders on
his tongue, each one prised off with enormous
effort.

Your father was a great warrior, in battle
the bravest man I ever saw. But he destroyed
the two families who gave him refuge. His
recklessness killed two sons who didn't need to
die.

This wasn't what I'd come to hear. I
remembered two head-stones, of Leo Zanardi, 8
and Luca Bonazzon, 26. The ones killed by the
Nazis? I ask him. That's what their head-stones
say, he said.

He didn't offer anything more. I wanted to
say that according to Arch Scott my father had
been a hero of the partigiani, but that wasn't
what Signor Gianni was disputing. The bravest
man I ever saw. In battle.

Then there was Donatella, where my father
had shown neither courage nor honour. I have

344

her letters to prove that. Una parola, she'd
written in her last letter, in February of
1946. Just one word and my beautiful daughter
and I will wait for you.
   One word.
   I said it. Cinzia?
   Yes, he said.

Clare read the words again, trying to make sure she'd understood
the meaning of that last 'Yes'. The simple 'Yes' that meant her
grandfather was Cinzia's father. The 'Yes' that meant Cinzia was
her father's half-sister. The 'Yes' that meant incest. There it was.
The crime, for which this diary was 'explanation but no excuse',
though in fact it was both. He had blindly, unknowingly, fallen
in love with his sister.

   She had read the last passages in silence. Now she leaned over
him. 'You loved your sister,' she said. 'There are worse crimes.'

   If he'd been listening, he'd have to respond. But there was
nothing.

56

<u>December 20, 1976.</u>
I don't know what to do. I do know what I have
to do, but I'm not sure I can do it.

Cinzia's been leaving messages at Aldo's
bar. Aldo is pleased that I have un' amica, he
thinks that seals the deal and I'll stay. He
has no idea that tutto e cambiato, again.

I keep thinking that there's an easy way
out of this. The truth shall set you free
and all that: I tell Cinzia the truth and
we're embarrassed for a while but stay friends
for each other. On any real scrutiny, it's
bullshit. We're lovers. The image of Signor
Gianni keeps coming back to me, crying out of
his one good eye, the other one dry, telling me
he's lost his wife and son and pleading with me
not to take his daughter. He doesn't mean don't
take her to London, he means don't tell her
that he isn't her father.

Cinzia was never told the truth. I can't make
a judgement on that, it's too late and I wasn't
there in the terrible confusion after the war
when these decisions were made. I could pretend
I come from the new world where this sort of
old shit doesn't get oxygen, and I can pretend
not to understand the sort of society that
needs all these secrets and lies to avoid shame.

Vergogna. Brutta figura.

But even as I write this, I realise how
ashamed I am of my father. I don't have any idea
what part he played in the death of those two
sons on the head-stones I saw, and I'll never
know. I came here to find something good in him.
Instead, all this distance away, at the other
end of the world, I can sense his awful shadow
over all of it, and over me still, and I know
now I'll never escape him. He didn't have the
courage to once acknowledge the declarations of
love by Donatella in her letters, or acknowledge
his daughter. The bravest man Signor Gianni ever
saw in battle ran away from his child like a
coward.

I told Signor Gianni that my father knew
what he had done and it had eaten him. I don't
know whether that helped. But it's some help to
me, I think, that I know where my father's howl
on the Moon Man's soles came from.

I'm glad it ate the bastard up, because his
cowardice has wrecked me.

Signor Gianni is asking me to do exactly
what my father did, run away. This time
there's no child. This time, he says, it's the
honourable thing to do, to save Cinzia from
losing her father after having just lost her
mother and her brother. Signor Gianni says she
has loved before, she'll love again.

I had to hold down my anger at his dismissal
of our love as just another of Cinzia's

liaisons, but what could I say?

Mi fai, tu. Mi fai.

It makes a terrible sense now.

December 21, 1976.

This morning I handed the keys to the apartment
and the Opel back to Aldo. He was crying. I
call him the uncle I never had, but I never
had a father like him either. His two sons were
there, holding on to his trouser legs. They're
lucky buggers. I said goodbye to the boys last
night at the bar. They all came, apart from
Beppino - I lied to Aldo, that I'd said my
goodbye to him in Venice - and there were tears
and I wanted to tell them why I was going,
but had to let them think I had been shamed by
being sacked and being told I wasn't wanted
and couldn't get over it. The worst thing is,
they understand, they think that's a correct
way to respond to my sacking and reinstatement.
Vergogna, the brutta figura. They hold no
grudges and I've promised them a mate I know
in London will come in the New year. Eric's a
running fullback with a prodigious boot and
will do better here with his young wife and
new baby than in London. They'll love him.
I've told Aldo to shift Paolo from fullback
to cover Franco's centre position. What about
you? asked Aldo. How will we cover you? I told
him it was nice of him to pretend that was a
problem.

This morning he handed me more messages from Cinzia, who now knows something's terribly wrong and will go to her grave thinking I'm a bastard. Her last message was simple: no pleading, no declarations of love like her mother made to my father. Dimmi qualcosa, caro. Tell me something, love. Tell me something.

But if I tell her anything, I'll have to tell her everything.

Signor Gianni said a broken heart is a wound that heals. Shame is forever. This way, it all dies with me.

I ask Aldo to give her a message from me: Mi fai, tu. Mi fai.

I'm writing this on the train somewhere west of Bologna, where any trace of Franco's blood will have been washed off the cobblestones by now. I've got the hang of this Italian keyboard since I was last sitting here, but what's the point. I won't be writing any more.

* * *

Clare laid the last page in her lap, took her father's cold hand in hers and held it against her wet cheek, feeling his sense of loss across the decades. 'Oh Dad,' she whispered. 'You poor man.'

She stayed like that for a long time, in the gentle measured rhythms of the hospital hum. The syringe driver nestled beside him on the bed made no sound. Nor did his breathing. She put her cheek close to his and felt the intermittent flutter. She sat back. Slowly it came to her: she had an aunt, if Cinzia was still alive. And there was more.

One of those names her father found on the gravestones at Gemona. She'd seen somewhere else. Somewhere close.

She reached into her sunshine yellow bag, drew out her wallet and took Renzo's card from where she'd stashed it among her receipts. She'd never had to use it — Renzo had always arrived before she'd needed to — but now she read it, understanding for the first time what it might mean. *Professore Lorenzo Lamonza.*

The Antipodes, 1945-50

57

His memory often played tricks, in league with his emotions. Sometimes he'd find himself crying, then couldn't remember what he'd been thinking about when the tears came. Often Franco, he suspected. Or Donatella. Or the wasted years of estrangement from Beppino. Certainly he could remember crying for little Leo and Luca, as he stood there so many years ago in front of the burnt remnants of the Bonazzon and Zanardi houses.

After taking Donatella's bicycle from the implement shed, the only building on the farm that the Gestapo hadn't razed, he'd ridden east towards Trieste with a vague notion of offering himself to the Gestapo at San Sabba in return for Luca's release. His bargaining chip would be Major Ferguson's unit up on Monte Canin. They were soldiers and could take care of themselves and, besides, the war might be over before the Nazis could do anything about them.

On reflection, he could see it was a stupid idea — the Nazis held all the cards, and they'd have imprisoned him as well as Luca if he'd offered himself to them on a plate. But his guilt in bringing Harry and the fire down on the families who had given him refuge overwhelmed whatever reason he had left and drove him east.

The Germans had turned the main road to Udine into a one-way highway going north as they tried to get their surviving troops and materiel back up through the Brennero to a last stand in the Fatherland. RAF and American aircraft were strafing and bombing them, and as he rode east through the burnt-out towns of Nimis and Attimis and Faedis towards Cividale, Joe could feel the earth shaking and see the columns of smoke delineating the highway over to his right and curling up through the crisp April air.

Joe rode past PG 57 at Grupignano and on towards Monfalcone unchallenged. All eyes, Italian and German alike, had turned inwards, trying to survive until the end of Armageddon and imagine where they might sit when that day came. A foolish peasant on a bicycle moving towards rather than away from the action was of no interest to anyone. He slept in abandoned sheds and empty storehouses, under the rafters of burnt-out homes, once in a bomb crater, relying on the improbability of two bombs landing in exactly the same place. There was no food and very little uncontaminated water. The plains of plenty had been laid waste, poisoned, scourged by the tide of ravenous black ants and by those who were hiding from them and by those who were pursuing them on land and from the air.

He was so weak that it took him several days to pedal to the main road between Venice and Trieste. Thirsty and ravenous, he approached a scout car under cover in a copse on the side of the otherwise deserted road. The soldiers were mending a puncture and he could smell tea. When they saw him they levelled their rifles, then told him, in English accents, to fuck off.

'I'm Private Joseph Lamont,' he told them, dredging the words from what already seemed long ago, 'of 24th Battalion, New Zealand Second Division.'

They were from the 12th Lancers, forward scouts for the Div and therefore honorary Kiwis, they said, as they gave him sweet tea and bread. When they discovered that he could speak Italian and the local dialect, they strapped Donatella's bike on the back of the car and took him with them, speeding north and east towards Monfalcone.

They caught the rest of the Lancers just after midday, stalled at the entrance to the long bridge over the Isonzo River. The Germans had prepared it for demolition and the Lancers were waiting for the sappers to come forward to defuse it. The Brits feared they'd be too late because they could hear the time fuse ticking on the nearest bulwark.

Joe knew it was something he could do, and he no longer cared what happened to him, so they lowered him over the parapet above the mine on a rope. He was so malnourished it only took one Lancer to hold him: they'd drawn straws, he remembered, and a lance corporal called Billy Mason had held the rope. Joe unscrewed the detonator and Billy hauled him back up and shook his hand, said he was good luck. Billy transferred Joe and Donatella's bike to his armoured car and the Lancers crossed the Isonzo and roared on towards Monfalcone.

They drove past the railway station at Ronchi dei Legionari, where he and Arch Scott had knocked on the door of the stationmaster's house, and then on into Monfalcone, where crowds lined the street to cheer the Lancers' armoured cars through, held back by troops wearing the red star on their caps.

These, and the pro-Tito slogans plastered on the walls, seemed to speak of Tito having beaten the Lancers to Trieste. But they soon came up against a German roadblock at an intersection and while they waited for New Zealand Bren carriers and tanks to come forward and force the Germans to hoist the white flag, the Brits speculated on how the Slavs could have come from the east and got past the Nazis and into Monfalcone. Joe, recalling the encounter with One-Eyed Jack, pointed to the low range of hills shadowing the curve of coast. 'The hills are theirs,' he said, 'they don't need the roads.'

There was more German resistance at Castello di Miramare, where the coast road tunnelled under a bluff, and Joe watched from a distance as RAF fighter bombers worked over the defenders. While they were waiting a troop of tanks fired out to sea and sank two German motor torpedo boats. When he was sure they'd finished firing, Joe asked one of the drivers sitting on the hatch of his Sherman if he'd come across Daniel Lamont, last heard of in Tuscany. The man, who introduced himself as Alby from Dunedin, said he hadn't heard of 'Dan' but told Joe he'd 'find out soon enough when HQ gets established in Trieste'.

There was another pocket of resistance on the skinny road along the cliff above the sea, but after a brief firefight the German commander marched towards them with a white flag. The Lancers told Joe that the man who walked out and accepted the German commander's surrender was Colonel Haddon Donald of the 22nd Battalion, Harry's battalion. Where was Harry now, he wondered, repatriated or back with his old unit? He would have moved heaven and earth to stay in the war.

Joe was no longer sure of the sequence of events after they got to Trieste. For the Lancers and the Kiwis Trieste was supposed to be the triumphant final flourish of a long and brutal campaign, but instead it was messy and dangerous. The radio messages coming in to the Lancers said that Tito's Slavs had been there for two days already. They hadn't managed to quell Nazi resistance but were shooting Italians on the street, anyone they suspected of being fascist. Partisan Italians were shooting fascist Italians and vice versa and there were also Chetniks there, fascist Slavs fighting Tito's communists. When Tito's soldiers saw the New Zealanders arriving, they turned their weapons on them and made it clear that Trieste was now part of Yugoslavia and they weren't giving it up. The Germans had retreated to four or five strongpoints within the city and wanted to surrender to the Kiwis, not the Yugoslavs.

One of the strongpoints was the Tribunale building on a square fronting the wharves, which the Lancers were directed to. Radio traffic said it was full of SS types who'd been ordered to surrender by the German area commander but had refused.

In the stalemate, Joe asked for the bike to be untied. One of the places highlighted on the Lancers' maps was La Risiera di San Sabba, the SS prison. They'd come in from the west and he reckoned San Sabba was about ten miles to the east of where they were. That side of the city was held by Tito and Billy was adamant that Joe should hold off until the Allies took full control, but Joe couldn't sit and wait. He unstrapped Donatella's bike and set off. Billy had insisted on giving him a Lancer's battle tunic and cap so that he wouldn't be mistaken for an Italian and shot by the Slavs. But Joe stuck the cap in his back pocket and tied the tunic around his waist, believing he had more chance of getting there as an Italian.

He'd ridden about a mile along the waterfront before he hit the first Slav roadblock. There was always an Italian-speaking Istrian among the Slavs, and Gianni Lamonza, Italian partigiano trying to get to San Sabba prison to save his brother-in-law, the leader of the Friuli brigade of the Garibaldis, was given directions and ushered straight through. The second roadblock was further round the coast, when he tried to turn inland up a street lined with squalid old industrial buildings. When he told them his story, the Slav sergeant said he was too late but gave him directions to a site further up that road, cordoned off by more of Tito's troops.

Behind the cordon was what was left of a six storey red-brick building with smaller three-storey wings on either side. The Germans had dynamited it two days before to obliterate the evidence of what had gone on inside. He was told there were no bodies so far but that two sacks of bones and human ashes had been recovered from the area at the front of the taller building, where the oven had been.

In 1975, the year before the terremoto wrecked his life again, he'd taken Nina, Donatella, Cinzia, Franco and Beppino back to San Sabba when it was opened as a museum. It looked as squalid and menacing to Joe as it had that day in 1945. They were shown the underground entry passage and the death cells where those awaiting execution and cremation were kept, often sharing their quarters with cadavers waiting for the ovens. There were seventeen smaller cells, the first two of which were used for torture and stripping the prisoners of their clothes and papers and watches and jewellery. Luca's identity papers had been found among them, the only evidence that he had died there.

Joe had stared unseeingly at the red brick walls while Nina had wailed for her son and Donatella, Cinzia, Beppino and Franco had broken down and cried with her, along with many of the families of others who had been murdered and burned there, Jews and partisans, Slovenians, Croats, Italians, political prisoners and hostages. Five thousand people, they were told, in a little over a year. Unable to join Nina and Donatella and Cinzia in prayer, Joe had stood there silently, still paralysed with shame thirty years later . . .

Now they were all dead too, Donatella, Nina, Franco and Beppino. Only Cinzia remained, and he himself, somehow.

58

Joe couldn't remember riding back along the waterfront to where he'd left the Lancers, but he must have done. The Lancers were gone, but the man Joe had been told was Colonel Donald was approaching the front steps of the Tribunale building carrying a white flag. Joe could see windows partly open with machine gun barrels pointing from them. The massive doors opened a crack and two SS officers appeared, unshaven, their tunics unbuttoned. One had a sub-machine gun and the other held a Luger in one hand and a half-empty brandy bottle in the other. There was an exchange of words, then the door slammed. Donald walked calmly back across the square with SS machine guns trained on his back, everyone watching expecting to see him torn in half at any moment.

Joe was about to ride on to find the Lancers when he heard the clank of tracks on hard concrete and had to stop himself from running. Instead he forced himself to watch as about twenty Shermans came into the square from the other end, worked their way to vantage points around the Tribunale building and began firing. Joe fell to the ground, clawing at the flagstones, then scrambled to his feet and ran.

He woke up on stone steps among the wharves that ran along the front of the city. It was dark and silent and he was hungry, thirsty and cold. He put on the Lancers' battle tunic, pulled the cap over his head and walked back towards the square. The tanks had gone and Colonel Donald had obviously decided to leave any surviving SS to Tito. Soldiers with the red star on their caps were swarming in through the holes punched in the three-foot-thick walls by the tanks.

At a loss, Joe walked back through a succession of big squares towards the western end of town, hoping to find the Lancers, other Kiwis, or maybe even Dan. There were few people on the streets and those who were carried weapons. Joe wondered if there was a curfew but was past caring and plodded on unarmed through an urban no man's land towards he knew not where. Trieste didn't feel like Italy. The piazze were too big and plain and so were the buildings. Grand and square and Teutonic. He felt like an alien: an insubstantial speck of half-life, drifting through the streets unseen. That must have been why no one shot him.

He climbed up through the city, hoping to reach the countryside and find a sheltered place where he could rest. As he ascended, he came to a residential neighbourhood of substantial villas and then, ahead of him, were lights and voices. It was a large taverna or dance hall with a terrazzo looking out over Trieste. Weak and thirsty, he hovered at the door, listening. Most of the raised voices he could hear were female and Italian.

He'd heard that sound before when Luca had taken him into Gemona to buy more chemicals for the dynamite. They'd passed a corner taverna and Luca had stopped. 'Senti,' he'd said. Listen. Joe could hear a babble of voices, men's. Joe would have said they were confidently holding forth and spoke good Italian, much more complex than he'd heard used among the partisans. 'That is the voice of fascism,' said Luca. 'It's not parade-ground ranting, it's not Mussolini on the dais, it's this vanity, this entitlement, these words like silk thread weaving a web to stifle liberty.'

When Joe put his good eye to the glass of the door in Trieste, he saw uniforms inside and a black kiwi on a shoulder epaulette, so he pushed inside and grimaced as he was hit by the light. He drank wine and beer because it seemed to be free, though each glass just made him thirstier for the next. There were a few Lancers there, but no one he knew. A Reg and a Johnny slapped him on the back and were too drunk to realise that he was a Kiwi underneath the tunic, with peasant shirt and pants and working boots. But the Italians they tried to introduce him to knew instantly where he'd come from and quickly moved on. They were well-dressed men and women and their daughters, who didn't look as if they'd suffered much. The war they were clearly worried about was the one that was about to begin, between Tito's communists and Italians who'd supported the fascists. Reg and Johnny were delighted that the Div, and the Lancers, had been offered billets by these wonderful people in their wonderful houses. They were a class of Italian whom Joe had never seen among the partigiani, and he drowned his ire with more wine when he realised that the naïve Kiwis and English had become their de facto protectors.

Joe said very little, tried to concentrate on eating and drinking and breathing away his anger, until, out on the terrace, he saw a tallish frame he thought he recognised. Joe pressed his way through the throng towards the man, who was talking in Italian to two beautiful young women dressed up to the nines, and tapped him on the shoulder, which bore a Kiwi epaulette and a lance corporal's stripe.

When the man turned his blue eyes on Joe, and blew out the smoke of the cigarette he'd been drawing on, Joe blurted, in dialect so that the young women would not understand, 'Luca e Leo li gà copài i todeschi, 'e boarìe le stà brusade, ma Donatella, che Dio a benediga, la sè drio spetarte.' *Luca and Leo have been murdered by the Gestapo, the farmhouses have been burned, but Donatella, God help her, is still waiting for you.*

'Have we met?' asked the man.

59

Could he be sure it was Harry? He had been once, but age hadn't helped his recall of the man whose face had turned to his that night. Back then Joe was unused to drinking. He'd been found comatose in his own vomit on the street next morning and had been delivered to one of the Div's mobile hospital units, where he woke with a sore head, dry retching. When he'd managed to keep some soup down, a neat wiry man, balding, came and sat down beside his bed. He introduced himself as Captain Foley from N Section, whose responsibility it was to repatriate Kiwi prisoners of war.

'We're at a bit of a loss here,' said Captain Foley. 'Who are you?'

* * *

Joe was interrogated and processed by N Section and given new ID papers, but stubbornly refused to hand over his false carta d'identità for Gianni Lamonza. They gave him a psychological test that he struggled with in his own language — he found he'd forgotten idiosyncratic English and when he was trying to collect his thoughts he would say, 'E allora' and Foley would say 'What?' and he would say 'Niente'. And Foley would say 'Can you please speak English?' and he would say, 'Magari' or 'Perforza' or 'Certo' or just 'Sì'.

When he told Foley about the heroic partigiani of the Garibaldi brigade, the captain asked, 'Aren't they communists?'

He also told them that he had fought alongside another New

Zealander and watched Foley's eyes very carefully when he mentioned Harry Spence. There wasn't a flicker of recognition so he said no more. The captain asked for the names of the families who'd given him refuge and the partisans he'd fought with. Joe was so conditioned not to supply this information that he hesitated to name them, but Foley said there might be some way to recognise their contribution, so he described what had happened to the Bonazzons and Zanardis and wept again when he spoke of Leo and Luca.

'Can you believe that?' he asked Foley. 'The Gestapo has a gun to your only son's head, and still you say nothing about two soldiers from the other end of the earth. Can you believe that?'

Foley asked whether he might be suffering from battle fatigue. Joe said that he hadn't been in many battles, tried to explain that it was a different sort of war, being hunted, having a poster displayed everywhere you turned with your face on it and a huge reward for your capture. The captain had been interested in the poster. When Joe gave him more details, Foley's only question was why Harry Spence had impersonated an officer, and Joe a corporal.

* * *

Joe was sent to Bari to wait with the rest of the troops for a ship home. He felt like an impostor in his stiff new uniform and found it difficult to fit into the military way, and was laughed at when he sometimes finished his sentences in dialect. He wasn't sure what assessment Captain Foley had made of his state of mind, but it must have been positive because in Bari they gave him the official notification of Dan's death.

They told him that Dan had died instantly in his tank on 27

July 1944 at La Romola in Tuscany, and they gave him a letter that had been found on his body.

This didn't make sense: incineration would have killed his brother. There were burn marks around the edge of the letter, and dried mud, which proved to be dust mixed with blood. By then he'd seen so many grotesque cadavers that he was grateful for the kindness of those who had decided that Dan's death had been quick and unknowing. The letter was written the day before he died. 26th July 1944. Castellare, Tuscany.

> *Joe,*
>
> *We're sweating blood for every inch of land we take. They're using Tigers like mobile gun emplacements. We have to send waves of Shermans against them. It needs 4 or 5 of us to take out every Tiger, so it's not a pretty equation for us tankers — three or four of us are dead ducks every time. The first one we came up against 3 days ago near Romita took out four of us before its own crew blew it up. The wreck was covered in hits, all our armour-piercing shells had bounced off, apart from the one that got in through a weld seam. I can't find out anything about you. You're not on any Red Cross lists. I hope you're somewhere safe, in Germany maybe, feeding up on sauerkraut and blood sausage. Hope the bastards are treating you good. We're coming to get you, little brother. Stay safe till we get there.*
>
> *Dan*

What had he been doing on the 27th of July the year before? Had he felt a tremor in his soul at Dan's passing? It would have been midsummer on the Bonazzon campi. He'd have been living in his cave out the back of the property and helping Bepi and Gigi in the fields before the sun got too high. Would it have been too early to be cropping beet? The maize would have been high enough to hide in. July was a couple of months before Major Ferguson arrived, so the Garibaldis would have been operating under Luca's directions, blowing up pylons and points with Joe's homemade dynamite.

There might have been a shadow on his soul about that time, he decided, but it wasn't Dan's. It must have been about then that Donatella had been invited to the dance by Klaus and later that night he had seen her pure happiness after she'd made love to Harry.

He couldn't sleep for the first five days after the ship left Bari for fear that if he closed his eyes he would be engulfed once again by the fire and flame of the *Nino Bixio*. But as time settled heavily on the placid ocean, and continued to pass as if nothing had happened, Joe gradually lost his fear of the sky. He walked round the deck most days and lay up there most nights, watching the men get bored with crown and anchor and begin schools of two-up, which ran for twenty-four hours. But Joe never played and no one pressed him on it: he wasn't the only one on board who spent the days staring out at the horizon, seeing pictures he couldn't talk about.

As time went on the manner of death, the how of it in that torrent of paranoia and shifting allegiances Joe had left behind on the northern plains of Italy, seemed to matter less. Death had come or it hadn't. The thing he couldn't understand was why it hadn't come for him. Or perhaps it had, but in a different way. The fear and dread that had been his companions for so long seemed to dissipate, and with them went any feeling at all.

60

His brother's widow Sandy had been waiting for him on the wharf at Wellington. There were cheers from the crowd and a band playing as they disembarked with their kitbags. Joe left his empty bag on the ship and walked off with Dan's letter, both his IDs and his paybook in his pockets.

Sandy was in a big coat with the collar turned up against the sharp edges of the wind. She hugged and kissed him then they clung to each other and cried for Dan. Despite the coat, in that close embrace there was no hiding the fact that she was pregnant.

She took him to a department store where old ladies with blue rinses sat sipping tea and eating pikelets with whipped cream and strawberry jam. Away from the excitement of the wharf everyone whispered in public, as if they had secrets to keep. Sandy whispered to him that she'd fallen in love with an American soldier she'd seen sitting by himself crying at the dance hall the nurse aides used to go to. He'd been about to embark for the islands next day. He'd told her the marines were being used as human waves against the Japanese and he would certainly die. 'But he didn't,' she said, smiling through her tears.

Joe was thinking that it had been almost a year since Sandy would have heard about Dan and become a widow. He was thinking that's just what happens in war. People lose their children, their brothers, their fathers, their houses, their fields and their husbands, and somehow have to go on.

He had been going to show Sandy Dan's last letter but it didn't seem right to do that, with his blood still on it. He could see that she was past that. She said she'd saved as much money as she could and was about to join her man in a small town in Arkansas so the baby could be born American. She'd withdrawn all Joe's army pay from the bank and handed it to him, the notes all neatly folded into a fat white envelope. 'You should check it's all there,' she'd said, but he didn't.

She asked him some questions about what had happened to him, why they hadn't heard anything for so long. Joe tried to explain, but couldn't find the words to describe the kind of war he'd been involved in. It already seemed like a dream, particularly afterwards, when he walked back through Wellington's cold streets past soldiers who looked just like him. They were happy, mostly drunk, some singing, some dancing with girls or with each other, some fighting.

Something about him must have alarmed Sandy. At one point she put her fingertips on his scar and shook her head and asked him, 'But what will you do, Joe?'

He'd not said goodbye. When Sandy had excused herself to go to the 'bathroom', she'd left her coat over the back of the chair, so he'd slipped the envelope of money into one of the side pockets and left.

He walked over the first hill to the botanical gardens. The night sky was obscured by low cloud: anyone up there looking for him would be blinded, so he lay down in a grassy glade and slept. Before he fell asleep, he remembered thinking how strange it was to be here. Back in the tearooms, when he'd been working out how much time had passed since Sandy had been told she was a widow, he'd realised something else about time. Out on that ship, maybe when they'd been crossing the Indian Ocean to Fremantle, he'd turned twenty-two.

61

Perhaps Sandy had been right to be alarmed at Joe's prospects. Perhaps she'd seen something in him that wouldn't sit easily in the world that awaited him back home. For what followed were lost years, he could see that now. He was like flotsam from the *Nino Bixio*, blown apart by the explosion but still floating, unable to find form or substance. He'd got a taste for the way alcohol softened not just memories but the sharp edges of the present.

The newspapers said New Zealand had lost more soldiers per capita than any nation other than Russia, but the scars of loss weren't visible. The country showed no sign of the terrible convulsions Joe had ridden through on Donatella's bicycle, the ash and smoke and rubble, the cratered roads and fields and wrecked vehicles, the burnt-out villages and a hungry terrified population made homeless refugees in their own land. In New Zealand, it seemed to Joe, a people not given to overt emotion were able to put it all behind them and continue on as if nothing had happened, and he became lost in the silence, a ghost more haunted than haunting, moving through the pristine emptiness of the landscape.

In Gemona he'd dreamt of going home to Oamaru, back to the mine at Ngapara. But although he'd never thought of it consciously, home had meant the proximity of Dan and Sandy, the remnants of his family. Sooner or later Malachy would die and loosen his grip on Ida and the others, but that might be years away yet. In the meantime there was no one for him down there.

Instead he went north through a land of plenty spotted with rickety wooden houses that looked as if they would not survive next year's spring growth. At Huntly, in country so flat and winter-wet it could have been the plains of the Veneto, he found a coal mine.

The Huntly East mine followed a split of the Taupiri seam that was twenty yards deep in places. In one shaft, already four yards high, an older Scottish miner on his shift, Robert Laing, told him that there were another eight or nine yards of coal under their feet. Robert had been in New Zealand since he was eighteen, had married here, but had never lost his tangy Scottish accent. He had keen black eyes separated by an angry red bulb of a nose, kept from exploding by deep veins of coal dust in the enlarged pores.

It was a much larger mine and workforce than at Ngapara, with lift cages and electrical jiggers that were all new to him, but the drilling and shovelling were constants. Joe liked being part of a larger body of men and although every miner had to keep his wits about him and know what he was doing, his name was just one of many tabs hanging on the day-shift board. He had a hut in the single men's quarters and kept largely to himself when not working, drinking in the local bar and falling easily into sleep.

As time went on, the fire of El Mreir largely left him alone and his dreams and nightmares and memories and imaginings became indistinguishable. He'd be singing 'Twinkle, twinkle little star' to Leo and Paola. Leo would be looking up at the imaginary heavens for his star when his eyes would fall on Joe and he would ask Donatella, 'What does this man want, Aunty?' Or he'd remember Luca in a debate in the hayloft with Harry, except that instead of Harry it was Il Pazzo with his glasses smashed and it wasn't a debate, it was an interrogation. He dreamed of Bepi and Nina, Gigi and Marisa, and wondered if they'd rebuilt their houses and replanted their campi. Mostly he dreamed and thought of Donatella, what had become of her, whether Harry had contacted her, whether her baby was a boy or girl. Either would have been welcomed by the extended family, he knew, but if its illegitimate provenance was known by the community, it might be easier for a boy to live with that. Besides, the Bonazzons and Zanardis had each lost a son.

After a year, he decided to write Donatella a letter. He wasn't sure how to write dialect and he knew the teacher in her would prefer to read Italian, but that was already slipping away. The letter looked clumsy to him when he reread it but he posted it anyway to the address he remembered and hoped that the houses had been rebuilt and there would be someone there to deliver it to.

He wasn't expecting a reply, but many months later one of the men told him there was a letter for him up on the board in the dining room. His heart had raced until he saw that the envelope was his own, returned to sender.

62

One late summer evening he was dozing on his bed. It was still twilight outside and he heard excited shouts. He ignored them for a while until something hit his hut with a thump. His startle response was still there — on the rare occasions anyone came to his hut, he'd be awake and on his feet, fearful and angry, before a hand had touched the door. On the rare occasions he lost his temper, he'd learnt to ask himself what he was afraid of. Fear was the trigger for fearless fury. But this time it was only a rugby ball that had hit the wall and was now lying a yard or two in front of his step. Nearby were several men in shorts and assorted rugby jerseys, hands on hips or knees, breathing heavily.

'Sorry mate, can you throw it back?' asked one of them. 'We're a bit knackered.'

Joe picked the ball up, flicked it around till his right fingertips had the seam, then spiralled it back to the nearest player. There was complete silence until he turned to go back inside.

'Taihoa!' He heard the ball being booted and turned back just in time to catch it.

Jack Taumata and Ernie Jones, Jonesy, were the main men behind the game of pick-up that happened most evenings until the start of club training. They insisted Joe join their games, then when autumn came they took him along to the Huntly clubrooms for the senior trials.

Rugby unlocked something in Joe he'd thought was dead — a childlike joy, an ability to lose himself completely in the moment. He'd been anxious before the first match, almost backed out, but from the time the ref's whistle blew for the beginning of the bruising, bustling, chaotic game he lost whatever was broken and watchful inside him and grew quiet and focused.

It was in the clubrooms that he met Robert Laing's daughter Iripeta. A big woman with the face of an angel, Peta already had a child, a toddler called Andrew. She said the boy's father had 'slung his hook' on hearing she was pregnant and was planting pine forests on the Central Plateau. Peta was tender and funny, earthy and easy with Joe. When she realised he was a virgin, she made sure his first experience was one to remember 'because mine was shit'. At twenty-five a late convert to that pleasure, Joe became a zealot. Sex, he discovered, was another way of losing himself and living in the present, but he was always careful to wear frenchies, even though Peta didn't seem overly concerned.

Through Peta, Joe was gradually absorbed into the Laings' family circle. Although Robert had no relations in New Zealand, Peta's mother Huia was part of a big Maori family with connections to the Ngaruawahia marae and endless cousins would identify themselves in the opposition teams or over drinks in the clubrooms afterwards.

Robert was a keen fisherman and owned a large dinghy with an outboard. After Joe had turned down a couple of invitations to go fishing, it had become easier to accept than to admit he was still a bit wary of boats. On an Indian summer's day, they'd caught no fish in the Waikato, broad and slow moving like the Kakanui and Livenza but about ten times larger, so they'd collected Huia, Peta and Andrew in Robert's old Bedford pick-up and driven to the launch ramp at Lake Ohakuri.

The sun shone down on them as they drifted across the placid waters and Robert tried everything he knew, spinning, then trolling without result. When he finally admitted defeat, they had a beer and sandwich picnic in the boat, then Joe had dived into the water in his clothes.

Down in the deep brown he finally felt the *Nino Bixio* let him go. When he surfaced, bursting up, he roared something ecstatic but unintelligible. Peta looked at him and giggled. Joe began laughing and it was infectious — Andrew, then Huia and finally Robert, pissing themselves about they knew not what, save that something had released its terrible grip on Joe and they were happy for him.

63

Joe had often wondered if he might have stayed in Huntly, built a life there. He'd gradually burrowed his way into the community, made a small space he could stand tall in, propped it with fellow miners and rugby team-mates, none of whom would regard him as a close mate — his failing not theirs — and with Peta and her extended family, Robert and Huia. When he was in Peta's welcoming arms he could think of nothing else but her, but when she wasn't there it was always Donatella's quiet eyes searching his. Old Mal had always said, 'Don't want what you can't have, boy', but in his dreams it was Donatella who was looking to him for something.

Joe didn't talk about the war with Peta because he didn't know what to say about it, how to describe it. The only conventional war he'd fought had finished at El Mreir, where he'd conclusively proven himself to be a coward. His lack of words wasn't a problem: none of the ex-soldiers down in the mine wanted to talk either. When Peta caressed his scar it didn't need any more explanation than the returned soldier with one leg who worked as a pay clerk in the mine office, or the missing brothers and husbands who had never come back. The war quickly became an unspoken narrative in the collective memory, a pain best forgotten, and Joe might never have talked about it again, but for a chance meeting with Arch Scott.

After a pre-season friendly against one of the South Auckland teams, it might have been in Manurewa, he saw a tall blond figure he recognised at the bar in the clubrooms. Arch Scott was carrying about four stone more than when Joe had last seen him at the station in Ronchi dei Legionari but the long friendly face was unmistakably the same. They found a couple of chairs at the end of a varnished chip-board table and talked, with a jug of warm draught between them. They began in English, swapping courtesies about their present situations, but gradually switched to Veneziano as their conversation ranged back to places and incidents they'd lived in that language and now found impossible to describe in English.

When Joe bought Arch another jug, Jonesy and his team-mates seemed to know what was going on and stayed at the bar so that Arch and Joe weren't disturbed.

Joe discovered that he and Arch had had very different wars behind enemy lines. After liberation from PG 107/7, Arch had stayed close to San Pietro di Livenza, where he had counselled and practised non-violence, for fear of the retribution the alternative might bring to the Italian families who'd sheltered them. He'd spent his time in the service of other prisoners, organising food and shelter, and trying to get them back to Allied lines. Two Kiwis had been caught and executed in his area, one of them, Dave Russell, quite close to him. That had knocked him, but he'd got forty-seven men off Caorle beach by British motor boat and submarine. Harry Spence hadn't been among them, which, in Joe's mind, made it more probable that the man he'd spoken to in Trieste had been Harry.

Arch said word of the heroics of Rico Zanardi and the Garibaldis had travelled south to San Pietro, that he'd been stunned by some of what he'd heard: the blowing up of a major rail bridge and engines in shunting yards and the execution of a Gestapo officer. He'd often wondered if all he'd heard could be true. When Joe confirmed it, Arch said it was a story that had to be told.

Joe agreed but wasn't actually sure. The bare facts of what they'd done were one thing but what had happened in and around them was quite another. Joe wished he'd gone back to San Pietro with Arch after the encounter with One-Eyed Jack above Monfalcone. If he'd done that, he wouldn't have brought Harry and Charlie down on the Bonazzons and Zanardis, and Luca and Leo would still be alive, and Donatella wouldn't have fallen in love with Harry.

Joe had had a question for Arch Scott that he couldn't ask anyone else. He'd wanted to ask Arch whether he felt anything, whether the feelings he could remember having before the war had come back. But once Arch began telling his story, Joe's question seemed redundant.

*   *   *

Arch had stayed on in San Pietro as interpreter and assistant for an English military governor who spoke no Italian, so he was present at the disbanding parades of local partisans, now called patriots, and sat in 'courts' dealing with long queues of people with queries and difficulties they tried to resolve, and helped to organise the delivery of food and commodities to a population who'd been caught in the crossfire of two huge armies fighting to the death.

'At first, I was happy enough to be involved,' Arch said. 'Happy to act as a peacemaker between my mates the patriots and the fascists they wanted to kill. I preached peace and tolerance, an end to fighting and hurting, asked them to forgive and forget, to try to look ahead towards a new Italy of harmony and love.' Arch shook his head hopelessly at the memory. 'Then the Allied Military Government held a reception at Portogruaro for local dignitaries and anyone else in the upper echelons with enough money or prestige to have himself invited. Watching those fawning sycophants that night gave me a gut's ache. Some well-to-do people were anti-German and had been very kind to us, but most of them were backing the winning side, you know? Good time Charlies, remnants of an effete aristocracy. There wasn't one partisan leader at that reception, but many British and Italian officers, resplendent in their uniforms, and of course plenty of lovely-looking Italian women ready to grab them by the balls. A stiff prick has no conscience, Joe,' said Arch, 'and the penis is mightier than the pen or the sword.'

'The same thing happened in Trieste,' said Joe.

Arch said he'd argued with the naïve military governor who began granting perks and preferences to these new acquaintances. It might have been why his repatriation orders suddenly came through.

'To those that have shall be given,' said Arch. 'I could see us winning the war and losing the peace. The northern Italians had been waiting for us with open arms until they saw former fascists giving parties and dances to high-ranking Allied officers, making millions of lire working for the Allies today as they had with the Germans yesterday. After two months of Allied occupation all the ordinary Italians saw was more unemployment, lower wages for workers and a huge black market as all the stuff hidden during the German occupation saw the light again.

'That reception at Portogruaro was the last function I attended. I turned down all the invitations to dine with people who wanted to sting me for favours, and spent any remaining spare time I had with my family and friends in San Pietro.'

Arch had tried desperately hard to stay in Italy and help where he could, arguing with Divisional HQ that they needed someone on the ground who knew the people, knew who was who and who had done what, but to no avail — he'd been forced to accept repatriation and go to England. He felt so let down that he told his OC that he no longer wanted to hold rank in the New Zealand army and handed in his one stripe.

Three months later he was put on a ship that stopped at Taranto, below Bari. Arch had planned to leave the ship there, abscond from the army and walk back to the Veneto. But the time in England had dulled his anger and his desire, beaten him down, enough for him to stay on board and go home. 'Just enough,' said Arch.

But since he'd been home he'd often wished that he'd jumped ship at Taranto. He felt that he'd deserted his family and friends back there and still felt bitter about how little the aftermath of war depended on the men who had fought it. But he'd written letters to the Antonel and Cusin families and friends who had supported him, and to the heroic priest, Don Antonio Andreazza, who had feigned madness when the Germans tortured him and had spent more than a year in an asylum out in the lagoon. And he'd sent another rugby ball over to San Pietro, after the one the prisoners had received in the Red Cross parcel at PG 107/7 had finally given up the ghost.

By the time Arch had finished talking, Joe had fallen back into a deep pool of feelings and memories that he'd been flitting fearfully across for five years like a dragonfly, skimming and touching without disturbing whatever was dwelling in the water below.

Back in his hut, the thing that stayed with Joe was what Arch had told him right at the end. 'Some never came back,' he'd said. 'The Hare Battalion. N Section never found them all.'

'Some would have died alone, unknown,' said Joe. 'Quite a few tried to cross the mountains into Switzerland, didn't they?'

'Some decided they didn't want to be found,' said Arch. 'Decided they preferred their Italian lives.'

That stayed with Joe. He didn't think consciously of going back just then, not until the shadow of Harry Spence fell across him once again.

Treviso, 2014

64

At 10.21 whatever within her father that was still clinging to life let go. There was no discernible change but the absence of breath. The butterfly wings had stopped beating. She stroked him, called to him, then remembered the button. A nurse arrived, checked for vital signs, then crossed herself and took Clare's hand. Clare kissed him and whispered, 'Bye, Dad', then had to brush her tears from the cold concavity of his cheek.

They left her there with him, she didn't know how long. She felt strangely at peace, as if this was a moment she'd lived before. Many times in fact: over the past eighteen months, it had seemed inevitable and imminent. At some point, Signor Abruzzi came and said, 'I'm sorry' in English, then spoke soothingly in Italian, words she didn't understand but in a tone of such sympathy and understanding that she wept again.

Then the nurses came back, along with the white-haired nun, who stood well back and watched, whispering what sounded like prayerful consolations to herself as the nurses clicked off the brakes on the wheels of his bed. Clare was past trying to protect her father from what might be nothing more than a customary blessing in a Catholic country. She looked at her father's face as he went. It seemed looser in death, less taut. Death is peace, she thought, life is pain. She wasn't sure whether she was thinking of his release or her future without him.

As they wheeled him away on the bed the nun touched her sleeve, whispered 'Thank you' in English, and was gone.

Clare sat there alone, seeing herself almost objectively as a woman in a chair in a hospital room with no bed, surrounded by flowers from people she didn't know. She was sure that if she waited here the person she'd thought she knew, even a little in so short a time, would come on cue, as he had since they'd arrived in Venice.

She knew she'd been clinging too hard to the sense Renzo gave her of a life beyond the mesh of bad relationships and dirty commerce. She'd hoped that somehow he might be a key to finding a new way, something more profound. It was an impossible burden to put on anyone, particularly someone you'd known for only a week, but to find that he was part of more duplicity was ruinous. Renzo had pretended to share what he knew, significant information about the truth of things. When he'd talked about particles that misbehaved when they weren't being watched, had he been talking about himself? Had he been using a professional code that she was supposed to be able to crack?

He was a Lamonza. He hadn't assigned himself to her and her father by accident. He was the son of Beppino — or of Cinzia — and had kept his name. A terrible thought struck her. That if he was Cinzia's son and had kept her name, it was probably because there was no father around. *Fuck*. Could he be her father's incestuous love child? Could history possibly repeat like that? She tried to calculate how much older he would have to be than her, whether he'd said what year he went to MIT, and felt a red blush at the remembered kiss. *How could he have allowed that to happen?* Then she remembered him saying that his father had died. She felt guilty at the relief that memory afforded her . . .

There was a tap on the door, as she knew there would be, and he let himself in, wearing his perfectly preppy uniform and his caring facade and crossed to her, with his heartfelt 'I'm so sorry's', then tried to kiss her.

She rose from her chair in alarm, held him off with stiff arms. 'Who the hell *are* you?'

He at least had the decency to look crestfallen. Then he reverted to that curious formality. 'I, too,' he said, 'am looking for the answer to that question. You must excuse me, Clare, for expecting to find it in you.'

65

Renzo drove her up towards the Dolomites. Clare didn't bother asking where they were going; it didn't matter. Presumably at the end of the journey there'd be some kind of explanation, but she felt washed out and quickly fell asleep in the warm peace of the car, waking only when he veered off a winding secondary road onto a rutted shingle track climbing up through russet vines.

The Audi scrambled up for about a kilometre to a crude wooden sign at the edge of the vineyard, *Osteria senza Oste*. 'Hostelry without hosts,' he told her.

She didn't really understand until he'd jammed the car's nose between two rows of vines and led her up a narrow path. A couple of hundred metres from the car was a simple wooden shelter built on a terrace with a couple of tables and chairs out front. There were gently undulating hills as far as she could see, covered in vines, turned golden in the autumn sun.

'You're looking due north,' he said, 'at prosecco country. It used to be a well-kept local secret in your father's time and these vintners weren't rich. Now these hills are a gold mine, but they've tried to preserve some of the old traditions. Come,' he said, 'I'll show you.'

Inside the shelter were bottles of prosecco and other wines, fresh bread, cheese and prosciutto on a board, with glasses and cutlery and a small basin.

'It runs on honesty,' said Renzo, putting some euros in a cup.

'How ironic,' she said. 'In Aldo's bar at the reunion, you pointed out Franco's photo and told me who he was, but never once said that he was your uncle.'

'Sins of omission, yes,' he said. 'I apologise.'

'But why keep it a secret?'

'I didn't make a secret of who I was. I gave you my card and my name, but I admit that I wasn't forthright about how I was connected, and who to.'

'Why not?'

'Take a seat outside and I'll bring us some lunch.'

'I'm not hungry,' she said.

'But you still need to eat something.'

She couldn't argue, but went out and sat looking at the vista until he appeared with two glasses of white wine, then a torn baguette with cheese and prosciutto. He was right: she was hungry — until he began talking again.

'How this started. I wanted to stay close to your father because I thought he might reveal something very important to me: who my grandfather is. I put that incorrectly. I know my grandfather is Gianni Lamonza, but I don't know who Gianni Lamonza *is*.'

'Why would my father have known anything about that?'

'Six months ago my grandfather had a minor stroke and was hospitalised. They discovered there were no medical records for Gianni Lamonza. He'd never been in hospital before or even visited a doctor. So I went through his personal items and found his old identity papers, his carta d'identità from the war, and presented them. The hospital passed them to the authorities, who confirmed they were forged.

He took a sip from his glass. 'Okay, that kind of fitted with the story we'd always been told, of his real ID papers being destroyed by the Germans in a prisoner of war camp. We were told that was why he took so long to be repatriated from

384

Germany to Italy. The Allied authorities couldn't determine who he was. So, the fact that his ID was forged, well, the aftermath of the war, it was a confusing time. So, while my grandfather was in hospital, I tried to trace his identity so that he could be issued with legitimate papers. Further investigation revealed he hadn't paid tax, registered as a voter, drawn any benefits. He'd lived in this society for ninety odd years like a ghost, leaving no official footprints.'

Clare didn't see how this could possibly be relevant to her father. She hoped it wouldn't be.

'There's more. Lamonza is a very unusual name: we were always told that his family was from a remote mountain valley up the back of Trentino, and that his family were all killed by the Germans, but I went through all the births, deaths and marriages records for the whole of the Brennero in the decade 1920 to 1930. There was no record of a Gianni Lamonza having being born. Not only is there no record of Gianni Lamonza, there is no record of any Lamonza *ever*. It doesn't exist as a family name, and it never has, as far as I can tell. So Gianni Lamonza, my grandfather, doesn't exist and neither does his family.

'I had no one to turn to. All the people who might have known anything about my grandfather's provenance — my grandmother, particularly — had been wiped out in the terremoto in 1976. He also lost Franco that year, when your father was here. It was a terrible time for him, as bad as the war, and he refuses to talk about either.'

'Doesn't he have to tell the authorities?'

'The case has been shelved. The man is more than ninety years old, after all, and he's one of the last surviving *confusioni* from the Second World War. But *I* want to know. You can understand that?'

'Of course.' She wanted to be able to agree with as much as possible of what he was saying, in the hope that he wouldn't require a revelation from her.

'The reason my grandfather was able to exist without ever having to have an official identity was because of my grandmother, Donatella. She was at the centre of everything, according to my father, Beppino, so when they lost her they all felt cast adrift. People who knew Beppino when he was young said he was a real live-wire, but he filled up with sorrow and then alcohol. Maybe he never got over the loss of Donatella and Franco. But he also fell out with my grandfather, and that didn't help. Over Bruce.'

Until this point, Renzo could have been addressing the vines and the view, but Clare now felt his eyes turning towards her, with real intent, as if his part in the story was drawing to a close and she was about to pick it up.

'Something happened back then. My grandfather sabotaged San Pietro's moment in the sun, which he'd spent two decades creating, and wrecked his relationship with his youngest son. Why?'

Clare was overtaken by a creeping fear. Where was this going? She didn't want to be the one holding the secret to anything and feared that the contents of the manila file would be the key to whatever Renzo was driving at. To avoid his eyes, she looked out at the golden vines and shivered.

'I'm sorry,' said Renzo. 'I can get you a blanket from the car?'

'I'm fine,' she said.

'My father used to talk of your father. He would have loved to have been at the reunion: whenever he talked of Bruce it was always in a tone of great respect. But with great regret also. Whatever happened back then to make Bruce leave was a sore point between my father and my grandfather. My father said Gianni had destroyed Bruce's figura, his respect, by sacking him as coach and dropping him from the team. I've never been brave enough to ask my grandfather what happened. Did your father talk about it?'

Not *talk*, no. She shook her head, not prepared to trust her voice.

'My father Beppino said there was something very strange about my grandfather's reaction to Bruce. That when he first saw your father at the market, he'd run away from him in shock. When Gianni had Bruce sacked, my father pleaded with him to reinstate him. Beppino and Gianni loved rugby, that was their biggest connection. They would happily talk rugby all day and night but Gianni refused to discuss Bruce or why he had sacked him and broken the team. Beppino said he'd never seen his father so intransigent and he got the impression from what little Gianni said that there was some kind of history, some kind of bad blood between him and Bruce. But how could that be? It's surely not possible. And yet my father said he got that strong feeling.'

Clare was mute with fear. 'I have no idea who your grandfather is,' she said, carefully. 'Dad never indicated to me that he knew anything about him.'

Which was true, as far as it went. That seemed to confirm something in Renzo, perhaps just his next question. 'I don't want to be indelicate,' he said, 'but did he ever talk about a woman called Cinzia?'

Oh Jesus, thought Clare.

'Cinzia was my father's sister, my aunt. Beppino said she

fell in love with Bruce.'

'Oh?'

'My father said that her relationship with Bruce was very short but was Le Grande Histoire d'Amour, the big affair — you understand? Maybe that was all that happened: Cinzia was the apple of my grandfather's eye and he was jealous of his daughter's love for Bruce and perhaps feared that he would take her away, back to New Zealand. You can perhaps understand that Gianni had lost his wife and his beloved eldest son, so the prospect of losing also his daughter . . .'

'I can understand that, yes.'

'But it still doesn't explain why my grandfather ran away at the market when he first saw Bruce, and when he had no idea that Bruce and Cinzia were interested in each other.'

Renzo seemed to have finished, and he hadn't ended with a question, yet it was there, palpable in the silence between them. *What do you know?*

It would be so easy to say it, just let the words go. *Cinzia wasn't your grandfather's child. Your grandfather knew that Bruce and Cinzia were brother and sister.* Just say it and let the heavy truth land like a cluster bomb and cause what damage it might.

It's not my place, she thought. *This* isn't my place. Her father, who had never appeared in court as far as she knew, used to say that it was an unspoken rule of cross-examination never to ask a question that you didn't know the answer to, because it might not be the one you were looking for and it could wreck your case. He never told her what to do if you were the one holding the wrecking ball, and the question had already been asked. As of this morning she had no family and she would love to claim her aunt, a woman she'd never met yet somehow felt she knew. But her father had held that truth to himself for nearly forty years. Was it right for her to just let it go? Is that what he'd intended by giving her the file?

She stared out at the view for some time, as if the answer to her dilemma might be there. Death and tragedy and betrayal seemed to arc back from her father this morning to God knows when. Yet all she could see was golden beauty, from one horizon to the other.

Dimmi qualcosa, caro, Cinzia had written to her father before he ran away without saying a word. *Tell me something, dear one.* Clare was no longer sure that Cinzia had been behind the little red door in Dorsoduro, no longer sure that Cinzia *could* have shut the door in her father's face. Now, before Clare said anything, she needed to be sure. Where was she now, the woman of her father's diary who had also been smashed by love? Did she recover? Did she find meaning in her life?

'I'd like to meet Cinzia,' she said, as casually as she could. 'If she's still around.'

Renzo looked surprised, but said, 'Of course.' Then he spoke again, awkwardly. 'I have one further confession to make,' he said. 'Another sin of omission.'

The Antipodes, 1951

66

Joe was never a very militant unionist. He'd joined the coal miners' union at Ngapara because that was a prerequisite of getting the job, and at Huntly East he'd joined the union again for much the same reason. After a childhood spent in servitude to Malachy Lamont on the farm at Devil's Bridge, any working conditions that allowed a break, any employment that gave workers any rights, any payment of money for work done, seemed enlightened.

Robert had dragged him along to union meetings, and he'd found there some of the same passion for workers' rights and aspirations for a more equitable society that Bepi and Gigi used to argue over in the fields. There was also another element he recognised: the fiery anger of Luca when he talked about the fascists, and the concept of class warfare where the workers' only recourse was to take up arms against their oppressors, the owners and employers. That element was small but vociferous and Joe watched the great bulk of miners hear them out and then get back to the business of making a rational case for better wages and conditions.

Robert Laing was one of the angry ones. His Scots burr was

more persuasive than most, partly because he carried the mine's institutional memory: of the forty-three miners who'd died in a methane explosion in 1914, and of the eleven men asphyxiated at nearby Glen Afton just before the war. But the principal cause of Robert's fury was that he'd not been allowed to fight for his adopted country because the war's hunger for coal had made mining an essential industry.

Joe had known none of this. His boss at Ngapara, Captain Nimmo, had enlisted, though he'd had to invent a new Christian name before the army would allow him in. When Joe thought back to the superficiality of his own reasons for enlisting and the horror that ensued, he felt Robert and his family might have been well served by the government intervention, but he said nothing.

Robert's anger was compounded during the war. In 1942 he'd been one of a thousand Huntly miners who'd gone out on strike when the owners of nearby Pukemiro mine had broken an agreement to top up wages. He'd been incensed — still was — when the government prosecuted the miners who'd gone out, then took control of the mine and suspended the sentences of those they'd collared so they could go back to work. 'We're mere pawns in a larger game,' proclaimed Robert, a chess enthusiast. 'A game where the bosses keep changing the rules so we have nae chance of winning!'

Four years into Joe's stay at Huntly, the union's treasurer retired. Joe had studied the previous year's financial report and thought he could remember enough from the accounting course he'd done at PG 57 to do the job. He'd had ulterior motives: he was keen to learn again and he was already thinking that he didn't want to spend the rest of his life down a mine. As the El Mreir nightmare receded and he lost his fear of the sky, his need for the security of earth above his head also faded. He could see a life above ground. Perhaps running his own business, maybe something relating to mining supplies.

In the meantime, as long as he was taking out Robert Laing's daughter there was no avoiding the union meetings and being treasurer made them slightly less boring. When Joe tried to pinpoint why, initially at least, he'd found the spirited discussions between Bepi and Gigi so interesting — and even the arguments between Luca and Harry and Donatella up in the hayloft — he thought it might have been because the subject under discussion back then was always how to make a better world, a brave new post-war world.

That sort of aspiration was seldom expressed at the union meetings. The agenda would be about the minutiae that directly affected the miners' well-being: safety matters, percentages, relativities, shift hours, holidays, smoko breaks — all good practical concerns but not exactly compelling.

*   *   *

Just before Christmas in 1950, a union rep came up from Wellington with the news that New Zealand's economy was booming. After more than a decade of restrictions and shortages, not to mention the Great Depression before that, their union was going to make sure that miners got a fair share of the national wealth they'd helped to create, not to mention compensation for the soaring cost of living.

'Christmas is finally coming for the workers,' the rep told them, 'if not this year, then next.'

That was the first Joe had heard of an economic boom. Huntly was not a pretty town and had seemed in the five years he'd been there to have become neither better nor worse off.

In early 1951 they'd been told the Arbitration Court had awarded a fifteen per cent wage increase to all workers. That certainly made a difference to Joe's pay packet and was greeted with quiet satisfaction by most of the miners, though not by Robert and his cronies, who thought it wasn't sufficient compensation for over a decade of selfless sacrifice by workers for the war effort and recovery.

'Enough is never enough,' was another of old Mal's maxims, applied usually when Joe and Dan pleaded for respite, but fifteen per cent was significant and voices like Robert's would have quickly been forgotten had it not been for the exclusion of watersiders from the largesse.

It turned out that 'all workers' actually meant workers covered by the industrial arbitration system, and technically the watersiders stood outside that because they were controlled by the Waterfront Industry Commission. This, according to the union reps who came to speak to the miners, was dominated by British shipping companies who offered the wharfies nine per cent. 'The same greedy bastards whose merchant ships were protected by our sailors,' said Robert.

In response, the Watersiders' Union refused to work overtime and there was, for Joe, a bewilderingly rapid escalation: the shipping companies wouldn't hire the wharfies unless they changed their stance about overtime, and when the wharfies resisted, they were locked out of the wharves, which came to a standstill.

On 21 February, the government said that the country's export-based economy was under threat and declared a state of emergency. The next morning, Joe stared dumbstruck at the headline in the *Waikato Times* and felt the blood drain from his face: 'New Zealand at War' read the quote from the Prime Minister, Sid Holland. Knowing that there were a thousand or so New Zealand soldiers in Korea, Joe feared that the situation had worsened and conscription might be imminent. But the body of the article confirmed that Holland was talking about the waterfront. The enemy was within. A few days later the government sent troops to Auckland and Wellington to do the wharfies' jobs.

At a hastily convened union gathering, Robert told the miners that this meeting was now illegal in so far as it supported or gave any information about their comrades on the wharves, that under newly imposed emergency regulations all newspapers and publications and media were rigidly censored, that police had been given sweeping powers of search and arrest, and that it was now an offence for citizens to assist strikers. 'Even giving food to the bairns of the strikers has been outlawed,' thundered Robert.

Even the workers were divided: the watersiders and their striking supporters were members of the Trade Union Congress, labelled communist not just by the government but also by a rival workers' organisation, the Federation of Labour, whose membership included the great majority of unions. The FOL leader was a man called Fintan Patrick Walsh, known to many as the Black Prince, but referred to dismissively by Robert as 'Tuohy, that gob-spittle Irish sheep shagger'.

This time, though, Robert couldn't be dismissed as a dyspeptic radical. The newspapers obediently stopped reporting the wharfies' side of the strike and the miners' information about what was happening on the waterfront came from illegally gestetnered leaflets and word of mouth from unionists in the know.

Joe's every instinct was to keep his head down and stay well clear as the stand-off worsened. Within weeks 22,000 workers went on strike in sympathy: freezing workers, drivers and, inevitably, miners. In a small mining town like Huntly, the shopkeepers and mining supply companies soon suffered too. The community rallied and, despite the emergency regulations, food got through, including the odd slaughtered sheep from local farmers and fresh vegetables from market gardeners.

Perhaps as a response to the crisis, Peta's husband came back from the forests.

* * *

Joe was in the habit of turning up at Peta's little brick house whenever he felt inclined. In mid-April, when the chimneys were already puffing grey smoke into the cooling air, he let himself through the back gate. There was a solidly built man swinging a shining axe, splitting logs like matchsticks, watched in awe by Andrew, now almost ready to start school. When the man saw Joe he offered a callused hand and introduced himself as Winston.

Joe had heard Peta talk about Win, and Joe could anyway see the son in the face of the father.

As they were shaking hands Peta appeared on the back porch, her eyes full of beseeching appeal. Joe fibbed to Win that he'd called by as part of his rounds as union treasurer to see everyone was okay. By that time Andrew had moved towards Joe and put his hand proprietorially on his trouser leg. 'Uncle Joe,' he said. Maybe Win knew, but they all went along with the fiction.

Win finished chopping the wood while Peta made a pot of

tea in the kitchen. 'It was fun, Joe,' she said, 'but he's the boy's father.'

She didn't need to say any more. Peta and Win were married and had a child. Joe could look out the window at father and son and see the family circle was complete. He and Peta had been making do with each other, being kind, giving comfort. That was something. That was enough.

They all sat on the back steps and slurped their tea. Win, unusually, asked Joe about his scar. When Joe said El Mreir, Win said he'd been with 28th Maori Battalion. The freight carried by those few words between them was almost insupportable. Win shook Joe's hand again, eyes brimming, called him brother.

It struck Joe as he walked away into the Huntly dusk that they'd all been making do since the war, making do with their jobs and lives while their souls tried to catch up with what had happened to them in those few years of cataclysm. Win away in the forests trying to work it out, Joe in the mine, both trying to reconcile who they'd been before the war with who they were now, to find some way of carrying what they knew. Win had come home to his family.

By the time he got back to his hut in the single men's quarters, Joe knew it was time to go. The new decade was upon them, the new half-century. It was time to put the old one behind them, time to expect something more than making do. That was what the watersiders wanted too. This wasn't Italy, mired in centuries-old divisions. New Zealand was an almost empty canvas: they could paint whatever pictures they wanted on it.

67

Is that how he'd ended up in Auckland that autumn? Had he been giving Peta time to reconstitute her family, or had he been wanting to get out of the mine anyway and the strike forced his hand? He could no longer remember, but Robert hadn't objected to his going, so he might have wanted to give his daughter and her husband a chance to make a go of it. State of mind was harder to remember than actual events but he thought he could recall being full of hope when he went north.

Peta had given him the address of a friend who might be able to put him up while he found some cheap accommodation, so he'd walked east to west across the city from the railway station, parallel to the port, down into the valley of Queen Street, up over the hill and down again into Freemans Bay.

At first he'd been impressed with what he'd seen — the grandness of the railway station's entrance fringed with columns of nascent phoenix palms, the flowery orderliness and old trees of Albert Park and the curving corrugated iron shop verandahs of the Victorian buildings in and around Queen Street. But by the time he'd climbed the hill to Hobson Street and begun descending into the valley behind, the stone had turned to wood, most of it blistered or unpainted, some of it so weathered and gnarled it was pulling the nails from the frames, leaving gaping holes into dank interiors. Many of the windows were broken. It was an overcast day with a cool southerly, a precursor to winter. These places already looked freezing. ·

He found Daisy Purdue's address, a tidy enough bungalow next door to a ramshackle villa that became a double storey at the back as it fell down the slope. He wouldn't have picked Daisy as a friend of Peta's. Where Peta was a big woman, relaxed and open, Daisy was a thin twig of twitching nerves. Where Peta never wore make-up, Daisy painted it on, even though her skin was like Peta's, brown satin. The common ground they had was generosity. Daisy offered him the sofa until he could get on his feet, much to the displeasure of the man who appeared to be her lover. Ted had hair so Brylcreemed it glinted like a helmet.

'Make sure it's just till you get on your feet,' said Ted.

'It's a bad time,' whispered Daisy to Joe, but didn't say why.

Joe was sure Ted had been drinking, though he was dressed in a spivvy suit and had arrived after dark in a shiny car. Daisy, her hair in curlers, cooked them dinner of sausages and mash and peas, which Ted didn't much like, then she went off to work, her blonded hair waved down on one side of her face, high heels, glitzy dress, looking, Joe thought, like a film star. Leaving Joe to Ted.

Living in Huntly surrounded by miners, Joe hadn't had much idea how the country perceived the striking wharfies until Ted 'put him right' about them and 'the rest of the fucking commie rabble who went out with them'.

Ted wanted to know where Joe stood, who he was, where he was from, what he was doing in Auckland. When Joe told him he'd been a miner but had come here to find different work, Ted considered that for a moment then said, 'Good on you.'

Looking for some connection, Joe had asked him who he'd been with in the war. Ted said he'd driven engines. 'Trains,' said Ted. 'I was exempted. But I'm well out of that: railways are dead money.'

Then he fell asleep on the sofa so Joe wrapped himself in his coat and went out and sat on the verandah. He looked out on the ramshackle villa next door and watched the comings and goings. After an hour or so, he thought he could make an educated guess about how many people lived there. About thirty, he reckoned. Many of them were young children, still running about barefoot in the darkness, constantly wiping snotty noses and runny eyes on dirty shirt sleeves or holey jerseys. There were at least two babies inside: he could hear one crying and one had what sounded like whooping cough. And an elderly couple settled down to sleep on the verandah, wrapping themselves in canvas and sackcloth. It wasn't the only house like that Joe had seen in the neighbourhood, just the closest.

After a couple of hours, Joe saw Daisy's bedroom light switch on, then off, and crept inside to make his bed on the sofa. Sometime before dawn he started at a hand on the door and saw Daisy tiptoeing past him, holding her high heels. He heard muffled conversation between her and Ted, then silence.

Ted had warned Joe not to make a row first thing, that he didn't need to get to the car-yard until mid-morning and Daisy usually got up mid-afternoon. Come morning, Joe didn't risk shaving or even making himself a cup of tea, simply cleared his stuff off the sofa, packed it away and let himself out the front door.

It was a fine clear autumn day as he climbed the hill to Ponsonby Road, which ran along the top of the ridge. The trams were still running, though some of the rails were already being lifted. He bought a *Herald* at Three Lamps and read the front page, then found a bench to sit on and went through the situations vacant. One job caught his eye, and it was close by, a sawmill and timber yard. As he walked down the hill to the yard nestling below the ridge, he could see, further west, corrugated iron roofs glinting up hill and down dale until they were lost in the green of the far hills.

At the entrance to the timber yard, a man walked him across to the manager's office past men in leather aprons pushing logs into huge revolving saws. Men at the other end pushed them back the other way while a conveyor belt took the off-cuts away, hovered over by a couple of men who pulled out the awkward lengths that might catch and block the belt. 'That's what you'll be doing,' the man yelled over the scream of the saws.

Joe didn't know if he could cope with the noise but he needn't have worried. When he joined a group of sorry-looking men in front of the manager's office, the first thing the manager said was, 'No strikers or my job's on the line.' Fully two-thirds of the group turned and walked back the way they'd come, Joe among them. There was no camaraderie in shame and the men quickly went their separate ways.

* * *

Joe bought a pint of milk and a loaf of bread and took it back to Daisy's house. Ted was gone so he had the place to himself. He made a cup of tea and a piece of toast and was careful to spread the butter and jam thinly.

During the afternoon, Daisy appeared from the bedroom, blonde hair straggled and sticking out like clumps of flax, blue shadows under her eyes. 'I have to drink,' she said. 'I can't do it sober.'

Joe made her a cuppa and she wrapped her dressing gown around herself and sat out on the verandah in the late afternoon sun. 'Be winter soon,' she said, shivering. Joe brought out his coat and she snuggled into that. 'Peta said you were a sweet man and to look after you,' she said. 'I'm sorry about Ted.'

Joe said that he and Ted were fine and that he'd soon be on his feet and gone.

Daisy saw right through that one. 'What will you do? This strike won't end any time soon, will it? They're blacking anyone associated with it.'

That night Ted brought someone home with him, a 'drinking buddy' he said by way of introduction. The stranger was dressed in a suit and tie, overhung by several chins. Joe had a strong feeling that he'd seen him before, that somewhere underneath that recent flesh was a face he knew. But the man gave no indication that he recognised Joe as he asked him quite aggressively what he thought was going to happen to the strikers. Before Joe could declare his ignorance the man said, 'Let me tell you what's going to happen.

'This is war to the death, make no mistake. These striking wharfies don't know the half of it yet: they'll be set upon by the police if they try to protest and if the police aren't up to flaying their hides, the government will send in the troops and the specials, like they did in 1913. There'll be blood on the streets. Any wharfies who stick to their guns will be blacklisted and will never work on the wharves again. They'll be pariahs wherever they go and there'll be no way back for them anywhere in this country.'

Joe said nothing, which the man took as encouragement. 'The waterfront is going to need a new labour force,' he said. 'Whoever signs up now to go to work on the wharves will be looked after, mark my words. You could be farting through silk.'

Still Joe said nothing, trying to remember where he'd seen this man's face before. He thought it might have been the war. Had they shared the fatal charge on El Mreir? Had he been in PG 57?

'Let me know,' the man said, rising. 'I could get you in on the ground floor.'

It was when he reached out to shake Joe's hand, and his shirt cuff rode up, and Joe saw the expensive watch on his wrist, that he knew. This was the man who'd offered Harry food for his watch when they'd arrived at the prison camp at Bari. The cookhouse wallah Harry had almost strangled.

* * *

Next morning, Joe rose before Ted and crept out past a different shiny car and climbed the hill to the Ponsonby Ridge. He found a discarded newspaper on the tram stop, intending to have another look at the jobs. He never got past the headline: 'Rail Bridge Damaged By Explosives. Saboteurs At Work In Huntly District'. The article detailed an attempt to destroy the railway bridge at Mahuta in the dead of night. Joe knew the bridge well: it took the coal from the open cast and underground mines back across to the main trunk line.

Alongside the headline was another column, headed 'Fiendish Act A Warning of Danger'. Sid Holland was quoted extensively. 'This diabolical act of sabotage will bring home to the people of New Zealand perhaps better than any warning I can give what dangers beset our country and the depth to which its enemies will descend to achieve their ends. I can think of nothing more fiendish or hideous . . .'

What words would the prime minister use if the country had suffered one iota of the damage Joe had seen in Italy? It was 'an infamous act of terrorism' perpetrated by an enemy that Joe had never seen but must have been all around him in Huntly. 'This is part and parcel of a desperate cold war that has come to our shores, in which life and limb are constantly in danger . . . the enemy is already within the gate . . .' The paper said it was May Day tomorrow, an international workers' holiday.

Joe didn't bother with the situations vacant. He walked back to Daisy's. Ted's shiny car was gone. He made himself a cup of tea and a piece of toast and sat out on the verandah.

Down where the boards of the porch swept under the abutment, several pairs of unblinking black eyes were watching him eat. He'd lived with rats all his life, at Devil's Bridge, the flour mill at Ngapara, the Veneto. He still remembered the rat looking at him after he, Charlie and Harry had eaten the chicken Harry had killed. But that had been in a shack out in the fields and he'd seen plenty more in such places, where animals lived or food was stored. In Freemans Bay rats lived where people ate and slept, where children played, and scurried openly across yards in the middle of the day.

* * *

That night, Ted came home drunk again after the six o'clock swill and castigated the fucking commie terrorist coal miners who had blown up the railway bridge at Huntly. Joe excused himself as soon as Daisy went off to work and waited on the verandah for Ted to fall asleep.

An ambulance came, no siren, and a small form was carried out of the house next door. Joe hadn't heard the whooping cough for a while and the little bundle the St John nurse carried away made no sound. He saw a black van stop further up the street but thought nothing of it. Its headlights were turned off, but no one got out.

He was halfway between wake and sleep, not sure whether he

was remembering or dreaming Donatella's eyes. She was telling him she was worried that an SS lieutenant on the Orvenco road bridge had noticed her comings and goings and was watching her. Joe had told Bepi about Donatella's fears and Bepi got a message to all their relations and friends around Gemona and Osoppo that if the Nazis came and asked about Donatella they were to say that, yes, they were expecting her at any time. Joe had wondered then, and still did, if the SS lieutenant was simply struck by her beauty. Donatella didn't look like a film star, she didn't look anything like Daisy, but she had something that drew the eyes of men.

Nothing had come of the SS lieutenant's interest but Joe had found it reassuring that even though by then she was Harry's lover she had brought her fears to him, not Harry. He'd often asked himself why. Whether she'd talked to him about her fears because she could sense the fear in him, or because fear was an emotion unknown to Harry, or whether there were some things deep in her heart that she felt safe sharing with Joe and no one else. He liked to think maybe that was it.

He was back there, somewhere in the Veneto in the last days of the war, not in his cave because there was a door, when he felt rather than heard a hand trying to turn the latch.

By the time the shoulder forced the door in, Joe was behind it with the iron poker in his hand. He stepped back half a pace as a black uniformed shape burst through, off balance, and smashed the poker down on the helmeted head. Before he could turn to swing at anyone else, he was hit from the side and splayed on the floor under several heavy men in black uniforms.

One of them grabbed a clump of his hair and twisted his head around. 'Is your name Joseph Lamont?' he yelled.

Joe was still confused about where he was. Should he give

404

out any information? Who would he endanger if he did?

A fist smashed his temple right above the scar and he slumped.

68

It wasn't San Sabba; the walls were concrete block not red brick. He felt groggy when he came round, but he knew that much. Part of his scar had been restitched. The men in black uniforms were New Zealand policemen in midnight blue. They took him from the cell where he'd woken up to an interview room with two chairs, a desk and no windows. There was a plainclothes detective there, mid-thirties, in braces and shirtsleeves and a much older overweight sergeant with a wooden baton. Neither identified himself or said why Joe was there.

'G'day Joe,' said the detective. 'You know that treason still carries the death penalty?'

'No,' said Joe.

'Hanging by the neck until you're dead,' said the sergeant.

'You should be aware,' continued the detective, 'that an act of terrorism like this could be construed as treason. A treacherous act against the country's national interest.'

Joe couldn't think of a response to that.

'Tell us what you know about the Huntly bridge.'

'I read in the paper that it was blown up,' said Joe.

'Dynamited,' confirmed the detective. 'The politicians are furious. Rabid dogs. They want blood.'

Joe just nodded, unsure what he was supposed to contribute. The detective had the kind of face you would be happy to trust, square and open, and eyes that appeared to smile as he looked at Joe expectantly.

'It's also true, is it not, that you're the treasurer of the Huntly branch of the coal miner's union that's struck in support of the wharfies?'

'I was, yes,' said Joe.

'Commie scum,' said the sergeant.

'And that you left Huntly three days ago under a cloud?'

'What cloud?' asked Joe.

'Why did you leave Huntly?'

'To come to Auckland. I wanted a change.'

'Not to cover your tracks?'

'What tracks?'

The detective sat down opposite Joe and leaned across the table. 'Tell me exactly where you were last night.'

'Where you found me?' asked Joe.

'The night before,' clarified the detective.

Joe told him he was in the same place, asleep on the sofa at Daisy Purdue's house in Freemans Bay.

'She's a working girl, isn't she?'

'She works,' said Joe. 'In a club in town.'

'Then she wouldn't have been there at night, would she?'

'Her man Ted was there.'

'We've spoken to him. He says he fell asleep early, can't vouch for whether you were there after that or not.'

'I was still there in the morning.'

'He says he didn't see you in the morning.'

'That's true,' conceded Joe. 'But Daisy saw me on the sofa when she came in from work.'

'So she says. But she's a prostitute and she's also a friend of Robert Laing's daughter, isn't she?'

'She's a friend of Peta's, yes.'

'How well do you know Robert Laing?'

'He was very good to me.'

It was clear the detective was feeling a good deal of frustration.

He blew out his cheeks, consulted his notes and lowered his voice conspiratorially. 'Listen son, we've had information which we're obliged to act on. You understand?'

'What information?'

'Anonymous information — at least as far as you're concerned. But from a very reliable source. Very. Someone I'd trust with my life.'

Joe had said nothing.

'From what our anonymous informant says, you're the expert,' said the detective.

'At what?' asked Joe.

'Blowing up bridges. Our information is that you're the gun. That in the war, up in northern Italy, you made your own dynamite and blew up pylons, railway point systems and bridges. Railway bridges. Is that true?'

No one had asked him that question before. He was still conditioned to deny it, but there was no point in doing that any more. 'It's true,' he said.

'According to our informant, the way the charges were set down in Huntly, it was your modus operandi.'

These words were new to Joe. Modus, he thought, might mean the same as moda in Italian, and operandi surely had something to do with operating, doing, but he wasn't sure. He was sure about one thing. 'If I'd set the charges the bridge wouldn't be still standing.'

'Smart little cunt.' The sergeant tried to kick the chair out from under Joe, but he was already rising when the policeman's boot hit the back legs. The chair crashed across the room into the wall. Before Joe could turn the sergeant whacked the baton into the back of his knee and his leg gave way. When he hit the floor the sergeant booted him in the back just underneath the ribs.

'Enough!' shouted the detective.

That was the end of the first interview. Joe was ordered to his feet. He couldn't stand straight for the pain in his kidney, but the sergeant pushed him, bent double, along the corridor back to his cell.

'You're gonna swing for this, you little commie shit,' he said as he pulled the iron door shut.

Joe couldn't sit because the pressure went straight down to his kidney and he couldn't lie straight because it seemed to stretch it. On the bunk, he lay on his back with the pillow pushed up under his shoulders to lift them a bit. He found if he kept his feet flat and his knees bent the pain was bearable until he had to piss. He wanted to go, but couldn't, then when it came it was red.

It wasn't just the kidney that kept Joe awake all night. He'd spoken to no one about the detail of what he did in Gemona, not even to Captain Foley of N Section or to Robert Laing or Peta. Nobody else in New Zealand could possibly know that he'd made the dynamite they'd used in Gemona. Nobody but Harry Spence.

By morning he had convinced himself he must be wrong, even though something else the detective had said was troubling him. He'd called the informant a very reliable source. 'Someone I'd trust with my life.' That was Harry, he thought: someone he'd trust with his life. He remembered that warm dry hand holding his as they crawled on their bellies in the dead of night through Nazi lines. Why would the man who'd saved his life countless times want to see him hanged? Had he been like Charlie and done something unforgivable? Joe couldn't think what that could have been, but if Harry the predator had him in his sights, he was dead meat.

* * *

Next morning, the detective had come to his cell. The sergeant had let him in but stayed outside. 'We've spoken again to Daisy Purdue,' he said. 'I'm prepared to concede that it's most unlikely you could have got down to Huntly, laid the explosive and got back to Auckland between the time Ted Gartner went to sleep and the time Daisy Purdue got back from work. Not impossible, but unlikely, given when the explosives were set. But you could have been an accessory.'

'I wasn't.'

'You didn't contribute advice or expertise to those who carried out this crime?'

'Lots of miners know about dynamite. They don't need me.'

'That's also true,' said the detective. He read through his notes again, then stood up. 'Might have to come back to you, son,' he said. 'But in the meantime, let me shake your hand. I saw action in Italy with the 22nd and what you did with the partisans was brilliant and brave.'

He shook Joe's hand and walked out of the cell, leaving the door open. Joe was unsure what he was supposed to do.

'Get a move on,' said the sergeant. 'Fuck off.'

The relief Joe felt to be hobbling along the streets of Auckland again quickly turned to anguish, then rage.

Daisy had left for work by the time he got back to Freemans Bay. When Ted drove up that evening in another shiny car, Joe was waiting for him on the verandah. He told Ted he wanted to talk to his friend with the watch and the gift of prophecy.

410

69

In the early morning darkness, Joe waited with a couple of other men up at Three Lamps. Joe thought he might have recognised them from the sawmill, but couldn't be sure. Their eyes didn't meet and they said nothing to one another. They didn't have to wait long. A truck with a big canopy over its tray pulled up. The tailgate was lowered and the canopy pulled aside enough for the men to climb on and join others already sitting on benches along either side of the tray.

They sat in silence, avoiding each other's gaze as the truck ground down the hill and eventually slowed and they heard the chants of a crowd — Joe couldn't make out many of the words being yelled, except 'fucking' and 'scabs'. A little further on, the truck stopped. The back flap was pulled apart and a policeman peered into the back briefly, then let the flap fall back. Joe glimpsed a tall wrought iron fence with a cordon of police holding back a surging crowd of wharfie pickets.

* * *

The *Doncaster Star* out of Southampton was already heading north up the Rangitoto stream that evening when the man with the watch found a mistake. One of the scabs who'd registered this morning with the new waterfront union hadn't been checked back out in the evening. It was the kind of mistake easily made under the pressure of getting the scabs safely through the picket lines without revealing their identities. He was confident that this Joseph Lamont character would be up there at Three Lamps with the others come morning.

At least that's what Joe was hoping would happen. There was no search of the hold that first night, or the second, so presumably no hue and cry raised by ship's radio. Maybe his name had been quietly expunged from the scab roster: the cookhouse wallah wouldn't have wanted any grief in his new venture. One lost soul more or less wouldn't make any difference.

Down among the wool bales and the smell of lanolin, Joe had three days' food and water. He made it last five and then made his wobbly way to the deck and asked for the captain.

George Hardwicke had the kind of what-oh English accent Kiwi soldiers had made fun of, usually attempting impersonations of General Auchinleck, but there was no levity in the anger Hardwicke directed at Joe. 'What on earth possessed you?'

The story Joe told Hardwicke wasn't about strikes and betrayals and death. It was a story of fighting with the partisans, of falling in love with an Italian woman he'd wanted to marry, but had been forced by the army to leave behind at the end of the war. He told Hardwicke he'd just found out by letter that she'd borne him a child, now six. He wanted to go back and assume his responsibilities as a husband and father.

Joe's story wasn't the whole truth, but it turned out to be the best truth for Captain Hardwicke, who had run the North Atlantic U-boat gauntlet during the war and seen many of his merchant seamen mates perish. He'd been forced into long absences from his young family, and he was a romantic.

When the *Doncaster Star* stopped for refuelling at Cape Town, Joe was told to keep his head down and out of sight. Similarly at Accra, where a load of copra was swung on board. Hardwicke told Joe he'd better get off before they reached

British customs at Southampton, so when the ship berthed at Lisbon to take on cork, Joe thanked Hardwicke and walked down the gangway into a warm Portuguese night.

* * *

On the ship, between long days scrubbing rust off iron with a wire brush, and spot painting, Joe had a surfeit of time to run back through exactly what the detective had said. His service with the 22nd, Harry's battalion, had confirmed the identity of the informant. Joe had been close to vomiting on the detective as he shook his hand.

Before Harry assassinated Il Pazzo, Joe had wanted to run, but knew Harry would have killed him with a bullet to the back of the neck, just like Charlie. Now he realised he'd made a terrible mistake in Trieste, that it must have been Harry at that party. Joe hadn't been accusatory exactly when he told Harry that Leo and Luca were dead, and that Donatella was still waiting for him, but just as Harry was the only person in New Zealand who knew about Joe's expertise with explosives, Joe was the only one who knew about Harry's shame.

Harry had always said that you didn't need an ideology, that it was enough to be against Jerry. You didn't have to be for anything, except freedom. His bid to have Joe hanged for treason painted a different picture of what he'd meant. Joe saw the empty canvas of the new world being smeared with the prejudices and divisions of the old: Malachy Lamont had broken his own family in two by dredging up the orange and the green, and Harry had now proven that post-war New Zealand was the same mess of red blood and black intent that had drowned Europe.

When he'd asked drunken Ted to take him to the cookhouse wallah that night after he'd been released from jail, he'd felt more isolated and alone in his own country than he'd ever felt in Gemona, and just as vulnerable. Back then, Harry was hunting Germans, not Joe.

70

Joe could remember every detail of the end of his journey, but not much of the journey itself. There were still transients wandering post-war Europe and the story of Gianni Lamonza, an Italian who'd emigrated to Australia, and was desperate to get back to see his mother before she died, was different in detail but not in kind from many others. He'd stayed off the main roads and been fed and watered by the people of the land, who seemed the same in Portugal and Spain and France as the contadini had been in the Veneto and Friuli. It had been a long trek that took him six weeks, though he hadn't walked much of it: he'd been driven in trucks and donkey carts and on the back of motorbikes. He'd slept occasionally in beds but more often in haylofts or out in the maize, and although the surroundings had given rise to bad dreams or memories, he mostly slept well in the knowledge that this time the sky was safe and there was no one looking for him.

The borders were problematic and he had to circumvent the customs posts: he had no passport and his Gianni Lamonza carta d'identità was no more likely to survive careful examination now than it had during the war. But that was easy: the walking tracks were well established and he crossed the alps from France in high summer on a track that might have been built by the Romans and came down the Tende River valley to Ventimiglia, where he boarded a train.

All the way he'd prepared himself for disappointment. Donatella might have married, she might not want him. When he'd seen from the train window the mountainous spine running along the Yugoslav border and dropping down to Gemona, far from feeling he'd come home he had to suppress a desire to flee.

And that feeling hadn't been helped by the burnt-out ruins of the Bonazzon and Zanardi houses. Not one stone or piece of timber had been repaired. There were labourers in Bepi and Gigi's campi: the owner had reclaimed the land. The mezzadria system seemed to have died with the war.

He'd followed one worker's directions to a much older Nina in a tiny flat at the bottom of the climb into town. She'd fallen on him and cried, then taken him to the hospital to see Bepi, who had succumbed to phlebitis in his legs. Propped up in the hospital bed he didn't look any smaller, but when he hugged Joe there was a strange lack of substance in that big frame, as if he'd been punctured. There were tears to be shed and news about Gigi and Marisa and Nonna Isabella before he could ask the question he'd come for.

If Nina and Bepi felt that he shouldn't contact Donatella, he didn't know what he would do. He wanted to be able to respect their decision but wasn't sure that he could. He thought he could probably count on Bepi's support but Nina could be more difficult. She'd been an increasingly isolated and forlorn figure towards the end of the war, watching her daughter fall in love with the man she never trusted. She'd always sensed, Joe thought, that he loved her daughter but in the face of Harry's confidence, Joe had done nothing to fight for her. Would that condemn him in Nina's eyes?

'Should I go to her?' he'd asked.

There was no hesitation from Nina. Donatella had had her baby in Venice where no one knew her and was teaching at a nursery school run by the Canossian Daughters of Charity. Her daughter, Cinzia, was at their primary school.

A daughter, thought Joe, as Bepi pulled a half-empty bottle of grappa from the bedside cabinet, put one finger to his lips and whispered: 'Un po' di riscaldamento?'

* * *

He'd taken the train back south with Bepi and Nina's blessing, but no certainty about what would happen. They had thought it better not to telephone Donatella in advance as she might try to avoid old painful thoughts, 'But,' said Bepi, 'there is no life without pain.'

From the station, he'd followed Bepi's directions to the vaporetto for Accademia. He'd never seen Venice before: he'd heard it sat on stilts in the middle of the sea and was surprised and reassured, as he looked out at the maze of tiny canals and streets, that it was built on land, in stone. Stone coursed by rivers, rivers of salt water.

He'd been over and over in his mind what he would say to Donatella when he saw her again. Why he loved her. How much he'd loved her even when she'd loved someone else. Every time he practised the words they sounded false to him and he hoped he'd have sufficient control not to say them. Or that she would say something to him that would help him to say the right thing to her.

About three in the afternoon, he alighted at the Accademia stop, walked past the grand wooden bridge and round to the right flanking a smaller canal. There stood the large convent school Bepi had described, with its own campanile and garden courtyard on the other side of a wrought iron gate, where some mothers had already begun gathering.

Then he saw her. She was walking across the courtyard garden towards the gate, surrounded by a bevy of little girls, too young to be her daughter. Other girls, older, were flowing out of classrooms on the other side of the courtyard. When Donatella's group reached the gate the small children dispersed to their mothers and she stood there, waving them goodbye and watching them go, until her eyes found him.

There was a moment when she looked stricken. Her hand went to her mouth and Joe didn't know whether she was appalled or simply stunned. As he moved towards her Joe remembered her last words to him as she left the blackened ruins of the family home with Leo's body in the cart.

'M'hai detto di tornare dai miei,' he managed. *You told me to go back to my own.* 'Eccomi.' *Here I am.* 'Sono tornato dai miei.' *Come back to my own.*

She said nothing.

He hadn't seen the child. There was a little girl standing a couple of yards behind Donatella, a still centre in a swirl of girls, considering him with her mother's serious eyes.

She was wearing a white dress and patent leather shoes with buckles. Her dark hair was short, urchin style, as if someone had held an upturned basin over her head and cut around the edges, so short you couldn't see any wave or curl or red in it. A fringe, though, under which those eyes were looking at him, searching for meaning, just as her mouth searched for a smile. He'd wondered how he would react to Harry's child. She must have sensed something in the way he was looking at her.

'Papà?' she asked.

Donatella turned towards the child. She said nothing that Joe could hear, but must have given her some signal. Perhaps it was just the absence of denial. The little girl suddenly ran forward and jumped into his arms. He'd hugged Cinzia and cried over her before he'd even embraced her mother.

Venice/San Pietro di Livenza, 2014

71

Cinzia had asked to meet them in Campo Santo Stefano. The first wind of winter was flowing east off the Adriatic but they found her at an outside table. When they took their seats beside her, Clare realised it was the same cafe her father had brought her to that first morning in Venice. This was where they met, she thought. *This was their place. This is where I should begin.*

It wasn't that easy. Suor Isabella had come straight from teaching, a black coat over her grey smock. She looked severe and drawn. Clare knew she had to give her some context. This time she couldn't just dump the file and run, as she had with Renzo.

He'd confessed at the Osteria senza Oste that the white-haired nun who had visited her father on his deathbed, Suor Isabella, was in fact his aunt, Cinzia. Clare had been dismayed, not so much by Renzo agreeing to do his aunt's bidding but that La Testa Calda of her father's diary, the redhead who had sworn and blasphemed and wanted so much from life and love, had betrothed herself to Christ. 'How long after Bruce left did that happen?' she'd asked Renzo.

Within a year, he thought.

Clare couldn't tell Renzo how indescribably disappointing it was that the woman she'd so identified with had succumbed to religion, had given up on her aspirations, had been defeated by love.

For Renzo, Cinzia's vocation had the benefit of logic: she'd spent her formative years in the Canossian school in Dorsoduro, had been educated by the sisters there, it was where her mother Donatella had taught. It made sense to him that, if Cinzia wanted to serve, that's where she would go. The order was a very pragmatic one, he said, with a big emphasis on serving the poor, women and children particularly.

Then again, as Clare was learning, Renzo was seldom surprised by anyone's behaviour. Curious, but not surprised. She supposed that if, like him, you believed the sub-atomic world defined the universe, and that anything that is possible, no matter how unlikely, happens all the time, it would be difficult to be surprised by anything. As much as she'd tried to get her head around the idea of Cinzia being a nun before they arrived at the cafe, it was still a shock: the severity of the grey and black, her urchin-cut white hair pressed under a soft wimple.

* * *

Renzo's sharing of his last 'sin of omission' had decided Clare. By the time they had left the golden prosecco vineyards behind and returned to Treviso, she knew she would give him the file. Her father had bequeathed her the secret: *Some good might come of it.* No good could possibly come from her holding onto the information, but telling Cinzia wasn't a decision she should have to make by herself. Back at his apartment, she'd handed him the file without preamble. 'You should read it,' she'd told him, 'before this goes any further.' It was, she knew, another test. *Show me what you do with secrets. Prove you're not another Nicholas.*

She'd left him to it and gone for a walk around safe, somnolent Treviso. Anxious, she kept getting lost until she remembered Renzo's maxim — left is right, right is right, straight ahead is right. By the time she found her way back, he'd have read her father's diary. Would he be upset, appalled, shocked, incredulous at the enormity of it, disgusted? She should have known better.

When he buzzed her in, he was exultant, waving the file in the air like a fly swat. 'This explains everything!' he said. 'Why San Pietro's glorious season in Serie A was ruined, why my grandfather sacked Bruce, why he fell out with my father!'

She could scarcely believe it. 'Is that all you take from it?'

'No, no, of course not. My aunt is your aunt — we're family, but not blood relations. Perfect!'

'Except that my aunt doesn't know she's my aunt, she doesn't know Gianni Lamonza isn't her father and she doesn't know she fell in love with her brother!'

'Yes, yes,' he agreed, though this was clearly an afterthought.

She'd guessed that he wouldn't be shocked, but she was surprised how little the central revelation of her father's diary meant to him. 'So the incest is no big deal?'

'Ethical man put taboos and constraints around consanguinity for good reason,' he said. 'It's a taboo that dates from the time when sex was inevitably reproductive rather than recreational. But, actually, we're all from the same singularity, we're all made up of bits of the same stardust, we exchange atoms with all living matter, so in the end we're all inextricably bound together.'

She had to laugh. Sometimes he sounded as full of New Age bullshit as Sarah. 'You think Cinzia will buy that?'

'That's what you want to do? Tell her?'

She nodded. 'Suor Isabella will regard it as a mortal sin, won't she?'

That slowed him down, but not for long.

'Truth is such a nebulous concept,' he said, reverting to the curious formality that meant he might be under some pressure. 'On the rare occasions we meet it, we must embrace it. Our aunt will understand that.'

She'd been so desperate to hear that answer: she wasn't sure what it proved about him, other than that he wasn't Nicholas. And he'd said *We* must embrace it. *Our* aunt.

'Forgiveness,' he said, 'depends on truth. That's what your father understood at the end of his life. That's why he was trying to find Cinzia.'

* * *

But now, sitting in front of Suor Isabella, Clare wasn't so sure. In the hospital room, she had deflected Clare's glance, never made genuine eye contact, but this time she took Clare's hand in hers and apologised for not introducing herself earlier.

'I wasn't sure whether you knew about my relationship with your father,' she said, with Renzo's slight American inflection. 'It was a long time ago, but I had no wish to cause any embarrassment.'

As her eyes searched Clare's, she saw the Cinzia of her father's diary.

'Ten days ago,' Clare began — *Was it only that long ago?* — 'I sat here with my father. He was reading this file.' Renzo shifted the little espresso cups to make a space on the table. 'I had no idea what was in it. I noticed that every time an older woman came by or crossed the piazza, he would look up from the file. I thought he was perving — you know?'

'Stava guardando le donne,' said Renzo.

'Understood,' said Cinzia. 'Please don't translate for me, nipote.'

'Scusami, Aunty.'

'I didn't know what was in the file,' said Clare. 'Now I do. He was looking for you.'

'Mio Dio.' Cinzia's right hand came up to her heart.

'My father wasn't well, he was very weak, but the next day he found Gianni Lamonza's door and knocked on it and asked for you.' Clare felt her voice waver. *And I turned away from him in his need.* 'Did Gianni tell you that?'

'No.'

'There's a reason he didn't. And it's the same reason that my father ran away back in 1976. In this file is his diary. He writes about a beautiful woman he fell in love with.'

'Yes,' said Cinzia, not responding to the flattery, looking puzzled and apprehensive. 'That's what it felt like. A fall. We fell into each other.'

'He writes about why he had to run away. The reason is shocking, I'm not sure you'll want to know it.'

Cinzia didn't look at all sure either. 'Do you know, nipote?' she asked Renzo.

'I have read it, yes.'

'Should I read it?'

'It's the truth, Aunty. I think you would want to know the truth.'

'Will it hurt me?'

'Yes,' said Renzo.

'Then why do I have to know it?'

Renzo shrugged as if it was self-evident. 'Because it's the truth.'

'It tells how much he loved you,' said Clare.

Cinzia tensed and looked as if she was about to run. Then she took a deep breath. 'It took me a long time to forgive him. Perhaps to truly forgive, you have to understand why, and I never did. Though, as you know, I did pray for him.' She shifted in her seat, adjusted her robes and coat, wrapped her arms about herself, as if to brace against what she was about to hear. Then she said: 'Tell me what it says. To my face.'

'Here?'

'No.'

Clare thought that the moment was over and she had blown it. Instead, Cinzia smiled at her.

'It would be unseemly for a Canossian sister to be seen crying in public over a lost love.'

They followed her across the piazza to where it narrowed on the way to the Rialto. Clare met Renzo's eyes and he shrugged, clearly having no idea where they were going. After about twenty metres Cinzia turned to her right and pushed through a large but inauspicious door. Their feet echoed off old flagstones up into cavernous shadows. When Clare's eyes adjusted to the darkness, she realised they were standing in the nave of a very old and ornate church. Suor Isabella was in front of them, clasping her hands together in prayer to a deserted altar.

I cannot do this. Not here.

'I'm not sure this is the right venue,' she whispered to Renzo. 'Can we run?'

'Either He's omnipotent or He isn't,' said Renzo. 'He'll hear everything if He exists or He'll hear nothing if He doesn't. Doesn't matter where it happens.'

He was smiling. How could he be so *secular*? So unimpressed with all this *stuff*? Part of her knew this exalted space with all the gold and trappings and grandeur wasn't so much to laud God as to intimidate His mere mortals into obeisance. Another part of her *was* that mortal.

Cinzia sat in the second to last wooden pew, turned away from the altar and patted the wood next to her. 'Sit here,' she said, 'tell me everything. Are you lovers?'

Clare wanted to say that it was Cinzia's confession, if there was to be one, but Renzo took her hand in his and said, 'Yes, Aunty.'

'I'm pleased,' said Cinzia, smiling. 'I think you're good together. Now. Tell me what I don't know.'

Clare knew she had to carry on, that it wouldn't be fair to let Renzo tell her. She just had to say the words.

'Gianni Lamonza is not your father.' She'd said it too loudly: there was an awful echo to her voice around the old stone and hovering plaster saints.

Cinzia looked immediately to Renzo. 'Are you sure?' she asked.

'It's all here,' said Renzo, indicating the manila file he was holding. 'He's Beppino's father and Franco's, but not yours.'

'But how can you be sure?'

'Because my grandfather was your father,' Clare whispered.

Clare watched those big eyes putting it together, then filling. She had to keep going now.

'That's what Bruce found out,' she said. 'That's why he left.'

Cinzia made a kind of choking sound, then turned away.

'Should we go?' Clare whispered. *Please God — though given the choice between the candidates here, He certainly wouldn't be helping her — let's get out of here.*

Cinzia shook her head as if to clear it. She wasn't looking at them, but Clare heard the echo of what she said. 'I didn't know him, really. Bruce.'

She spoke just as her father had described, giving his name, so curt and banal, a sonorous cadence.

'Yet it was like meeting someone I had been waiting for all my life.'

Clare didn't dare speak.

'When he went away, I was . . . like the ones who die in battle. Caduto. Fallen.'

Cinzia turned back to them and took the file out of Renzo's hands before Clare could claim it. Her eyes looked ethereal, pinpricks of light in the shadows. 'Tell me about my father. Tell me about the man I was waiting for.'

Clare told her what she knew. That she'd never met Harry Spence because he died so young, but that he must have been a handsome and charismatic young warrior when he fought alongside the partisans, when Donatella Bonazzon fell in love with him. 'We don't know why he didn't come back to Donatella, but you'll read in the file that he became a tortured soul in later years. Perhaps that was why.'

Cinzia asked for photographs of him. Clare was sure there would be some among her father's effects at home and promised to send them, along with photos of Bruce himself. When they rose to leave, Cinzia hugged them at the door and said she'd stay for a while.

'Will you be all right, Aunty?' asked Renzo.

'In His eyes? My God is not a harsh God, nipoti. If Cinzia

and Bruce were innocent at the time it happened,' she said, 'they are still innocent.'

'Will you tell him?'

'Papà?' Her eyes were as clear and direct as ever, but blinked tears. She shrugged, helpless, hopeless. 'I don't know.'

As they walked back through Campo Santo Stefano, Clare was merely relieved to be out in the chill wind, but Renzo was exultant. 'Did you hear what she said?'

'Which bit?'

'She was calling me nipote, nephew. But at the end, she said nipoti. Plural. *Us.*'

When they crossed back over Accademia to the vaporetto, Clare stopped at the top of the bridge and looked out at Venice. It was the same view towards La Salute that she'd been admiring when she'd spotted her father on the far side and followed him into Dorsoduro. This time the cold wind made her flinch and the hard clear light reflecting off the chop in the Grand Canal hurt her eyes.

72

When she'd first seen Renzo's apartment, she'd almost fled back to the Continental. She'd become used to making snap judgements on the interiors of homes: furnishings, furniture, bric-a-brac, smells, whether to recommend a commercial cleaner or a professional home stager. Renzo's apartment looked as if it had been dressed for sale: clean, contemporary, sterile, too many cushions. There were no personal touches, apart from photos of his family, formal and framed, all clustered together on the coffee table in his living room. She could recognise Franco among them, Cinzia in her habit, an older couple who must have been his father and mother, and his wife, Sofia — a longish face with big, kind eyes. The walls were bare.

The absence of autobiography was telling: this was a man marking time, she thought, a man still in some kind of grief limbo waiting for something else to happen, for a new life to overtake him. His animation for the mysteries of cosmology might be compensation for the impoverishment of his personal life, but he'd at least been honest about that: 'I'm telling you what saved me,' he'd said.

A dangerous man to become entangled with, maybe. Then again, she'd always been so careful and where had it got her? Why should she and Renzo not be lost and dangerous together?

She should have guessed that he'd look kind of dressed even when naked. Light olive skin with a pelt of silky black hair from his collar bone to his darker-skinned penis, but none on his shoulders or back. He looked as if he was wearing a vest and leggings over his powerful, slightly bowed legs. 'Don't ever wax,' she told him.

She'd come without even having to tell him what she liked. It had taken six months of careful hints with Nicholas, and even then it felt like a favour. With Renzo, the sex had been so simple and good that Clare had become afraid and defensive. She'd tried to point out the shortcomings of the relationship, as if sabotaging it might protect her. Like telling him she'd only known him for five minutes.

'Physicists don't recognise time in that way,' he'd said calmly. 'The whole of reality exists at once. There's no now, no then, no tomorrow — this might be why physics is in trouble but while we sort it out, the orthodox view would be that whether I've known you for five minutes or five thousand years, it's all the same.'

No use then traversing her feeling that her twenties had been a disaster of confusion and uncertainty and she didn't want to waste her thirties, that if he was going to make her unhappy now was the time. 'I'm on the rebound,' she'd said on another occasion.

'Elasticity is a universal property, stasis is unnatural.'

It was hard to come up with a feisty response. By the time she'd worked out what he might have meant, the moment was gone. She'd tried being more direct. 'What I know best is loveless marriage. Duplicity. Fraud. Betrayal.'

'What I know best is love and loyalty. Perhaps also obligation and a little boredom, if I'm honest. Perhaps we could meet somewhere in between?'

'Maybe you're still grieving for your wife.'

'There's a part of me that will always grieve. That is part of my life, unless I stop living. What can I do?'

'My family might be cursed.'

430

'That implies the existence of God or an interested universe. I'm not sure about God, but I know that the universe doesn't care about you one way or the other.'

He touched her wrist when they talked. Constantly. She found it so erotic it was embarrassing. She wanted him all the time, everywhere, but worried that if she told him he'd be shocked. Maybe she was being too careful: though formal and constrained in the way he dressed, intellectually he was a naked wild man who embraced the stars. She'd been right: they fitted. He was a lazy lover in the best sense. Nicholas had always been in a hurry to get his rocks off, as if she might change her mind halfway through. There'd been something desperate about him, and self-absorbed. Renzo was responsive but happy in the moment, not always looking to force the next.

That gave her room to get more excited, to take the initiative. There'd been no discussion of sexual history and he hadn't asked once about contraception. Was that trust? She hadn't told him she was pregnant.

What she'd wanted to be able to say to him was that *our* family might be cursed. To warn him, because *we're connected too*. So she'd given him the file. Maybe his delight in this tenuous connection through his aunt to New Zealand, this opposite place to Italy, this antipodes, the idea of his family embodying these opposites, appealed to the particle physicist in him. He loved the romance of Aotearoa, how far away it was, that his connection spanned the globe and gifted him another part of the universe with a different night sky. He seemed to know so much about it already: he described the intensity of light and shadow, the chiaroscuro, and a different palette: green and blue, he thought, 'not the terracotta and ochre of Italy'.

She admitted she was dreading going home: that it meant

the end of anonymity and the resumption of responsibility, of duties, of big decisions waiting to be made and implemented: the matrimonial property; the fraud case against Nicholas; to fight or not to fight. She still didn't mention the baby.

'I could come with you,' he said. 'For a little while at least. If it would help.'

'It's such a long way.'

Those dark lights in his eyes. 'Imagine following the curvature of the earth through day and night!'

She trusted what he'd told her in that little restaurant beside the Sile, that he preferred the truth, even if difficult. She believed that if she decided to keep the baby, it wouldn't be a problem for him. He had such a holistic view of the universe that he didn't have a proprietary bone in his body — they were all atoms of the universe derived from the same singularity, we all belong to each other, et cetera et cetera: she was sure he would embrace the child as his own. She loved him for that, but it wasn't his decision.

*   *   *

A true lawyer to the last, her father had left written instructions for Clare. He'd wanted to be cremated immediately 'to save on repatriation costs', even though they would have been covered by his insurance. He wanted 'no fuss, no ceremony'. He'd also been very specific about what he wanted to happen to his ashes: 'simple wishes' he called them, a handful spread here, a handful there. She wasn't looking forward to standing alone on that crag at Tokarahi where they'd once stood together, where her grandfather had howled in sorrow, but she'd do what she had to do.

Clare had trawled the internet for an urn that had a screw-top rather than a sealed lid, but the on-line catalogue was bewildering. Did she want what remained of her father preserved in original Venetian blown glass or in pietra serizzo stone? Stainless steel or hand-cast brass? Or perhaps biodegradable *from renewable paper produced in a sustainable manner*, or bamboo with a magnetic lid? Could she see him in a container that looked like a phallus or a gherkin, or in one that looked like a chocolate box? In an imitation giant acorn in russet brown or moss green, or in a heart-shaped biodegradable corn-starch heart *with a soft natural feel*, or in sand-gel *guaranteed to biodegrade within three months if buried, or within three days if immersed in water*? By way of decoration, would she prefer sculpted motifs or accent bands or gold-leaf decorations *intricately hand decorated by skilled artisans*, or handmade paper flowers, or a solid gold bow? Or perhaps just a bloody great sculpture of a horse or a lion or other *personally meaningful* statuette on top?

Renzo hadn't helped by telling her, in his informative way, that cremated remains aren't really ashes at all, they're actually particles — what else! — of bone too dense to be fully vaporised by the heat, and that some of them can still look like bone, not ashes, and by the way did your father have any metal dental work because that stuff can survive the fire too?

She'd burst into tears. He'd held her and told her it was only the second time she'd cried for her father, and that it was good. When she'd stopped crying, he'd suggested they buy a clear glass preserving jar, because then they'd have easy access and would have a running gauge on how much they were dispersing at each location. Her father had also asked that Clare keep some of his ashes 'if she wanted' and Renzo suggested that once they'd spread the last handful in accordance with his instructions, she'd have a better idea of what sized receptacle she'd need for what was left over.

So Broochay travelled back to San Pietro for the last time in an Agee jar with an airtight seal, and they sat him on the table in Aldo's bar so he could see and hear the fine speeches that were made in his honour by his old team-mates and dirigenti. As much as they tried valiantly to celebrate his life, Clare felt again that unspoken sense of regret and melancholy. Now she understood why. Renzo felt it too and while pretending to translate whispered to her that he wished he could tell them why Bruce had gone away.

Renzo now felt able to point out his grandfather. Gianni Lamonza featured prominently in many of the photos around the walls of the dining room, usually in the middle of the front row, captain or vice-captain as a young man, then progressing to the dirigenti, sitting in a dark suit with his wonky eye ever lower in his face and more askew as he hit middle age. Renzo pointed out there were no recent photographs: his grandfather, a founding member of the club in the early 1950s, had never set foot in San Pietro again after the embarrassment of the game in Sicily in 1976, when his youngest son had turned against him and he'd lost face in front of the dirigenti by sacking Bruce.

What a waste, she thought, as she looked at all the smiling faces of mostly young men in their happy pomp, then at these same men around her at the long table, desiccated as if the years were gradually leaching the juice from them. She could barely look at the photo of her father and Franco, the due coglioni of San Pietro. God, how handsome Franco had been, and how much of Renzo she could now see in him!

When the meal was finished and all the speeches made, several of the men told her they could not come to the ground for the spreading of the ashes, and kissed her and wished her well. In the car, Renzo explained that some of them might have religious reservations, that the Catholic church still had problems with scattering ashes because it meant the denial of the resurrection of the body. 'They can tolerate his ashes sitting on the table because they want to believe the best of Bruce and tell themselves that he wouldn't have denied the resurrection before he died. But scattering his ashes is a step too far.'

There were also questions of local regulation, because the rugby field was commune land, so Aldo, a councillor, suggested they do it at night. They lined up a few of the cars beside the clubhouse, left the motors running and headlights on and then walked to the centre of the field. Clare looked out at the low concrete stand where the crowd had chanted 'Terr-on-i!' and Big Dom had scaled the wire fence to climb into the Calabrians. It seemed inconceivable that anything like that could happen now.

The grass was already wet with dew when Renzo unscrewed the lid of the jar and Clare reached in and took a handful of the gritty shards and flakes. The cold easterly was still blowing so she was careful to turn her back to the wind and get the men in a semi-circle behind her. Aldo stilled her arm and said something that sounded like an invocation.

'In bocca al lupo, caro amico.'

'In the mouth of the wolf, dear friend,' translated Renzo.

Clare brought her arm back, then through and upwards. The particles of her father's bones were light enough to be taken away by the wind. Maybe tomorrow they'd be sitting on the dew when the sun rose.

There were more hugs for Clare, more whiskery kisses. Aldo stood, a heavy figure propped on his slender stick, tears streaming, and waved them away. As Renzo backed the car around, they could still see him out there on the gleaming grass, his back to them and the wind.

She ached to tell the old man what she knew: that her father had left and ruined their one moment in the big time through no fault of San Pietro's. But she realised that secret was no longer her burden. It was like the game of pass the parcel at her childhood birthday parties, but this time the parcel contained a booby prize. Cinzia had ended up holding it when the music stopped. Her turn to decide what happened next.

That thought was still in her head when Renzo took the call from Cinzia.

Dorsoduro, 2014

73

I giorni se strassinava e i ani i volava via. No podeva ricordarse de geri e de staltrogeri, ma ghe gera momenti del pasato che i restava dentro de iù, come che i fosse qua desso. Face e vosi che vegniva fora vive come gera sempre sta vive, anca se 'l saveva che i gera tuti morti. *The days dragged and the years flew. He couldn't remember yesterday from the day before, but moments from his past still sat within him like a presence. Faces and voices welling up as alive as they ever had been, though he knew they were all dead.* Franco and Beppino, Donatella, Luca, little Leo, Bepi and Nina, Gigi and Marisa, his brother Dan and the dark pervasive shadow of Harry Spence. They were more real to him now than the newspapers he tried to read every morning with the one eye that still accepted the light, where Bunga Bunga Berlusconi, a convicted tax fraudster and exploiter of underage *puttane*, and Grillo, a professional comedian, danced across the national conscience with impunity, reducing political discourse to farce.

He considered it a failing of the left that such fools from the right were able to hold onto power and popular sentiment, and wondered whether Franco, moderated by age and guided by his uncle Luca, might have been the leader the left needed, and whether those who ordered Franco's death in Bologna knew that too. There'd been an inquiry that proved Franco had been shot before the demonstration turned violent, that it turned violent only because Franco had been shot. Someone had whispered in that carabiniere's ear: someone, left or right, was afraid of Franco's leadership and had ordered a political assassination. Ciò nonostante, his son was dead.

Of everything that had happened, closing Franco's eyes was perhaps the hardest. He tried to keep the memory of the light in those eyes alive inside him: despite Cinzia's efforts on His behalf, he didn't believe in God any more, not even a socialist or non-sectarian God. The only immortality people had was in the memories of those who knew them.

Ten years ago, he'd travelled alone to the war cemetery at Girone in the low hills just south of Florence, where his brother Daniel was buried. He'd stood in front of a white stone tablet, one of over sixteen hundred patterned across a vast sward surrounded by cedars and cypresses. Daniel had been killed and buried further south, then exhumed and reinterred there. He'd stared at his brother's name, engraved between a laurel wreath and a cross, but felt nothing. It was war: hundreds of thousands of people, perhaps millions, had died and his brother was one of them.

Then he'd taken the train back north to Bologna and found a small plaque in Via Mascarella, close to the spot where Franco had been shot: *Franco Lamonza, Qui Assassinato dalla Ferocia Armata di Regime.* He'd held himself together until he'd read the words at the bottom: *Franco è vivo e lotta insieme con noi. Franco lives and struggles together with us.*

Then he'd wailed and crumpled to his knees beside the wall.

He'd wanted to shout: 'Non è vero! Non è vero!' *It isn't true! He's dead!* He'd felt clamped in a dreadful maw of loss and waste. Maybe war was a cataclysm more intelligible than this arbitrary shot by a carabiniere. He could ask 'Why him?' on behalf of his son in a way that he couldn't for his brother in a war where millions had died. After a while, a woman in sturdy shoes had come to help him up, a demented elderly man. He didn't tell her who he was, but composed himself, thanked her and made his way back to the railway station.

Now the interrogators were about to arrive: his daughter Cinzia, who had been unusually insistent on this meeting; his grandson Renzo, the extraordinary boy who always had the sky in his head; and a young woman who was the daughter of Bruce and granddaughter of Harry. Cinzia had insisted that this young woman be there too. What did that mean? Before agreeing to meet her, he'd asked his grandson to describe her. Did she have light blue eyes the colour of a snow-fed lake? Was her hair dark blonde? He'd said yes, and that she had a lovely smile. That had worried him. Does the smile tease you? he'd asked. Is she sincere? Has she a buon cuore, a good heart?

Just days or perhaps weeks ago, he'd slammed the door on Bruce because it had been such a shock to have him suddenly there, tall and spectral and scarcely recognisable except as the son of his father, asking for Cinzia. Now, according to Renzo, Bruce was dead. And Bruce's father too, apparently, for many, many years. Years when he'd needlessly lived with the fear, the cold dread, that Harry Spence would reappear with his cruel smile to claim Cinzia and wreck his tenuously built reality and family. Now Harry and Bruce were both gone, did that make a difference to what he should divulge?

He hadn't been ready when Bruce had knocked at his door,

but now he had to be. His daughter and Harry's granddaughter and his own grandson were the ones who would carry his memories into the future, keep alive those who might otherwise die with him. He had to decide which of the faces and voices, the loves and losses, the blood and betrayals, the secrets and lies, was worthy of light and life beyond his own.

And first he had to tell his daughter and grandson who he was: as Gianni Lamonza he'd lived a lie, a lie full of integrity and honour, he believed, but a lie nevertheless.

Where to begin? With himself, surely.

74

He'd got work down at the market below the Rialto, helping to unload the barche, the barges, in the early morning and cleaning up in the early afternoon. The men and women at the market knew who Gianni Lamonza was from the moment he opened his mouth: his dialect was Venetian but with the subtle differences in inflection and some words that told them he was from Gemona. Some of them called him Mountain Goat because he had encouraged that provenance and because he was so agile in leaping from barca to land. But it was no longer the mountains he looked towards north and west across the laguna, but the rivers.

He'd got to know Sandro, the owner of one of the barche that delivered produce to the market. Sandro was a volatile bully who shaved his head, beard and moustache once a year on the first day of summer and then didn't touch either for another twelve months. Gianni had a way of teasing him that deflected the worst of his tirades and when his latest off-sider quit, he went with Sandro on his barge, across the laguna to the Sile and up the coast to Cortellazzo, the entrance to the Piave, and further north to Caorle, nestled round the mouth of the Livenza, where Arch Scott had brought prisoners of war to be taken to safety off the beach.

He would be away for a couple of days at a time, puttering up and down those gorgeous rivers, collecting produce from the farmers and delivering it across the laguna to the market in Venice. His favourite was probably the Sile, spring-fed and constant in flow and volume, which would take them right up to the old gates of Treviso, where legend had it Attila the Hun had been stopped.

They often passed the little beach on the Livenza where Joe and the other prisoners had swum. They passed PG 107/7, the huge farmhouse that had served as their prison. They picked up produce from the estate at the wharf where Joe had surprised Harry with the woman who'd given them her husband's clothes before they escaped from San Pietro that night after the armistice.

From the water he saw the best side of the old towns because they had been built to face the river, not the road. Otherwise nondescript little towns, like Casale Sul Sile and San Pietro, had a purposeful beauty when seen from the water. They had towers and piazze that faced the wharf and he could watch the life of the towns unfolding as he drifted by on Sandro's barca.

One day, early evening, passing San Pietro, he saw half a dozen kids of about twelve or thirteen in the piazza by the wharf kicking a ball. That wasn't unusual: what was unusual was that it was a rugby ball. Joe asked Sandro to put in to the wharf.

*   *   *

Gianni and Donatella had found they didn't need to tell stories about themselves: the people around them filled in the spaces using the information they had. In that way he'd become the Gianni Lamonza they'd always known. So it was with Cinzia, then with Franco and Beppino. Joe Lamont became almost forgotten by the few people who had known him.

The most dangerous times were when they visited Bepi and Nina in Gemona, and Gigi and Marisa. Bepi didn't live much longer, but liked to tell stories. His favourite was the one about the soldier called Giuseppe who'd come from the other end of the earth to fight with the Garibaldis and then returned to marry his daughter and become a Venetian called Gianni. Bepi would have loved to tell his grandchildren that story but never did: it became, like the rest of the Bonazzon and Zanardi families' history with Joe Lamont, too dangerous to ever speak of.

Neither Bepi and Nina nor Gigi and Marisa ever blamed Joe for the loss of their sons. Joe sometimes allowed himself to think that to some small extent having Gianni in the family as a son-in-law was at least some compensation for the loss of Luca, but Leo's execution crippled Gigi and Marisa for the rest of their lives, and was the reason neither family ever returned to the campi they used to farm.

Thanks to Peta, Joe had known enough not to try to seduce Donatella, but to wait until she came to him. They'd slept together from the first but as wounded friends, not lovers. They never once discussed Harry but he was often there between them. It had been nearly six weeks, the beginning of winter, before her hand had reached across the bed and alighted on his bare chest and she'd lifted her nightdress and straddled him.

Could he say she ever loved him the way he loved her, felt at the mere sight of her the kind of unbidden exaltation of the human heart described by the hymns they used to sing at the basilica in Reed Street? He told himself it didn't matter: she showed him a knowing tenderness, a deep empathy out of which passion gradually surfaced, irregular and raw, with a needy intensity that sometimes scared him. It was enough, as they carefully reconstructed their lives in the tiny house in Dorsoduro.

Venetians knew La Serenissima was a place of ghosts, and Gianni Lamonza could understand its attraction for the spirits of those long dead: where else would they find that virtually nothing changed as the centuries flowed by? He came to like the thought that Joe Lamont had become another of Venice's ghosts, but it was something of a private joke until that day down at the market in 1976 when he'd seen a spectre that turned his blood to water. Harry Spence walking towards him. With his daughter who was Harry's daughter.

He'd been taking courgette flowers from the crate and laying them out on the banco, when he'd looked up. He could still see it now. Cinzia turning to say something to Harry, putting her hand on his as she talked in that intimate way he'd thought she reserved for him. It was like a blow to the head. He could feel his brain bouncing off the inside of his skull, bruising and fizzing. Was it an illusion? Was his drinking and grief over Donatella making him mad? Was his good eye failing? He looked again, carefully, and it *was* Harry, more real than when he'd last seen him in Trieste thirty odd years before. He could feel the skein of lies that held together what was left of his world fraying and breaking. He staggered away from the banco, then ran, as Beppino and Cinzia called out after him, 'Papà! Papà!'

He knew what he must do to Harry's son, and he'd done it. But now, nearly forty years later, he was paralysed by doubt. His relationship with Beppino had never recovered from the sacking of Harry's son. And that same weekend Franco had died on the streets of Bologna: explanation enough, surely, for Cinzia being so broken.

Had it been worth it, for the preservation of a lie? He no longer knew, but more and more he would see the expectancy in Donatella's eyes, urging him to speak before it was too late. Truth must be their final legacy to their only survivors, Cinzia and Renzo: the truth and what sat behind that truth, family and connection. Whoever the Spences now were, well, so be it. Harry was Harry but Bruce had been much admired in San Pietro by all his children not just Cinzia, and he had done the honourable and unselfish thing. Renzo had spoken highly of Harry's granddaughter, and he would have to trust that.

For much of his life as Gianni Lamonza, he'd tried to forget the young soldier Joe Lamont and what the war had done to him, but as he got older, memories had come back to him from even earlier. One in particular, of himself as a boy looking out from the old Ardgowan school towards the sun in the west making rippling shadows of the soft folds in the Waiareka Valley, where the river glided and riffled deep blue and green in the gorge close by the mine and the mill at Ngapara, before the land rose up in tiered whitestone to the snow of the Kakanuis. After El Mreir that memory had become part of his nightmare, but gradually that pristine vista had returned to him here among the hemmed stone and water of Venice. It might be too late for Cinzia, but he wanted to pass that on to Renzo and his descendants: the solace of that majestic space.

A rap on the door wrenched him back. Before he could lever himself out of the chair, Cinzia had let herself in. Her white dress. He could no longer see her properly but there was still the pleasure of her touch and her smell of sandalwood and incense as she hugged him and helped him out of his chair and onto his feet.

'I saw them coming, Papà,' she said. 'They're almost here. Sei pronto per questo?' *Are you ready for this?*

Now the moment was upon him, he wasn't sure. So much death, so much pain. Where to begin?

There was another knock on the door, his grandson's gentle tap, he knew. With Harry's granddaughter. If he saw too much of Harry in her, would fear freeze his tongue and take away his voice?

As Cinzia moved to open the door, he caught Donatella's eyes searching his and knew where he must begin.

Love. Surviving. Enduring. That had to be the beginning of it and, he hoped, the end.

E allora . . .

Ends

Acknowledgements

The Antipodeans is a mix of historical and fictional characters and events. For those readers who wish to know which is which, there is all sorts of material in the public domain, but I can recommend some of my inspirations and sources.

In respect of the World War II strand, I am indebted mainly to the late Arch Scott's *Dark of the Moon*, Susan Jacobs' books, *Fighting With the Enemy* and *In Love and War*, and also to *Signor Kiwi*, the story of Frank Gardner's exploits.

Other important resources were: *In Peace and War* by Haddon Donald (thank you Bruce Stainton); *I Silenzi Della Guerra* and *San Stino — Tra Storia Memoria* by Lucia Antonel; *To the Gateways of Florence*, edited by Stefano Fusi; and *The Waiareka Warriors* by Lindsay Malcolm, as well as numerous BBC Horizon programmes and the film, *Particle Fever*.

Many people also helped with research. My thanks to Adrienne Simpson, Senior Archivist at the Gisborne Public Library, Helen McIlwraith, Charge Nurse at the Haematology Ward of Auckland Hospital, Tim Collins Smith, Dr Joel Cayford PhD (Atomic Physics), and Milanese journalist Simone Battaglia, who provided me with research on Franco Lorusso, a member of Lotta Continua (and a rugby player for Pisaro) who was shot dead on the streets of Bologna on 11 March 1977. Venetian writer Elvis Lucchese helped me with Venetian dialect, which is not often written.

Both Elvis and Simone were recommended to me by my friend Vittorio Munari, who also assisted me with research, read a draft of the novel for me, and provided a base for my research trips to the Veneto and Friuli. Paolo and Anna Gasparello showed me the Treviso they love.

Susan Jacobs and Elvis Lucchese also read early drafts of this novel and helped me move forward with it. The biggest advances happened under the guidance of my editor, Anna Rogers, and, quite late in the piece, Edoardo Brugnatelli. My thanks to Kevin Chapman and the team from Upstart Press, Warren Adler and Jane Hingston particularly, for their enduring patience and support during that process.

San Pietro di Livenza is a fictional town, a conflation of Arch Scott's beloved San Stino di Livenza and my own village, Casale Sul Sile. For the 1976 strand, I drew heavily on my own experience there and also on that of my Caimani friends from that time. I thank all of them.

The Katherine Mansfield Menton Fellowship enabled Mary and me to spend the necessary time in Europe. Our forays to the Veneto and Friuli during my tenure of the 2013 Menton Fellowship were invaluable and inspirational.

Thanks also to my wife Mary, first reader, confidante, navigator, and shoe enthusiast, and to the late Michael Gifkins, my agent, for his diligence, wisdom and enthusiasm. Months after his death, as this novel moved towards publication and that process precipitated the kinds of questions that inevitably arise, I found myself reflexively reaching for the phone, looking forward to Michael's happy chat and scurrilous gossip as much as his informed steer on matters literary.